On
Wing
and a
Prayer

Ruby Jackson and her husband live in a small village in Surrey. Ruby, who worked for an international charity, now writes full time, with a particular interest in how women cope under pressure. When she's not writing she is probably in their large garden coping with weeds.

Also by Ruby Jackson

Churchill's Angels
Wave Me Goodbye
A Christmas Gift

Ruby Jackson

On a
Wing
and a
Prayer

HARPER

Harper
An imprint of HarperCollins*Publishers*
1 London Bridge Street,
London SE1 9GF

www.harpercollins.co.uk

A catalogue record for this book
is available from the British Library

ISBN: 978-0-00-750629-3

Set in Sabon by Born Group using Atomik ePublisher from Easypress

Printed and bound in Great Britain by
Clays Ltd, St Ives plc

MIX
Paper from
responsible sources
FSC
www.fsc.org **FSC** C007454

ACKNOWLEDGEMENTS

Lizzie Surguy of the Goring Hotel was massively helpful as I tried to paint an accurate picture of this beautiful hotel during WWII. Thank you, Lizzy. The website for the Ritz Hotel was very informative.

My personal knowledge of motorcycles was gained during one summer of hanging on to a delightful American marine as we roared around Virginia. WWII websites, as always, filled in the many blanks.

Many thanks are owed to my old friend Tom Wilson from California who constantly found me "impossible" to find articles and news footage of US activities in WWII, thus making it possible for me to actually see the men and machines about which I was writing. One or two of the Americans in this book owe a great deal to the many American military families for whom I babysat in my college years. Their generosity is the stuff of legend. After graduation, I spent three months touring the US on Greyhound buses and visiting families I had met while in college. Only when I started writing this book did I realise how much I had learned from those terrific people. You know who you are.

I owe a great deal to the encouragement and support of my editor, Kate Bradley, and my agent, Teresa Chris, and where would I be without the eagle eye of Yvonne Holland? *Chapeau*, Yvonne.

Thank you, Sarah Gardiner, for patiently digging me out of technical holes.

A senior officer in a Scottish regiment has been an unfailing help in matters of military detail.

Since this is the fourth in a series I will confess here that I omitted to thank several important sources of help in a previous book, *Wave Me Goodbye*:

My good friend, Aline Templeton, sent me an article featuring the late Dowager Duchess of Northumberland. Lady Alice was inspired by this wonderful lady's wartime activities.

And thank you to Mateuz Wcislo, a Polish engineer who kindly translated some phrases into Polish for me.

And for this fourth book I need to acknowledge the patient help and guidance of Rebecca Webster, archivist at the Institute of Education of the University of London.

As always I owe a huge debt to librarians in the Arbroath library.

And last but not least, I have to thank my friend and colleague, Tamara McKinley, who assured me that I could write a saga.

For Patrick O'Donnell and
Dr Gary Colner with much love.

ONE

April 1942

'It's still so strange not to see Daisy sound asleep when I wake up early, Dad. The house is so quiet; when will it feel normal?'

Fred looked up from the front page of the Sunday paper. 'When it is normal, pet, and your mum and me is hoping that'll be soon. You're an absolute godsend, our Rose. Kept your mum sane, you have.' He went back to the lead article.

Rose stood quietly for a moment. Was this the time to say something, to say that she had been thinking for rather a long time that she needed a change, a chance to do something different? Could she say, 'Remember in February when I had a bad head cold and didn't go to evensong? Remember I caught Mr Churchill on the wireless, heard the whole thing, instead of catching just a bit as usual? I thought then – I've got to do something more, like Daisy and the others. When this war ends I'd like to have done something besides factory work'? She looked over at her father, relaxing in his armchair, his

1

waistcoat for once unbuttoned, and decided not to disturb his one morning of relative peace and quiet.

She folded up the section of the Sunday paper she had been reading and almost slapped it down on the little table between them, inadvertently causing her father to jump. 'Sorry, didn't mean to do that. I'm off for a run. Nothing but doom and gloom in the *Post* this morning.'

'Don't forget Miss Partridge is taking her Sunday dinner with us – suppose we'll have to call it "lunch" since it's Miss Partridge – so don't be late.'

Rose promised she wouldn't be and, after changing her 'going to church clothes' for something suitable for running, she hurried away. Effortlessly, she jogged out of the town, past houses where heavily laden and sweetly scented lilac trees leaned over garden walls, tantalising passers-by with their perfume; past Dartford Grammar School, where she pretended not to see the enormous reserve water supply tank, which had been installed the year the war broke out as one of the many preparations for conflict. Would an enemy aircraft bomb it and flood the many lovely gardens in this part of the town? She hoped not. Since May of the year before, England had been experiencing a lull in the bombing raids from Germany and from the closer German bases in occupied Holland and France. But the worst part of a lull was that one never knew when it would end. In some ways this uncertainty was worse than nightly attacks. At least then people knew what to expect.

Rose changed direction to run through Central Park, formerly a favourite meeting place for local residents, especially on Sundays when families strolled among the flowerbeds. These days anxious parents preferred to stay at home rather than take a Sunday walk with one eye always on the sky and ears straining for the threatening sound of aircraft. Out of the park she ran, further and further into the countryside, now carpeted with spring flowers. She wondered if she had ever seen such stretches of golden buttercups; they were everywhere. Who could not feel happy just by seeing them? Fruit trees, too, showed off their mantles of pink or white blossom as they swayed in the gentle breeze. Who could believe that this glorious garden could possibly be a small part of a huge battlefield?

Rose began to run towards the river, revelling in the feeling of absolute freedom, enjoying stretching her long legs. She stopped, not because she was tired or stiff but because she wanted to stand still and breathe in the clear air. How absolutely beautiful it was. Everything was perfect. The blue sky was decorated with the remains of white vapour trails, showing where aircraft had passed. In the fields below and around her, green shoots were poking up through the soil and, some distance away, untethered horses were grazing. Smiling, Rose pretended that there was no war; there had never been a war and all was well with the world. She decided to run as far as Ellingham ponds, those little man-made pools that had been created when gravel and sand quarrying had stopped just before war had broken out. Horses had drunk from them; migrating birds or local wildfowl had nested there. The ponds were hardly objects of beauty now: every one was camouflaged with wire netting on a floating wooden frame, so that German airmen, sent to destroy the nearby Vickers munitions works, could not use reflections from the water as an aid to navigation.

Eventually she came to a halt, remembering that Miss Partridge was coming to Sunday dinner. *Heavens, being late will certainly spoil a perfect Sunday,* she thought as she began to trot slowly back along the way that she had come, *and I do want to see Miss Partridge.*

She reached the rather rough road that wound its way across the area, and was about to quicken her pace when she heard the sound of a speeding motorbike. It sounded as if it was on this country pathway. *What an odd place to ride a motorbike,* Rose thought as she jumped off the pathway and onto the wide grass verge.

Rose's older brothers had taught her to drive before she left school at the age of fourteen, and she was accustomed to delivering groceries in the family van, but their parents had never allowed either of their twin daughters to ride a motorcycle. 'They're too heavy for girls,' Sam, their eldest brother, had agreed. 'If you can't lift it, you shouldn't be riding it.' Nothing the girls had said had persuaded him to change his mind.

The roar of the engine grew louder and closer. Rose moved further back on the verge, noting, with growing concern, both the poor surface of the road and the sound of the accelerating bike. Before she could think another thought or move a muscle, the bike was there and then . . . was gone.

'Wow. Fantastic, what a speed, lucky—' Rose began aloud, just as she heard a screech of brakes, followed by a thud. She listened but there was nothing but a terrifying silence.

For a fraction of a moment, she felt rooted to the spot, but the adrenalin lifted her out of the almost trance-like state and Rose Petrie, former junior sports champion, began to run. She was round the corner in moments. The motorbike was lying on its side across the pathway. Her stomach lurched in horror as she saw the driver pinned underneath. Rose kneeled down beside the machine and tentatively examined the unconscious man. How young he was, and how very, very still. His eyes were closed and there was severe grazing on one side of his jaw; blood was seeping from a wound in his forehead and mixing horribly with the dirt and gravel on his face.

Rose had no idea if he was alive or dead. She remembered her brother's words – 'If you can't lift it, you shouldn't be riding it' – and wondered if it would even be wise to attempt to lift the machine off the young man's body. Should she try somehow to clean his poor face? Water? In the wonderful films she had seen with her sister and their friends, the wounded hero was always given a sip of water. If she ran back to one of the ponds perhaps she could manage to wet a cloth, but she had no cloth. She looked again at the motorcycle, which was possibly crushing something important while she hesitated. Rose seemed to remember that any implement sticking into the body of an injured person should not be removed until qualified medical personnel were on hand, but what was she supposed to do with a machine that might well be crushing this man to death?

Thank God, Rose thought as she felt a faint pulse in the neck. Could he hear her if she spoke, and would that help him? 'I'm going to try to move your bike,' she said as calmly as she could. *Oh God, what if I drop it back onto him?* 'I'm really very strong,' she continued, hoping against hope that her low voice was reaching him, perhaps giving him some comfort. 'I work in a munitions factory and lift machinery every day. You wouldn't believe how heavy some of that stuff is.'

There was no response and so Rose stood up, took a deep breath, bent down, grasped the body of the bike firmly, and, having assessed in which direction to move, began to lift. The trapped rider groaned. *He's alive, he's alive. I can do this.* In another moment she had the bike on the grass verge. She wanted to fall down beside it, as every muscle in her well-toned body seemed to be complaining, but instead she looked for something with which to wipe the blood from his face.

Why did I change? She was wearing only a shirt and her shorts. Then she heard a voice, faint but clear.

'Help me.'

Immediately she was back on her knees beside the injured man. 'I'm going for help,' she said. 'I wish I could stay with you but there's no one else here.' She was pulling her shirt out of her shorts. Desperately she tried to tear off the bottom but the material resisted.

Rose looked around and her eyes lit up as she saw a large shard of glass from the broken headlamp. She picked it up and feverishly sawed at the shirt. At last there was a tear, which allowed her to rip it apart.

Praying that it was clean, she folded it and gently wiped the blood from the man's face. 'I wish I could do more for you but I'll get help . . .'

The whisper was so faint that she had almost to put her ear to his damaged face. 'Dispatch. Pocket. Urgent . . . Take.'

Again Rose looked round, hoping desperately that someone – anyone – was within hailing distance. No one.

She felt a touch on her hand. 'Please.'

'Of course, I'll do what I can.' With a hand now marked by his blood she tried the pocket of his leather jacket. Nothing. 'It's a dispatch. An inside pocket. Do you have . . . ?'

His eyes blinked as if answering her. Rose reached inside his jacket, hoping that she was doing no damage to his poor body. There was a pocket, and inside was a fairly thick envelope. 'Got it,' she said. 'I'll run for help and then deliv—'

The eyelids fluttered again and the voice was fainter than before. 'Urgent. Please.'

'I'll do it. Trust me. I'll get you some help. Trust me,' she repeated. 'I'll deliver your letter and I will bring help.' As she spoke the last words she was already running. She had not run competitively since she was a schoolgirl, but she was fit and well. She tried to forget the injured, possibly dying dispatch rider, and the message that seemed to be burning a hole through her shirt. She had read the word on the front. 'SILVERTIDES'. She knew the name only because she had occasionally delivered tea to the kitchen door of the great house. It was at least three miles away and she had a single mode of transport – her long legs.

Rose kept going. As she ran she remembered the words of her coach from those long-ago school days. 'Long and longer strides for the first twenty paces; then accelerate until you think you can't go any faster. Relax facial muscles.' She almost flew, her long stride eating up the uneven ground. She tried not to think of the letter she was carrying, or the dispatch rider who had insisted that he be left, possibly to die, in order that the dispatch might reach its destination. The young man was in the military and was obviously about the same age as her brother Phil.

Twenty-three is too young to die, she thought fiercely, remembering the loss of her brother Ron, who had been even younger when he had given his life for his country.

'Empty your head, girl, empty your head,' came the order from the long-ago voice, and obediently Rose forced herself to concentrate on nothing but finishing the race.

She ran as she had never run before, oblivious of her screaming muscles, her labouring breath, her tears. *Heel, outside of foot, rock off with the toes, over and over again; push with your ankles, drive with your elbows*. For a moment she was in a bubble as she pulled remembered advice up from her subconscious, which helped her think only of technique and not of injured dispatch riders or important messages.

Ahead stood the gates of Silvertides Estate. With her last ounce of energy she reached them, clung to the bars to prevent her body sliding, exhausted, to the ground, and pressed the bell.

'Don't fuss, Mum, it was no more than a cross-country run.'

Rose had had a refreshing bath and was now sitting in the scrupulously tidy front room, not the kitchen, so seriously had her parents taken her story of the afternoon's events. Of course she had been much too late for Sunday dinner and was now pressingly aware of growing hunger.

'Quite an adventure, our Rose, but your mum and me think you're making light of it.'

''Course not, Dad. Only sorry I missed Miss Partridge.'

'She said the same about you, love, but she'd promised

to do geometry or some other maths subject with George – sharp as a tack is our George.'

Delighted to have young George Preston's prowess become the subject of discussion, Rose congratulated her father again for taking in the orphaned youngster, who had initially caused the family a great deal of bother, culminating in vandalism and an attack that had put her twin sister, Daisy, in hospital.

But Fred had had years of experience in dealing with daughters who did not want to be the focus of his attention. 'Come on, Rose. Rose ran, Rose saw accident, Rose helped injured rider, Rose delivered letter. Rose came home. There has to be more to it than that.'

'Aw, Dad,' moaned Rose, using exactly the tone of voice she had used as a disgruntled child, 'he was speeding on a poor surface and a pothole caught the front tyre. He and the bike went up in the air – I think, I didn't see it – and the bike landed on top of him. He asked me to deliver his dispatch and I did. Possibly I spoke to a butler sort of person, quite grand and with a posh voice, but he said not to worry, it was in their hands. I sat in a lovely room and a maid brought me tea; they'll have got an ambulance . . . can't be sure.'

Is he alive? Did they find him? They had promised to go immediately and they said they would get him a doctor.

A long-ignored memory surfaced. This was not the first time she had run for help. She had tried to black out all memory of that day on Dartford Heath, when Daisy had stayed beside two unbearably sad, dead bodies, and Rose, the faster runner, almost traumatised by shock and horror, had conquered her threatening hysteria and run for help.

9

'Didn't want to warm it too quick, Rose; nothing worse than dried-up food. Eat that up and then off to bed with you or you'll never do your shift tonight.' Her mother had come in from the kitchen at just the right moment, for Rose wanted to be left alone to think.

Sitting in an armchair in the front room with a plate of food in her hands took her straight back to childhood. Unwell? Unhappy? Either situation could be mended by sitting in a comfortable chair in the front room, eating a plate of Mum's best stew. Not that this stew could measure up to the 'before this dratted war' stews; far more vegetables than meat – thank goodness carrots were not rationed – and a gravy Mum was near ashamed of. But so far the Petrie family had managed to avoid tinned stew. 'Can't be sure what's in it,' muttered Flora as she arranged the tins on their grocery shop shelves.

As she ate her lunch, Rose could remember nothing but the face of the dispatch rider and the feel of the gates at Silvertides as her exhausted body collapsed against them. Maybe it would all come back tomorrow. She wondered if she would ever find out about the injured rider. She knew enough about dispatch riders to realise that she would never learn what was in the so-vital letter. But it had to be really important. His face swam before her tired eyes and his voice whispered, 'Urgent, please.'

I tried, she thought to console herself. *I hope it was enough.*

Two days later Rose was standing at her workbench on the factory floor. She was dirty and hungry and very, very tired. More than anything she longed for the shift to be over so that she could go home.

Rose's shift supervisor appeared at her bench. 'Petrie, got a minute? Boss wants you in his office.'

'What's wrong, Bill?' Rose could think of no reason for a summons to the office.

'He'll tell you hisself and that'll save me guessing, won't it?'

Rose straightened up, took off her overall and the scarf that covered her hair, and walked off to the office, where she hesitated before knocking on the door.

'You sent for me, Mr Salveson,' she said, noting that as well as her boss and his secretary there was a second man in the room.

'Come in, Rose. Mr Porter here would like to talk to you.'

Vaguely Rose felt that she knew the second man but could not place him. 'I don't understand, Mr Salveson.'

'The local newspaper would like to talk to you, Miss Petrie, about your wonderful action in delivering the dispatch for the gallant boy who died trying to do his duty.'

Rose was speechless. The secretary saw the colour drain from her face and shouted in time for Mr Salveson to catch Rose before she fell to the floor. He lowered her into a chair and gestured to his secretary to fetch a glass of water, which he held to Rose's lips.

She pushed it away. 'Dead? He died?'

'Yes, one of our stringers heard about it. The house-keeper at Silvertides told us how you ran with it. Seems his lordship had to go back to London before he could talk to you.'

Rose forced herself to stand up. 'I'd like to go home now, Mr Salveson.'

'We need an interview,' said the reporter.

'No,' said Rose quietly, and looked at her employer.

'Are you sure, Rose? People should hear about your courage.'

Courage? What courage had she needed to run a few miles with a letter? The boy, the dead boy, had had courage. 'I won't talk to the press, Mr Salveson, and the hooter's gone.'

'You heard her, Porter. Miss Petrie doesn't seek publicity. I'll drive you home, Rose. I can see you've had a bit of a shock.'

'No, thank you, Mr Salveson. I'll be fine with Stan Crisp. He'll see me home.'

The disgruntled reporter left angrily and Rose went to catch her friend, Stan, before he headed off in the opposite direction. Really she wanted to be alone, but she could not be sure that the reporter would not follow her. If he did, she knew that Stan would not allow him to bother her. She did not tell him the whole truth, merely that she felt faint and would feel better if he was with her.

She always felt better when Stan was there.

TWO

May 1942

'Stan, won't you please come to the spring dance with me?'

Stan looked across the table at Rose and sighed.

'Stan?' she persisted unhappily.

'Yes? Sorry, Rose, I thought you were going to ask someone else. Charlie's a good dancer. Why don't you ask him?'

'I have asked, and everyone is either working that night or has already got a partner.' She looked down at her hands, afraid to meet his eyes. 'Why do none of them ever ask me out?' She smiled then, thinking that she might have found the answer. 'Is it because they think we're an item?'

Rose, Daisy and Stan had started school on the same day and had been friends ever since. Rose and Stan had always been particularly close, and Stan's grandmother, with whom he had lived since his parents had died in a flu epidemic, always referred to Stan and Rose as the perfect couple.

'Now that we're grown up, we'll have to ask your granny to stop matchmaking.'

Stan looked around the room, as if hoping he might find an answer to her question written on one of the walls of the ancient tavern. He straightened his backbone. 'It's not Gran, Rose. Can I tell you the truth?'

'I've got bad breath? For goodness' sake, Stan, what is it?'

'You scare everyone to death, pet, simple as that. Blokes don't want to be second best – all the time.'

'Scare everyone, me? How? And if I do scare everyone,' she said, her voice heavy with sarcasm and throbbing with hurt, 'why don't I scare you?' She stood up as if to leave.

'Sit down, Rose,' said Stan gently, and he pulled in her hand. 'Maybe I should have said something years ago, but I like you just the way you are, and . . .' he hesitated for a moment and then jumped in, 'more importantly, I know that the right man for you will love you just as you are.'

'Thank you very much, I'm sure.' Rose felt physically sick. Stan, her oldest friend, the man she had got so used to being with – what was he saying?

'Rose—' he began, but she gave him no time.

'The right man?' she repeated angrily. 'The right man? Not you, then. So will you please tell me what's wrong with me? Ivy Jones has dated every man in Dartford and she hasn't a single brain cell in her fluffy little head.'

'She knows how to talk to lads—'

'And I don't,' she interrupted him. 'I've been talking to lads since I first opened my mouth.'

'You talk like you're a lad, Rose; comes of having three brothers.'

Rose looked at him quizzically; she did not understand what he was saying.

14

'You want me to pretend that I know nothing about football? And I mustn't be caught changing a tyre on my dad's van? If that's the case, why is it that every single last one of our friends has been more than happy to have me change tyres, replace fan belts, cheaper than the local garage . . . ? I could go on.'

Damn. He had hurt her and he could think of nothing to say that would improve the situation, but he was her friend and he tried. 'You run faster, jump further, climb higher, swim better; dash it, Rose, if they let girls play football you'd be everyone's favourite centre-half, and more than one of us has said as how Sally isn't the only girl in our class as could've gone to a university. And now your picture's been in the paper about trying to save that dispatch rider. My gran was hurt you didn't tell her so she could buy the paper. But never mind that; you had your reasons for keeping it quiet. That was just like you, Rose. That's what I mean. The things you do. Nobody measures up, Rose. We all love you, but you're too good for any of us. You should join up, you should, and have a chance to meet other men. I'm going to enlist as soon as I can; still got to convince my gran.'

She looked at him in astonishment. 'One, there isn't a picture in the paper because I told the reporter to go away.' She took out her hankie, a very pretty one that her friend Sally Brewer had given her last Christmas, and blew her nose. 'And two, what do you mean, enlist? Why? You're doing war work – have been since you were fifteen.'

'Not enough, not when there's lads out there willing to get killed for us; lads like your dispatch rider, and your brothers. And you talked about it, Rose, before Daisy went.'

'I can't compete with Daisy. Are you scared of her too?'

15

Stan ran his fingers through his hair in obvious exasperation. 'Maybe if I hadn't left school at fourteen I'd have learned the words to explain. It's not just the things you're good at; it's more than that, but I can't say exactly. But somewhere there's the right bloke, Rose – maybe in Dartford, maybe in London; maybe, like for Daisy, in one of the foreign countries. Hanging around with me won't help you find him.' A huge grin creased his pleasant face and he punched the air with his hand. 'League, that's the word, like football teams. I'm right fond of you, Rose, but I'm not in your league.'

Again Rose got to her feet. She hadn't really wanted to come to the Long Reach Tavern as it was unpleasantly close to where the motorcyclist's accident had occurred, but it had always been one of the favourite places of their intimate group and she would have found not wanting to go difficult to explain. 'I want to go home, Stan. Expecting a letter from Sam or Grace. Don't enlist without telling me, will you?'

'I won't,' he said – but behind his back he had his fingers crossed.

Rose's heart seemed to feel a slight pang. For the first time in their relationship, he was unable to meet her eyes. 'You won't tell me, or you have enlisted already?'

'I wanted to tell you first thing but the right words wouldn't come.'

She stared at her oldest friend, hurt and anger warring with each other. 'Then let me help you. "Rose, guess what. I've enlisted in the XX." That help?'

She turned and almost ran from the room, and Stan felt in his pockets for some loose change which he threw down on the table before hurrying after her.

Her bicycle was gone and there was no sign of her on the path. Stan wheeled his own machine towards the road, shaking his head in exasperation. Over fifteen years of friendship, and few cross words, but with a couple of ill-thought-out sentences he had blown it. He began to pedal towards Dartford. He knew he would never catch her – unless she wanted to be caught – but he cycled as quickly as he could, hoping that she would have waited for him somewhere.

Rose cycled home, thoughts whirling around in her brain as furiously as the wheels on her bicycle. *Not in your league . . . the right man . . . joining up.*

'You're not the only one who can join up, Stan,' she yelled, to the world, though pleased that there was no one within hearing distance. 'You're not the only one who feels second best, even though no one has ever refused to take you to a dance.' Conveniently she forgot that Stan had a shift on the Saturday evening.

When she had gone far enough that she knew he would be unable to catch her, she got off her bicycle and sat down on the rough grass. She tried to rub away the tears but they kept falling. *Stan doesn't love me; what'll his gran say? She wants us to marry; I know she does. Scared? Those great big lads are scared of me? Me?*

As the enormity of what Stan had said really struck her, Rose cried great broken sobs. After a few minutes she pulled herself together, sniffed loudly, blew her nose on the end of her shirt and stood up.

'You're not the only one who wants to do more with your life, Stan Crisp. Rose Petrie does too and, watch out, she will.'

'Enlisted?'

'Yes, Mum.'

'No.'

The small word seemed to echo around the kitchen, even bouncing off the clean white walls, before finally disappearing in a sigh.

'No,' repeated Flora Petrie, staring in distress at the only one of her five children still at home. 'You don't mean it, Rose, you can't. Are you doing this because of a tiff with Stan? We knew he'd been at army recruiting; we hear everything in the shop. We wasn't sure whether to tell you or not. It was between you and Stan, we decided. But hear me out, Rose: you're already doing more than your share in the factory. And remember, you was bombed, you ended up in hospital. Not to mention delivering that dispatch to some admiral or general or something at Silvertides. God alone knows what goes on in that house. Boats could come right up the Thames Estuary bringing who knows what.' She ended on a sob. 'I can't lose you too.'

Rose fought back a tear. She had been sure that her mother had got used to the idea of her enlisting; they had discussed it so often since the outbreak of war. 'Please, how many times do we have to go over this? Don't make it any harder than it already is.'

Mother and daughter, equally distressed, looked at each other.

There was the sound of hurried footsteps on the stairs. 'Flora, love, we've gone over this a million times. Rose has to have her chance like the others.' Fred Petrie had come up from the family's grocery shop, upon hearing the raised voices, to join in. 'Come on, I need my dinner, and Rose needs hers too if she wants a sleep before her shift.'

Flora fixed on the word 'chance'.

'Her chance to be killed, like my Ron or that lad on the motorbike. Wonder what *his* mum feels like.'

Rose stood up, towering over her parents. 'That's it, Mum. I'll let you know when I'm going, but I *am* going.'

Without another word, she walked out.

She was angry. Of course she understood her mother's concerns – had she not lost one son to this ghastly war? Her eldest son had been a soldier, an injured prisoner of war and, finally, an escaped prisoner, now found and repatriated. Her third son was with his beloved navy, 'somewhere at sea', and her other daughter, Daisy, Rose's twin, was an Air Transport Auxiliary pilot. Rose, who had worked in the local Vickers munitions factory since before the outbreak of war, had remained at home as a loving support, burying her own ambition to be, as she believed, of more value to the war effort as a member of one of the women's services. Now, after almost three years of waiting and hoping, Rose had asked her employers to release her so that she could enlist. To say that she was surprised to have had her request granted so quickly would be an understatement. Her immediate boss had informed her that the company would write a recommendation asking that Rose Petrie be allowed to join the Women's Transport Service, part of the Auxiliary Territorial Service.

'We'll be sorry to lose you, Rose, grand worker that you are, but if you want to be in the ATS then we feel it's our duty to help you,' said her shift foreman. 'Mind you, we shouldn't have had to read about the heroism of one of Vickers' workers in a small paragraph in the local paper. Too modest by half, our Rose, and why they had to use an old school photograph, I'll never know.'

Rose, who had refused to be interviewed or to have her photograph taken, had been unaware that the newspaper had photographs from her school sports days in their files. They had produced their article anyway, without her cooperation. She could still see nothing heroic about running for help and would have preferred it if the incident had never come to light.

'You'd think I swam through shark-infested waters, the way they're carrying on,' she wrote in a letter to her sister. 'Yes, I delivered the dispatch and I hope it was worth it, but that boy died, Daisy. He's the hero. A hero would have been able to save him, not leave him alone to die. I can still see his face and hear his voice . . .'

Rose had not really expected her mother to be delighted when the letter of acceptance arrived, but neither had she expected such strong opposition. After all, it could scarcely be called a surprise. Rose loved her parents and hoped to continue to be a tower of strength to them, but it would have to be from whichever posting she was given. Her training post was to be in Surrey, a joy to both Rose and her parents as it was no great distance from Dartford. Should Fred be unable to find petrol, her parents would visit by train or, if Rose were to be given a pass, she could travel home. Rose was determined not to feel guilty: because she was looking forward with delight to being away from home, away from the cosy flat where she had lived all her life, away from the factory where she had spent several years, and especially away from embarrassing memories of Stan's comments.

Her thoughts flew to Grace Paterson, an old school friend. Grace had simply walked out of her home and disappeared for almost a year. No one had had the slightest idea where she was or what had happened to her. Maybe I should do the same, Rose thought. Just pack my little bag and melt into the night.

Envisaging her mother's distress if she were to do such a thing, Rose quickly changed her mind. She could never bring herself to disappear without warning. She sighed. How lovely it would be not to have a conscience. Life would be so simple.

The date had been fixed. In two weeks' time, Rose Petrie would show herself at Number 7 ATS training centre in the lovely Surrey town of Guildford. After induction and training, she would become a fully credited auxiliary. Flora, Rose felt, would cope as she had coped with every situation this war had thrown at her.

'It's only down the road, Mum. I'll come home every minute of leave I get. Maybe I'll be able to give you a hand in the shop now and again. You'll see. You'll hardly know I'm not here.'

Flora pretended that she believed what her daughter was saying, while Fred explored every known avenue – and a few shady formerly unknown ones – but was unable to source extra petrol. His daughter reminded him that she was of age and perfectly capable of starting her adventure on her own.

'For heaven's sake, Dad, a training camp can't be anywhere near as scary as a munitions factory, and you and Mum managed to let me do that on my own.'

'You weren't on your own, love; for a while you had our Daisy here supporting you.'

Some days later, Rose went shopping for her exciting new venture. She had been told that her uniform would be provided, and so she had packed a few changes of clothes for off-duty hours, if there would be any. Discovering the frock she would have worn to the spring dance – had Stan taken her – she pushed it to the very back of her wardrobe. She was sure she would never want to go dancing again. She was joining the ATS and would be dedicated to her work, to her new career, she decided rather grandly.

Her parents had told her to make a list of the personal items she would want to take with her. 'You're welcome to anything that's in the shop, love. Me and your mum'll be happy to pay for it,' Fred had said, but Rose wanted the excitement of going shopping for this amazing adventure, which, even before it had properly begun, she was finding both exhilarating and frightening.

'Stockings, pyjamas, white petticoat, white thread, black thread, darning wool, elastic – if I can find any – shampoo, toothpaste, deodorant.' The list seemed endless. 'Unbelievable, Mum, the list of things we can't live without.'

'We've learned to do without, lass; hardly notice any more that we haven't seen a banana in years. Here, have a look in this,' Flora said as she handed her daughter a catalogue. Flora hid her misery well. She would never accept that all five of her children were, as she put it, in the Forces – the four still alive, that was – but she could pretend, she hoped, until Rose was gone.

Looking at the advertisements in her father's catalogues was an important part of searching for 'best price'. Fred had no space on his packed shelves for deodorants but they were listed in the catalogues. Flora had found one with a catchy name: ODO-RO-NO – 'The greater the strain, the greater the risk of underarm odour.'

Rose laughed. It practically claimed that no matter how hard she worked, there would be no unpleasant smells. 'Not too expensive either, Mum. We'll have a look in the town.'

Palmolive soap was listed at thruppence ha'penny per bar and Rose decided to buy two or three bars, if possible. Soap had been rationed in February, as fat and oil had been deemed more necessary for food production than for cleanliness.

'I'm sure we has some Lifebuoy soap in the flat. I been saving mine,' Flora offered. 'We has to take your coupons for soap, love; iron-clad rules, your dad has.' She looked at the items heaped on her daughter's bed. 'Is there anything left that hasn't been rationed, love?'

'I expect chocolate, sweets and biscuits will be on the list before long.'

'Best to stock up on what's available. Your dad hears rumours when he goes to the distribution centres.'

Rose smiled. 'Every Saturday since I've been old enough for pocket money, I've bought a tube of Rolos. Could I survive without them?'

Flora, who ate few sweets but was, she had to admit, a little too round, looked with affection and a little envy at her tall, slender daughter, who ate everything and anything and yet never gained weight. ''Course you could; we gets used to anything after a while, but as it happens there's some Rolos in the shop and I could put some in a tin for you so they'll keep.'

Rose's wage was not going to be quite as much as she had earned in the factory and so she would be compelled to be more frugal – and she'd have no parents there ready and willing to hand over the odd shilling 'till the end of the week'.

She had seen nothing of Stan since she had left the factory and there was an unaccustomed dull ache in her insides. None of the lads fancy me, she told herself, not even Stan. Daisy knocks them down like skittles and we're twins. What's wrong with me?

Try as she did, she could not understand what Stan had tried to tell her. 'Not in her league', indeed. What a load of old tripe. Was it possible that Stan had palled with her because no one fancied him? No, Stan wasn't like that. She had written to Daisy about it and Daisy had tried to console her.

> You and Stan have been friends for ever and friendship
> is very important. He does love you and I think you
> love him the same way, as a dear and special friend.
> Don't let go of that, Rose. Tomas is my friend, but our
> love for each other is so much more than that and
> you'll know it when it comes. It's like being run over
> by a Spitfire, knocks you for six. Absolutely wonderful.

'Thanks a lot, Daisy, I don't think,' Rose had said angrily, and got on with her packing.

It was young George who brought her news of Stan. She had gone down to Central Park for a last walk round and bumped into her foster brother on his way home.

'Got a letter for you, Rosie,' he had said with a cheeky grin.

24

'Rose, not Rosie, you horrible little boy – and how come you've got a letter for me?'

George had lived with the Petries since his mother and brother had been killed in an air raid. Nothing had been heard from his layabout father since and, frankly, no one missed him. The two years of regular food and sleep, plus affection and guidance, meant that the boy was completely at ease with all the Petries, and he merely laughed. They walked along together companionably while he searched through his pockets. 'Got it last night but you was in bed when I got back from the pictures and you was up before me this morning. Now where can it be?'

'If this is some kind of a horrible boy joke, I will tie you to my—'

Eventually George hastily pulled out the rather grubby, crumpled envelope before Rose could think of something nasty to do to him. 'Here,' he said with a grin. 'Your chap kissed it lovingly, made me want to be—'

'You have no idea how sick you'll be if you utter one more word, Georgie Porgie.'

George was bright in more ways than mathematics and he handed over the letter and walked sedately beside her. 'Blimey, Rose, you're not going to wait till we get home. Maybe he wants a quick reply.'

'Then he can wait,' muttered Rose, and she began to stride out so that, fit as he was, young George was no match for her speed and had to trot to keep up as they rushed home.

Once inside, Rose hurried up the stairs that led from the family shop and from the back door she called, 'I'll be there in a minute, Mum,' and went into her bedroom, closing the door behind her. She flopped into the old chair that had worn the same flowered cotton cover for as long as she could remember. For a few years she and Daisy had been able to sit in it together comfortably, but as they'd grown they'd had to take turns – one in the chair, the unlucky one on the bed. Since her twin had gone off to join the ATA, Rose had been able to make constant use of the chair, which made her miss her sister more than ever.

'Well, let's see what Stan has to say, Daisy,' she said aloud. The letter had been written the day before and had Stan's Dartford address on it.

Dear Rose,

I have joined the army. I'm the lowest of the privates in The Queen's Own Royal West Kent Regiment. I never meant to hurt you, never. You're my best friend, have been since we was five. That's a long time and I don't want nothing to spoil it. I love you, Rose, can't think of another word for what I feel but I do know it's not the love that you need for marriage. Please write to me because if I'm going overseas . . .

Please understand, Rose. I don't know. Maybe it was them Spitfires sent out to help the people in Malta and every last one of them bombed to bits before they could even get off the ground. Maybe it's these raids on lovely bits of England. Gran took me on a trip to Bath once – couldn't believe it was real and now thousands and thousands of buildings is damaged. Gran's right cross about Bath and about me joining up but I'm making her an allowance, same as I give her now. She's not old, Rose. I suppose you always think your gran is old but she's not and the neighbours both sides say they'll keep an eye on her. She'll always know where I am. I'll write to both of you when I can.

George said as you have joined up too. I bet you're in the ATS and one day we'll see you driving all them famous people around London.

Love,
Stan

Oh, Stan, I know, and I love you too.

There was a PS, but he'd very effectively scored it out. Rose tried to decipher it but could make nothing of it. She got out of the chair and lay down on the bed. Stan was gone, and unless his grandmother had his address she would have to wait until he wrote to her – if he ever did. At least she could get a letter written and Mum or Dad could get the address when Stan's gran came in for her rations.

She got up, found her writing pad and started writing.

Dear Stan,

I'm ashamed of myself. Imagine falling out over a dance I never really wanted to go to anyway. Stupid.

You'll be a great soldier. I am very proud of you and I bet they make you a general. I hope the West Kents have a nice uniform.

I think I'll be going away soon too. Don't worry about your gran. With the neighbours and Mum and Dad, she'll be all right.

Please answer this,
Your friend always,
Rose

She stood up, sniffed, wiped her eyes which had gone all teary, tidied her hair and went downstairs to join what was left of her family.

THREE

Guildford, Late May 1942

'Think yourselves lucky, girls. When I joined the ATS we were definitely the military's poorest relation. Some of us were without a uniform for months and had to wear out our own clothes, and I do mean wear out. The ATS is not a stroll in the park. If we were lucky we got a badge. Three years later and you're getting everything, including your knickers.'

'Which no woman in her right mind would want to wear.'

'Very funny, Petrie, or was it you, Fowler? Maybe they're not Selfridges' best but, believe you me, you'll be glad of them in the winter.'

Rose, who had been standing quietly among the new recruits or auxiliaries, as ordinary members of the Auxiliary Territorial Service were now called, said nothing but merely waited till she was given her uniform. She had made no remarks, no matter what the commanding officer thought. Her stomach was churning with excitement that she was to be – at long last – an actual servicewoman.

'Hope we have your size, Goldilocks. You're tall but you're slim. Any good with a needle?'

'Not very, ma'am, but my mother is.'

'And did you bring Mummy with you?'

Rose blushed furiously, but contented herself with reflecting that she could, if so inclined, pick up this bossy little bantam and toss her in a wastepaper basket. She said nothing and watched the separate pieces of uniform pile up on the table. A lightweight serge khaki tunic was joined by a matching two-gore skirt, which she hoped would reach her knees, two khaki shirts and a tie. Slip-on cloth epaulettes with the ATS logo stitched on followed the battledress trousers, which the new controller had insisted upon as being much more sensible for the work the ATS auxiliaries were called upon to do, preserving modesty in some cases and simply being more comfortable in others. A cap, some unbelievably ugly green stockings, khaki knickers that were, if possible, even uglier, heavy black shoes and robust boots completed the pile.

'I've given you the longest items we have, Petrie, but I'm afraid they'll all be too loose.'

In some despair, Rose spoke tentatively. 'Didn't the army expect tall women, ma'am?'

'Of course women of all sizes were expected, and I myself have dressed at least three over the years who were much taller than you, Petrie; at least six feet in height, and broad too. I'll keep my eyes open for items that will fit a little better, but in the meantime there are several seamstresses who'll be happy to help out. In fact we have one auxiliary who did tailoring at an exclusive address on Bond Street in London. Look at the notice board in the canteen. Names and units are there.'

The group, having received their issue, returned to the rather Spartan hut that they were to live in for the foreseeable future. It contained iron beds, some cupboards, a few chairs, and a picture of Eleanor Roosevelt, wife of the President of the United States, who had toured the camp in August.

'Shouldn't she be in the lecture rooms with the King and the PM?' Rose asked, but no one answered, being too involved in comparing uniforms.

Rose was not a vain woman, personal vanity not having been encouraged by the Petrie parents, but when she saw herself dressed in uniform for the first time, she wanted to weep. The tunic was wearable if she tightened the half-belt at the back till it was almost nonexistent, but the skirt, although long enough, was so loose that it fell down, leaving her standing in her new knickers. Since leaving school, only her twin sister, Daisy, or their mother had seen Rose in her underwear and she was embarrassed.

'Why did I ever leave Dartford?' she said aloud. The uniform looked so unprofessional and, although she was at a base in Surrey, which was not too far from home, the new intake had been told not to expect leave for some time. Were she to post the absolutely necessary items home, it could take weeks for them to get there, be altered and be sent back.

'Don't worry, Rose.' Another girl, whose name she had not yet learned, came over from her bed. 'I'll take the skirt in for you after tea, and they'll all be here to admire the stunning new khaki issue, so try to take it in your stride. With those blue eyes and that glorious golden hair, the colours will suit. And as for modesty, three months at a boarding school and you wouldn't have

30

an inhibition left. That's about all I learned, apart from a bit of sewing – both skills equally useful in the ATS.'

'You're very kind. I can sew on buttons, jobs like that, but—'

'Always better to leave it to the professional. I'm Cleo Fitzpatrick, by the way, which is, believe it or not, short for Cleopatra. My father was stationed in Egypt when I was born; I still haven't discovered a really good way of paying him back.'

Rose, who had a very happy home life, looked at Cleo's face and relaxed as she saw that the girl was joking. She was obviously as fond of her parents as Rose was of hers. 'My twin sister and I always hated being called after flowers.'

Cleo looked up at Rose. 'But you suit your name, and what about your sister? Are you identical?'

Before replying, Rose reached for her shoulder bag, took out her purse and retrieved a small black-and-white snapshot taken on the beach at Dover before the war. 'I'm obviously the giant looming over two of the others, but which one d'you think is Daisy?'

Cleo examined the picture for some time. 'None of them even has the same eyes or hair. That one maybe, the taller one.'

'That gorgeous creature is our friend Sally. The sweet little one in gingham is my twin sister.'

'No, you're not serious.'

'Cross my heart. She's in the ATA, believe it or not, and a pilot. Been in since '41.'

There was no time for further chat as several other girls poured in. 'Quick, you two, the boiler's on in the washhouse. First come first served.'

The accommodation on this training base was basic. It consisted of huts of all shapes and sizes. The toilet block was a long rectangle built over a pit. A slight wall separated each toilet, but at this time there were no doors. Girls like Cleo who had spent years in boarding schools and were used to dressing and undressing in front of other girls were much more relaxed about this situation than those who had been raised to keep all matters of personal hygiene private. Rose hated it and longed for the day when her induction period was finished and she would be transferred, she hoped, to more comfortable living quarters. There was only one washhouse for the group and a limited supply of hot water was available, and only in the evenings. The new auxiliaries soon worked out a rota system – 'another thing boarding school taught,' said Cleo.

The oldest auxiliary in Rose's hut was a thirty-eight-year-old widow from Derby, who told the others that she had joined up when her twenty-year-old son had insisted on joining the army.

'"Join the army and see the world, Mum," he said, and I, tears streaming down my face, begged him to reconsider. He's all I got in the world, see, but – "I got a chance to do something grand, Mum," he said, "and, just think, I'll be able to give you a bit of a hand. All my food's provided, and my uniform, plus I get paid. You'll see, we'll be able to put a bit aside for that cottage you've always wanted. The war's an opportunity for them as is willing to take it."'

Chrissy Wade explained her situation to the girls during a welcome break. 'An opportunity to get killed is what I told him, so what could I do but join up? Had a cleaning job afore the war and a lot of opportunity there was there, I don't think. Hope this lot don't give me all the cleaning to do in the ATS.' She had laughed then, and the younger women laughed with her, already liking her spirit.

The others were, like Rose, in their twenties. They included waitresses, beauticians, seamstresses, shop assistants, factory workers like Rose, and even two university students: Cleo, and a shy, rather intense girl from Poole named Phyllis.

'You two will be officers in no time,' said Chrissy, 'that's what my lad said. Ten lads signed up with him and one went straight for training to be an officer.'

'I hope not,' said Cleo.

'You couldn't be an officer, Cleo,' Rose teased her. 'How embarrassing for the ATS to have an officer with two left feet.'

'Don't officers just stand looking rather splendid while the others march?' Phyllis, who hardly spoke, surprised them all by joining in.

It was obvious to Rose that Phyllis was joking, but most of the others seemed to take her remark seriously. Except Cleo.

'That lets you out too, Phyllis. You're too small to be splendid.'

'Thanks very much. I'll remind you that Queen Victoria was small.'

'Like a little Christmas pudding,' Rose surprised herself by suggesting. Everyone laughed.

The trainees were up by seven o'clock, their sleep having been somewhat disturbed by the almost constant droning of aircraft. Rose, like thousands of other people living in the south of England, had become used to the sound of planes flying overhead night after night, and she could recognise the sound of enemy aircraft.

'They're ours,' she mumbled several times during the night. 'Go back to sleep.'

They slept and woke, dozed and woke again, and by eight o'clock were washed, dressed, beds made, room tidied, and in the canteen for breakfast. Rose, who had shared the cleaning of their little shop and their homely flat above it, had hoped that cleaning would not be on her list of daily tasks.

'I don't mind keeping my own area clean, and I'll clean up after myself, but I didn't join the ATS for domestic duties.'

After breakfast came the dreaded drill. Learning to march certainly woke them up every morning. Cleo complained loudly that her boarding school had not included marching in its comprehensive syllabus. 'Honestly, Rose, it looks so bleep-bleep simple when we see regular soldiers on the parade ground, but it's far from easy. And that drill sergeant yelling in my ear only makes me mix up my feet. I'd do better if you were teaching it. Why do we always have to be bullied by men? Makes something in me rebel. But right now I'm thinking of drawing a great big R on one of these ghastly, clumpy shoes.'

'Just make sure it's on the right, right shoe,' teased Rose.

In a way, however, Rose agreed. Would they ever learn to keep in line, stay in place, to use the correct foot or the proper stride, especially since they were of varying heights? Could they possibly master standing to attention, standing at ease, halting smartly when on the march,

34

and would they ever learn to salute properly? Rose, with brothers in the Forces, found herself wishing she had paid attention when they had wanted to show her.

She was quietly glad that at school she had been on the very successful athletics team and so set herself to rapidly mastering the drills.

Aptitude tests – or trade tests, as the girls called them – came after all the marching and drilling. Scores attained in these tests would be used to decide where each ATS auxiliary would work. Rose worried that, as a working-class girl who left school at fourteen, she might be sent to work in the kitchens.

'What do you think, Cleo? You went to a posh boarding school till you were seventeen. Some of the others have had secretarial training. You girls will get the best jobs. Girls like me will end up peeling potatoes or waiting tables.'

'Rubbish, Rose. You have more experience in driving and in looking after cars than anyone – in our hut, at least. I learned to drive but I've never even put in petrol, and as for oil and keeping the blinking thing chugging along – that is all far beyond me.'

Rose laughed. 'Don't you have any brothers? Mine were always taking engines apart—'

Cleo interrupted. 'And putting them back together.'

'Exactly.'

Rose wrote to her parents during her first week of training.

If the King himself, God bless him, was to come into the camp, I would not be ashamed of my salute. But if Mr Churchill comes, and Sergeant Glover says as how

35

he often has a quick visit somewhere, do we salute him? He's not in the army and he's not a royal. I'm not going to worry. Sergeant Glover knows everything.

Last night, as in two o'clock in the morning!!!!, we had a practice of what to do in an air raid. It was just an alert but it frightened the life out of most of us. We have to wear these uncomfortable steel helmets – can you imagine, steel? They're really heavy but Sergeant Glover says they can be the difference between life and death. Don't worry, Mum, I'll wear mine.

Would you believe we had a talk on obeying orders? 'Orders must be obeyed immediately and without question. Your life could depend on your ability to master this simple skill.' Never thought I'd be grateful to have had the Dartford Dragon as my teacher in elementary school. I've already made a friend, although everyone in our hut is friendly. Some is quite posh and some in between, like Cleo, my new chum, who has done a lovely job of altering my uniform. You'd have cried if you'd seen me before she fixed it. I could have wrapped the skirt round me twice. The underwear is awful, can't think why they gave it to us, unless some girls is so poor they hasn't got changes – isn't that a shame? – and we've got this huge furry coat-like thing that reaches almost to my ankles. Cleo's trailed on the ground till she had time to fix it. She did look funny – a bit like Charlie Chaplin waddling along like a duck – but Sergeant Glover says we'll be glad of our Teddy Bear coats in the winter.

Cleo had indeed made a beautiful job of tailoring Rose's uniform and, as her appearance improved, so did her confidence. When she had worked in the Vickers munitions factory in Dartford, she had become expert at keeping her long hair safe inside a net; now she made one thick plait, wound it into a tight ring and fastened it with kirby grips. No matter how active she was, it stayed inside her cap.

Somehow, knowing that she looked professional made it easier for her to believe that she would succeed. Once or twice she had felt that she was struggling in the aptitude tests but consoled herself with the knowledge that she had done her best. Her ambition was to be a driver; surely the men in charge would see that she had years of experience, not only of driving but also of vehicle maintenance. She knew that driving the Prime Minister was probably an impossible dream. People say that dreams can come true but, in the meantime, decided Private Petrie, any driving would do.

She managed to go home twice during her time in Guildford. Once she took Cleo with her, worrying all the time about Flora's nervousness around people she did not know. Her worries were for nothing. Cleo might have a retired army officer for a father and might have been educated at boarding school, two possible reasons for Flora to feel anxious, but Cleo endeared herself to Fred and Flora immediately.

'Boarding school and then the ATS,' sighed Flora. 'You'll need a good tea, pet.'

Rose and Fred exchanged an affectionate smile over Flora's head. The much-loved wife and mother had found another lost lamb. The first one, young George, arrived home from Old Manor Farm, which was tenanted by the Petries' long-time friend Alf Humble, in time for the

37

'good tea', and was immediately fascinated by this exciting creature with the exotic name.

'Do you know all about the real Cleopatra?' he asked Cleo immediately, as he munched happily into his sugarless carrot cake.

Cleo thought quickly. It was obvious to her that the boy was anxious to show his knowledge.

'Well, I was born in Egypt and my dad said she was an Egyptian queen; I don't know much about her except that someone rolled her up in a carpet.'

George was delighted to show her the difference between historical fact and fiction. 'Miss Partridge told me all about Cleopatra and Julius Caesar. Do you know who Caesar was?'

Cleo had a sinking feeling that she might be doomed to spend her entire forty-eight hours' leave reliving her secondary education. It was obvious that the boy remembered every word spoken by the wonderful Miss Partridge. 'I do indeed, George,' she said, ignoring the disappointed look on his thin face. 'We could talk about Roman history but isn't Sergeant Petrie coming tonight? He'll want to talk to his sister, won't he?'

Flora's face had worn an enormous smile when she had told the girls that, hearing of Rose's expected visit, Sam had requested – and been given – a twenty-four-hour pass. 'He'll be here soon,' she said, 'and he'll have news of Grace and of Daisy.'

So it proved.

Sam arrived just as his father was on his way out to do his usual fire-watching shift. Fred had time only to hug his son, and say, 'I'll catch you at breakfast, lad,' before hurrying off.

Cleo looked somewhat shocked as Flora brought out yet another tin. 'Doesn't rationing affect grocers?' she asked, and was immediately ashamed of herself. 'Oh gosh, Mrs Petrie, I didn't mean that the way it came out.'

Rose laughed. 'My parents are as honest as the day is long, Cleo, but Mum has made stretching rations into a science. In other words, when she's expecting one of us, she and Dad do without and all rations are saved.' She looked across at her mother, who was pretending not to hear. 'They think we don't know but we do.'

'My mother's housekeeper was exactly like that, Mrs Petrie,' said Cleo, anxious to make reparation for her insensitive remark. 'Probably mothers all over the country are doing without so that their children can have everything they need. Are meals still good in the army, Sam?'

Sam smiled at her. 'Depends on where the army is. It wasn't too good in the POW camps, except when we got Red Cross parcels. We got them from the Yanks, the Canadians, and our own. Camp I was in, we had some trouble with guards; they sometimes pinched our stuff. Mind you, I don't think the poor beggars got much more to eat than we did. We traded with them sometimes. Everybody got cigarettes and I exchanged mine for other things – vitamin C tablets, writing paper.'

'You got parcels from America? But they weren't in the war then, Sam. They only joined after the Japs bombed them at Pearl Harbor just before Christmas last year.'

'They still gave aid. Every country in sympathy with the Allies did a bit. The parcels went to a Red Cross centre in Geneva, I think, and the Swiss distributed them to every camp. Nobody cared where the parcels came from. The notes inside were in several languages: Yugoslav,

French, English, Polish – a lot more. We'll never forget the Red Cross or the St John. And you'll see, now that the Yanks are in, they'll come to Britain and they'll fight with us in Europe.'

Cleo was deeply moved. 'I've been a bit sheltered, Sam, I'm afraid. I didn't know any of that about the Red Cross parcels. Good people everywhere. Makes me proud to have joined up.'

'We've got a friend in the Land Army, Cleo,' put in George. 'She's Sam's sweetheart, isn't she, Sam?'

Sam stood up and looked at his mother. 'Isn't it time for little boys to go to bed, Mum?'

'I was just saying about Grace so you could tell Cleo about farm food,' said the aggrieved George.

'Well, actually—' began Cleo, but before she could say another word they heard the doorbell.

'I'll get it, Mum,' called Rose, already running quickly down the wooden stairs to the back door.

'Sally Brewer, I don't believe it.' Rose's excited voice rang out on the staircase. 'Mum, Sam, George, you'll never guess who's here.'

George jumped up. 'Sally's a film star,' he boasted somewhat erroneously, going to meet her. He stopped before running down the stairs and called back, 'A real one.'

It was a lovely reunion: Rose, Sally and Sam actually there in the familiar, comfortable living room, with Grace and Daisy present in spirit. Phil was at sea. The family was conscious, as always, that since Ron had been killed it could never be complete again, but they did not burden others with their personal sorrows. They welcomed Sally, who had come down from London, where she had had the smallest of small parts in an actual West End play.

Her news, which she had hoped would excite Rose, was that she was going to be in a musical – in Guildford.

Rose, and Cleo, who was almost as star-struck as George, groaned. 'We've finished training. We're leaving Guildford.'

They cheered up when Sally told them all manner of stories connected with her time in the theatre, actors and actresses she had met, screen tests she had had for film-makers and the, admittedly, tiny parts she had had in propaganda films. 'I actually stood beside Noël Coward for three whole minutes in a film.'

'The real Noël Coward. Wow.' Cleo breathed out the word in awe.

Sally added Cleo to her list of 'suitable friends to be invited', and then organised the group into writing round-robin letters to Daisy, Grace and Phil. 'Everyone writes a sentence about anything and signs it, and we'll keep going till everyone has written at least one sentence on each letter.'

'But I don't know them, Sally,' Cleo pointed out.

'They won't mind, and besides, you're bound to meet them one day. Seems to me the whole world wants to be looked after by the Petries, and Flora and Fred want to look after everyone. Relax and enjoy!'

Much later than ten o'clock George, grudgingly, went off to bed, as did Flora, and Sam walked Sally back to her home.

'We always thought Sam was sweet on Sally,' Rose told Cleo as they brushed their hair before turning off the very dim bedroom light. 'But you couldn't doubt where his heart really is when you see him with Grace. Funny old thing, love.'

41

'Hysterical,' agreed Cleo.

They were asleep in minutes.

The great day came. The intensive study and hard work of just three weeks – which somehow seemed to have been much longer – were behind them.

With the exception of Chrissy, the occupants of Rose's hut were wide awake by five-thirty; few of them had been able to sleep at all.

Would anyone be told that she just did not measure up? They had been together for such a short time but they were a team, a family, supporting one another, and today they would be parted and perhaps would never see each other again. It was a sobering thought for all but the two 'boarding school girls', who were quite used to meeting and parting.

'Royal Mail, girls, fabulous invention, and there is the telephone,' said Cleo. 'Let's make a pact to meet somewhere every year. All suggestions for suitable venues gladly received.'

'Officer material if ever I saw it,' said Avril Hunter. 'Were you head girl, by any chance, Cleo?'

'God, no,' said Cleo, adjusting her beautifully tailored skirt. 'For some obscure reason I did become a prefect and possibly became the teeniest bit bossy; it was that lovely magenta stripe on my grey blazer – went to my head, it did.' She waited till the laughter died down before continuing, 'Rose is definitely head girl material: popular, bright, attractive, and, to top it all, she's an athlete. Bet they make her an officer.'

'All my brains are in my legs,' said Rose, blushing furiously. She was moved to hear that she was popular

– Daisy was always the instantly popular twin. She really did not want to be selected for officer training. She could hear Stan's voice – Stan who had not answered what she thought of as her 'apologetic little letter'. 'Not in your league, Rose.' Despite her churning stomach, she pulled herself together. Whatever happened today was the beginning of something, and if army recruits worked half as hard as ATS recruits, he probably had no time for writing letters.

Everyone in the new intake confessed to a churning tummy. Would a girl be selected for cooking, cleaning, waiting tables in mess halls, as a storekeeper or a telephonist? Would the two university students be asked to train as translators – both had studied at least one foreign language – or might something even more secret and necessary be their lot? Who might become a lorry driver, a motorbike messenger, a mechanic or perhaps even an engineer or electrician? And those were not the only jobs available. With the necessary skills, a woman might be trained in wireless telegraphy, to use the newly developed radar systems. Yes, the opportunities were there.

The early morning hours seemed to crawl by. Would it ever be ten o'clock? But, of course, ten o'clock came, as usual.

By lunchtime, with many of them in a state almost of euphoria, they trooped into the canteen. Chrissy could scarcely contain herself and had tried to avoid lunch so that she could sit down and write to her son. 'Can you imagine, girls?' she asked them several times. 'They don't want me to clean. They think I'm secretarial material. What will my lad say when I tell him his mum's going to be a secretary?'

No one was unkind enough to tell her that, since she could not type and knew nothing about shorthand, she had a long way to go.

'You'll get there, Chrissy, and secretaries make lots more money than cleaners. That cottage with roses round the door is just a matter of time.'

No one from Rose's group had been selected for officer training.

Cleo had been selected for driver training. At the most, she could drive and, thanks to Rose, she now knew where to put petrol; Phyllis had been chosen for reasons even she could not begin to understand to join an anti-aircraft crew, looking out for enemy aircraft with the help of radar and searchlights.

'Please don't do any firing until you can recognise every type of plane in existence,' Rose warned her, half seriously. 'Don't want you shooting down my sister.'

'Only men fire guns.'

'That doesn't fill me with confidence,' retorted Rose, and again everyone laughed.

Next they turned on Rose. 'Come on, Rose, why so quiet and modest? What job have they given you? Chauffeur to the American general?'

Rose smiled and tried gamely to hide her bitter disappointment as she said, 'No, very sensibly they've put me down as a mechanic – trainee, that is; it's usually a man's job. What's your betting they still give me a woman's wages?'

Each of the young women had been told that her wages would be two-thirds of that earned by the men. For Chrissy, it was still better than she had earned as a cleaner, and was, in her eyes, a definite step up.

Cleo hugged Rose. 'I'm so sorry, Rose. They should have made you a driver. Probably there's been a mistake. They'll discover that and change your posting.'

'I'll be a good mechanic, Cleo. Honestly, I'm delighted; I was always afraid they'd throw me out altogether. Pity we won't be together, though. It's been fun.'

Promising to keep in touch, they continued to walk back towards their hut, where already packing-up was going on.

Cleo stopped. 'I'm going to make a bet that by this time next year you'll be a driver.'

Rose tried to smile. 'For Mr Churchill, naturally.'

'Of course. Just wait and see.'

Two days later, the newly 'embodied' auxiliaries boarded a bus heading for the station, the first step to their new posts where each one would have the rank of private. Cleo, in the window seat, noticed as the bus drove out that there was some unusual activity at the toilet block.

'Goodness me. Don't look, Rose; it'll just upset you.'

Naturally Rose had to look. She sighed. 'Let's be charitable and say we're glad for the next lot of trainees.'

The girls turned their heads again, looking towards the exciting future. Behind them auxiliary staff were – after many requests – hanging curtains on the fronts of the toilet cubicles.

FOUR

It could have been worse. She might have been sent to Scotland. Not, thought Rose, that there was anything wrong with Scotland, but it was just so very far away from Dartford.

Preston was not too far really, and what she had seen from the train looked almost familiar. They were not stationed in the town itself but a few miles out. There was a river, the Ribble. Rose liked the sound of water flowing, jumping over stones on its way to the sea. She thought it would be pleasant to walk, run or cycle in the area around the base. It was mainly moorland and there was a high point called a fell not too far away. It was called Beacon Fell, possibly because beacons were lit on it on special days or to warn nearby inhabitants that trouble was coming.

She wondered if the beacon would be lit to warn of an air raid, then scolded herself for being silly. If she ever got time off she could get a train from Preston to London, and then another from London to Dartford.

Cleo was in a place called Arundel. She'd have to look that up, but niggles in her brain hinted that Arundel was a lot closer to Dartford than it was to Preston. A really bright spot, however, was that Chrissy was here with her. To arrive at a new base and know not one person there would have been awful.

'Pity we're not in the same billet, Rose, but for me it's lovely to know at least one person.'

They were sitting in the canteen enjoying their dinner of corned beef, potatoes and carrots – at least Rose was. Chrissy was merely pushing her carrots around.

'I'm delighted you're here too,' said Rose, 'but you don't look too happy, Chrissy. I'll fetch us a nice cup of tea and you can tell me what's bothering you . . . if you want to, that is.'

She walked across to the tea trolley and poured two cups of tea. 'Good heavens,' she said aloud. 'It's too weak to run out of the pot.'

'Very funny, Petrie. We're lucky to be getting any tea at all. Kitchen does its best, but with rationing—'

'Rationing? When was tea rationed?'

'You been in outer space, girl?' asked the irate cook. 'At least two years.'

'Since 1940? I was working in a munitions factory in '40, but my parents sell tea, high-end market as well as the housewife's choice, and I don't remember a word about it.'

'Parents don't tell their offspring everything.'

Rose thanked the cook, apologised for complaining and then walked back to her table, remembering recent conversations about parents and the sacrifices they were prepared to make for their children.

'Here you go, Chrissy, can't exactly stand a spoon up in it, but it's hot, wet and sweet enough!'

'Just the way I like it,' said Chrissy with an attempt at a smile.

Rose sat down beside her. 'What is it? You can tell me and I'll help if I can.'

Chrissy looked at Rose for a long moment. 'It's my Alan,' she said at last, 'my son. I haven't had a word from him in weeks and I'm worried sick.'

'Where is he?'

'That's it. I don't know. He said in his last letter as he might be going overseas. Really excited, he was, and I pretended I were, an' all. See the world: Paris, France, the mysterious East.'

'Letters from overseas take much longer than from – where was he stationed?'

'Aldershot.'

'That must have been nice, not an awful long way from Guildford. Did he write to you in Guildford?'

'Yes, but he won't know this address if he didn't get my letter telling him.'

'That won't matter, Chrissy. If he sends a letter to Guildford it'll be sent on to you. Happens every day of the week, but try not to worry.'

Rose knew all about worrying over absent loved ones. They had waited for letters from Ron, and Flora would always treasure the few he had written before his death in action. Rose could not speak of her brother's death to anyone, and especially not to a woman who was worried about her only son.

'My brother Phil's at sea, Chrissy. Sometimes it's months between letters and then five or six arrive at the same time. He numbers them now and so Mum knows if one's missing. Sometimes they do get lost and sometimes the lost one turns up months later. And when my brother Sam was on active service, Mum got letters every week and then it was months between . . . It doesn't mean he's not writing, Chrissy, just that there's a hold-up somewhere. You have to stay positive.'

'I'm sorry to be such a nuisance, Rose. I'm trying to concentrate on the typing and the shorthand but then I start worrying about Alan and I can't see the keys or the symbols – all I can see is Alan's face.'

That was what it must have been like for Mum and Dad with the boys. Did I give them half the sympathy I'm giving Chrissy? I hope so.

'You haven't touched your tea. Don't blame you really. Doesn't even smell like tea. We lived above the shop and if we weren't smelling Mum's baking, we were smelling tea leaves – lovely. Some of them's really exotic, you know, from China and places like that.' She picked up Chrissy's cup. 'I'll fetch you another cuppa.'

'No, this is fine, Rose. You've been a grand help.'

'Haven't done anything but, Chrissy, maybe if you try to concentrate on how proud of his mum, the secretary, Alan's going to be . . .'

'I will, and thanks.'

'Nice of you to join us, Petrie.'

The senior mechanic was not pleased to see Rose walk in after he had started talking. She had been late leaving Chrissy and then her attention had been caught by the sight of a long line of army vehicles, each obviously in dire need of care and attention. Her heart had leaped with anticipation as she saw some vehicles that she recognised: an Austin light utility with its spare wheel anchored neatly on top of the driver's cabin; a Bedford fifteen-hundredweight general service lorry. Each vehicle bore a large red L, and each one was surrounded by trainees and, surprisingly, soldiers. Everyone stood gazing hopefully into the engines, as if by merely looking they would understand all the mysteries inside.

'Sorry, Sergeant, won't happen again, sir.'

'Better not, or you're out on your ear. Keeping our vehicles moving is about as important a job as there is. What do you know about motorcycles?'

For a second Rose felt faint as she saw again the young man pinned under the motorcycle, and heard his voice: 'Urgent, please.'

'Very little, sir.' She thought quickly. 'I'd recognise a Harley-Davidson. If you can't lift it, you can't ride it.'

The sergeant's face, red with anger, stared into Rose's. 'Is that a girly attempt at humour?'

'No, sir. I heard it somewhere.'

'Right, you're a big girl, let's see how many of them you can lift.'

He led the way across the machine shop to where motorcycles in various stages of disrepair were lying. 'Pick them up, Petrie, and if you value your skin, don't drop any.'

'I hardly think that's a sensible use of Private Petrie's abilities, Sergeant Norris.' Neither Rose nor the sergeant had heard Junior Commander Strong enter. 'As far as possible, I hope she will never need to lift a motorcycle but, in the meantime, a working knowledge of the engine would be helpful.'

'Yes, ma'am.'

'Good. Petrie, do try not to be late. The machines won't repair themselves.'

'Yes, ma'am.'

The officer turned and walked out of the workroom, leaving Rose and Sergeant Norris looking at each other while everyone else determined to look anywhere but at them.

'Get to it then, girl.'

To Rose the smell of oil was almost as pleasant as that of exotic tea leaves from 'the mysterious East'; she almost revelled in it. Soon her hands were oil- and grease-marked. As a qualified mechanic, Corporal Church instructed her painstakingly.

'What have you worked on before, Rose?' Corporal Church asked.

'My dad's van and the occasional old banger some of the lads had.'

'This is your first bike, then?'

Again Rose pictured the crashed motorcycle. 'Yes, Corporal.'

The corporal smiled, and her rather plain face seemed to light up with an inner glow. 'Good start. We'll take this one apart and put it back together again.'

It sounded simple.

'Bit fiddly,' said Rose, an hour or so later as she handed over the unfinished job.

'Maybe so, but you're well on the way, Rose.' Once more the mechanic surprised Rose with her friendly smile. 'I'll finish this off. While I'm doing that, you can clean those parts lying over there. Keep them in exactly the order you find them; in other words, pick up a part, clean said part, put it down exactly where it was to start with. Got it?'

'Yes, Corporal.'

For the rest of the afternoon, Rose scarcely lifted her head as she examined and cleaned the motorcycle parts. She found minor and, unfortunately, major dents in some pieces, but was pleased that she was able to repair them. Sally's fingernails wouldn't handle this little lot, she thought with a smile as she remembered her actress friend. She looked at her own long and very dirty fingers with their short blunt nails.

'Better get used to it, Rose.'

Rose smiled at the mechanic. 'I'm admiring them, Corporal. These dirty hands bring me one step closer.' She stopped, embarrassed.

'Closer to what?'

It was impossible to tell the exact truth, which was to be a driver, although, since she had not passed into the unit for drivers, Rose felt deep down that her dream was further away than ever. 'To be a fully qualified mechanic,' she said, crossing her fingers behind her back as she spoke.

Corporal Church stood up and stretched to her full height – which was considerably less than Rose's. 'A few weeks on bikes, Private Petrie. Do well and I'll give you an ambulance. Get that going for us and I might just be able to find a staff car that needs a little tender care.'

In spite of what she thought of as a bad start, Rose returned to her billet, a long and fairly wide Nissen hut, in a happy frame of mind. She had started to learn and had achieved a little. She had been reprimanded by the senior mechanic but admitted that she had been careless about time-keeping. He was right to tell me off, she told herself, and he took it on the chin when he caught it from the junior commander. And Corporal Church is a superb mechanic. I like her. There's something about her, nice and calm and competent. I get the feeling that she's very fair too.

Dear Mum and Dad,

If you're planning on putting a packet of tea in my sock at Christmas, could I please have it a little early, like now? Food's not bad; we had some decent gravy today, which covered up the smell of the corned beef very well, and hid the taste and all. I told you about Chrissy as trained with me. She's here too, which is lovely because she's a nice woman, but she's worried sick about her son. A really good cuppa would make quite a difference, I think. He's not long shipped out and she hasn't had a letter since he left. Have you had a letter from our Phil?

Rose stopped for a moment and shouted, 'I wish this blasted war was over.' Feeling slightly better, she returned to her letter.

Has Daisy said anything about Tomas, about where his family is? That was another horror story when we were catching up with the news. A whole village in Bohemia, which I'm told is part of Czechoslovakia, was burned down and everybody killed. It's called Lidice, the village that is. Really awful. I hope Tomas's family isn't from there. Good news is the Americans

53

have defeated the Japanese at a place called Midway, which I think is an island in the Pacific Ocean. All our senior officers were cheering so it must be something special. It was Mr Fischer who used to explain all the news to Daisy, wasn't it? Daisy said she bumped into him somewhere, didn't she? Wonder where he is because I would really like someone to explain all this.

I miss you. Today I got started on engines but they were motorcycle engines and I never worked on one before. The chief mechanic is pretty grumpy. No, actually that's not fair, I was late and he was angry. Afraid I didn't cover myself with glory as I just could not get the hang of what he was trying to explain and he got more and more impatient. I met a really nice mechanic though, a corporal, so we can't be friends since I'm just a private, but there's something about her, Mum, you know. You get a feeling sometimes, doesn't matter if they're rich or poor, but something in the face or the eyes tells you this is a good person. Well, that's Corporal Church and she was ever so supportive.

Say hello to everybody in your letters and remind our Daisy she's got a twin sister in case she's forgotten. Ha-ha.

Love to all,
Rose

Rose finished her letter, put it in an envelope, which she addressed and sealed before looking around the room, aware for the first time in several minutes that other girls had entered the hut while she had been writing and were now making themselves comfortable on beds or chairs.

'How you can concentrate, Rose?' said Vera Harding, who was about the same age as Rose. 'Who were you writing to, Laurence Olivier or Clark Gable?'

'Top secret.'

'If I'd annoyed the chief mechanic the way you did today, Rose,' a second girl entered the conversation, 'I'd have been studying the manual.'

Immediately several voices joined in, some siding with Rose. 'She's wet behind the ear, Ella. Don't worry, Rose, most of us cried for days the first time we had to work on an engine.'

'Why did they accept you if you know nothing about motorcycles? I take it you have some experience with machines?' Ella Barker went on.

'Yes, I can drive and I—'

'We can all drive.' It was Ella again, like a dog after a bone.

Rose looked at her for a time before replying. 'I am so pleased for you,' she said coldly, and smiled a little as Ella blushed.

Several of the young women in the billet began to laugh.

'Oh, Rose, oh, lovely English rose. At last someone who can give as good as she gets,' said Vera. 'Our Ella, Barker by name and barker by nature.' She ignored Ella's mutterings and continued, 'Now, do come and tell us all about yourself, and all about the handsome soldier you were writing to.'

'Sorry, Vera, I was writing home, and now I will study the manual.'

But for some time she was not allowed to return to her studies as various young women introduced themselves. By the time they all crowded around the wireless to listen to their favourite programmes, it seemed to Rose that she had known everyone in the billet, even the formidable Ella, for much longer than the short while she had been in Preston.

Having worked very hard all day, the girls were quite happy to get into bed at lights out. Rose lay for some time going over the events of the day and the evening. I miss Mum and Dad and George, she thought to herself, but these women are all in the same boat as I am, and they're making an effort – well, most of them – to get on with everyone else. I'll learn all about motorbikes – if our Daisy can go from driving cars to flying a blooming great plane, I can learn about bikes. Again the image of the dispatch rider pinned under his bike came into her head. I'll learn for you, she decided, and maybe I'll even be brave enough to ride one of them . . .

'I'm not promising,' she whispered as she fell asleep.

Next morning she joined several of her roommates for breakfast. From across the room she saw Chrissy, seemingly quite happily chatting to the women at her table. Rose waved and was delighted when Chrissy too raised her hand in greeting. Letters were delivered every day; maybe today she would hear from her son and maybe Rose Petrie would get a delivery of tea leaves.

By the end of the first week, Rose was thoroughly enjoying the work and the companionship of all the other women. Work was going well, and Sergeant Norris had even congratulated her on her aptitude and application.

'Well, well, teacher's pet,' laughed Vera as they walked back to their billet one evening after the last class. 'Aptitude and application. He'll have you a motorcycle dispatch rider before you can shake a stick.'

'I sincerely hope not. It's cars I want to drive, although ambulance drivers are needed, aren't they?'

'Every kind of driver is needed, Rose. Drivers have accidents; they get strafed or bombed just like any other soldier. There's risks everywhere.'

Vera had looked and sounded rather tense as she spoke, and Rose had the feeling that there was something on her mind. She decided to wait until her new friend was prepared to share it and so she decided to change the subject. 'What are you wearing to the dance on Saturday night? I've only got one suitable frock with me and everyone will be tired of it after a while.'

'I don't dance.'

Rose was quiet for a moment, thinking. Then she made up her mind. 'I went to lots of dances at our local church hall and at the Palais,' she said. 'I bet there was a Palais in your town too, Vera, but could I just say that if you have religious reasons for not dancing then, of course, I'll respect that, but . . .' She stopped, wondering how best to carry on now that she had started. 'But if you haven't had time or opportunity to learn how to dance, I think I could teach you.'

They had reached their hut. 'We could have some tea and a listen to the wireless if no one's having a lie-down,' suggested Vera without answering Rose's question.

'Just time to have a shower and wash my hair.' Ella, who also shared the billet, was on her way out as Rose and Vera went in.

'We'll save you some tea,' Vera called after her, but Ella waved a hand as if to say, 'No, thanks.'

'Hello, ladies, anyone for a cuppa?' Vera addressed the women inside.

'It's made already, girls, and Susan's mum sent a bar of chocolate,' Ada Plumtree, the oldest ATS member in their hut, called to them. She counted quickly. 'Two squares each if we eat quickly. Now, who's going to the dance on Saturday? There's rumours of Yanks in the area.'

'Not Yanks, Poles,' Susan argued, 'but who cares, they'll be as tall as the Yanks.'

'But, unfortunately, a helluva lot poorer,' Vera said, and everyone laughed.

'You're a married woman, Ada. You shouldn't be interested in other men.'

'I'm married, love, not dead. You going, Rose? There's bound to be at least one taller than you.'

The happy chattering went on as they relaxed after a full day of hard work.

Ella came back from the shower room to join them. 'Anyone got a spare towel? I dropped mine and it's too wet to dry my hair. I can't go into the lecture room with water dripping down my neck.'

A dry towel was produced and Ella sat vigorously rubbing her short fair hair while the others talked of the various nationalities that might turn up at the base's Saturday night dance. For many of them this dance would be the first frivolous evening they had spent in some time.

'Any POWs coming?' one of the girls asked, stunning her companions into silence.

'Prisoners? My mother would have a fit. They're the enemy.'

'They're human beings,' said Rose. 'My brother was a POW in Germany,' and then she laughed.

'What's funny, Rose? Being a prisoner anywhere isn't funny.'

'Sorry, Ada, I was about to say my brother would have loved to go to a dance. He's a good dancer. Then I remembered there weren't any women in the camps and he wouldn't have danced with a man for all the tea in China.'

'Funny things, men,' said Ada. 'God bless them every one.'

'My hair'll do, girls. We'd better get off to the canteen or we won't have time to have a decent meal before the lecture.'

The lecture turned out to be three short films on the care and maintenance of military vehicles, including motorcycles and Churchill tanks.

'Good Lord,' said Ella, as they walked home in the gathering darkness, 'from the sublime to the ridiculous. You take it all in, Rose?'

'Absolutely. I would love to drive one of those giants. The Churchill must be named after the Prime Minister, don't you think? I'll ask if I can work on one of them.'

'You're going to be lucky to get to work on a beaten-up old ambulance. Got any idea of the cost of one of them tanks?'

Ada joined Ella in teasing Rose. 'You joined the wrong branch of the service, chum, if you're set on driving. Maintenance only gets to keep them running.'

'I can hope.'

They stopped walking so suddenly that they bumped into one another. 'Didn't you ask to be a mechanic, Rose?'

'No, when I was joining I did ask about being a driver but when we took the tests the marks I got showed that maintenance is where I'm best suited. Aptitude, they call it.'

'But you can drive?'

'I told you that already, Vera. I've been driving since I was ten – tall for my age – but our dad and my brothers – had three of them – taught my sister and me how to repair and maintain.' She stopped talking, wondering if it would be thought boastful to show her pride in her twin sister. In for a penny? No, another time.

The women walked on without speaking, quite happy to be tired and to know that they had done their best all day and had, perhaps, improved their skills. They reached their Nissen hut and Ella startled Rose by breaking the silence.

'Any of these gorgeous brothers of yours available?'

'For what?' Rose asked without thinking.

The others laughed; when she realised what Ella meant, Rose laughed too. 'Sam's spoken for,' she said. 'No wedding yet, but soon, we hope. Phil's available but he's a sailor and you'll have to catch up with him. We never know where he is until he's been – if you know what I mean.'

'Hope he's nowhere near Malta. It's really getting a battering. You don't believe the Germans would really try to starve a whole island to death, do you?'

'Awful things happen in wars – on every side,' said Vera in the voice of someone who has seen and heard everything.

'Put the kettle on, somebody,' called a voice from a bed near the door, 'and come in or stay out, but make up your minds.'

Calling out apologies, they hurried inside, closing the door behind them. A few girls appeared to be asleep; others were sitting up in bed, reading magazines or writing letters.

'Last one in makes the cocoa,' called out the first voice, and soon the hut was quiet as some busied themselves with ironing uniforms, polishing shoes, or putting in curlers, making and serving cocoa to their roommates, just a few of the tasks that had to be done every night before sleep claimed them.

Rose was drifting off when she heard a voice from a bed near her. 'You told us about two of your brothers, Rose. Is the third one available?'

The question brought back all the grief and sorrow caused by Ron's death. How to answer? Pretend to be asleep? Would the question be asked again in the morning?

'Afraid not, Ella. He's unavailable.'

'Shame, but who knows, maybe the answer to a maiden's prayer will be at the dance on Saturday.'

'Shut up and let people sleep or you'll be unable to walk, never mind dance.'

Rose did not recognise that harsh voice but she did agree with her sentiments. Happily so did Ella.

Saturday came and the Nissen hut was full of excitement as the young women prepared to have a wonderful time at the rare social evening. Flora had persuaded Rose to take the pretty dress with her and, although she had worried that the dress might make her remember the embarrassing conversation with Stan, Rose had packed it – after all, she had no idea what she might be doing in the next few months. She did think of Stan, but that was because – at long last – a letter from him had arrived, and not because seeing the dress made her sad. She was delighted to have something both new and pretty to wear.

Short and sweet, said Rose to herself as she reread Stan's letter – a bit like you, Stan.

Dear Rose,

I got your letter. It was great to hear from you. I heard from a lad in my squad that ATS takes the same ranks as regular army so we'll both be privates by now, unless you've gone to be an officer and if you have, and you should, I'll be thrilled for you. I'll even salute. That would be so easy, as I've looked up to you, in more ways than one, all my life. I've done basic training and found muscles I never knew I had. They're quite glad I'm good at gym as there are competitions among the regiments. We're shipping out, can't tell you where even if I knew, which I don't, but please write to me again, Rose.

I really like being in the army and I hope you do too.

Stan

'Come on, girls, time to change from pumpkins to Cinderellas.'

The young women, in varying stages of undress, looked at Ada and laughed.

'Cinderella didn't change into a pumpkin. It was a coach, all silver and gold and with red plush cushions.' Ella heard what she was saying and stopped. 'That didn't come out right. The pumpkin changed into the coach. Cinderella didn't change into anything, did she?'

'A beautiful princess,' answered at least three of the girls.

'And this rich, handsome, completely unattached and therefore available prince fell in love with her,' said Vera.

'Absolutely. And, who knows, tonight may be the night. Anyone have any lipstick?' Ella was rooting through a very untidy drawer as she spoke.

Rose picked up her ATS shoulder bag and took two lipsticks out of it. 'Almost gone,' she said as she held them up. 'Tangee Natural pink in this one and Theatrical Red in this, but I did find refills in Boots.' She had been delighted to find the Tangee priced at one and ten, but her favourite red had been a whopping five shillings. 'I get the Theatrical Red first, but you're all welcome after that.'

Vera offered the ubiquitous Evening in Paris toilet water, an offer eagerly accepted. Rose slipped on the pretty cotton dress with its sweetheart neckline and almost full green-and-blue patterned skirt. It was some time since material had been widely available, but there was enough in the skirt to make sure that there would be a discreet, tantalising glimpse of the two petticoats she was wearing with it, one white and the other blue. She smiled as she remembered her disappointment that Stan had not taken her dancing in it.

Must have hurt my pride and not my heart, she decided, but she was quietly glad that she and Stan were still friends.

She looked over at Vera, who had changed out of her uniform into a simple blouse and skirt.

'Come on, girls,' said Ella. 'Destiny awaits.'

'Let's hope he's tall, dark and handsome, with no spots,' said Ada, and the unmarried girls shrieked in pretended horror.

The gym was already crowded when the women got there, and the noise from the band and conversations being conducted at a volume guaranteed to defeat the musicians was almost deafening, sure proof that the evening was going well. There was no time to look for a table as each girl was whisked onto the floor almost before she had removed her coat. It was only after some time that a breathless Rose saw that Vera was not dancing and was sitting alone at a table. Rose excused herself from her over-eager partner and joined her roommate.

'You're too pretty not to have been asked to dance, Vera. May I ask why you're not up on the floor?'

Vera looked at her with suspiciously moist eyes and tried to smile. 'Scruples, I suppose, Rose, and I am enjoying the music and watching all the dancers, really.'

'I have scruples too, Vera. Bet you ten bob almost every person in the room has some.'

'But they're not all engaged – well, almost engaged – to a prisoner of war.'

'A dance is just a dance, nothing more, and I'm sure that if we asked we'd find there's someone bravely dancing here who is married to a prisoner of war.'

Vera sniffed. 'You don't understand. You have absolutely no idea what it's like to be waiting for someone. I promised James, I shouldn't be here enjoying myself while who-knows-what's happening to him.'

She stood up as if preparing to leave, but Rose touched her hand. 'Sit down for a minute, Vera, and we can have a beer or some cider. Look, there's a friend of mine, Chrissy Wade. She'll go to the bar for us.'

Since Vera seemed to accept this, Rose waved frantically at Chrissy, who saw her, gave a happy smile and made her way over to join them.

'Hello, this is fun, isn't it? That music makes me feel as young as you two.'

Rose introduced Vera and asked Chrissy if she would mind standing in the line to get drinks for all three of them while she and Vera had a private conversation.

Chrissy was happy to help and, when she had gone, Rose turned again to Vera. 'You said "almost engaged". So you're not engaged to your prisoner of war but you love him and he loves you?'

'I think so.'

Now what? Rose felt totally inadequate. Was this what Stan had meant when he said she spoke like a man? Did that mean she also thought like one, for she could not think of a single thing to say to cheer up the other girl. As always in times of stress, she found herself taking a deep breath. 'Vera, you don't think you love him?'

'That's what's so awful. I know I don't love him – if loving means going all soft inside like when I see Jimmy Stewart at the pictures. I never get like that with James, but we've been paired off for years and he enlisted when he was seventeen and begged me to save myself for him and I promised, and I think that means I shouldn't want to dance with other men, especially since poor James is in a POW camp. He's only twenty and that's so sad. You have no idea.'

Rose was delighted to see Chrissy making her wary way across the dance floor.

When they were sitting, glasses in hands, and had taken at least one sip, Rose said, 'Chrissy, how old is your Alan?'

Chrissy did not answer immediately; it was almost as if she had to try to remember. 'Hard to believe he's twenty,' she said at last.

'About your James's age, Vera,' pointed out Rose as she turned back again to Chrissy. 'Does he have a girl?'

'No, and where's he supposed to meet one on a troop ship or in the desert, I do not know.'

'He could have our Vera here. She's got a lad that doesn't want her to have any fun while he's deployed.

And it's worse now,' she added quickly, as she could see anger sparkling in Vera's eyes, 'because he's a POW.'

As soon as she spoke, Rose knew that Vera did not understand her meaning. She had wanted to explain that Vera was determined to make life as pleasant as possible for her own beloved prisoner of war, wanted to assure him that she was true to him.

But Vera was standing, her face rigid with anger. 'I did not say that, Rose Petrie. I said he wanted me to keep myself for him, and he's ever so brave. He was a dispatch rider and got caught by a patrol and now he's a prisoner of war.'

'Then I'm sure he wants you to be dancing with a nice lad, Vera, instead of sitting here talking to Rose and me,' said Chrissy gently. She looked around the room. 'Like that one with the ginger hair over there,' she said in a tone loud enough for the soldier to hear. 'Honestly, Vera, if your James loves you, he knows a dance is just a dance. You're not marrying the chap.'

'Well, well, well, am I in luck? Three lovely ladies all by themselves.' The tall, ginger-haired soldier smiled, walked over to the table, said, 'May I?' and without waiting for a reply, sat down. 'Corporal Terry Webster,' he said.

'Hello,' Vera began bravely. 'I had a chum at school called Terry.'

'Don't tell me,' said the soldier, holding his hand out as if to brush away Vera's words. 'Bet she was a saintly girl whose name was Theresa. Am I right?' He laughed.

His laugh was pleasant. Rose looked across the table and smiled at him. Corporal Webster was a few inches taller than she was, and the width of his shoulders told of the strength in those long arms.

'And, Viking Princess, my hair is not, as your lovely friend said, ginger. It's called *châtain clair,* translating, for those who don't *parlez-vous*, as clear chestnut.'

'Much nicer than ginger,' agreed Rose, who was surprised to find herself drawn to the young man, so different from any of the other young men she knew. He was at ease and friendly, confident but not overwhelming, and there was more than a hint of sophistication about him. In the same situation, Stan would have been tongue-tied. She smiled as she thought of her old friend. 'And do you *parlez-vous*, Corporal?'

'Terry, please, and let's just say I wouldn't go thirsty in Paris.'

'Glad to hear that. Now this is Chrissy, and this is Vera.'

'And I'm Ada,' said another voice, and Ada appeared from the direction of the bar, obviously ready to chat to a handsome young man. 'Now, if you haven't had time, tell us all about yourself.'

Terry smiled at her out of startlingly green eyes. 'I'd rather hear all about you.'

'Behave yourself,' said Rose, forgetting for a moment that he was not one of her brothers.

He laughed and called over some friends. The rest of the girls joined them and the evening went with a swing. Everyone danced, including Vera, who, after a few minutes of arguing with her conscience, relaxed and began to enjoy the evening.

'I'll write to James,' she told Rose. 'It's only talking to other men and dancing, but all my friends are here too, aren't they?'

She looked so worried that Rose reassured her.

She wrote to her sister Daisy later that night expressing her doubts.

It's none of my business, of course, Daisy, but the poor little thing doesn't seem to know if she loves him or not. She's promised to save herself for him, and if that means what I think it means, then she's not in much danger on a dance floor with over a hundred other people on it.

We have alerts here all the time and I hate the sound of the big bombers, but if I pretend that you're flying one of them – and, yes, I know you're not a fighter pilot – then the noise doesn't bother me so much. Sometimes the rumbling and droning goes on for ages and I can't see a thing because they're too high up or there's beastly weather with thick, dark clouds.

Met a nice chap called Terry. He's taking me to the cinema next Saturday and I'm looking forward to it. He says a fantastic film has just come out in London. It's called *Mrs. Miniver*, with Greer Garson. Isn't she one of Sally's idols? It's got superb reviews and we're crossing fingers it's in Preston. And – would you believe – Terry's taller than me and he's broad and somehow seems to be much bigger. Says he was a swimmer when he was at school, and, let me tell you, he looks as if he can hold his own. Plus he's got the most gorgeous green eyes you ever saw in your entire life.

Any chance we can get leave together or meet some- where? I miss you, Daisy, even more than I miss Mum and Dad. Is that awful? Just I can't imagine telling Mum about Terry's beautiful eyes.

Rose

PS. He says I'm a Viking princess, daft, isn't he!!

The following Saturday, Rose spent the afternoon preparing for her date. She washed her long hair and brushed it dry so that it rippled over her shoulders and shone like gold. Unfortunately she could not find even the smallest piece of mascara with which to darken her fair lashes, but excitement was making her lovely blue eyes sparkle and so she decided that she would do. She was trying to decide between a dark-blue shirtwaist dress with a little white collar and a light-green fitted jacket to be worn with a pleated grey skirt when Chrissy announced that her date had arrived. Rose grabbed the dress, which was closer and easier to haul over her head, slipped on black peep-toed shoes, picked up a white cardigan and her handbag and hurried out to meet him, slowing down as she got to the end of the pathway so that her breathing had time to get back to normal.

There was no mistaking the admiration in his green eyes.

'Well, Miss Petrie, you look like something out of a magazine.'

'Thank you, kind sir, I think,' teased Rose as he gallantly opened the passenger door of the small Morris car.

'You should wear your hair down all the time, Rose,' said Terry as he started the engine. 'Now I think you look like a princess in a fairy story.'

'Not Viking?'

He laughed. 'Absolutely a Viking princess. I'm the luckiest man in the British Army.'

Terry had managed to borrow a friend's car and, as he helped her into the rather elderly vehicle, Rose found herself hoping that it would last the journey; she certainly did not want to spend time working on the ancient car in her pretty dress.

Terry did not start the engine immediately and Rose looked at him. He looked rather crestfallen.

'What is it, Terry? Has something happened?'

He sighed and leaned back in the seat. 'Rose, I'm so sorry, but we won't be going to *Mrs. Miniver*.'

Rose was disappointed as the new film was garnering rave reviews. 'Too bad, Terry. Sold out?'

'No. It hasn't got up this far yet. Something about how many copies of the film there are.'

Rose smiled. Having grown up with Sally, whose father was the projectionist in a cinema, she knew all there was to know about releases. 'It's all right, Terry. What's on?'

'You're a darling, Rose. I just knew you wouldn't fuss. *Suspicion* is playing, Alfred Hitchcock.'

'Super. I love Hitchcock's films, don't you?'

'Wow, thanks, Rose. I was so worried, having practically promised *Mrs. Miniver*.' He started the car and, happily without any breakdowns, they drove off into town. They saw the thriller, shared a bar of Batger's vanilla fudge, and enjoyed themselves immensely.

Rose was happy. Terry had not touched her at all during the film, except when he touched her hand as they shared pieces of the recently rationed sweets, and he took her hand naturally as they walked back to the car.

He drove straight back to the camp, parked and walked her to her Nissen hut where they stood at a door for a few minutes. Rose was slightly nervous. What was she supposed to do?

'May I kiss you good night, Rose? I realise we've only just met, but you're so lovely, so special.'

He was not afraid of her. Rose was cheering inside. She nodded and he took her in his arms and kissed her very gently on the lips. Rose felt her stomach flip-flop while wonderful and completely new feelings swam through her body.

'Good night, my gorgeous Viking,' he whispered against her ear. 'I'll see you as soon as I can, maybe next weekend?'

'I'll look forward to it,' whispered Rose, and he looked at her for a moment before once more kissing her.

They said good night again and then Terry turned and walked back to the borrowed car.

FIVE

York, August 1942

The train puffed slowly out of the station. Rose grasped the metal bar that stretched across the window, looked out, and said her silent goodbyes to her second posting.

She had not expected to be transferred again so soon; after all, they had been at Preston for only a few months. But less than a month after the dance, several girls had departed to 'pastures new', and Rose had been amongst those summoned to the commander's office.

'Have to lose you, I'm afraid, Petrie; seems you're needed elsewhere. We do want you to know that the ATS is proud to have you in our midst and that it has been decided – unanimously – that we can best make use of your skills in the drivers' pool. I'm sure there's no need to tell you that the utmost discretion is expected at all times. You will leave for York tomorrow to begin driver training.'

Her mind in a whirl of impressions, memories, hopes, Rose saluted and left the room. Where had the weeks gone? She had never climbed the fell, or even spent much time in the town.

You weren't on holiday, Rose, she told herself. You were learning a trade and you've done it. I don't know how, but it seems I'm going to be a driver – or a driver mechanic. Why so sudden? Did someone read that silly newspaper article? That got me accepted in the first place. But I don't care. Just as long as no one talks about it and I don't have to see it.

She was so excited that she pulled her skirt up to her knees and jumped over a bench. Realising what she had done, she looked around furtively, praying that no one had seen her. She breathed with relief; the parade ground appeared to be empty. Rose was so pleased with her new appointment that she was sure that anyone she passed could tell that her entire system was afloat with millions of tiny bubbles. She sighed but told herself that it was just as well there had been no time to become really close to Terry. That was a sad thought. A slight pang ran through her as she remembered their first meeting and their few dates. He had been a perfect host at the cinema, neither too pushy nor too restrained. He knew exactly how attractive he was, and being actively pursued by a virile, attractive man had certainly boosted Rose's morale. Their second date had been at a dance in town and Rose had been surprised to see how Terry assumed that she would not want to dance with anyone else.

'The lady's with me,' had been his remark to one of the men in Rose's own motor pool. He had not been pleased when Rose had laughingly insisted that she was going to dance with her colleague.

'You're my date.'

'Yes, Terry, but it's a dance and you can't expect me to ignore my colleagues.'

Terry had given in, but with poor grace. This is moving a little too fast, Rose decided, telling herself firmly that she had not joined the ATS to find a substitute for Stan but to become a properly qualified driver. She had given up hoping to join the élite drivers' corps – someone had said those drivers were all civilians – but the war couldn't last for ever and she, Private Rose Petrie, would be well qualified for a new and exciting civilian life.

Her euphoria melted away as suddenly as it had come. She wanted to achieve her dreams through hard work and ability, nothing else. She could not forget her encounter with the dispatch rider, which had ended so tragically for him and for those who loved him. She would always be happy that she had been able to help him but she did not want to profit in any way from his death.

You already have, a nasty little voice in her head said.

Rose brushed away the voice and allowed herself to think of her recent progress. In the few weeks in Preston after the dance, Corporal Church had been true to her word. Having got to grips, so to speak, with motor-cycles, Rose had been allowed to work on an ambulance. Silently and at length she had thanked her three brothers and her father for teaching her everything they knew.

'There was a mix-up, Petrie,' Corporal Church had said after Rose, beaming from ear to ear, had almost floated out of the office after hearing the news. 'Don't ask me what, but just enjoy yourself.' She had pointed to a dilapidated old ambulance, one door hanging open and the bonnet up. 'Get that bugger working and I'll let you work on a staff car, a fairly new Ford. I've got a ten-bob bet on that you can do it, so don't let me down.'

Later the corporal had pocketed a ten-shilling note, thanked Rose and, in the following days, had allowed her to work on the engines of both a three-ton truck and a Bedford fifteen-hundredweight utility van. Rose had found the van marginally more difficult than her father's, and the three-ton truck trickier, more modern and definitely more powerful. But she had loved every sweaty, oily moment.

'A joy to drive, Corporal,' she reported.

'Don't get too used to it, Petrie. We have loads more of them big bruisers in Mechanised Transport,' she explained, pointing to the truck, 'than we do of the gorgeous staff cars. I've heard there's a Daimler armoured car. Wouldn't that be a nifty Christmas present?'

Now, once more on her way to what could be an exciting and fulfilling post, Rose unfolded the issue of the *Dartford Chronicle* that her mother had sent because there was a picture of their actress friend Sally Brewer on the front page. Sally was in naval uniform, one beautiful hand smeared with engine oil and the other holding a can of a new miracle concoction that was guaranteed to remove dirty oil from anything.

In an inside page Rose found a different type of advertisement. 'Girls wanted to make Vidor Batteries. Aged 18 and over.' Rose giggled at that line but assured herself it was the girls, not the batteries, that had to have reached that exciting age. '21/6 per wk. 43-hr wk. Holidays with pay plus piece-work earnings.'

'Piece-work earnings' sounded rather nice. Just think, if I'd stayed at home I could have applied for that, Rose mused, knowing full well that, even if her assignments had not yet been what she had dreamed of, she was still where she wanted to be.

She thought of Terry, whom she had known for such a short time. He had definitely not seen her as 'one of the blokes'. Rose knew what she looked like and knew that she was quite attractive, if on the tall side, but Terry had made her feel feminine and even pretty. She had always thought that men found sophisticated girls like Sally or delicately formed girls like Daisy attractive, but she was in no doubt at all about Terry's feelings. He had cycled over to her unit, a week after the dance at which he had behaved as if he owned Rose, and had apologised.

'Being with you makes me feel so great, Rose. I just want to keep you to myself, you're so lovely; but I behaved like a cad and it'll never happen again.'

Rose had forgiven him, and when, a few days later, she had told him of her new posting, he took it very well.

'York isn't a long way away, Rose, and I can borrow a bike and come up when we have time off. Let's not just drift.'

'I won't drift, Terry. I'm a really strong swimmer.'

He had laughed with joy and kissed her then, a kiss that seemed to fill her with both ecstasy and longing; longing for what, she did not know, but she would keep in touch with Terry and, yes, she would be kissed like that again.

SIX

Rose had never visited York but was familiar with it from photographs in magazines and on calendars. She had looked forward to her first glimpse of the historic city. She knew that York had been bombed in April but was still stunned by how much the picture in her head differed from the new reality. The station and the railway lines had suffered, and evidence of destruction and repair were everywhere. The only building she recognised was York Minster, still standing unchallenged among ruins of houses, churches and schools.

She had travelled with an older woman, Gladys Archer, a lance corporal, who had come north from London. On the way to the camp, the drive through the old city had sickened both of them. The devastation of war was everywhere. There were huge craters in several streets, together with piles of broken glass and rubble, still uncollected. Skeletons of homes and businesses stood out against the lovely summer sky. Rose was relieved to reach the camp.

Less than an hour later, she was meeting her room-mates and unpacking her kitbag.

'Well, Petrie, still delighted to be in the Auxiliary Territorial Service?' asked a very pretty young woman, smiling brightly at Rose out of beautiful, very dark eyes as she handed her a mug of hot sweet Camp coffee. 'I'm Francesca Rossi, and I do prefer Francesca, but call me Fran if it's easier.'

'Yes, Francesca, I'm still delighted,' answered Rose, and all the young women in the Nissen hut laughed. 'I'm Rose and, believe it or not, I even like that coffee.'

'Real coffee's fearfully expensive, but the bottled mixture does make a pleasant change from the terrible tea,' said Francesca.

Gladys, who confessed to a headache after all the travelling, glared at the pretty young woman. 'What would an Italian know about tea?'

'I know all about tea,' Rose said hurriedly as she saw what appeared to be the beginning of an unpleasant scene, 'and quite a lot about coffee.'

Francesca smiled her beautiful smile. 'I can answer Gladys, Rose,' she said. 'I am sure her bark is, as you might say, worse than her bite. Firstly, Gladys, I am not Italian. My grandparents were Italians who were happy and grateful to come to England many years ago. My father, Giuseppe, was born in England and was a British citizen and that made him very proud. He fought for his country – this country – in the Great War and was gassed. His lungs were so badly injured that he lived only until 1921. I was born three weeks after his death and so I too am British, but of English and Italian descent. And yes, we have an ice-cream shop . . .'

'Best ice cream in the whole of Yorkshire,' another girl put in.

Francesca laughed. 'Yes, it is, thank you, and in the café Nonno makes the best lunches.'

'Sold,' said Rose. 'When are we free to go? And what does Nonno mean?'

'Italy is still on Jerry's side.' Gladys seemed not to want to let go.

'Grampa,' Francesca answered the second question. 'But very soon Italy will join the Allies because most Italians are unhappy with Il Duce, Benito Mussolini. Unfortunately some people here are very angry with Italians, even those whose families have lived in this country for many years. This is unfair. We are loyal British citizens whose ancestors came from Italy and, even after what happened to Nonno, we pray for the day when Italy and England will be allies.'

'Can't come soon enough,' Gladys conceded, sitting down on an empty chair.

Rose looked at Francesca and saw her lovely dark Italian eyes were sparkling with tears she was trying hard not to shed. 'Francesca, can you tell us what happened to your grandfather?'

'Everything is well now, Rose, but we will never forget it. We prefer not to speak of it, but the very day that Italy declared war against Britain, Nonno was arrested and interned. All the years he has lived and worked here and they called him "of hostile origin" . . . For him, thankfully, imprisonment lasted only a few months.'

Both Rose and Gladys gasped. 'How awful for you, Fran,' said Gladys. 'I'm sorry I was grumpy.'

Francesca seemed determined to remain calm and friendly. 'I have been in this camp several months, and I'm very happy – with everything,' she added, looking over mischievously at Gladys. 'And, Rose, you will be happy with the appalling engine the transport officer will find for you to work on, no?'

She means yes, thought Rose, but she smiled. Apart from the fact that Francesca was very friendly and determined to remain polite, even when others were being rather churlish, she was an Italian – no, she was British of Italian descent.

'No, Francesca, I was looking forward to actually driving a truck or a car or even a Jeep; instead you say I'll be in overalls, as usual, and covered in oil and gunge.'

'The driving will come, Rose. The maintenance is as important, if not even more important, than being able to drive whatever one is asked to drive. What if you are taking a politician or a general to an important meeting and the car goes phut two miles from the venue? What do you do?'

'Fix it, I hope.' Rose smiled at Francesca. 'I see your point, but everything seems to take so long.'

Francesca offered her a box of biscuits. 'Have some. They're Italian.'

'And quite delicious,' said Gladys, determined to show her better nature. 'Forgive my bad mood.'

'I think everyone in the world has a bad mood sometimes, Gladys, and, believe me, you're an amateur. An Italian, like Nonno, in a bad mood is a force of nature. Maybe we can all go to my nonno's café for lunch when we next have time off. I'll tell him, cook as for Italians: that way, we don't get chicken and chips.'

'But what about his bad mood?'

'You'll see a good mood – a beautiful sight. Maybe he'll sing. A force of nature, remember? You'll tremble and say, "What does he do with all this energy when he's angry?"'

'He uses as much energy being angry as he does when he's happy?' Gladys was laughing.

'Exactly. Now who has an afternoon off soon?'

Rose smiled. She would miss her friends from Preston, just as she had missed the friends she had made at Guildford, but she knew she would like most of these hard-working, dedicated women just as much.

'There's a very pretty girl here called Francesca,' she wrote to Stan later.

She's about twenty-one, I think. And then there's a woman, Gladys, who must be about thirty; she can be touchy but maybe that's because she's a lance corporal in a billet with several privates. Bit of a shame we have to move around so much. We say we're going to keep up but it's almost impossible to find time to write home, never mind write letters to all the lovely people I've met. I remember Grace Paterson telling us she'd made a really good friend at her training farm, but when she did get around to writing the friend had moved. Maybe Grace's letter is travelling all over England looking for her. Who knows?

She was going to add that Grace had Sam to write to now but that seemed a little insensitive. After all, Grace and Sam were in love. Stan and Rose were not. We're best friends, she decided, and always will be.

'I'm off duty on Sunday afternoon, Francesca,' she said later that evening when she met Francesca in the washroom, a place where the girls seemed to spend an

81

inordinate amount of time. Many of them liked washing small items of clothing every night and hanging them up to dry in the warm, damp atmosphere rather than sending them to the efficient but often time-consuming laundry service.

'Lovely.' Francesca smiled broadly. 'I am too. We'll sweet-talk someone at the stables to take us in. Maybe Gladys will come too.' She looked at Rose who had the strangest expression on her face. 'Is there is a problem, Rose?'

'Stables? I didn't know we had stables and, even if I did, I think my riding skills aren't up to riding a horse all the way to York. And what on earth would we do with them once we got to your granddad's café?'

To Rose's surprise Francesca burst out laughing. The fact that even her laughter was attractive and highly contagious did not, in that moment, actually endear her new friend to Rose.

'My riding is limited to hanging onto the mane of a great carthorse; lovely animal, but I prefer car seats.'

Francesca patted her gently as if she was a small child. 'We're not going to ride in, Rose, although I must admit it would be quite lovely. No, no horses. The only mode of transport in our stables is on four or more wheels – well, there could be a bicycle or two . . .'

'Before I pick you up and—' began Rose.

'Cavalry officers refer to "the stables" when they are talking about vehicle storage. I have a chum in the Blues and Royals. One picks up their jargon.'

'Does one indeed?' asked Rose.

'There's the loveliest MTWO,' began Francesca with a worried look at her new friend.

'I understand our own jargon, thank you: motorised transport warrant officer.'

'He's become rather a close family friend, Rose. Indeed, after a slice or two of Nonno's lasagne, he is putty in my hands. I'm sure if anyone is going into York on Sunday, we'll be offered a lift.'

And so it proved. Warrant Officer Starling himself had to visit the town and would be pleased to drop the girls off at the café and pick them up later.

Immediately after the all-ranks church service on Sunday, the three young women hurried to change out of their uniforms. The prospect of a few hours with no heavy stockings, no shirt and tie was delightful. Rose and Francesca, who were slender, laughed to see that they were both wearing almost identical dresses. The dresses had been fashioned taking into account the new austerity. They were A-line and reached just below the knee; material was in short supply and so there was very little swing to the skirts. Francesca, with her dark colouring, had chosen the shirtwaist in red and white, whereas Rose, a blonde, was wearing a very similar dress in light green, but with white cuffs on the short sleeves, and a white collar. The buttons on her bodice were dark green while those on Francesca's were white. Gladys, slightly more mature in age and figure, had chosen to wear a floral skirt and a simple white blouse with a blue cardigan thrown around her shoulders.

'Wish I was a bit skinnier, like you two,' she grumbled.

'Well, they do say Bile Beans are the answer, Gladys. At least, according to an advertisement in one of Dad's catalogues, they're all you need "for radiant health and a lovely figure",' Rose said mock-seriously. Gladys looked at her questioningly. 'Is a word of that true? Bile Beans?'

'She's teasing, Gladys. You don't need to be thinner; you look very nice.'

The opinion of the warrant officer was the same. 'And very nice too,' he said as he looked at his passengers. He himself was in uniform as he really did have a delivery to make in York.

Rose and Gladys enjoyed their second glimpse of the famous city. They saw the spires of the fabled minster rising up into the skyline, long before they reached the outskirts.

'Will we have time to see it, Fran?' asked Gladys. 'I'd love to get a postcard for my mum.'

'Great idea,' echoed Rose. Propaganda was already reminding the populace to keep in mind members of the Forces in their Christmas mailings and, although Rose felt it too early to even think of Christmas, she knew her family would love postcards. 'My sister was here, before the bombing.'

'Then she is one of the lucky ones,' said Francesca with a heavy sigh. 'For some reason they didn't bomb the minster and fires never reached it, but thousands of houses were destroyed. It will take years to replace them or repair the damage.'

Rose felt cold. 'All those homes. It's ghastly. There must have been so much loss of life.'

'You'd think so, wouldn't you? The raiders came at night when most people were sound asleep in bed. We were. But somehow, can you believe it, only about three hundred people died. Have you ever been bombed?' Francesca looked at her two friends.

Gladys had never experienced an air raid in her home town, but Rose, of course, had lived through many, as Dartford lay directly in the path of enemy aircraft heading for London from Berlin. 'Dartford's had some bad times, hospital wards destroyed, some houses, but apart from in London, I've never seen anything like this. It's frightening.'

''Course, I'm not telling you anything you shouldn't know,' Warrant Officer Starling piped up suddenly, 'but they say as some Luftwaffe general thought it was a good idea to destroy all the cities in England that featured in a German guidebook: Bath, York, Norwich, Canterbury and others. They made a right mess of Canterbury, missed the cathedral but destroyed the medieval centre. We can build new houses but we can't rebuild our past, our history.' He stopped, as if suddenly embarrassed by his own eloquence.

'You're so right, sir,' said Rose, 'but we can make certain that we remember it.'

'Come on. We've gone all doomy and gloomy,' complained Gladys. 'We're off base, we're going out to a delicious lunch and every girl in the unit will be jealous when we report back. Where are you dropping us, Officer?'

'Right here,' said Warrant Officer Starling as he drew up close to a shining café window over which hung a very pretty blue-and-white awning.

'We used to have the Italian colours,' said Francesca sadly, 'but after . . . Nonno decided it was better to change.'

'It looks lovely,' the girls agreed and, after thanking their driver, walked with Francesca into the little café.

Mrs Rossi, Francesca's mother, hurried out to meet them. Rose had assumed that middle-aged Italian matrons were usually of average height and rather round, but Francesca's mother was an older edition of her daughter, slender and very beautiful, with dark sparkling eyes and the longest eyelashes Rose had ever seen.

'Welcome, welcome,' she called out, her accent not Italian but Yorkshire. 'Papa has the lasagne ready and he has saved a little of his own wine for you.' She waved at Warrant Officer Starling, who was returning to his lorry, and Rose was surprised to see how different, even tender, he looked as he waved back. 'We are saving lunch for you, Enrico, whenever you come.'

Once again he raised his hand in farewell as he returned to his vehicle.

'Enrico?' said Gladys.

'Italian for Henry. It's very nice,' said Francesca, with a slight note of pride or concern in her voice. 'Mamma has been alone for too many years. Come and meet Nonno.'

'Very nice indeed,' Gladys whispered to Rose as they followed mother and daughter towards the exquisite, mouth-watering smells that were coming from the back of the building.

Francesca's grandfather was tall and broad-shouldered, but very thin – as if, perhaps, he did not eat his own cooking, or perhaps as a result of his imprisonment. He welcomed them as warmly as any Italian Rose had ever seen in the Hollywood films she had enjoyed as she grew up. In no time at all, it was as if they had known one another always. They sat at a large round table and ate lasagne, but only after they had eaten all the other delicious dishes he had prepared for them. When they told him how incredibly wonderful it all was, he sighed deeply.

'Ah, before the war, before the war I could make such dishes and I will again. This is very humble food,' he shrugged, dismissing the feast he had just served, 'but I am glad you like it. Only the best is good enough for friends of our little Francesca.'

'Ice cream, Nonno, please. Many on the base say your ice cream is the best anywhere, don't they, Rose, Gladys – and the café too?'

'Yes, and some were surprised that you're open on a Sunday afternoon,' said Rose, who had been wondering if she had enough money in her purse to pay for such a lovely meal.

Signor Rossi laughed, a laugh as hearty as his lasagne. 'Open? The café is not open; this is the house kitchen. I cook today only for family,' he gestured towards his daughter-in-law and his granddaughter, 'and welcome friends.'

Rose blushed to the roots of her hair. She was feeling quite stupid. As far as she could remember, she had not been invited to join the Rossis for lunch. They had talked about visiting the café but surely only as customers. She could just imagine her mother's reaction if she thought her daughter had gone to lunch with friends and had not taken flowers, chocolates, or even a packet of special tea.

'You are hot, Rose. I fetch the *gelato* and that will cool you down.'

Francesca and her grandfather got up from the table, collected the plates, cutlery and serving dishes and turned to go into the scullery behind them, flashing breathtaking smiles as they did so. Rose looked at Gladys, who did not seem to be worrying as she was. She was surprised when Mrs Rossi reached over and patted her hand gently. 'They're Italian, Rose, and everything is perfect. Now, I'm almost pure Yorkshire and know you're squirming with embarrassment. But that's my Francesca and I wouldn't have her any other way. Since she could walk she has been bringing people home. "Come," she would say, holding out her little hand to reassure them. "Come." Nonno has always encouraged her; she is the light of his life.'

'You're very kind, Mrs Rossi.'

Before Francesca's mother could reply, there was a knock on the door of the café. 'That will be Enrico. Excuse me.'

'Let's walk around York while the WO eats,' suggested Francesca, and Rose and Gladys were absolutely delighted to leave Mrs Rossi and the warrant officer alone.

Francesca took them to York Minster and they enjoyed visiting the glorious building. Then they wandered among the surrounding streets, gazing in awe as Francesca pointed out one interesting site after another, and buying post-cards. 'They say that house has been there for hundreds of years,' she said, pointing. 'And there's a room dedicated to each period during which it's been standing. So there's a Jacobean room and an Elizabethan, and a Georgian and a Victorian and whatever else. You must come back when we have more time. And we should explore the Shambles, the street where all the butchers had their shops in the Middle Ages, and Parliament Street and Fossgate . . .' Francesca spoke at length about her home town and Rose wondered what there was in Dartford that she could show off with such pride.

The ancient Holy Trinity Church, of course.

Gladys was not, by inclination, a sightseer and was glad to return to the Rossi café where they found Warrant Officer Starling waiting for them.

'Almost had to leave you three. Come on, Fran, shout cheerio and get in the lorry; you two, an' all.'

Rose thought wistfully of that pleasant family-centred afternoon quite often in the week that followed. Prior to joining the ATS she had believed that she knew almost everything there was to know about driving and the care and maintenance of smaller engines. She soon realised that this was very far from the case. Her initial feeling on first seeing the engine of a thirty-hundredweight lorry – small by military standards – was one of excitement.

'Magnificent,' she breathed.

The more she gazed in awe, the more terrified she became. This monster wasn't remotely like the shop's van. That engine she could take apart and put together again. Would she ever master this great beast and its bigger relatives? Simply changing a wheel would be a problem. She remembered struggling to lift the motor-cycle from the dispatch rider. That had taken time and the cycle weighed a lot less than this lorry.

But I was extra careful because I was afraid of injuring him. That made a difference.

'Come on, Rose,' she instructed herself, 'this is just another step on the road you want to take. So get cracking.'

She determined to think positively. She had stripped the engine of her dad's van before she was twelve. Surely, not ten years later, she could learn how to get the best out of this one and others like it.

It was with renewed vigour that she attended to instructions and demonstrations.

She received a quick note from Daisy telling her how, initially, Daisy had found some of the planes she was asked to fly rather frightening.

And just with a little notebook full of instructions, Rose. I like to think that our generation is smoothing a path for women in the future. The outlook for women is changing for the better. Just such a pity that it's taking a world war to do it. I look forward to seeing you cruising down the high street in a three-tonner – unless you prefer to show off in an armoured Daimler with Mr Churchill. Pity you won't ever be asked to drive the King. Nearest I've ever got to him is a signed picture in an office.

Tomas is hoping to come to Dartford with me for Sunday dinner sometime soon. High time he met Mum and Dad. We want to go out to the Humbles so that we can put some flowers there for Adair, but I think his cousin is home on sick leave.

Anyway, it would be great if you had time off too.
Love,
Daisy

That letter cheered Rose as she contemplated the joy of meeting again the man who would one day become her brother-in-law. Nothing official had been said, but the family now took Tomas's position in their lives for granted. It had never occurred to Rose when she had accosted the tall, slender Air Force pilot in Dartford that Christmas that she was meeting someone who was to become part of the family. A little time can make such a big difference.

She worked even harder as she contemplated the joy of seeing the family and having news to share.

The day came when she was allowed to drive a lorry. There was no important journey to be made; it was merely to move the vehicle from the workshop area to its habitual parking spot in the depot.

'What's taking you so long, Petrie? Are you going to stand looking at it all night or do you plan to park the damned thing?'

Warrant Officer Starling definitely had two personas: the gentle, cheerful, friendly man who loved Francesca's widowed mother, and the professional soldier who had no favourites but who treated everyone, including Francesca, with the same brusque professionalism. Francesca and her friends preferred the first one.

'I'll put it away, sir.'

'Nice of you,' he said sarcastically. 'Now get on with it.'

Still she stood when she should have been climbing into the cabin.

'It's a truck, Private; you have driven a truck before?'

'Lorries, sir, much smaller.'

'It's a big lorry, Private, just a big lorry, and you've got nice long legs to reach the brake and the clutch – a doddle. Now move out.'

'Sir.' Rose snapped to attention. A big lorry, that's all it is: a huge grocery van.

She reached up, grabbed the door handle and hauled herself up. Wow, how high above the ground she was. She sat for a moment feeling the seat under her and making herself familiar with the cabin. For several days they had enjoyed perfect summer weather, but all day rain had been threatening. It chose that moment to start. Rose looked at the windows and tried to remember where the controls for the wipers were. She started the engine. Woohoo, she thought. Lovely, lovely purring engine. The windscreen wipers functioned beautifully and she let go of the brake, accelerated a little and felt the huge vehicle move smoothly. All she had to do now was drive it to the Motorised Transport Depot. Luckily that was not too far away and she began to relax as the superbly tuned machine responded to her commands.

And then . . . disaster. Coming down the road straight towards her was another truck, a vehicle almost twice the size and weight of hers.

'Get over,' she yelled, waving her left hand furiously, but of course the driver could see but not hear her. 'It's on the wrong side of the road,' she whispered. How could he not be aware of his mistake? The truck was going to smash right into her.

It happened so quickly that she scarcely had time to think, and her brain and body worked instinctively. Rose wrenched the wheel round to the right and, protesting furiously, the large vehicle swung around while at the same time, the other driver seemed to have become aware of the situation and yanked his wheel – unfortunately to the left.

They were still heading straight towards each other. For a single mad moment, Rose wanted to close her eyes so as not to witness the inevitable crash but, in the nick of time, she hauled again on the wheel. The great vehicle obeyed her frantic instructions and swung even further to the right, almost grazing the other truck. Next it careened off the wet road, easily dismissing the slight barrier between the actual road and the field, and charged off across the grassy land where, luckily, because of the rain, no one was walking or playing a quick game of football.

'Don't slam on the brakes.' The voice in her head was her father's. To brake had been Rose's first intention but now, that well-loved voice echoing in her ears, she managed to stop her legs trembling so much and ease off the accelerator. The truck began to slow its tempestuous charge and gradually it drew to a complete halt, smack in the middle of the recreation field.

Rose slumped over the wheel as reaction hit her and the trembling began again.

'Are you planning on staying here all bloody night, Petrie, or would you like to park this bloody expensive bit of equipment where it belongs?'

Two swearwords in less than two seconds – a record for Warrant Officer Starling, who was standing beside the truck, shouting in through the slightly open window.

Rose's head snapped up. 'No, sir. Yes, sir. At once, sir.'

She had time to wonder how on earth he had got there so quickly. Had he been watching her majestic, if somewhat slow exit?

'I'd go now, Rose,' Starling said gently. 'I wouldn't want you to hear the vocabulary I use when I make mincemeat of the idiot driving that one.'

The other truck was now stationary on the road, its hapless driver being extremely sick over the front-right wheelbase.

'Back her up; don't turn her. This isn't a racing track.'

Rose was incapable of speech. She managed a salute, started the engine and began very, very slowly to back the truck across the field, hoping to do no more damage to the recreation area.

If he was watching, Warrant Officer Starling would expect to see her driving confidently and not hesitantly.

A doddle? Who had said driving the lorry was a doddle? She could not remember – perhaps she had used the word herself, perhaps it was the WO.

'This is easier than I thought,' said Rose to herself as she finally reached the road and straightened the lorry so that it was facing towards the vehicle depot.

In less than five minutes she had parked the truck in the correct place, locked it, hung the keys on the proper peg and was walking quickly back down the hill to her quarters.

'I don't half need a bath!' she declared as she slumped into a chair.

'It must have been dirtier in a munitions factory, Rose,' Gladys, who was sorting through a drawer, reminded her.

'Dustier, Gladys. You seem to know about factories. Did you work in one too, before the war?'

'Usual story: left school at fourteen, got a job in a glove factory. I made thousands and thousands of gloves. The air was full of fibre; can't rightly remember what the older women called it – ooze or oose, something like that. And then the war came and I joined up right away. Started in the kitchens and worked my way up. Before this damned war is over I want to make sergeant. I can't wait to see my husband's face when I do. He had me believing I was stupid.'

'Husband?'

Gladys wore no rings and had said nothing at all about her private life, but most of the women were still new to one another and personal information tended – depending on the individual personality – to be given slowly or all at once. Gladys and Rose were of the first group.

'Former. And no, I have no idea where the sod is, but if – when – I make sergeant, I'll find him.' She began to laugh and it was so infectious that Rose found herself laughing too.

'High time we freshened ourselves for tea,' said Gladys when they were calm. 'If we go now we might be lucky with the hot water.'

'Rose, Rose, I found this.' Francesca was hurrying in just as they were hurrying out. She was waving an envelope. 'Very masculine writing.'

'Then it's probably from my dad,' teased Rose. She thanked Francesca and took the letter. 'I'll follow you along, Gladys.'

She sat down on her bed and opened the envelope.

Dear Rose,

I have a PASS this weekend. I'm delivering someone to Durham – or somewhere thereabouts – and I'll nip in to see you. 18.00 hours Saturday. OK? Glad rags.

T x

SEVEN

Rose's meeting with Terry at the weekend was short and sweet. As promised he arrived at six o'clock on the Saturday evening. Rose, as commanded, was in her 'glad rags'. Terry was not. He was in uniform.

Rose heard an unfamiliar voice. 'I can give you twenty minutes for a quick chat, Corporal, or whatever else you can get up to in twenty minutes, but this vehicle has to be stabled before it's missed.'

Rose had been really pleased to see Terry waving to her out of the window of the small pick-up. She had expected him to arrive in whatever vehicle was being used for transporting his passenger, but was surprised to see that it was he who was the passenger.

He jumped out easily and together they watched the pick-up move away.

'Change of plan, Rose,' he said as he gave her a quick hug. 'My VIP will eventually end up in London. He was supposed to stay overnight in Durham, but I'm now driving him to an RAF station where he'll get a plane to London. Afraid I have to return the car to base and, if I'm lucky, catch a train or wait until something is returning to Preston. Could we walk or maybe grab a cup of something?'

Rose had been brought up in a house where tea was treated with great respect and so 'grabbing a cup of something' was always the last port in the proverbial storm. 'A walk would be nice.'

He took her hand and they began to walk around the station, where she pointed out the scene of her upsetting encounter with a truck on the wrong side of the road. 'I pulled over to the right to get out of his way but he pulled to his left to get to where he should have been in the first place.'

Terry hugged her to him as if she was very delicate and needed extra care in handling. 'Good God, Rose, you could have been killed. Was he a Yank? They all drive on the wrong side of the road.'

Rose had rather enjoyed being treated as if she was made of some delicate porcelain but she stepped out of his arms, taking his hand instead. 'Not all of them, surely, Terry, but I have no idea who was driving. Probably I should have pulled left. That way I would have gone into the rec ground on the other side. But look at it; it's a good job they don't play cricket here. I churned up the field quite a bit.'

Terry examined the damage and shrugged. 'A roller would take care of it – but don't suggest it or you may end up becoming their new groundsman.'

They laughed together and, tension over, wandered quite happily around the field, hand in hand, which, to Rose, felt intimate and exciting, chatting of this and that.

'We heard that two of our ships, *Eagle* and *Manchester* got sunk recently, Terry. Did you hear? I don't know exactly when. I seem to be the last person on the base to hear any news because I hardly ever have time to read a newspaper, though I listen to the news on the wireless every chance I get. My brother Phil wasn't on either of the ships and that's great.' Rose felt that she was boring her companion, who said nothing at all as she rambled on. 'Blimey, that sounded selfish. I'm sorry for all the lads and their families. And HMS *Eagle* was going to Malta with supplies so the brave people there are affected too.'

'There's a war on, Rose. These things happen every day. If we heard everything we probably couldn't function. Now forget the bloody war and pay attention to me.' He pulled her round gently so that she was facing him, holding her so close to him that she could feel his heart beating. 'Oh, Rose,' he almost groaned her name. 'When do you have a few days' leave? Let's plan a weekend together in York.' He put his face close to hers and kissed her cheek and then her ear.

Every nerve in Rose's body seemed to respond. 'Terry—' she began, but he interrupted.

'I can't stop thinking of you. Morning, noon and night. Do you feel the same way about me? You must. I can feel you tremble and respond. You can't deny your feelings, Rose, lovely, lovely Rose. Tell me you think of me too.'

Rose had thought of Terry often, but no thought of a weekend together – with all that possibly entailed – had entered her head. She pulled away from him. 'Yes, I think of you, but what kind of girl do you take me for, Terry? You can't think that I'm the type of girl who goes off for a weekend with a man I've met three times – no matter how much I like him.'

He let his arms drop to his sides. 'This is the fourth time and, damn it, Rose, I respect you. Nothing would happen that you didn't want to happen. But there's a war on. People are getting killed every day. We have to grab life while we can. Women are different now, doing men's jobs. A girl can do what she wants with her life. Old rules don't apply.'

Part of her agreed with him – and she was well aware that being held in the way that he had held her was sending exciting shivers coursing through her body – but a larger part knew that her parents would be disappointed in her if she were to spend a weekend with a man she barely knew. In fact, she was quite sure that Flora would be unhappy if she were to spend a weekend with a man to whom she was not married, and she certainly had given no thought at all to any idea of marrying Terry.

'You're too fast for me, Terry. I like you a lot and, yes, as I said, I do think about you . . .' She thought for a moment and said honestly, 'I think about you quite a lot. I've heard all the arguments about experiencing everything in case we get killed and, honestly, I don't know what I would do if I was in love . . .'

'I love you, Rose, and I'm sure you feel the same way about me. When we were so close now, didn't you just want that to go on and on? Maybe get closer?'

'In time, Terry. It's too fast—' she began.

'Frigid bitch.'

She was shocked to hear the phrase spat at her face viciously as he pushed her away so fiercely that, had she not been so athletic, she would have fallen heavily.

'Leading men on. The world is full of bitches like you. And I drove all the way up here just to see you. Well, it won't happen again.'

He left a stunned Rose standing speechless on the pavement while he took off across the field to where the pick-up was parked. She had said no; said that their relationship was moving too quickly for her. Was that so terrible, too much of a blow to his masculine pride?

Doubts ran through her head. Had he actually brought a VIP up to York? Was he driving the very important someone-or-other to an RAF station? I'll never know now, Rose thought. She looked around, hoping against hope that no one had witnessed the rather embarrassing encounter. One or two ATS personnel were walking around, one with a dog. She realised that she was cold and trembling. She could not meet anyone she knew; they would know immediately that something had happened. *Frigid bitch*. What a ghastly expression. Rose dashed the tears from her eyes. I'm not frigid, I liked it when he kissed me, but I don't want anything serious yet. Is that so awful? Mum would say, 'Oh, Rose, you haven't got the brains you were born with.' How would Daisy have handled that? Or Sally?

Rose forced herself to calm down and returned to her billet as casually as possible. 'He had to drive a VIP, so no date,' she murmured, and, picking up her sports clothes, went off to the recreation hall to see if she could find someone to beat at badminton.

Rose returned from the badminton courts feeling pleasantly tired but quite pleased with herself. She had beaten a sergeant – which was not, in the opinion of one or two of her friends, a particularly smart thing to do; but since the sergeant had asked that a return match be played when he had recovered both his pride and his equilibrium, she disagreed. She had also played in a mixed foursome where she was obviously the most experienced player, so that her team won easily. The others were happy to have met someone who could probably help them improve their games.

'If you ever have time, Rose.'

She had agreed, and it was only when she was walking into the mess hall with Gladys and Francesca that she again remembered Terry's wounding words and all her doubts came flooding back. She heard Stan's voice: 'I'm not in your league, Rose.'

Somewhere there had to be a man who would love her even if she were better at some things than he was.

She wrote, of course, to her twin sister, the one person in the world who would never be shocked or horrified or angry about any of the thoughts that were racing around in her head.

I felt humiliated, Daisy, worse than when Stan told me the lads were all scared of me, so scared that they didn't even want to . . . well, get a bit closer. I'm tired of being one of the lads, but I don't want to be bullied into something I'm not sure of or ready for.

Her letter reached Daisy when, for once, Daisy had a free morning, and so a reply was dispatched much more quickly than usual.

Poor old Rose. Your Terry was not a nice character and you're much better off without him. I have to remind you that Stan was very brave to tell you what he did. It couldn't have been easy. Not in his league. Silly Rose, that proves he knows you're very special.

Stan loves you but not the way Tomas loves me –
and that doesn't mean you're not an attractive
woman. You're gorgeous and just haven't met the
right chap yet. Stan's not the only decent man in the
world, Rose; there are lots of them. I've been blessed
to love two wonderful men, Adair and my darling
Tomas. We're hoping to have good news for our
families soon but in the meantime we very rarely see
each other and so can't make definite plans. Stop
looking for Mr Right and one day you'll fall over
him. Just see if you don't.

All my love – of the sisterly kind!!!

Daisy

Very funny, Daisy, said Rose as she read the letter but,
as always, communication from her sister cheered her.
Rose was no closer to knowing when she could get back
to Dartford. Apart from seeing her family, she had hoped
to meet Cleo, who was now in London, but the supply
of military vehicles needing careful attention continued
to grow.

'A full week as soon as it can be managed, Petrie,' was
the usual reply to any request for a short pass.

'Don't forget there's a war on,' she told herself
gloomily. But how could anyone forget? The girls had
been miserable when sweets and chocolate had been
rationed in the previous month, but if that wasn't bad
enough, biscuits were added to the long list of rationed
foods. Signs of war, especially death, were everywhere.
Not even the Royal Family was exempt. On 25 August,
the King's youngest brother, Prince George, Duke of
Kent, was killed in an air crash near Wick in Scotland.

'War's no respecter of anyone,' said Gladys, as she looked at sad newspaper photographs of the beautiful young duchess. 'She was a princess before she married Prince George,' Gladys informed them all. 'Greek, I think. And there's a baby boy just born as will never meet its father.'

'Terribly sad,' said Rose. 'Can't begin to think of how sad the poor woman is when she should be really happy.'

'Oh, Rose, there are many, many mothers mourning the father of their children. But it shows that the royals are just as much at risk as anyone else. They are suffering too. Buckingham Palace was damaged and even the Houses of Parliament.'

'It's all ghastly,' said Rose, 'but as far as the palace and Parliament are concerned, I would imagine those were deliberate targets. Let's find something cheerful to talk about. Didn't someone say that *ITMA*'s coming back again? I love hearing "Can I do you now, sir?" Absolutely guaranteed to get my parents laughing.'

'Didn't I hear something about moving it to the seaside and calling it *It's That Sand Again*?' Gladys asked. 'Doesn't seem to matter since I seem to be somewhere else whenever there's anything funny on.'

'Well, they never did say we'd be working office hours, but there is a social in my church hall in two weeks,' Francesca announced. 'Anyone who's off on that Saturday evening is more than welcome. I can tell you two that things haven't been very nice lately. Some of our customers have stopped coming and Nonno is afraid he'll be interned again. So many men of Italian descent have been already, and conditions in these camps can be poor . . .' She forced a smile. 'But no more of those worries – back to the social. Mum and Nonno are helping with the food and they're hoping that loyal customers will support him. There'll be dancing too and – this is my mother talking – a small but very select band. That probably means a piano and an accordion, if Father Geddes can find someone. Two shillings covers admittance and supper; drinks extra but any profit goes to the Spitfire Fund.'

'I'm up for that,' said Rose. 'Count me in.'

Others agreed too, depending on the availability of transport. One girl said it would be against her principles to support the Catholic Church.

'Golly,' said Gladys, 'I had no idea Spitfires had a religious affiliation. Learn something new every day. Pity they're not C of E, but I'll come, Fran, if I can get into my party frock.'

Rose had fallen into an easy friendship with Francesca and her family. The Rossis were extremely hospitable and seemed genuinely delighted when Francesca brought friends home. Francesca's grandfather was pleased that Rose's family were shopkeepers and he liked to chat with her.

'The Emperor Napoleon said that England was a nation of shopkeepers, Rose, but now you see that we Italians are becoming English shopkeepers too.'

Chiara Rossi smiled, pleased to see that already it was as if Rose and the Rossis had known one another all their lives.

'Enrico is on duty the evening of the church social, Rose, and so he will not be here to bring my Francesca home. If you have an overnight pass, would you stay the night here? Nonno is really too old for late nights and, if you are here, he will not stay awake fretting if she comes home with the dawn.'

'She won't come home with the dawn if she's with me, Mrs Rossi. We're both on duty mid-morning.'

'Good, it is settled then. And you must call me Chiara, please Rose.'

Early on the evening of the dance Rose and Francesca were able to get a lift from some soldiers from a nearby base who were going into York. Carrying their party dresses, shoes and overnight things, the young women clambered into the back of a Leyland breakdown lorry.

'Pray we don't see a vehicle in trouble, girls. We'd have to stop,' grinned the corporal who'd helped them on board.

But it was a perfect early autumn evening and the road remained clear. The soldiers jumped down and gallantly caught their overnight bags and then the girls as they lowered themselves onto the pavement just a few steps from the Rossis' front door.

'There is plenty of hot water for washing,' said Francesca's mother as she welcomed them, 'and I have the ironing board ready in the kitchen if the dresses need pressing. But first we will have supper.'

'But, Mamma, we will eat at the social.'

'Nonno is preparing pasta with pesto especially for Rose. Now, go, put your things in the bedroom and hurry back.'

It was, thought Rose, like being a child again, and so like being at home that she felt her eyes begin to prickle as if she might cry.

'Lovely, Mrs Rossi . . . Chiara, although I have no idea what pesto is.'

'A sauce, delicate and utterly delicious.'

The girls hurried to the bedroom and Rose smiled with pleasure. The furnishings were perhaps more feminine and rather more expensive than those in the room she had shared with Daisy, but basically they were the same. Two beds, but with matching quilts, one chair covered in the same material as the curtains, a very pretty soft-grey carpet, a white dressing table that any girl would have envied and, on the wall close to it, a porcelain hand basin with gold taps in the shape of dolphins.

'How lovely, Francesca.'

'Oh, good, I'm so glad you like it. It was refurnished for my sixteenth birthday and I had quite a job persuading Nonno not to order everything in pink. I do love having my own washbasin. Three people and one bathroom makes for disastrous mornings.'

'Think what it's like having seven,' said Rose, remembering frantic mornings when every Petrie was at home.

'Good and bad, Rose. I have my own little sink with my beautiful taps, but do you think I would not trade them, without thought, for my father?' She decided that she had been too serious. 'Forgive me. The discussion over the death of the King's brother reminded me that I too never knew my father.' She smiled. 'But I have Nonno, grandfather and father rolled into one. Quick, I smell the pesto.'

They hurried along the corridor and down the stairs to the kitchen, only to be enveloped in Mr Rossi's arms. 'Rosa and my little Francesca,' he said. 'Come, I have made something special.'

They sat down at the table where Rose was surprised to see that the plates and bowls were of blue glass. The serving dishes were blue with exquisite flowers rioting over them.

106

'From Sicily,' explained Chiara as she saw Rose admiring them. 'And, Papa, what is in your pesto sauce?' She turned to Rose. 'It should have basil leaves but there is no basil. In spring he uses wild garlic leaves, equally delicious . . .'

'But only if you pick before the flowers come, Rosa,' said Nonno, 'and yes, Francesca, I have not the wild garlic so just eat, yes.'

For some reason that was when Rose remembered Sam and the generous Italians who had sheltered him in Tuscany and the Italian priests who had seen that letters from escaped prisoners of war eventually reached their parents. While they ate the delicious food, she told the Rossis all about Sam and about Grace, whom he loved.

'And, would you believe, even Grace thought that Sam was in love with our friend Sally.'

'That is a good happy story, Rosa. I think my compatriots would say, "We must care for this boy because he needs us. One day, who knows, a child of ours may need the help of a stranger."'

'I wish everyone thought the way you do, Mr Rossi.'

'Most people do,' he said with a smile. 'And now you two must make beautiful for the social. Mamma and I have packed the boxes, Francesca, and we must go now. Mamma will take her keys and so you make sure to take yours.' Then he spoke in Italian and Rose had no idea what he was saying.

Francesca, however, laughed. 'So typically Italian, Rose. One of Mamma's friends has her nephew staying for the weekend – Nicco, he's eight and an angel. But that doesn't matter. What matters is that Nicco wants to come home with Nonno, who will leave the social early, and so tomorrow morning we will have another place at the table. Five, almost as difficult as at your house.'

They laughed and hurried off to change.

Francesca wore a rather prim, short-sleeved white blouse but her skirt was a glorious red circle of pure silk. Around her waist was a broad black belt and on her feet she wore toeless black court shoes. She tied back her hair with a silk scarf the exact colour of her skirt. Rose wore her last summer's best dress of green cotton, with a sprinkling of yellow buttercups embroidered around both the hem and the sweetheart neckline. On her feet were heeled white sandals.

'You look super,' she told Francesca. 'That skirt is glorious. I don't think I've ever seen real silk.'

'Thank you. I love it. It began life as my Yorkshire grandmother's parlour curtains. Mamma found them in a trunk and had a skirt made for me and a blouse for herself. Waste not, want not – or should it be, "Make do and mend"?'

'Either or both. You'll be the belle of the ball.'

Francesca laughed. 'Everyone's seen it before.' She hesitated and then walked over to her lovely dressing table. 'Would you like to wear these? They're daisies, not buttercups, but they would look lovely in your hair.' She held out two bone hair clasps. Each was a large white daisy with a bright yellow centre.

Rose, who had been feeling a trifle underdressed for a social, looked at the lovely clasps, took them from Francesca and held one on each side of her hair which, for once, she had allowed to hang down her back. 'I'd love to borrow them, thanks, Francesca, and they do, if I may say so, look great.' She fished in her bag. 'The least I can do is let you use my Theatrical Red,' she said, handing her friend her lipstick.

'Matches perfectly. Thank you.'

Feeling quite pleased with themselves, the girls picked up their coats and hurried downstairs.

'The hall is just around the corner and we can make a grand entrance. Have you been to a church social before?'

'Of course. I'm C of E and our vicar, Mr Tiverton, really tries to make the church the heart of the community.'

'Then you'll be quite used to all Nonno's customers coming up to ask you a million personal questions – oh, and the priests, of course. There's two of them: Father Geddes, who pretends that he hasn't a serious bone in his body, and Father Danco, a Belgian refugee, who has *only* terribly serious bones in his. Poor man, he ministers especially to local refugees – we have several – and I suppose it's hard to laugh when you've been forced to flee from your home.'

'Don't worry, Francesca. I just know I'm going to have a really wonderful time.'

They did. They chatted for a few minutes to Francesca's mother and grandfather, their friends and the eight-year-old Nicco, who was, as Francesca had said, delightful. Next, as Francesca had forewarned, they ran the gauntlet of the elderly but razor-sharp priest. Rose was introduced to so many people that she eventually gave up trying to find some way to remember them. Besides, I'll probably never meet any of them again, she decided.

They were in great demand, but Francesca confessed to Rose that she was still 'rather fond' of her cavalryman. 'He's in North Africa and writes as often as he can.'

Rose enjoyed meeting everyone but was slightly wary of several of the young men who approached their table.

The food was good, especially when they took into account how very difficult it was to source ingredients these days. The music was also very good; Father Danco was an extremely talented pianist, and there was the church's elderly lady organist, who was also an excellent if rather playful clarinettist. No accordion player turned up until after the interval. He had spent the first part of the evening playing for the Boys' Brigade in a Unitarian Church hall a few streets away. Again, the whole atmosphere was so redolent of Dartford that Rose felt happily nostalgic.

A friend of the unnamed 'cavalryman' had promised to drive the girls back to their unit at seven the next morning, and so they promised Nonno and Chiara that they would slip in quietly before midnight.

'At least an hour before midnight would be very nice,' said Chiara when she kissed them as she, Nonno and young Nicco were leaving, their boxes now completely empty – a sure sign of a good party.

The girls laughed and went back into the hall, only to be immediately snatched by ardent young men and whirled back onto the dance floor.

When the music stopped, before the band could play an encore, Rose thanked her last dance partner, assured him, yes, I'd love to see you again, and hurried across the floor to where Francesca stood like a brilliant light surrounded by adoring moths of all shapes and sizes. Three times more they danced and then Rose refused. 'Sorry, boys, it's been lovely, but we're on duty first thing. 'Bye.'

Francesca laughed. 'They're so sweet. Some of them know David. I'll write to him tomorrow and pass on all their good wishes.'

'You won't have time, Cinderella,' said Rose. 'Another friend of David's will be outside your front door at seven o'clock tomorrow morning, so let's hurry.'

'These streetlights are a pain,' complained Francesca. 'They're so faint they're almost . . .' She stopped, stood completely motionless on the pavement and pointed with a shaking hand. 'Was that lightning, Rose, or did I see a flame?'

'I was looking at the streetlight . . .' began Rose, turning and peering through the darkness.

'Mamma! Nonno!'

Francesca emitted a blood-curdling scream and began to run. A mere two hundred yards away, on the street where the Rossis' house stood, flames were intermittently hurtling into the dark sky.

'It could be anything on the street,' Rose tried to console her as she easily outdistanced the younger girl. In no time at all, she had turned the corner onto the street. Her heart seemed to stop beating as she saw dense smoke belching from the café's windows.

'No, no, no.' Rose could feel her blood rushing through her veins as she stopped directly in front of the building. There was much more smoke than flame, but she knew the fire was gaining. She hurried to the door and stepped on something that crunched beneath her feet. Glass. But surely . . .

'Mamma, Nonno.' A sweating, panting Francesca was beside her, hammering on the door.

'Your keys. Quickly. Nicco is in there too.'

'I dropped my bag.' Francesca screamed again, 'Mamma, Nonno, wake up!'

'Quiet, quiet, calm. We'll get in.' Rose took off her shoes and broke the glass that remained in the café door.

She put her arm through and tried to open the door from that side, but it was useless. The door was locked. She turned back to the sobbing, desperate Francesca. 'I'm going to squeeze through the window. Go and find someone, anyone; there will be an ARP warden and he'll have been alerted to the flames. Go.'

'I can't, Rose,' she almost screamed. 'My mother, Nonno, little Nicco, we have to get them.'

Rose looked her straight in the eye, her voice calm and low. 'Go, Francesca,' she urged her again. 'I'm more supple than you. Run.'

Francesca hesitated for a second and then turned and, as quickly as she could, retraced her steps along the sleeping street, her desperate calls for help growing fainter and fainter as she moved away. Rose desperately tried to work out the best plan of action. Obviously the Rossis had been overcome by smoke and she knew that smoke inhalation was very dangerous, but the building was now very much alight, and if help didn't come soon . . . She could not bear to think of the consequences. Rose took off her shoes and used the heels to hammer down the glass shards that were stuck to the door frame, knowing that she would be cut to ribbons if they impeded her entry. Having used as much time as she thought she could possibly spare, she rolled her dress up to protect her chest, put her arms and upper body through the opening and, praying that one of the sleepers might hear, she called their names as loudly as she could. Smoke filled her mouth, her throat and then her lungs, but she bent down until her hands found the glass-covered floor and, her mind full of the thought of the possible death of yet another innocent child, she walked her hands forward. Her body painfully followed as her legs were scraped across the broken lower frame of the door until she thought she could bear it no more. Her eyes stung from the smoke, her lungs were full of it, but the thought of how much more the three helpless people in the house – one of them an innocent child – had inhaled, made her brave. With a last surge of energy, Rose forced her protesting body into a roll and felt some slight relief as her battered legs lifted into the air and she found herself in the room. Surely she heard the clanging of the fire brigade getting louder, closer? Her roll had banged her against the bottom of the staircase – as yet undamaged by the fire, which she could see racing towards her from the café. The welcome noise of the fire engine reinvigorated her and somehow, coughing and choking, the torn skirt of her summer frock now held over her nose and mouth, she was able to struggle up the staircase. Something that felt like a lump of lead at the pit of her stomach reminded her that she had no idea where the boy, Nicco, was sleeping. So small, so small, it would take such a little amount of inhaled smoke to kill him.

That knowledge served to strengthen her, and Rose pulled herself on up the staircase, hearing the crack and hiss of flames advancing behind her. She sobbed a little but did not need to look to know that the fire was now well established. The corridor was lit only by the glow of the flames and she realised that she was confused. Which door led to which room?

'Nicco,' she gasped. 'Chiara, Nonno,' but there was no answer. She tried the first: it was a store cupboard. She staggered to the next and could see the outline of a bed near the window. She threw herself towards it and – oh, with what relief she felt it lift under the pressure of her exhausted arms. Clean air flew into the room and, with it, voices. Rose turned from the window and staggered to the bed. Chiara lay there. Was she dead? Rose pulled back the covers and, thankful to feel a slight rise and fall of Chiara's ribcage, managed to lift the slim body up into her arms.

Please let me get her to the window.

Almost immediately another bulky, dark figure seemed to materialise beside her. 'I'll take her, love,' a masculine voice said gently. 'Come on, you too. Let's get you both out of here.'

'No, there's a child and an old man.' She stumbled from the loose grip of the fireman who had Chiara in a professional lift and was trying to lift the struggling Rose. 'Save her,' Rose beseeched him and, turning, went back out into the corridor. Flames jumped from the top of the stairs to the wooden doors and Rose tried not to think of the horror that had to be inside the room at the end of the corridor, which was ablaze.

She wanted to scream with fear and misery, but there was a child to find. 'Nicco . . .' She could scarcely hear her own rasping voice as she tried another door. The handle burned her hand but the door opened and there, in front of a slightly open window, was a small folding bed. Flame shot up beside her through the wooden floor but somehow she kept going and reached the bed where the child lay very still. Rose bent to lift the small body but her strength was gone. She felt herself slipping, slipping, heard another deep voice say, 'She's got the boy,' and then – nothing.

EIGHT

October 1942

How brave her friend was being. Rose knew how much Francesca mourned her beloved grandfather, for Signor Rossi had died in his burning bedroom. She had almost given up hope that those responsible for setting the fire that had injured her mother, Rose and young Nicco – and killed Nonno – would ever be found. The local police were doing their best to investigate, but it appeared that no one had seen or heard anything on that dreadful night, and there was no clear evidence pointing to anyone in particular. Local police were following all leads to possible suspects, as Nonno's café had not been the only target of thieves and arsonists. For the moment the arsonists appeared to have been very clever, or very lucky – perhaps both.

Rose, Francesca, her mother and Nicco were taken to hospital. Francesca had not been injured, or exposed to the smoke, but she was suffering from exhaustion and shock. After a night in hospital, being carefully monitored by trained staff, she was allowed to return to her unit. Rose, suffering from smoke inhalation, shock, and severe cuts on her body and legs, remained hospitalised for a week, longer than her Dartford stay for the injury sustained when the munitions factory had experienced bomb damage. Little Nicco's terrified parents gave thanks for the fact that Chiara had allowed their little boy to sleep beside an open window. He would be hospitalised for a little longer, but cold, night air and brave firemen had definitely saved his life.

It was only when her parents arrived a few days after the fire that Rose learned that Mr Rossi had died in the blaze that had destroyed his life's work. She understood too why Francesca had not come to see her.

'Lovely girl, Rose. She's back in your billet, on light duty. When she visits the hospital, she spends all her time with her mother,' Fred told her.

'Chiara will recover, won't she?' asked Rose in trepidation.

'So says the very handsome soldier who spends as much time with Mrs Rossi as Fran does.'

Rose tried to smile. At least Mrs Rossi and her daughter had Warrant Officer Starling to help them.

Francesca did write a short note, which was delivered by WO Starling on the day that Rose's parents returned to Dartford, where they had left their dear friend Miss Partridge in charge of both the shop and their foster son, George.

Dearest Rose,
    It is impossible to thank you. You saved my mother's life.
    Casa mia è casa tua.
    Francesca

116

Rose felt the tears welling up in her eyes and fought to control them. 'I didn't do enough; twice in my life I didn't manage to do enough.'

Warrant Officer Starling patted her hand in a somewhat embarrassed fashion. 'The firemen say Chiara would have died if it hadn't been for you. That's two of us in your debt, Rose. Signor Rossi didn't stand a chance, but the doctors swear he would have known nothing of what happened.' He smiled. 'Now get better and get back to work, and don't think this makes any difference.' He moved towards the door, where he turned. 'Except when we're off duty.'

Lucky Chiara, thought Rose. He is a good man and, as far as I can tell, he really, really loves her. She relaxed back against the pillows and was almost asleep when she heard a beloved voice say, 'Sorry, Nurse, we won't wake her; we'll sit for a minute just looking at her.'

'Daisy.'

The twin sisters hugged each other as if they would never let go. It was the slighter Daisy who, looking unbelievably smart in her ATA uniform, let go first. 'Rose, this is Tomas.'

Rose had been aware of another figure, tall and slim, but had been so overcome by seeing her sister that his presence had not really registered. 'Tomas, it's so lovely to see you again, but why, how . . . I'm sorry, this all feels like a dream.'

He bent down and kissed her forehead. 'You will permit, Rose?' he said as he moved aside to make room for Daisy.

'If it's a dream, it's the shortest one. We must go, Rose. Too many strings have been pulled and I mustn't take advantage. I'm flying Tomas up to the north of Scotland, a place called Wick, if we can find it, and then I'll deliver the plane to somewhere near Edinburgh.'

'How will you get to your base?'

'Usual way, hitch. Don't worry about us. We're old hands, but although I was absolutely stunned when I heard about the fire, the timing did work out beautifully . . . and stop looking at my hands. There are no rings there.'

Tomas laughed. 'She plays hard to get, Rose. Now, before we go, is there anything you need, anything we can get for you, or do? Just mention.'

Rose was still holding Francesca's note. 'You don't happen to speak Italian?'

Daisy took the paper and handed it to Tomas. 'Easier to ask what he doesn't speak. He is so clever,' she said with proprietary pride.

Tomas ignored her and took the note. He read it and smiled. 'Very simple, Rose. Your friend says her house is yours. It doesn't mean literally, but it means that you are as close as a valued family member.'

'You are wonderful, Rose Petrie,' said Daisy. 'Take care of yourself. No more jumping into burning buildings. Promise.'

'I actually rolled in, but I promise.'

She watched the ward door close quietly behind them. *My sister was here and her Tomas. First WO Starling and then Tomas.* She remembered Daisy's note: 'Stop looking for Mr Right and one day you'll fall over him.' *All right, Daisy, but I want one just like yours.*

*

A few days later she was back on duty. Francesca had been there to meet her as she arrived back at the base. The girls hugged and stood for a few minutes just being aware that they were alive.

'I'm sorry I didn't come, Rose, but Mamma . . .'

'I know. You must believe that they'll find who did it, Francesca. They'll question everyone who has ever said a nasty word about Italy or Italians.'

Francesca tried to smile. 'Let's not tell them about Gladys, Italians and tea.'

'Good to laugh, Francesca,' Rose continued as they walked to their billet, 'but how are you both doing, really?'

'Rose, how would you feel if someone you loved very much was burned to death, your mother and two friends were injured, and you lost your home and everything you owned? It will take time.'

'I know, dearest Francesca. Just remember that I'm here.'

'You are special to both of us, Rose. Now let's deal with the others.'

They were warmly welcomed and, after the initial enquiries as to Rose's health, it was ATS life as usual.

'You don't want to ride motorbikes, do you, Petrie?'

'I'd prefer not, sir,' replied Rose, carefully looking at Warrant Officer Starling's left ear instead of meeting his eyes.

'But you can ride a bicycle?'

'Yes, sir.'

'Then give this a try. I'm considering asking permission to purchase several of them to facilitate speedier movements around the station.'

Starling smiled, as if he were a conjuror doing tricks at a children's party, and pulled a container aside to reveal a surprisingly small two-wheeled object.

'What is it, sir?' Rose asked.

'It's a prototype of the Excelsior Welbike, Private – basically a very small motorbike.'

'A Welbike?'

'That is what I said. Now, if I'm not taking up too much of your valuable time, get on it and start the engine.'

Rose looked at the strange little machine in front of her. More than anything it reminded her of a child's scooter. It had a seat, and handlebars that seemed to be perched much higher than the seat although, thankfully, as on a normal bicycle, that could be adjusted. It had two wheels, each less than half the diameter of a bicycle wheel.

'I can't find the brake – or the lights. How will it help in the winter?'

'There's a rear brake and I want you to test it. No lights? We won't break the law then, will we?'

'Sir.'

Rose adjusted the seat and mounted. 'Nice balance,' she said.

'The War Office is delighted that it meets with your approval,' said Starling with his usual sarcasm. 'Now, go round the camp putting it through its paces. Quite small fuel tank; adequate power. I'll be interested in the mileage.'

Mileage, thought Rose as she turned on the engine; this could take some time.

Half an hour later she returned to the depot. 'No suspension, sir, but, thankfully, the rear brake does work. I got some odd looks as I went round perched like a parrot on a wire.'

He laughed. 'You must learn to accept progress, Petrie. You are a bit on the tall side to be comfortable on it, but that's a small price to pay. How did it handle?'

Rose, who had felt rather silly perched on the too-small Welbike, had to admit that the little machine handled very well and did build up speed very quickly.

'Good. I'll have one of the shorter women try it out before I make a decision. Dismissed.'

Rose saluted and turned to the depot door when his voice stopped her.

'Rose, tell me truthfully, how's Francesca doing? Her mum's worried. She tries to behave as she always did, bright as a button, but it doesn't ring true.'

'Sir—' began Rose, but he stopped her.

'Please, Rose, Chiara's worried. She's angry that Francesca didn't ask for an extension of her compassionate leave. She would have got it. I haven't the right to interfere . . . had thought Christmas might be the right time to move on. We've known each other for almost seven years. Francesca never knew her dad and so there hasn't been a problem. Sorry, you don't need to . . .'

Rose smiled at the usually so-controlled warrant officer. She wanted to advise him to keep to his original plans for Christmas, but she hesitated; he moved so quickly from friend to boss. She dared not 'step out of line', to use her brothers' phrase. 'Francesca knows she could have asked for more time, sir, but she felt it was better to get back to her normal duties as quickly as possible. Not that she's finished with grieving. I've no idea how to help her there.' She hesitated and then spoke again. 'I lost my brother Ron early in the war, but I've never been in her position. I do know she misses her grandfather and she worries about her mother. Frankly, I think she's worried that there could be another attack. You must know that the police have said that whoever torched the Rossis' premises dropped a canister of smoke quietly through the letterbox. That put Chiara, Nonno and little Nicco to sleep. That wasn't done out of kindness, so that they wouldn't know what was happening. It was deliberate so that no one would be alert enough to go for help. That's sick hatred. Francesca is angry because she stayed later at the dance than she had promised. She feels guilty and has convinced herself that if only she'd gone home earlier, she might have seen who did it, might have been able to stop it.'

'Might have died herself, more like, and you too. Four, five deaths because some twisted soul doesn't like Italians. Doesn't bear thinking of. Go home with her when you can spare the time, Rose. Chiara likes you.'

'I like her too. So she's found a place to live?'

'No, not yet. We found her a flat in a big house. Woman who owns it can't really afford to live there any more – no real income, poor old thing – and she's afraid that she'll be forced to take in lodgers. I can understand that. Elderly woman with no family to help her could be a bit scared of strangers, especially ones she couldn't understand. Eventually Chiara will get some insurance money that will help her rebuild. The Government's too stretched to help out, and if they did have a bit of cash it would go to the poor sods bombed out. The house and café will have to be demolished and that'll take time – she's bottom of a huge list. There's one or two pieces that could be repaired, things that belonged to Chiara's husband or to Signor Rossi. Unfortunately, what the fire

122

and smoke didn't destroy, the water did; but, thanks to you, Rose, she's alive.'

Rose remembered standing in the smoke-filled room, praying that she would not drop the unconscious woman. 'A fireman was there.'

'So you said, but the firemen say they couldn't have saved both of them without you. Dismissed, Private,' he said brusquely, changing from friend to senior officer in a blink.

Rose, not having been offered the use of the Welbike to whisk her back to her billet, was at the end of the line for supper. Nothing appealed to her and she was suddenly very, very tired. 'A mug of tea will be enough, Gladys,' she said to her other close friend in the unit.

Gladys fetched a tray of tea and two clean cups. 'Fran's gone for a swim. Good for her to get a bit of exercise.' She was quiet for a moment as she poured tea, but then said what was bothering her. 'You were a long time up at the depot, Grace. Didn't go unnoticed, if you get my meaning. Is everything all right?'

'Boss has a new toy called a Welbike. It's supposed to be for front-line troops. Basically it can be dismantled and carried like other kit. I tried it out for him, manoeuvred or guided it, I don't know which, all round the station, timing each journey.'

Gladys reached for the sugar. 'Good Lord, what's a Well Bike like?'

'One word, one L – don't ask why because I don't know. It's a cross between a bicycle, a motorbike and a toy, if you ask me, and dashed uncomfortable for someone of my height. Even with the seat lifted, my knees were tucked under my chin. And no one need worry about my

123

being closeted with the WO, Gladys. Most of the time, I was out around the camp making a laughing stock of myself; lots of personnel, including the Methodist chaplain, saw me.'

'Good. There's been a little gossip about Francesca, Francesca's mother and Starling . . .'

'No one's business who the WO chooses to walk out with.'

'I know that, and most people in this camp know that, but Mildred says she overheard two girls saying he'd hugged Fran when she arrived back from the hospital. Not a sensible thing for a senior officer to do.'

'He's human, Gladys, and emotion got to him. Believe me, he is very deeply in love with her mother.' She realised she was probably breaking Starling's confidence and asked Gladys not to mention what she had told her. 'C'mon, I think I've got a rather squashed tube of Rolos in my bag. They'll do for supper.'

'Should have tried the barley soup, Rose. Seemingly the Ministry of Food, would you believe, has been asking the British housewife for her cooking secrets and this recipe was picked up and tried out: barley, onions, carrots, salt and pepper, a cup or so of milk and water. Takes about two hours plus soaking time but I'll give it a try on my next leave.'

They walked back to their billet, meeting Francesca on the way.

'Had a good swim, Francesca?'

'Great, thanks. My mind seems to be able to shut off from everything when I'm in a pool. Nonno used to say it was because my family is Sicilian and happiest in water.'

'I feel exactly the same, but the water's hot and in a nice, deep bath tub.'

Such a relief to laugh.

'It's lovely and warm in here,' said Gladys as she pushed open the door. 'Your hair will dry in no time.' She waited for a moment and then added, 'How's everything going, Fran?'

They took off their coats and joined two other women who were sitting knitting beside the stove.

'Slowly. There is so much demolition work and rebuilding to be done in York. We are at the bottom of a very long list.'

The others smiled at Francesca. 'Such a shame, Fran,' said one as she began to wind a ball of red wool. 'Hope your poor mother got settled somewhere, Christmas coming and all.'

'Yes, thank you. She has been lucky enough to rent a furnished flat from a house owner who thinks Mamma is a lesser evil than some refugees or evacuees. The business community has been helpful too, and some of my grandfather's associates are trying to find suitable premises so that she can reopen the business, after Christmas probably. Our customers are very faithful and there have been many offers of help.'

'Pity she'll miss the Christmas business, Fran,' a second woman said. 'I remember last year there was ever such lovely Christmas treats.'

That was obviously a comforting remark, for Rose saw Francesca's eyes brighten as if at some lovely memory.

'Orders taken, ladies. Mamma did all the baking, you know; Nonno was the chef and ice-cream maker.' Her voice seemed to stick in her throat. She stopped for a moment to compose herself and then, with a bright if somewhat artificial smile, said, 'I'll bring in some samples the next time I go h . . . the next time I visit Mamma.'

Francesca's voice had stumbled slightly and Rose stood up. 'Would you believe I forgot I had some sweets to share and, since we've mentioned Christmas, won't you tell us what you two are knitting? Red wool – has to be Father Christmas, right?'

The conversation moved easily to hopes for Christmas and the New Year until, calm and relaxed, the young women, only too aware of their early starts, decided to take themselves off to bed. Rose's last thought before she fell asleep was that one of the knitters had mentioned that the writer Agatha Christie's latest book, *The Body in the Library*, had been published not long ago. That would make the perfect Christmas present for her dad.

NINE

November 1942

'We do what . . . ma'am?'

Rose was so surprised that she barely managed to squeeze the 'ma'am' in there, so that the small but imposing woman standing glaring at her could not accuse her of incivility.

'Fill them every morning, and empty them every night. And next time I have to repeat an instruction to you, Petrie, you will find yourself in the guardhouse.'

Despite the fact that the top of her cap barely reached the bottom of Rose's top pocket, Corporal Holland was quite formidable. What she lacked in height she more than made up for in width and sarcasm. 'Do I make myself clear?'

'Yes, ma'am.' This time Rose's unruly tongue had almost let the word 'sir' slip out instead of 'ma'am'. Not that Rose meant to be rude, but dealing with – or rather, being dealt with – by anyone like Miss Holland was a new and unpleasant experience for her. Her own nature was rather sunny, and before she joined the Auxiliary

Territorial Service, the people she met had tended to respond in kind to her pleasant manner. Corporal Holland was impervious to sunshine, or so it seemed to the disheartened new driver mechanic.

'Get on with it, then.'

'Yes, ma'am.'

'Preferably before the radiators freeze, Petrie.'

Freeze? Good Lord. Why didn't I think of that and why didn't she explain? Rose asked herself. In all her years of driving she did not remember ever having to empty the van's radiator in case of a freeze. Winters in lovely Kent could be extremely cold. The van had a radiator but, try as she might, she did not remember a time when it had frozen. Her father and brothers had never spared the girls the dirtier or more unpleasant tasks of vehicle maintenance, but she had never, as far as she could remember, emptied a radiator.

Of course, our vans were always kept in the lock-up at night, and yes, Dad always threw an old rug over the bonnet.

'And fill 'em all up before drill in the morning.' The words floated across the parade ground, followed by a rather disheartening laugh.

Rose looked after the small figure, reflecting that if this was a page in one of the comics George read, Corporal Holland would step on a particularly slippery section of ice and . . . No, she would not proceed with that line of thought.

There was no garaging available for all the trucks, vans, cars and bicycles on this base. Feeling slightly stupid, Rose set to work with a will. She blew on her very cold fingers and set herself to emptying twenty-six radiators. It was cold work but, she tried to tell herself enthusiastically, it was yet another step forward. She was going to look at every unpleasant task in the same way. Everything she learned took her a little closer to the dream job.

'Come on, ladies, move over and let Rose into the fire. She's blue.' Gladys, the only corporal in the hut and therefore very much the senior, began to rearrange the seating arrangements of the other women. The Nissen hut was comfortably warm as the large round stove sent out tremendous heat, and Rose was warm again very quickly. As usual, because the windows were carefully taped closed, the air was heavy and unpleasant. The mug of steaming, hot Camp coffee pushed into her icy fingers helped.

'Whose skirt is that drying on the stove? I'm not looking because I don't want to know, but take if off there now and, blimey, don't be so stupid again.' Once again the strident tones were those of Gladys. 'That's a bloody fire hazard. Do it again and I'll put you on a charge.'

The offending article was whisked away with an apology. 'Sorry, got caught in the rain, Corporal.'

'So did half the blooming ATS but they're drying their knickers in the laundry room like rational human beings.'

Several young women were now totally down-hearted, one or two looking helplessly at the round clock face on the wall, almost willing it to sing out, 'Supper time.'

Rose looked across at Gladys and smiled. She knew the tragic fire had affected many more than those directly involved. '"To begin with you will drive – and maintain – a selected vehicle,"' she quoted loudly into the gloom. 'Except for anytime anyone wants you to do horrid tasks like emptying radiators on the coldest night of the year so far.'

'Blimey, Rose, you didn't fall for that "drive and maintain a whatever" palaver?' asked Francesca, her vocabulary showing that she was as English as anyone in the room.

'I did. When I was told I was to train as a driver mechanic, I really believed that I would actually, occasionally, get to drive a blooming car, instead of ruining my beautiful hands –' she held her slowly thawing hands out to the group – 'by stripping down engines, fixing gear boxes and emptying and refilling bleep-bleep radiators. My father always said I was naïve. I believe everything anyone tells me.'

'Especially men,' said two or three of the women at the same time.

Everyone, including Rose, laughed. She said nothing, having no desire to talk about men, especially not Terry.

'When will they let me drive a Wolseley 18? Now there's a car. Or a Daimler would be nice, especially one of those fabulous armoured ones. Can't you just smell the finest leather upholstery? Car heaven.'

'Maybe the WO still has nightmares where he sees you driving his newest lorry. He wakes screaming as he watches you being chased across the recreation ground by a gigantic truck.'

'Thanks a lot,' said Rose, pretending to glare at the offending speaker. 'C'mon, I'm thawed out, just in time to freeze again on the way to supper.'

The women bundled themselves up in their Teddy Bear coats and ventured out. It was a frosty evening, stars twinkling like friendly little messengers from the blue-black sky, and the moon a bright white light.

'Bomber's moon,' whispered someone. 'Who's going to get it tonight?'

No one answered, each alone with her thoughts. Rose thought of the tall Czechoslovakian whom her sister loved. He had said something about an exciting new plane that he had watched on its test flight.

'Have said probably too much already, ladies, but if we get it into mass production, it will change the course of history,' he'd told them.

Where are you tonight, Tomas, and you, Daisy, and Phil?

How she hated the phrase 'somewhere at sea'.

They reached the Nissen hut where they would eat, and carefully Rose glued a smile to her face. She had a feeling that many of the others had done exactly the same.

They downed hearty bowls of hot nourishing soup with dumplings, a nice change from the more usual thick slices of bread labelled Wartime Loaf. This was thick and heavy, but no one who ate it left the table hungry. When Rose had first joined the ATS, meals had been accompanied by many mutters of, 'Do you remember . . . ?' but now, as the beginning of the fourth year of this war drew closer, there were few mutterings of disapproval as the women fuelled themselves for the work ahead.

They finished with blisteringly hot strong tea and something called a biscuit, which threatened to break teeth. Occasionally Flora and Fred sent a few ounces of tea to Rose but, as with the tea that had been sent up to cheer Rose's friend, Chrissy, the girls saved Petrie tea for their Nissen hut.

'Dash it all, it's snowing,' called one of the girls who had peeked out. 'Snow in November. Why couldn't it wait for Christmas?'

Arm in arm, they walked back to the billet singing 'Jingle Bells'.

'Noise like that shouldn't be allowed,' yelled some others, heading off hurriedly towards another hut, but Rose's group merely laughed and continued singing until they were snugly inside their hut.

'Guess what I found in the office, Rose – something guaranteed to cheer you up.' Gladys, her own cheery face bright red from the severe cold, handed Rose several envelopes. 'Must be your birthday.'

Rose stood up and took the letters. 'Are you sure they're all for me?'

'No, I grabbed the nearest handful. Of course they're for you. I'm off to wash my unmentionables but I'll be back in time for the wireless.'

Rose thanked her friend and sat down, the first envelope already opened.

The feelings of righteous anger that even a short note from Terry instilled in her were surprising. She could hear his voice as she read the note, apologising, begging and pleading. He couldn't believe he'd spoken the way he had. She was right to be angry but he would do anything . . . She could read no more. She crumpled up the page – Basildon Bond, white, with the address printed at the top right hand in black, very tasteful – and tossed it into the stove where it blazed for a second and then disappeared for ever. Turning to

132

her other letters, she opened the one with her mother's handwriting on the envelope. That was the last letter she read for some time.

Dear Rose,

I'm sorry to have to tell you like this, pet, but I couldn't let you know any other way. Mrs Robertson as lives across the stair from Stan's gran came in to get Mrs Crisp's rations. She told us Mrs Crisp had a telegram from the army. I'm very sorry, Rose, but Stan was killed three weeks ago. The officer as wrote about Stan says it was quick and he wouldn't have known anything about it. He also said as how Stan was one of the nicest young men he had ever had in his command and that he would have put Stan forward for promotion. He's buried over there, poor lad, and his gran will be told the address of the place as soon as they can.

I know you'll be upset and I wish I was there with you, but we hope maybe we'll see you at Christmas. Mr Tiverton will say words about Stan at the Christmas service.

Your dad and me are thrilled you're doing so well. We're so proud of you.

Love,
Mum and Dad and George

The letter, together with the others, slipped through Rose's fingers to the floor and she sat and looked at the flames. Why? Why Stan? And why had she not known? Surely their bond was so strong that she should have felt something? Why had she been able to sit reading a note from a man she despised when Stan, her oldest and dearest friend, had died? No, he had not died. He had been killed in battle.

Rose did not hear the concerned words from the other young women as they watched her stare blindly into the fire, looking for what? An answer to an unanswerable question?

'Rose, are you all right?'

'Rose, how about a cuppa?'

Rose ignored them all; she heard nothing but her mother's voice saying the unspeakable. Stan. Leaping to her feet, she ran out of the room.

The others looked at one another doubtfully. 'It's snowing, damn it. I'm going after her.' Mildred Fleming grabbed her Teddy Bear coat and moved to follow Rose from the cosy Nissen hut.

'So two of you will be laid up; it's snowing. Bet you two bob she feels the cold and comes back,' said another girl as she held a toasting fork up to the fire.

But Mildred, having grabbed a second coat, ran out without another word.

Snow was whirling around outside, swooping high and then diving low and hurling itself against Mildred's face. She stopped for a moment to get her bearings and adjust the heavy coat as she peered into the swirling white darkness.

Nothing.

She thought of calling out but something told her that Rose would not appreciate notoriety. She struggled on, remembering that if she turned right at the end of the walkway, she would come to a grassy area where there were some seats. If Rose, who had looked quite unlike herself, was distressed by news in the letter she had been reading, then she would probably want a place where she could sit and think or weep or even shout in anger.

Mildred reached the main road and was about to turn right when a figure loomed up directly in front of her.

'Rose?'

'I grew a foot since I went to wash my undies?'

'Gladys, thank goodness it's you. Rose read one or two of her letters, dropped them on the floor and ran out like a bat out of hell.'

There was silence and then Gladys said, 'Where's your torch?'

Mildred shrugged. 'I thought only of a coat for her.'

'Come on then. I have a torch.' The two women walked quickly, Gladys sweeping the torch's beam from side to side. Two empty seats, a wastebasket, but no Rose.

'She must have gone back. We missed her in the dark, that's all. Let's hurry, Mildred; if she hasn't I'll have to alert the boss.'

They turned and began the difficult walk back to their hut.

'Wait, what was that?'

'What can you hear in this wind? It's nothing, let's get back and send out an alert.'

'Possibly nothing but . . .' Gladys tried to send the light directly across the prevailing wind. It wavered. Surely there was nothing there. 'Rose, Rose, my dear.'

Rose was hunched on a wooden bench, tears and snow mingling on her cold cheeks.

'Quick.' Gladys took one look and went into action immediately. 'Put the larger coat around her and help me get her up. She's so cold. Come on, Rose, walk, walk I tell you.'

Awkwardly, Rose stumbled to her feet, so that the coat Mildred had thrown round her shoulders fell to the ground. Mildred picked it up, shook it and put it round her again. Rose shivered a little and then said, 'Thanks, Mildred.'

'Faster,' ordered Gladys. 'We're heading for the laundry because it's right steamy in there and we can all have a chance to warm up.'

'Gl . . . Gl . . . Gl . . .' Rose tried to speak but her whole body was trembling and shivering with cold.

'Not a word. No excuses, no explanations. With luck everyone will have gone.'

One solitary eighteen-year-old private was still using the clothes wringer. She glanced at them curiously but a glare from Gladys, a corporal, had her hurriedly turning her back and carrying on with her work.

'That towel just been dried, pet?' Gladys, now smiling, had cast a quick look over the girl's laundry. 'Great. I'll borrow it for a minute, if I may.'

'We don't want any talk in the camp, Rose,' Gladys whispered. 'Play along with me, pet.'

Even in her distress, Rose understood that Gladys was trying to ensure that no one found out about her hysterical outburst. 'I'm fine, Gladys.'

'We know,' Gladys said more loudly. 'That's why you were chosen for the manoeuvre. How stupid of me not to realise you'd be absolutely soaked.'

Gently Gladys patted Rose's face with the warm towel until it was dry. 'Do you need to undo your hair?'

In answer Rose put the towel around her head like a scarf. She smiled sadly and shook her head.

136

'We'll get this to you tomorrow, Private,' Gladys addressed the young private. 'All right? Good, now, mum's the word.'

The girl, both delighted and terrified to have been part of something obviously risky, even dangerous, gathered her laundry together and left, and Rose and her friends sat letting the damp warmth penetrate their bones.

'Sorry,' croaked Rose after a while.

'Nothing to be sorry about,' said a small chorus of voices.

'You had a letter, Rose. Bad news? Do you want to talk?'

Rose nodded, her face a white mask of misery and despair. 'You never expect it. My brother and now Stan. Seems worse because he was happy in the army. Why Stan?'

'Was he very special, Rose?' Mildred dared to ask.

Rose nodded. 'Very. I've known him all my life. We met in Sunday school, aged about three.' She smiled as a memory of Stan and herself as shepherds, dressed in costumes fashioned from spare mattress ticking, lightened her grief for a moment. 'We were in the same class at school, in the same sports team, same cycling club, left school the same day and started working at Vickers the same day.' She sobbed and then said, 'And his poor gran. Dear God, she's got nobody. Why did it have to be Stan?'

The tears started again and the others suggested that they return to their much more comfortable Nissen hut, have some cocoa and go to bed.

'Not going to say anything trite, Rose, but you do need to get thoroughly warm and then into bed for a good night's sleep.'

Rose, now aware that the others had spent the evening almost as miserably as she had, nodded and got to her feet. She hugged each of her friends without saying a word, smiled at Mildred as she took someone else's too-short Teddy Bear coat and walked out again.

Gladys told Francesca of Rose's tragic loss when she returned from her stint of volunteering in the station library.

'I've never seen her like it,' Gladys said. 'She was really cut up at your granddad's funeral, but this was scary. I had no idea she was walking out with someone at home. She said he was a school friend but I think there was much more to it.'

'She loved him. He was like one of her brothers. Poor Rose. Pity she can't go home; there'll be something in the church. Being part of it might make her feel better.'

'I'll do what I can, Fran, and if you could say something on the q.t. to Warrant Officer Starling . . .'

Francesca did talk to the senior officer who, although sympathetic, was bound by rules.

'Sorry, Francesca,' was the message passed on to Gladys. 'I wish I could but I can't help Rose. She's just not close enough; she's not a blood relation. Several of you are down for a week at Christmas. Best I can do is to try to get Rose on – if she's not there already.'

Rose, meanwhile, unaware that her friends were applying pressure on her behalf, went through the next few weeks like an automaton. She worked as hard, perhaps even harder than ever, but to Starling it seemed as if her heart was not in what she was learning. He was careful to treat her exactly as he had always done, and once or twice thought he saw a slight look of gratitude.

Gladys, Francesca and even Chiara tried to do the same, but Rose held her grief very close to herself and accepted none of Chiara's invitations to see the new flat.

'I need to write to Stan's grandmother first, Francesca. The words come out all wrong. Tell your mum, thank you, and I'll look forward to seeing her as soon as possible.'

Even Rose knew that her words seemed stilted, but while images of Stan at various stages in their long friendship kept flitting through her head, she could behave in no other way.

She forced herself to write home.

Dear Mum and Dad,

Thank you for letting me know the sad news about Stan. I am trying to write to Mrs Crisp but it's hard to find the right words. It wouldn't be easy to speak them either. What can I say? The truth. He was my best friend all my life and as close to me as my sister and my brothers. Mrs C used to drop little hints about us getting married and I think, for a while, I thought that would be the way too, but Stan was brave enough to tell me he didn't love me. Poor Stan, he tried to make it nice. I love you, Rose, always have but . . . You see, the truth is he wasn't in love with me and after a while I knew I had never been in love with him either. I thought loving and being in love were the same . . .

'Oh, blast, blast, this is rubbish.'

Fiercely, she crumpled the paper into a ball and dropped it into the mouth of the stove that belched forth heat. She took another sheet and began again.

Dear Mum and Dad,

I am fine. Thank you for telling me about my dear friend Stan. I am very sorry and I will write to his gran. Does she have anyone else?

The dates of Christmas leave will be out soon. I'd love to come home but don't get your hopes up. You'll have Daisy. Wouldn't it be special if Sam and Grace were free too? Is Tomas coming? It would make Christmas very special. Oh, say hello to the Humbles. Do you remember the pig we fattened and the delicious ham? Maybe you fed a pig this year too?

Rose.

She read it, was dissatisfied, but knew that she could do no better. How could she have forgotten to send her love? She looked at the unsatisfactory note, turned the full stop after 'Rose' into a comma and added 'with lots of love'. Feeling slightly better, she sat down to write to Cleo Fitzpatrick, her first ATS friend. She should write to Mrs Crisp. Tomorrow, she promised.

TEN

Rose woke before her alarm the next morning and was delighted to feel more like her old self. Was it because she had finally written to her parents and to the delightful Cleopatra? Her sister had once accused her of feeling guilty all the time. 'You'll wear yourself out, Rose. It's impossible to please everyone. You're too much of a perfectionist and you ask too much of yourself. Relax.' Rose had been annoyed but every now and again she heard Daisy's voice and wondered if perhaps she could be right.

It had stopped snowing. Only a light covering on the ground told them of the snowfalls there had been. The sky was now clear and stars were twinkling brightly.

'Christmas weather,' said Mildred as they walked, bundled up in their unglamorous, heavy but definitely warm coats, to the canteen for breakfast.

'Where's Fran?'

'Francesca,' said Rose deliberately, 'is cleaning her shoes. We'll save her a place.'

'What a mouthful. Francesca. Besides, that's Italian, and she says she's English.'

'It's her name, Gladys, and she likes it.'

'Anyone got leave?' Mildred changed the subject.

'We'll hear this week, I think, and not before time,' said Gladys as they reached the door and opened it to the delicious smell of – what? Could it be bacon?

'It's Spam.' Mildred had gone exploring while Rose and Gladys had found a table near the stove. 'But there's scrambled eggs and I actually think there's one or two real ones in the mix. Cook says porridge will be ready in a minute, thick enough to dance on, and he's got golden syrup, if we beat the rush. Will we wait for Fran?'

No one answered as the door opened, letting in an icy draught and a crowd of personnel, male and female, and there, at the end of the line, Francesca Rossi.

'I'll keep the seats warm. Spam and eggs for me, please, Rose.' Gladys commandeered four chairs and sat down to wait.

Another woman from their billet joined her and appropriated the other chairs. 'We should just put the hut number,' she suggested with a laugh. 'Be easier. Francesca went to a Catholic school – ate in what the nuns called the Refectory, but everyone was assigned a place and it was always the same.'

'Yes, but they always knew how many were coming in to eat. It's different every mealtime here, so first come first served, which is why we're near the food and the heat.'

A few minutes later Gladys was joined by Rose and Mildred, followed not long after that by Francesca and the others carrying trays.

By now there was a constant babble of voices and the clanging of pots and cutlery, though the large room grew marginally quieter as people began to eat.

It seemed that Christmas leave was on everyone's mind.

'Fran's mum has sent us in an Italian Christmas cake,' Gladys told the women. 'That is extremely kind of her, Fran, and I'll send a note as from our billet.'

'Not necessary, Gladys. It's a bit of advertising too, you see, not just being kind. Did you see it, Rose?'

Before Rose could say anything, Gladys answered. 'No one's seen it yet, Fran. I asked Cook to put it in the larder and, when you want it, we'll have him take it out for you. No point in it sitting out all day while we're at work.'

Francesca was not too happy with that decision. 'I'd rather like people to see it, Gladys, and taste it, and the fresher the better. Could you ask for it at teatime, please? No hard sell, ladies, but Mamma's going to need all the help she can get to start her business again.'

'If it's as tasty as the Christmas cake I bought from the café last year, you'll love it, girls,' said another of the women at the table. 'My family really likes trying different things, except my gran. I don't think she's ever tried anything different.'

'Fine, Rose, I agree with you; it looks good, but you have to admit that it looks nothing like a real Christmas cake – not even a sprig of artificial holly or a cardboard Santa.'

Gladys, who had arranged for Chiara's Christmas cake to be put in the centre of a large table so that everyone who entered the canteen would see it immediately, was delighted to see a wry smile cross Rose's unhappy face. 'All right, I suppose it's real in Italy and, bless her, she's sharing it, but, for me, a Christmas cake has to have marzipan and thick white icing, lots of icing holly leaves and berries, of course, and perhaps a snowman, maybe a little tin reindeer.'

'The very essence of Christmas,' said Rose with a smile.

'Exactly, but you forgot a fir tree.' She looked at Rose and Mildred, who appeared doubtful. 'I always baked a very big cake. In October, I seem to remember, and then the puddings. Will the cooks make puddings?'

'I suppose so. My brother Sam has been in the army since 1935 and he always had cake and Christmas pud. But if you get leave, Gladys, you can bake your own cake at home.'

'Wouldn't be the same. And there's only me now. That's one of the things I really like about army life – there's always someone to talk to, isn't there?'

Rose was quiet. She could not think of a moment in her entire life when she had felt alone. If she were to be given Christmas leave, she would return to a happy family home where she would be surrounded by family and friends, and where there would always be room for someone who was alone.

'Gladys,' she wanted to say, 'if I get leave you're more than welcome to come home with me.' Her more practical side reminded her that even if Phil did not return home for Christmas, there would be so many others filling the family quarters above the shop. Daisy was bringing her Tomas, Sam was bringing Grace, if Grace was given leave. That was possibly doubtful, as her employer, Lady Alice, had been so generous already. Was Sally planning to spend Christmas in Dartford? If so, she – Rose – could stay at the Brewers'. A solution? No, she could not leave Gladys in a house full of strangers.

Mildred started to laugh. 'Oh, Rose, you'll never make a poker player. Thank God that you have a big family. If Gladys and I get leave she can come home with me. Not Buckingham Palace, but a genuine welcome just the same. I live with my sister and her man, but he's overseas. She'll love the extra company; doesn't have a family yet, poor thing.'

Rose, who had finished breakfast, stood up. 'You're a marvel, Mildred. I was worrying about her. We'll talk later. Right now I have an intimate date with . . .' she waited for a second . . . 'a British artillery tractor. Tell Francesca good luck from me with the cake.'

She wrapped her heavy coat around her and walked out of the noisy, almost airless room, into the bracing cold of a late November day. Even this military camp looked better with its sprinklings of frost and snow. The weather, and the thought that – no matter where she would be – it would soon be Christmas, her favourite time of the year, put a spring in her step. She went through the list of Christmas cards she must buy, write and send. Stan? Rose stopped, her happy feeling cut short. One less card this year, one less gift. She bowed her head, thinking of her friend and of her brother Ron, casualties of this hateful war. Rose lifted her head and, through eyes blurry with tears, looked into the future. She could not let grief prevent her functioning. Yes, Christmas was coming; there would be gifts to buy and to post. She must add Chiara to her list. At the thought of Chiara, her endless kindness, her personal immeasurable grief, and her own inability to visit, Rose realised that she must now begin to look forward, to stop moving around in a semi-dream state.

I'll miss you for ever, Stan, and you too, Nonno, but I must remember the living.

Head held high, eyes clear, Rose reached the depot where several other mechanics were already working. They called hello and one added, 'Before you start, Rose, Boss wants you in the office.'

What could he want? Rapidly Rose ran through her last jobs. Yes, everything had been done according to rules and she had left her station as clean and tidy as she could possibly get it.

'Come in, Petrie,' Starling called, although she had only knocked, not given her name.

'Two bits of news, Petrie: one definitely good, the other a mixed blessing, as it were.'

Less than five minutes later she left the office, trying hard not to grin from ear to ear. His good news, which made her want to jump in the air and shout hooray, was that she had been given a week's holiday over the Christmas period. She could, with luck, travel to Dartford on Wednesday the 23rd and return to York a week later. The trains, she decided, would all be extra busy on the way south, but perhaps would not be quite so busy on the way back north. Then she remembered that the 30th was the day before New Year's Eve, known as Hogmanay in Scotland, and so every Scot who could travel home would be on that train. Uncomfortable travel conditions were unimportant. Rose Petrie was going home for Christmas and that was wonderful.

Rose was absolutely thrilled with what Warrant Officer Starling had called a mixed blessing. To her immense surprise she had been promoted and was now a lance corporal. She supposed that he had christened her promotion 'a mixed blessing', as it meant a little more money and much more responsibility. But, right now, in her state of euphoria, all she could think about was how delighted her parents would be about her achievement. She pictured their dear faces. She would not write, but tell them when she arrived. Occasionally she had imagined how pleasant it would be to be promoted. Now, one daydream had come true, and Lance Corporal Petrie would be home for Christmas. She could already hear her mother's voice. 'Our Rose, a lance corporal! Who'd have thought it?'

She wondered if her father would find a bottle of sherry with which to celebrate the event or might he remember the generosity of Squadron Leader Adair Maxwell who had once sent the family fine wine?

Poor Adair. Poor Daisy.

No, there was no need to shed tears for Daisy, who would be bringing her 'darling Tomas' home for Christmas.

Rose walked back to the area where several ATS personnel were working, only to be met by a cheer and some back-slapping.

'Well done, Lance Corporal.'

Blushing with embarrassment and pleasure, Rose pulled on her overalls and got to work.

After tea that evening, and after the many congratulations that came her way, Rose managed to write some letters. The first was to her parents.

Dear Mum, Dad and George,
    I'm coming home for Christmas. Leave starts 23
Dec. but I've no idea what time I'll get a train or even

if I will catch one, and I have to be on duty 31 Dec.,
08.00 hrs. But somewhere in there, there's almost a
week, and I'm so happy. Could you let me know
who's going to be sleeping in the house, as there's a
friend here who has no one to go to? Don't worry too
much as Mildred, another ATS friend, says Gladys,
that's Gladys Archer, is welcome to go home with her
as she has room. Neither of them has heard about
leave yet!! That's the army for you.

Just then, right in the middle of writing the letter, she
remembered Stan and heard him say how he would salute
her when she became an officer. Rose had to blow her
nose loudly and say her watering eyes were a result of
the dusty atmosphere of the machine shop. When she
recovered, she went on with her letter.

What has George grown out of this year? I haven't
had time to spend money or coupons and I could get
him something for Christmas. Hope we've time to
go to the market, Mum, as I am badly in need of
something for special occasions. [She had glossed
over the destruction of her pretty summer frock.]
I'm bringing you a delicious Italian Christmas cake,
Mum. Don't want you baking and cooking all hours.
    Love,
    Rose

She wrote to Chiara, to Daisy, to Sam, to Chrissy and
to Cleo.

When she had finished she stood up and stretched.
'Six letters,' she said. 'That has got to be an ATS record.'

'And I bet you'll send them all Christmas cards too,' said Mildred. 'You should have waited and saved on stamps.'

'Christmas cards? I haven't bought any yet.'

'My mother says every Christmas card she has ever sent is hanging in an art gallery in Florence,' said Francesca with a smile.

'Wow, is your mum an artist, Fran?'

'Not good enough to hang in an art gallery, Mildred. Nonno took us to Italy once. Do you remember when we were schoolgirls and no one anywhere talked of war? Mamma went to a famous gallery while we went for ice cream. When she came out we knew that she had been crying; her make-up was all over her face. She had seen many very famous paintings and had recognised every single one from Christmas cards. I need to go back there some day and see them for myself.'

'Sounds a wonderful idea, Francesca. I'll come,' Rose promised. 'My brother has good memories of Italy. Who knows, maybe he'll come too.'

'We'll hire a bus,' laughed Gladys. 'I never saw a painting as could make me cry – not from happiness, anyway.'

That remark made them all laugh.

Later, Rose managed to catch Francesca alone as they walked to the toilet block. 'I wrote to your mum, Francesca, and I'll post it tomorrow, but I was asking her if I could visit on Saturday morning.'

Spontaneously, Francesca hugged her. 'Oh, she'll be so pleased to see you. I'm going to stay with her on Friday night and so I'll be there too. She'll be delighted about your promotion.'

'That's nice, but I want to order one of her super cakes to take home with me.'

'She'll be thrilled to bake for your family.'

'I know, but I'll say it's for a Grace Paterson. She's an old friend and my brother's in love with her. Chiara's too generous, Francesca, and right now she needs to think of her future and let me buy a cake.'

Francesca laughed. 'Between you and Enrico she hasn't a chance to do anything else. Now we had better hurry or they'll think we are lost in the snow.'

The visit to Francesca's mother was a happy occasion. She called herself 'pure Yorkshire' but it was with Italian exuberance that she hugged Rose.

'Rosa, *cara*,' she said. 'Oh, it is so good to see you.'

'I'm sorry it's taken me so long.'

'Nonsense; we were all dealing with trauma in our different ways but you're here now and you need to see my cakes.'

She was delighted to add Grace Paterson's order to the orders that had already come in from the station. The large top-floor flat was full of the delicious smell of baking and Rose had fun picking out the scents that reminded her of Christmas at home.

'Cloves,' she called, 'and ginger. Treacle and baking itself, such a super smell.'

'Almonds,' added Francesca, 'and melting chocolate.'

'But there's something else. The kitchen is full of it.'

'Mamma, you're roasting chestnuts.'

'Yes, we can't have Christmas without roast chestnuts.'

'I smell something else,' said Rose as they walked into the kitchen. 'I know what it is but I can't think.'

'Brandy,' said Chiara. 'Lots and lots of brandy. Now come and taste these *cenci*, but not too much or you will spoil the lunch.'

Rose picked up one of the fried pastry ribbons and bit into it. 'Delicious, Chiara. Quite wonderful, and so different.'

'And so easy. I'll teach you, but not today. Today we salute the new lance corporal and thank her for all she has done for our family.'

It was a wonderful morning, finished with a delicious meal. As Rose cycled back to the camp she knew that she would never forget helping prepare an Italian Christmas in a little kitchen in an old house in York.

Back at her billet she found that, already, Cleo had written with her congratulations.

How I'd love to be there to sew on your stripe. Remember to use a slender needle and tiny, tiny stitches – and the right colour, of course. When are we going to meet, Lance Corporal? Every time I get anywhere near you, you take off to somewhere else. Most uncivil of the military.

I take up a new post in London after the New Year. It's probable that I'll be there for the duration. Surely you can pop down to civilisation for a weekend? I have a darling little flat – yes, I know, the idle rich – but there's a minuscule guest room where you are more than welcome to rest your weary head.

Have a wonderful Christmas and love to everyone, including my friend George.

Rose smiled. How thrilled George would be to know that Cleo remembered him.

The days between receiving the news of her promotion and the start of her leave were busier than ever. To raise money for a military charity, the camp put on a remarkably professional pantomime and, somewhat to her surprise, Rose found herself cast as 'The Giant' in *Jack and the Giant Killer*.

She did her best to act and was grateful that no one asked her to sing.

In a newspaper she saw a picture of a foreign military officer being driven to Buckingham Palace in the rather splendid 1937 model of the Wolseley 18, a four-door saloon car.

'Wouldn't mind driving that beauty one day,' she murmured, unaware that Henry Starling was standing behind her.

'Huge engine, Rose, two to three litres, lots of power. Driver'd feel it through his – or her – hands on the steering wheel, but happens you're more likely to see a Daimler in a British depot. The King likes them, and foreigners like to like what the Royal Family likes. Late 1940, it was, I saw a spanking new Daimler four-door all-weather tourer. Now that's a car to dream about.'

In a second he changed from friend to Boss. 'And driving luxury cars is only a dream, Lance Corporal. Right now, there's the engine of a British artillery tractor with your name in big letters on it. Be great if you could do something with it before you go off to wherever.'

'Yes, sir.'

Rose lifted her tool kit, made sure she had her protective goggles, and went off to find her project. She would certainly recognise the important machine when she saw it.

Three days later she took it out for a test drive. She chose the field where she had ruined the grass as she wanted to be quite sure that she would hear every sound made by the engine.

'Purring like a kitten, sir,' she said as she signed in the valuable machine.

'You're a genius, Rose. There's lots of lads will have reason to be grateful to you, although they'll never know.'

'It's my job, sir.'

'I know and you're damned good at it.' He turned to walk out and stopped at the large sliding doors. 'I'm grateful to you too, Rose. Chiara's almost her old self these days. Have a good Christmas.'

And he was gone.

Rose had never met anyone quite like Warrant Officer Starling. She admired and respected him. He could be abrupt but he was always fair. He was a completely different man when he was with Chiara – kind and gentle, never impatient.

'Happy Christmas, Enrico,' she whispered after him.

Sally had gathered up all the silver chains that, last year, they had made from the lining of tea boxes, and brought them to the Petries', since they were the family doing the most Christmas entertaining this year. She had heaped them up on one of the armchairs in the front room and gone off to a rehearsal for the Christmas review that ENSA was staging at a naval base on the south coast. Rose, so used to waking very early, stumbled on the chains when she wandered into the front room on the morning after her arrival from York. She stood, in her blue flannel pyjamas, looking at them and laughing. She picked up two of them, and wrapped them around her neck, as if they were those fashionable furs worn by rich ladies that had little beady-eyed heads hanging from one end.

'Ravishing,' said a voice, and there was Sam. 'Keep yourself warm in your silver fur, Rose, and I'll make us a cup of tea.'

Less than ten minutes later he returned with two mugs. 'Enjoy a mug while you can. Mum has decided we deserve only the best china. Dad's in the bathroom; I'll get him a mug when I hear the water run out.'

Rose sat drinking in both her hot tea and her beloved older brother. He was Sam, the old Sam, the real Sam, and she wanted to weep with the joy of it.

'When does Grace arrive?'

At the word 'Grace', his face became wreathed in a smile. 'You'll not believe it, Rose, but she's driving down with Lady Alice, and so I've no real idea of when she'll get here. Mid-afternoon, I hope. She's going to sleep over at the Brewers' since we're bursting at the seams. Grace's Polish friends are with Lady Alice too. You remember them, don't you? Really nice girls, refugees really. Grace likes them both and says that Eva is a beautiful singer. They've been invited for Christmas at the lord's house in Mayfair: isn't that nice? Grace thinks Lady Alice wants important people to hear Eva's voice.'

'Can you believe it, Sam? Daisy flying planes. Your Grace driving in a posh car with a titled lady. You, safe home and back with your regiment.'

Sam laughed. 'The world is changing for the better.' He looked at her steadily. 'Is it better for you, Rose?'

Rose thought for a moment, but since she had thought of nothing else for almost a year, she was merely marshalling her thoughts. 'I've been in the ATS almost a year, Sam, and I'm no nearer being allowed to be a driver, but I can fix anything and I really do think I could drive anything anyone asked me to drive. Plus, I've already been promoted – that has to be a good sign. So, yes, life is better.'

'Great. Plans for today? I'm going over to the Brewers' to fetch Grace.'

Rose gulped down some hot tea. 'Mrs Crisp, my friend Stan's gran,' she said. 'I have no idea what to say to her but I must see her.'

In the end it was not nearly as bad as Rose had thought it would be. Stan's grandmother had turned her front room into a shrine. There were pictures of Stan everywhere: some in uniform, obviously provided by his regiment, but there were a few from his childhood as well. Two of these were not actual photographs but images of Stan cut from newspapers. There he remained, fourteen years old, in running shorts or football kit. Tears stung Rose's eyes.

'It's all right, Rose love. I know what good friends you were, all his life. He were a good lad, my Stan. Well, he's with his dad now, isn't he? That has to be good, my son and my grandson together.'

'It's a lovely thought, Mrs Crisp.'

'Not a thought, lass. It's something I know. Now, let's go into the kitchen and have a cuppa and you can tell me all about the ATS. I don't even know what that means.'

An hour or so later, Rose left, having promised to be at the Christmas Eve service and to 'pop in' again before she returned to camp.

'I'm not going myself – a bit too late for me – but Mr Tiverton'll say the same nice words about Stan tomorrow at the Christmas Day service.'

Rose walked away, feeling the old lady's eyes on her until she turned the corner, and there, walking towards her, was her twin sister, accompanied by their friend Grace, and, tall and distinguished-looking in air force uniform, Tomas. The sisters ran into each other's arms. Rose and Grace hugged too, and Tomas greeted Rose with a chaste kiss on each cheek, reminding her of the other sad loss, Francesca's grandfather. But this was time for joy and happiness, not dwelling on sadness.

'This is going to be a wonderful Christmas,' said Daisy as she smiled up at Tomas. 'We have some shopping to do, Rose. Want to come along?'

Rose would have enjoyed shopping with them, but it was so obvious that they were happy together and, since they did not see each other very often, she would go home and leave them alone.

'I'd love to,' she said, 'but I have a few presents still to wrap. I'll walk along to the crossroads with you.'

'You'll never guess what's happened to the Luciana Billiard Room,' Daisy said.

Rose looked puzzled, as if, in the months that she had been away from home, she had forgotten her home town. Tomas merely held Daisy's hand and listened to their chatter.

'The Luciana, Rose, you know, just off the High Street; it's now one of those British Restaurants. You've seen the slogan, "Good food at reasonable prices". Many elderly residents are eating there, and refugees. More and more refugees are arriving because of all the ghastly things happening in Europe.'

She looked up at Tomas, remembering perhaps that he had left his home in Czechoslovakia in order to join the Royal Air Force and fight for freedom for all.

'Christmas Eve, ladies,' he said. 'For a few hours we will think of peace and goodwill to all men.'

When the shop closed late that night, Tomas asked Fred for a moment of his time and the family waited on tenterhooks in the front room, listening to the latest Christmas song from the United States, 'White Christmas', while they tried to arrange all the favourite Christmas decorations, especially the silver chains.

'Do we have to sit through this with you too, Sam?' asked young George, which made them all laugh – even Grace, who blushed furiously.

'Seems this young man wants to ask our Daisy to marry him, Flora,' said Fred when they came upstairs. 'Seems to me he's a good lad so we'll leave them to it.'

Grace and Sam looked across the room at each other, sharing some unspoken communication, and stood up. 'Time to get ready for the service, Mum,' said Sam, 'or we'll never get seats together.'

Flora and Fred could not help feeling very proud of their children as they all stood and sang together during the lovely candle-lit service. They had been aware, as always, that two of their number were missing: Phil, whom they worried over endlessly, and poor young Ron who had given his life for his country. Flora's eyes misted over but already she was counting Grace and Tomas as part of her beloved family. Her mother's heart went out to the tall, courageous, lovely Rose who had bowed her head to hide her tears as Mr Tiverton had spoken of the loss to the community of several serving men, among whom was Private Stanley Crisp.

Father Christmas can't bring back my dear Ron. I wish he would bring Phil; that would be a lovely Christmas present. Her thoughts went on. *But I know what I really want for Christmas, a lovely man for my lovely daughter.* She looked at Tomas and smiled. *And if he's as nice as Tomas, I don't care where he comes from.*

ELEVEN

North-East England, January 1943

Rose gritted her teeth, at the same time straining every muscle in an attempt to remain in control of the lorry as it hurtled its weaving way down the snow-covered road. She was losing the battle to stabilise the heavy lorry's direction and so could not even attempt to slow it down. Should she push the brake, she knew the vehicle would jump the barrier onto the verge and carry on, faster and faster, down the slope towards who-knew-what. She could see nothing ahead but blackness.

For the first time ever, her favourite lorry had refused to obey her instructions. It had, in fact, been unable to do so, since the terrifying and totally unexpected blow-out of the left rear tyre.

Rose and Gladys were taking a platoon of ATS personnel and equipment to a military camp near Stamford Bridge. It was very dark but there was scarcely any traffic, and for that Rose had been grateful. She could, she decided, get to the camp in less than an hour. With any luck, the girls would get a few hours' sleep before they began their exercise next morning.

And then, out of nowhere, a loud bang, followed by terrified screams from the women in the back, and an unfamiliar flapping noise that she later recognised as burst rubber bouncing on the road.

'Hold on to your hats, girls, I can't stop the damned thing. Just pray there isn't a river down there.'

'Can't you brake, Rose; at least slow us down?'

Rose, every muscle tense, unclenched her teeth again and said, as calmly as she could, 'Braking is dangerous, Gladys.'

Her mind was working furiously. 'Never brake in a skid.' That was Sam's voice.

'Step on the accelerator, just for a second; sounds insane but it works' – Corporal Church.

'A blow-out will make your vehicle pull violently, so gently, gently, counter-steer to try to stay in lane.'

'Yes, sir,' said Rose in reply to Warrant Officer Starling's voice replaying in her head.

Gladys was clearly anxious. 'Accelerating wasn't a good move.'

Rose knew that if she gave in to panic, there would be no hope for any of them. 'Trust me, it was a good move.'

Nothing had worked and the lorry's weight and the terrain were in charge. All Rose could hope was that they were not sliding towards the edge of a cliff.

'What can I do?' whispered Gladys through chattering teeth. 'Dear God, can I do anything?'

'Praying's good. Or try to calm the girls.'

But it was terrified screams that accompanied the lorry on its self-destructive careering down the slope to what . . . ?

'Oh God, there's a—'

The information Gladys was about to give was lost for ever as the front wheels of the military vehicle hit the edge of whatever barrier lay before them. Accompanied by the shattering of glass, the scraping of metal and the hysterical cries of several young women as they were thrown around under the canvas cover at the back, the vehicle turned almost gracefully onto its side and began to sink slowly into . . . what?

Initially, Rose lay stunned but she recovered quickly, only to discover that she was firmly wedged against the door, her nose and mouth squashed against the window. She tried to move but the not inconsiderable weight of Gladys was on top of her and still from the back came moans and groans and occasional feeble cries for help.

'Anything hurt, Gladys – really badly, I mean?'

She felt Gladys move. 'No, don't think so, and I'm able to move. I'll try to get off you but I'm completely disorientated; I've got to get out to those girls somehow, and I've no idea where I'll land. It's so bloody dark.'

'Tut, tut. You were praying a minute ago, Gladys.' Rose thought quickly. 'Auxiliaries,' she called in her most authoritative voice, 'everyone all right?' She listened for a moment but stopped as something very cold and wet lapped against her face. She sniffed and tried to wiggle her hand under her but could feel nothing. *How am I going to get these girls out of here?* Her feelings were ambivalent: gratitude that the liquid was not petrol but concern that a great deal of cold water was entering the cab. They had stopped but now they were sinking – but into what?

161

'Girls,' she called, 'can anyone hear me?' There was no answer.

'Think they've jumped out the flap, Rose. Didn't you feel the back end lift?'

'Hard to feel anything with you on top of me. Call again, Gladys. Is anyone left in the back?'

The sound of murmuring and some hysterical weeping from outside assured her that the new ATS recruits had managed to get out. She hoped no one was hurt but now was not the time to find out. 'Try to shout out to the girls, Gladys. Why on earth isn't anyone trying to open the damned door?' She felt Gladys tentatively attempt to turn.

'I can see faces, Rose; the girls are having no luck in opening the door.'

Cold water filled Rose's mouth and she choked and spluttered. 'Pray they do before I drown. What's this damn river? I must be well off the route as I don't remember a river.'

Gladys moved again. 'Thank God, Rose, I've got my feet free, but I'm stuck on the gear lever, and why did I decide to wear my new skirt? Damn thing's ruined and it's around my waist.'

'The river, Gladys?' Rose was gathering her strength in an attempt to push the corporal off into the small space between the seat and the windscreen.

'There's no river. I checked the map carefully before we left. It's got to be a ditch or one of them ha-ha things.'

The sobs and weeping outside stopped abruptly and the two trapped in the cab heard male voices accompanied by excited cries from some of the girls: 'Yanks, Yanks, the Yanks are here.'

'Well, lookee here, Sergeant. Isn't this the prettiest little nest of birds you ever did see?'

An American accent, a very distinctive one, seemed to be coming from above her. As a child, Rose had learned to love that particular sound and even to imitate it while sitting entranced in the projectionist's booth at her local cinema in Dartford. For a fraction of a second she wondered if she was dead, and then Gladys shrieked.

'Pardon me, ma'am –' the accent was American but different from the first one – 'Master Sergeant Bradley Hastings at your service. We are about to pull your truck out of the ditch. The other young ladies have exited the vehicle and are quite safe. I'm afraid I can't get this door open and if you ladies are not injured it's possibly better to lift the vehicle with you still inside. Otherwise, we'll need to smash in the door. Ma'am?'

'Gladys, why did you scream?'

'Nothing. Really stupid.' Why on earth did Gladys sound embarrassed? 'I felt something like a hand on my thigh . . . this damned skirt.'

'Maybe it was a fish.'

'No, ma'am, I apologise,' the more authoritative voice said, but with just the hint of a smile, 'Private Arvizo was merely groping, sorry . . . reaching for the handle through the shattered window. But don't worry, we'll get you out on a wing and a prayer.'

A wing and a prayer. Isn't that something from an old film? 'Lift the truck, Sergeant,' came the strangled sound of Rose's voice. The water was still seeping into the cab and she was scarcely able to breathe as Gladys continued to crush her against the thankfully unbroken side window.

163

They heard orders being given in that same pleasant but businesslike voice, some male laughter quickly quietened and then, with an unpleasant sucking sound, everything changed. They felt the lorry being lifted, carried a few feet and then turned right way up, before being set down on blessedly firm ground. They fell back against the seats.

'My God, how many of them are there?' asked Rose, but there was no one to answer.

A uniformed arm reached in – and the door opened. Gladys, her skirt still riding higher on her thighs than she'd have liked, almost fell out into a circle of smiling concerned faces, both male and female. Rose, conscious that she had lost her cap, allowing her long blonde hair to escape from its restraints and cascade over her shoulders, tried to maintain some dignity as she edged along the seat.

The same strong arm reached in and a tanned hand was offered. 'Let me help you, Miss Venus rising from the waves.'

He spoke so quietly that Rose was sure that only she had heard his remark. Startled, she looked up into smiling eyes of a most unusual shade of blue, almost lilac. For a moment they stayed looking at each other. Rose recovered first. 'Thank you, Sergeant, I can manage.' She swung her long legs out of the lorry and onto the ground.

The girls who had been thrown around in the back of the lorry were now proving that they had sustained no serious injuries by making friends as quickly as possible with the group of American soldiers.

'I'll have some mechanics check the vehicle, ma'am,' the sergeant offered, 'but I think it might be safer to tow it to your base.'

164

He had addressed Rose, probably assuming that she was senior, but Gladys, of senior rank, being a corporal now, answered him.

'You're very kind, Sergeant, but several of us are qualified mechanics, including Lance Corporal Petrie here. I would, however, be very grateful if you could shine some light on the lorry while they check it.'

'Yes, ma'am,' said the sergeant, who saluted before walking off to give his platoon their orders.

The examination, watched by the Americans and interrupted by occasional intelligent suggestions from them, proved that the vehicle was unfit to drive.

'The rear offside wheel is shredded, ma'am; needs to be replaced. Arvizo, radio ahead and explain the situation.' The sergeant turned again to Gladys. 'I think, if you'll permit, ma'am, we'll tow you to your base.'

'Gladys, did you hear what that American said when he helped me out?'

'You certainly made a conquest there, Rose; it's that glorious hair. Mind you, he's a bit of all right. Love the voice and the eyes. In fact he looks like one of them movie actors.'

'Yes, and I just bet any one of those silly girls out there has told him so.'

Rose turned from the mirror, which she had been using to try to see the bruises on her back and shoulders. 'What did he say?' she asked nonchalantly. 'Something about Venus.'

'Beware of men who compare you to paintings of naked goddesses.' Gladys looked at her second in command. 'It's an Italian painting, ask Fran or her mum. I think

165

it's called *The Birth of Venus*. She's starkers, standing on a shell, and her crowning glory is long enough to cover the naughty bits.'

'Is it nice? I mean, have you seen it?'

'Oh, yes, we pop over to Italy every bank holiday.' Gladys watched Rose's face. 'God, Rose, you believe me. Too naïve for your own good.'

Rose smiled quietly. She was more than secure enough to know that, no matter what anyone said, she was not naïve. She had grown up in a loving family with three older brothers and a twin sister and had worked for several years in a munitions factory – impossible, she felt strongly, to be naïve in these circumstances. She sat down to pull on her stockings. 'I've never met a Yank before, Gladys. They were nice fellows, don't you think?'

'When I recover from Arvizo squeezing my thigh, I'll tell you.'

The two women laughed.

'He was looking for the handle,' spluttered Rose.

'Like hell he was. Door handles are on doors, not an arm's length into the vehicle. Naïve Rose, Auntie Gladys is really going to have to look after you.' Gladys finished brushing her hair, took out a lipstick refill that had less than a quarter of an inch left and lightly applied it. 'Let's see if there's anything edible left in the canteen.'

The two women, one tall and slender, and the other of slightly less than average height and a little on the heavy side, pulled on their Teddy Bear coats, which were generously proportioned, and long and wide enough to fit round almost any woman. ATS personnel, especially those who, like women in other branches of the services, had had to do without a greatcoat for more than a year, loved them. One or two of the younger and better-dressed recruits had objected to the coats, but Gladys had pointed out the advantages.

'Picture yourself in nothing but a skirt and tunic and your God-knows-what, and probably ninety denier, sludge-green stockings at two o'clock on a freezing January morning, dismantling an engine with your tiny frozen fingers, and you'll thank God for your Teddy Bear. You can pull on every jumper you own under it, and nobody will know but you – and me.'

Now all the girls were in the canteen telling everyone who would listen, and several who would prefer not to, all about their exciting afternoon, and especially about their rescue by the American platoon.

'Muscles? You wouldn't believe it. The sergeant is straight out of a film; gorgeous eyes – well, he just told some of them to stand on one side of the ditch, some on the other and they picked up the lorry with Lance Corporal Petrie and Corporal Archer inside; carried them like babies in a cot and set them down so gently on the grass. I almost wish I'd stayed in the back waiting for rescue.'

There was a great deal of laughter and much excited chattering as there had been rumours for some time that the Americans were expected.

'Warrant Officer Starling offered them tea,' one of the girls who had been in the lorry hurried to tell her audience, 'but Sergeant Hastings refused – very nicely – and explained that they had to return to base. They'll "drop by" sometime, Sergeant Hastings said. Won't it be wonderful? And, by the way, what's a Master Sergeant?'

'A sergeant with points,' laughed Gladys. 'They have all sorts of non-coms in the US Army, but master's pretty good.'

'And don't get too excited about them popping in for a cuppa, Marge,' Rose cautioned. 'They say Americans are all very well-mannered and I'm sure he meant it, but there is a war on.'

Marge almost skipped with excitement. 'That's why they're here. People say they bring everything with them from America, even their food.'

Gloomily, Gladys and Rose looked at their Spam fritters. 'Even after three thousand miles of ocean, I bet it tastes better than this,' said Gladys. 'Come back, Arvizo, all is forgiven.'

An investigation into the accident was undertaken and Rose was not held culpable. Instead she was congratulated for her professional handling of the incident. A lecture was given on dealing with a blow-out. Attendance was mandatory.

Together with their senior officers, the American platoon that had rescued the unit in such difficult circumstances was invited to visit the camp on the first Sunday after the ATS women's horrifying experience in an out-of-control truck. It was only then that one or two of the girls had realised that some of the American soldiers were black.

For a few hours, between being good hosts and showing the Americans over the station, the women talked of nothing but military matters, US versus British transport vehicles – the Americans seemed to call everything a vehicle whether it was a car, an ambulance, a small lorry or a massive truck – and the progress of the war in every far-flung corner of the world. But when the visit was over, Gladys's unit gathered in her hut, made tea and talked about men: black, white and everything in between.

'Why, Corporal, why didn't I notice that the chap who carried me up the slope was black?'

'Because it didn't matter, I suppose, Jean,' answered Gladys, who was feeling just a little out of her depth. 'You were in shock and were aware only of broad shoulders and big, strong arms,' she finished rather suggestively.

The girl laughed. 'He would have to be strong to lift me. I never met anyone black before, never even saw a black person, except in films. Paul Robeson, wonderful. It was so dark, so scary, that all I knew was that whoever was carrying me was strong and wasn't going to drop me in the ha-ha thing.'

'That would have been a ha-ha moment, Jean.' Rose, who had to admit to herself that she had noticed no one but Sergeant Hastings and the audacious but likable Private Arvizo, tried to lighten the discussion.

'Didn't he have the loveliest voice?' Jean finished in a flush of embarrassment. 'Paul Robeson, I mean. *Sanders of the River*.'

'Released 1935,' said Rose, who had watched the film several times in the projection booth at her local cinema, 'which means those of us outside London didn't see it until the following year. I think a new one came out last year, *Tales of New York*, or was it *Manhattan*? We'll get it in the summer, I suppose.'

'I hope I said thank you.'

'Have one of Fran's mum's sugarless, butterless biscuits,' suggested Gladys, who was unsure if Jean wanted to thank the American singer or the soldier who had carried her to safety. She supposed it was the latter.

They were interrupted by a loud knock on the door. When it was opened a letter was handed in. 'For Lance

Corporal Petrie,' said Mildred who, having been closest to the door, had received the letter. She held the envelope up and looked at it very carefully.

'Now, who could this be from? Could it be from a big, tall, absolutely gorgeous master sergeant with wavy brown hair?'

'Stop being so silly, Private,' said Rose crossly as she took the letter. She had spoken to Bradley Hastings earlier.

'Call me Brad,' he had said as they'd walked around the ATS camp, and a small frisson of excitement had trilled through her. She had felt slightly off balance, but she had pulled herself together, and thanked the American sergeant and his platoon for their help. She hadn't the slightest intention of telling him that he had a lovely voice, although he did.

No, it's not, she told herself. It's just different.

She looked at the envelope and did not recognise the handwriting, but that meant nothing. Notes were carried across the camp every day of the week. 'Possibly from Warrant Officer Starling. I'll have a quick look at it.'

Mildred and probably one or two of the others were disappointed to see Rose grabbing her Teddy Bear coat and going outside. 'It is from him. Lucky girl.'

'None of our business, Mildred,' Gladys reminded her, 'and it's high time we tidied up in here and got ready for supper.'

The young women did as she asked but Gladys could sense that each and every one was glancing at the door every few minutes, waiting for Rose to return. They waited in vain.

Rose was sitting in the camp's nondenominational chapel, the only place she could think of where no one would speak to her. The note was from Brad Hastings and was a polite invitation to something called 'a hop' on the following Saturday evening. He explained that a general invitation would be sent to the camp commander, but he hoped that Rose would allow him to pick her up and return her to camp.

A hop? That's dancing. Very nice. I'd love to go with him, but what on earth will I wear?

Rose had meant to spend some time wandering through the Dartford shops at Christmas. How lovely not to have to rush; what fun to return to favourite haunts, perhaps to bump into old friends, to see what was available, hoping there would be a dress, or even a blouse, that just had to be bought. Flora had refused the offer of her coupons for George, saying that he had everything he needed, and so Daisy and Rose had clubbed together to buy their foster brother his first watch, putting aside personal shopping until later. 'Later' never came, for family excitement over the unexpected Christmas Day announcement of not one but two engagements had made everything else unimportant.

The Brewers, missing Sally, had joined the Petries on Christmas Day, and even Miss Partridge had been persuaded to visit them. Daisy had come to the Christmas dinner table wearing an exquisite ruby ring and Grace had happily shown her lovely, but much more modest, diamond. No plans had been made for wedding dates but the young couples were blissfully happy and smiled constantly as they accepted congratulations.

'We don't even know whether Tomas's family gets our letters,' said Daisy bravely.

'I would marry Grace tomorrow,' said Sam, 'but we'll wait until the world is a better place.'

Daisy and Tomas had gone their separate ways on Boxing Day, and Sam had had to leave a day later. Rose had so longed to have an hour or two with her sister and Grace; better still if Sally were there, but nothing had worked out. Instead Rose and Grace had muffled up and gone for a walk. Rose had told Grace all about her friends in the ATS and Grace had told Rose about Eva and Katia, the two Polish refugees who were with her at Whitefields Court, and about her experiences, good and bad, in finding out about her family.

'They, the law firm, are still trying to find out about my father, but it's not easy after all these years and with all the papers destroyed in air raids. But I've got a bank account, Rose, with money from my grandmother. Sam knows about it and he agrees with my plan for it. We'll tell everyone when it's time.'

'Sounds mysterious and exciting, Grace, and I'll wait. C'mon. Let's get back. I'm freezing.'

Next day Grace and Rose travelled together to London, where Rose waited for her train to York and a very nervous Grace made her way to Lord Whitefields' London home. Lady Alice was waiting there to drive the three Land Girls back to Whitefields Court.

It had been a Christmas to remember, and Rose knew she would relive the happy moments over and over again in the months to come, but she had not restocked her wardrobe and now had nothing to wear for her date with Brad Hastings.

TWELVE

Rose was not the only ATS member who had had a lovely Christmas.

On New Year's Eve, Warrant Officer Harry (Enrico) Starling had plucked up courage to ask the question that, for several years, he had hinted at and dreamed of asking.

'Chiara, will you marry me?'

On their first day back in camp the women had shared their experiences. Gladys had had a lovely time with Mildred and her sister, Rose had the engagements of her sister and brother to talk about, but Francesca had told Rose, and no one else, of her mother's engagement to WO Starling.

'They plan to marry sometime this year, Rose, but Mamma feels it's too soon after Nonno's death to announce it. To be honest, I think the Italian community has almost given up hope of her ever marrying again.'

'I think you'd have to be blind not to see they love each other.'

Francesca laughed. 'Exactly. At Midnight Mass, more than one whispered, "Nice to see your dear mamma looking so happy, Francesca." They're probably planning the menu for the wedding breakfast.'

'And the clothes.'

The women in Rose's platoon were thrilled to be invited to the dance at the American base and, of course, several begged for time off to shop. Every sewing machine in the camp was commandeered, as those with clever fingers altered out-of-date frocks.

Neither Rose nor Francesca felt that she owned an outfit worthy of the 'hop'.

'Everything I owned went up in smoke,' said Francesca ruefully. 'Replacing clothes was the last thing on my mind.'

'Almost everything I own is in Dartford – and much good they'll do either of us.'

They mulled over the problem for some time, but no solution presented itself and then, on Thursday morning, Francesca received a letter from her mother. She read it, becoming more and more excited with every word.

'What is it?'

'St Jude, the patron saint of hopeless cases.'

Rose looked at her friend. 'You've lost me. St Jude?'

'Yes, lovely, lovely St Jude. I said a prayer and Mamma has written . . .'

'You are so superstitious, Francesca.'

'You won't laugh, *amica mia*, if something suits you. Mamma went shopping for clothes, as befits a newly engaged woman. Being a desperately poor newly engaged woman, she went to a charity shop run by the WVS.'

'You mean . . . ?'

'She filled a suitcase, maybe a little too full – sales do that to her – and so she wants to see if we can

174

use anything. If we went in before seven on Saturday morning, we could have a quick look and be back . . . I'm on duty at ten.' She looked enquiringly at Rose.

'Twelve till three.'

'Might just work out. Even if nothing's perfect, too long, too big, it's got to be better than an old blouse and skirt.'

'I did bring a navy shirtwaist for the spring,' confessed Rose.

'Good. It'll be perfect for lunch with Brad some Sunday. I'll ask my stepfather-to-be to let Mamma know we're coming.'

'Thanks, Francesca, I have to run.'

Rose checked that her uniform was perfect and hurried up to the depot where she had been working on the engine of a Bedford semi-trailer. She stood beside the workbench, her sleeves rolled up, her hair bound in a turban in an attempt to keep it free of oil, dirt and rust. Her hands were filthy and, catching a glimpse of her nails, she sighed.

'In the office, Petrie, now.'

Rose straightened up, wiped her oily hands on a filthy rag and followed WO Starling into his office, wondering, as she did so, what could possibly have happened. At work Starling was the consummate professional and very rarely showed ill-temper.

'Sir?'

'God, you're a mess, but you're the best I've got. I want you to go and get yourself cleaned up and, in your uniform, back here in thirty minutes. What are you waiting for? Move.'

'Sir.'

Twenty-three minutes later, Rose, breathing quick, shallow breaths, was back in the depot.

'Give or take a minute, Rose,' Starling said with a laugh. 'Right, there's a job waiting for you at the airport. Sign out the van that's just outside; it has fuel. Take yourself off to the airport. A car and one or two passengers will be there within the hour. Take them to this address, wait for them, and drive them back to the airport. Get back here when you can.'

Her heart leaped with excitement. She was actually going to drive a VIP or perhaps two of them.

'You can stop grinning, Lance Corporal, and I hope someone thinks to offer you something to eat.'

Eat? How trivial, how mundane.

Rose lowered herself into the driver's seat of the van, closed the door and yelled, 'I am a driver!'

Then, feeling rather silly and hoping no one had seen or heard her, she drove off.

Her journey to the airport was uneventful. Snow still lay on the hedges and on the fields on either side, but the road itself was clear. She reported in, was told her passengers were delayed, and was invited to make herself familiar with the car she would be driving.

'Beauty like you should have a Rolls, love. Afraid all we've got today's an elderly Austin, but it'll get them there.'

Rose smiled ruefully and thanked the mechanic, who suggested she 'grab a cuppa char' while she had the chance.

By the time she was alerted to the arrival of her passengers, she could have had a three-course lunch, but 'There's a war on', singing in her head, helped her remain patient. She was surprised and thrilled to find that another car had been found to replace the elderly one she had been promised, and it exceeded all her expectations. It was a four-door Daimler all-weather tourer, and not even two years old.

'Take it right up to the strip. Fewer people who know who comes and goes the better.'

Rose saluted and, her heart beating so strongly with excitement that she felt everyone on the airfield must hear it, she gently released the brake and allowed the beautiful machine to purr gently forwards. She got out so as to be on hand to open the rear door for her passenger or passengers, and, one hand on the door, she stood and watched a small dot of silver light in the sky become larger and larger, until she could not only hear but see the small plane.

Her stomach lurched at the thought that maybe, just maybe, Daisy was the pilot.

'Gosh, it's lovely. What's it called?' she asked the engineer, who was waiting beside her.

'Percival Petrel: pretty little girl, isn't she? Carries passengers, cargo, you name it. Today it's top brass. One – and a secretary, or maybe bodyguard. Got a long drive ahead of you, have you?'

Rose laughed. 'Now, even if I know, you don't really expect me to tell you. Here they come.'

Rose stood to attention and saluted. Two men, one tall and slim and the other shorter and even thinner, approached the car. Rose held the door open and the tall slim man nodded to her and eased himself into the car, while his companion went round to the other side and let himself in.

Rose had memorised her instructions, and so she started the engine immediately and drove somewhat slowly until she reached the main road. Then she accelerated and drove confidently, the powerful machine obeying her slightest command. She heard nothing from her passengers. There was a speaking tube; should her VIP need to talk to her, he could.

She drove steadily, luxuriating in the feeling of being in charge of this car, of finding it responsive to every move she made.

What price Dad's van now?

She allowed herself to wonder about her passengers. Who were they and in what way were they important to the war effort? She would never know and did not really care. It was enough to know that they were helping bring an end to this senseless conflict, and that she, Lance Corporal Rose Petrie, was helping them.

She came to a crossroads, which of course had no directions on its pointing arms, and suffered a momentary loss of memory. Right, left, straight ahead?

'Straight ahead,' said a voice.

'Thank you, sir.'

She had heard that voice before. Where? On the wireless? After all, how many truly important people had she met in her life?

She drove on, determined not to put a foot wrong and, at last, there they were. Great gates held open by uniformed soldiers, a long winding driveway flanked by dense bushes, a massive house.

She drew up at the foot of a flight of stone steps and got out, but already there was a soldier at the passenger door. Rose's passengers got out, nodded to Rose and began to walk up the stairs.

The taller one stopped, turned. 'I thought I'd seen you before. Glad the ATS got you, Miss Petrie.' With a smile he turned, climbed the rest of the stairs and disappeared into the house.

Rose stared after them. 'The butler from Silvertides,' she murmured to herself.

Her instructions were to wait for her passengers and so she got back into the car. It was freezing cold outside and she had no overcoat with her. She peered through the frosting window. How she would have loved to walk around, just following the driveway, but she was not a casual visitor. She settled herself, as best she could, into her seat.

'They'll be a few hours, love.' One of the soldiers had opened her door. 'You'll be better off in the kitchen. Cook'll give you a bite to eat and, don't worry, you'll be told in plenty of time when they're moving.'

He showed Rose where the steps were that led to the kitchens in the basement. There Rose was met by a delightful wall of heat, accompanied by the delicious smell of roasting beef.

'Help yourself to a cup of coffee, pet. Milk and sugar's on the table. Upstairs they like brown with their coffee, but there's both.'

'Thank you.'

The cook was swathed in a massive white apron, from the bottom of which peeped military trousers and military boots. Rose smiled. Because of the apron and the cook's hat, she had not been sure whether she was talking to a man or a woman. A man, definitely.

He went about a myriad of tasks with clinical efficiency and Rose drank delicious coffee and watched him.

'You staying over, lass? These meetings can last an hour or they can go on for days.'

'I'm supposed to drive my passengers back to the airport.'

'Well, if you need a kip, there's at least thirty bedrooms with empty beds.' He laughed uproariously at this and Rose sat, enjoying the coffee and the warmth, and assured herself that if there had been any doubt that she was not returning to camp she would have been told to pack.

Some time later, after the men upstairs had had a meal, Rose and the cook enjoyed the leftovers.

'That really was outstanding, Cook. My mum's a good cook and some army meals aren't too bad at all, but I've never eaten anything like that before.'

He laughed. 'I was training at a posh place in London when my call-up came. When this blooming war is over, they say I'll get my job back, but I have plans of my own. Ever in London?'

'My home's in Dartford, so occasionally.'

'Well, then—' began the cook, but whatever he wanted to say was lost for ever as Rose was summoned to attend her passengers. They stood for a few minutes, shaking hands and talking animatedly, and then the slightly shorter man saluted and hurried down the steps and into the car. 'Take me back to the airport,' he ordered, and Rose was surprised to hear an American accent. 'If you're needed later, they'll call you.'

Call? Rose, who was desperately trying to place the man's face, which was vaguely familiar, and the voice, wondered what 'call' meant. The butler would be highly unlikely to shout to her.

Must be American for get in touch, she decided, but said only, 'Yes, sir,' and drove back to the airport.

It's all really exciting, she thought. This must be what a driver's life is like, chopping and changing, depending on what the important people need to be done. She was just wondering if it was likely that she would ever return to that great house when she realised who her VIP really was, and was so thrilled that she had to force herself to be calm and contained. No wonder they managed to find a really special car.

That night she wrote to her family about her first driving experience. She told them about the coincidence of meeting the man she could only refer to as 'the butler' and was delighted to tell them that he had recognised her and called her by name. But the best she saved for last.

> I can't tell you the name of my VIP yet. I didn't really
> recognise him at first, didn't really look at him because
> I was so happy to see the butler, but I did think I'd
> heard the voice before. He is so important I can hardly
> believe they allowed me to drive. Funny old world,
> isn't it? Hope I did well and that they'll give me
> another assignment.

But when she lay in bed that night, going over the events of the day and looking forward to the dance and her date with Sergeant Bradley Hastings, she wondered what he would think if she were to tell him she had driven Dwight Eisenhower, Supreme Commander, Allied Force of the North African Theatre of Operations, back to the airport.

THIRTEEN

Chiara had spread all the clothes she thought might be of some use to her daughter or Rose on the sofa, the chairs, and even the dining table of the furnished flat she was renting.

With scarcely hidden regret, Francesca rejected a midnight-blue sequined cocktail dress. 'Not for a hop, Mamma – that's too formal.'

'But it would be enchanting on you.'

'Perhaps, but we need to be able to move. That black skirt with all those red poppies would be perfect for you or for Rose.'

Rose held up the skirt. 'Was this originally curtains, Chiara? I haven't seen so much material in a skirt for years. Your colouring is perfect for it.'

'Only a tall, slim woman could wear this, Rose, and that's you, my dear.'

Rose held the skirt against her and lifted one of the sides up as if she were dancing. 'Only problem is I could get into it twice. I'm afraid the owner was tall – and fat.'

They put the skirt aside while they examined some of the other clothes. There was a smart suit and a business-like dress that Francesca thought would be useful, if altered to fit her.

'But I have coupons, Mamma, and I want to buy new clothes.' She stopped as she remembered that she hoped to be buying a new dress to wear as bridesmaid at her mother's wedding. 'But these two are worth altering, don't you agree, Rose?'

'Yes, I love the two-piece costume. Reminds me of one we all saved up to buy for a friend who was going to drama school. Can you imagine, someone at school with me was able to go to university if she wanted?'

'My cousin, Luigi, was going to the university but he joined the army to fight for Italy. Then he found he was fighting for Germany.'

'Girls, remember why you're here.'

Rose and Francesca laughed and started examining the clothes again. 'I only need something for the dance tonight,' sighed Rose, 'and I like the skirt but . . . I wish I wasn't such a beanpole.'

'Rose Petrie,' scolded Chiara, 'you are tall and slender and can wear anything, including this skirt, because I picked up a wide elasticised black belt, which will hold up the skirt no matter how hopping the hop is.'

Naturally Rose had to try and she pulled on the skirt over her trousers. Then she and Chiara waltzed around the room until, breathless, they sank onto the sofa.

'Oh, what fun to laugh again,' said Chiara, her eyes brimming with unshed tears. 'Don't look gloomy, girls, I'm crying because I'm happy. Now, Rose, a black blouse would be wonderful.'

Rose shook her head. 'Sorry, no.'

'Then white will have to do. And Francesca, surely

there is something here that maybe I can turn up or sew a flower on, or something?'

Nothing was found among the clothes set aside for the girls, but among those spread on the bed in Chiara's bedroom was a beautifully tailored blue-and-white polka-dot day dress. There was just enough material in the skirt to make exuberant dancing possible.

Francesca looked at it. 'It's a lovely frock, Mamma, but too long, and if you cut it, it will be too short for you.'

'Silly, sweet girl,' said Chiara. 'Rose, dear, help her into it while I get my scissors.'

Americans seemed to be everywhere. The accents, familiar from films, were now heard on the streets, in the pubs and in British military camps. Everyone in Rose's platoon had accepted the invitation to the 'hop' on the American base, but Rose was the only one to be picked up two hours before the festivities started.

Brad drove himself over in a vehicle he called a Jeep. Rose had seen one or two of these all-surface vehicles travelling around the countryside but she had never seen one up close.

'You'll have to tell me if you're uncomfortable, Rose. I've never actually been a passenger in one. The Government loves them; they can drive up and over everything.'

'So it's mainly for driving in rough country, through woods, that sort of thing?'

'I guess. A test driver drove one clear up the steps of the Capitol building in DC, just to demonstrate its power.'

'My brothers would love it,' said Rose, smiling as she remembered Sam, Phil and Ron learning to drive and then passing on their skills to their twin sisters.

Naturally he asked how many brothers she had and she said, 'Two,' then asked about his family.

But Brad was an only child and had no light chatter about family.

For a few awkward miles, they talked about recent daylight bombings, not only in London but in Reading.

'Must be frightening, hearing the planes approaching and being able to do nothing but wait.'

Rose, who had lived through nights of bombing and had been slightly injured in one daylight raid, merely nodded, and so Brad went quiet. But conversation did become easier.

'Tell me more about your family, Rose; sounds like fun.' Brad was, basically, a quiet man, but he was a good listener and seemed to enjoy Rose's chatter about her family and her friends.

'Wow, you must have had a great time growing up. I did too, mostly, but we always had to borrow other kids during vacations and stuff. I think my parents liked that; meant they didn't have to worry about entertaining me.'

He was quiet for a moment or two. 'That didn't sound nice. My parents were both professionals and always busy.'

Rose thought of her own 'always busy' parents, who had made time to be with their children. 'We entertained one another,' she said, and then added, 'By the way, Sergeant, where are we going?'

He stepped on the brake and the Jeep screeched to a halt. 'Excuse me, ma'am. I'm sorry; I worked it all out in my head so often I thought I already asked. Rose, Miss Petrie, I want so badly to go to an English pub. Is that OK for a lady? I mean, there are some places in my home town I certainly wouldn't take you to.'

Rose laughed and he looked at her and laughed too.

'Dumb Yank.'

'Of course not. English pubs are, on the whole, lovely places. We used to go on summer Sundays to a lovely country one in Kent. That's where my home is, Kent. My parents would have cider and sandwiches and we had lemonade – and sandwiches and cakes too.'

'Sounds great. So let's find us a pub that has cider and sandwiches.'

'Would you settle for beer and sandwiches?'

'Warm English beer. I've been told about that.' He did not add that he thought anything at all would taste good if he was in the company of this lovely woman.

Brad had been advised to go to the Abbot's Inn, a pub not far from the American base. 'Been there since the Middle Ages, Rose, so they say. Is that credible?'

'This is England, Brad. It could be older. So could the beer.'

He laughed then, a full-throated hearty laugh.

'Oh, you are just a tonic, Rose. Let's find the old pub and the older beer; we don't really have too much time if we want to get to the dance.'

They found the pub, a very elderly building that time seemed to have squashed into the ground, so that Brad and even Rose had to bend to avoid hitting their heads on ancient oak lintels.

'My dad would love this.'

'What about your mother, or don't American ladies go to pubs?'

'Mom's way too Ivy League, Daughters of the American Revolution. She likes the Ritz, Claridge's, places like that.'

'She's visited England then?' Grace asked, and added quickly, 'Brad, that's all too nosy. I sound as if I'm prying but that's not . . .' She could not continue. He had been so easy to talk to, so calm, so . . . so . . . She could not find words. 'Come on. Let's get you a beer and a sandwich.'

He laughed, took her hand – which made her jump, as if an electric shock had travelled through her body – and guided her through an unnecessarily dark room to a table. He ordered beer and sandwiches.

'Cheese and pickle,' he was told.

'Wait and see,' suggested Rose when he asked her what that meant.

When the sandwiches arrived, Rose found herself wishing she had a camera or could draw – anything to preserve the look on his handsome face.

'Boy, if that's a sandwich, I can't wait to get you a *real* sandwich.'

'This is real. The English invented sandwiches.'

'And we sure improved them. But don't worry, we'll feed you at the base.'

'Is it true Americans bring all their food with them?'

'You wouldn't want us homing in on your rationed goods, would you?'

Rose had not considered what difficulties having thousands of Allied troops in the country might cause, and said so. 'But tell me about the town where you grew up. Please,' she added, in case he might think her rude.

He took a bite of his slim, white, crust-less sandwich and smiled. 'Good, if a tad different,' he said, and then told her about growing up between Washington DC, the capital, and a little place in Connecticut, which he obviously loved. Then he looked at his watch and she saw his muscular tanned arm and had to forcibly stop herself from putting her hand out to touch it.

What on earth is happening to me? Is this being knocked down by a Spitfire?

'We'll be late if we don't move,' he said.

She wanted only to sit there and watch his face and listen to his warm, attractive voice, but she stood up and let him help her on with her coat, conscious all the time of his hands on her shoulders.

They chatted all the way to the base. Yes, 'A cheese and pickle sandwich was very good', and, 'I'd love to see one of those redbirds.'

'Redbird is the nickname; they're really called red cardinals. My mom used to say that seeing one brought good luck. I guess that's because they're not really a northern bird and so they're still kinda rare in the north-east. Tell you one thing, though – you'll hear them before you see them and sometimes you can't be sure until you actually see the bird because they don't just say "tweet-tweet". They have a whole bunch of different songs; maybe they do it just to fool us.'

It was definitely the oddest conversation Rose had ever had with a man and, as she was helped out of the car by his warm, tanned, strong hand, Rose knew that she had never enjoyed one so much.

The rest of the evening was just as interesting.

The room chosen for the dance was sparkling clean and had been decorated with British and American flags, streamers and a great many red, white or blue balloons. Every table had a white paper table covering, and in the middle of the table stood a ceramic pot holding a small British flag and a small American one. Rose wondered if every American soldier studied music, for the band boasted over a dozen skilled musicians.

Rose and Brad joined a table where Francesca, Gladys and Mildred were sitting and, in no time at all, the table was overcrowded. No one moved to a different table. Private Arvizo was there and, when he saw where Gladys was sitting, he upended the chair next to her, unseating the young soldier who was already there and sat down himself.

Francesca gestured to the empty seat beside her, the soldier sat down, drinks were brought, and the music began.

Rose had heard American music on the radio and she had seen films in which there was dancing, but she had never listened to anything like the music being played that night. Neither had she ever danced to music with that beat.

Jive, jitterbug, swing, Lindy Hop; the words and the music swirled around her. Somehow everyone was on the floor, and Rose laughed as she saw Gladys frantically moving Arvizo's hands nearer to her waist. He was unrepentant, though, and the hands kept sliding.

'Stop dancing with him, Gladys, if he's making you angry,' Rose said as they took a few minutes' rest while some of the men went to bring food to the table, and Francesca and Mildred went to freshen up.

'He's not making me angry, he's making me laugh, and laughter is so good. Did you ever have a dog, Rose? No, then trust me. Arvizo's like a big exuberant puppy, all over you and not an ounce of badness in him. Besides, Lance Corporal, you seem welded to your gorgeous sergeant, so don't talk.'

Rose blushed furiously. 'He's not my sergeant.'

Gladys reached over and patted Rose's hand. 'That's not what anyone on this base thinks, Rose, from the lowliest private to the commanding general.'

'Don't be silly. We hardly know each other.'

Gladys looked up. 'Here he comes and, believe me, you're the only person in the room he sees.'

Brad grinned at them as he reached the table; he was balancing several laden plates in his hands. 'We brought some of everything. Hope you like pinto beans. Arvizo here has a Mexican grandmother and he sweet-talked Cookie into fixing them just like his grandma makes.'

'A culinary masterpiece,' confided Arvizo. 'I begged them to do all Mexican-American but do you know what he said? He said, "You're not the only ethnic minority on this base." They've fixed corn-pone for the Southerners and hamburgers made from the finest Texas beef for Easterners like the sergeant here.' He was pointing to each food as he mentioned them.

'Dare I try corn-pone?' Rose asked Brad.

'Sure, it's only bread, and have a burger and some of these Tex-Mex beans.'

The others returned to the table, their plates just as heavily loaded, and the evening went on, eating, dancing, talking, or sometimes sitting back quietly and listening to the band.

Rose listened to music she was unaware of having heard before. The instruments were piano, two guitars, a saxophone and a trumpet.

'It's so sad.'

Brad covered her hands with his. 'That's the blues, Rose. Mood music, full of longing for something lost, very Southern.' He squeezed her hand. 'Don't you like it? I'll tell them to play something else.'

'No, it's beautiful.'

The others agreed and Rose, embarrassed, slid her hands away, whispering something about 'freshening up'.

Immediately Brad stood, followed by Arvizo as Gladys too stood up.

'Wow, do these Yanks move quickly,' said Gladys as they stood, side by side, tidying their hair and reapplying lipstick. 'Your Bradley is a real gentleman. Didn't you see how he stood up?'

But Rose said nothing. She felt her life was now whirling like the frenzied rhythm of the jive and it was just too fast for her.

FOURTEEN

London, March 1943

On the Monday after the dance Rose was sent to London. She was told very little, merely to pack for several days and to tell no one where she was going.

That meant Brad too. Rose had no way of contacting him, but she asked Francesca to tell him – if he should come to the camp, or if a call came for her in the station call box – that Rose was sorry and would contact him when she returned. She felt this was dreadfully rude, but she consoled herself with the knowledge that he too was a professional and would understand.

When the dance ended he had driven her back to the camp and had escorted her to the door of her billet. They had been quiet on the drive back, quiet in fact from the last interval, when a few of the musicians had played blues music mainly for themselves.

'Did I say something wrong, Rose?' He stood at the door, looking down into her eyes, his own eyes troubled.

'Oh, no, Brad, it was a wonderful evening. I think I'm rather tired, and certainly too full of delicious food.'

'Me too.' They stood still and silent. Then he smiled but it was not his normal delightful smile, more a passable attempt. 'May I see you again? Maybe visit York, have dinner; or there are theatres and movie houses in York too.'

'That all sounds lovely.'

'Great. There has to be a call box on the base somewhere. I'll find it and call you.'

Again they stood. Rose wondered if he would kiss her and admitted to herself that she wanted him to, but no, this had been their first date. If he kissed her, would he think her fast if she responded, and if she did not, would he call her frigid, as Terry had done? She took a quick, small step back.

'You're right. It's late and it's cold. Good night, Rose.' He stood for a heartbeat longer, leaned forward, and she felt his lips, soft as drifting thistledown, on hers; then, with a quick wave, he was back on the road and had vaulted effortlessly into his Jeep.

'I hope it doesn't snow,' she called after him, and he laughed and raised his hand in farewell.

There was another of the daylight raids on London just before Rose went there. The greatest loss of life was at Bethnal Green Tube Station, where terrified travellers had stampeded. Rose was very aware of the probability of another raid while she was in the capital; she tried not to think of that, though, but to focus her mind on the job she was going to be asked to do. Once in London she took a taxi to the address she had been given in Whitehall. As she stood before the enormous building, which spoke of power and prestige, she thought: somewhere in there is a person who is expecting me. Who, in there, knows Rose Petrie's name?

The only way to find out was to go in.

Rose lifted her ATS kitbag, straightened her shoulders, and walked up the long flight of stairs and into the building. It was unbelievably quiet inside, the only sound being the staccato rap of leather soles on tiled floors as civilians and military personnel walked the corridors. A receptionist sat behind a desk and she looked up when Rose approached. There was no welcome on her cold, expressionless face.

'Yes?'

'Lance Corporal Rose Petrie reporting.' Again she had to swallow the word 'sir', which tried so hard to jump out.

'Take your kitbag to the cloakroom, and then sit down over there until you're sent for.'

Rose had been taught to say thank you when anyone did anything for her, but she set her face – *everybody's overworked, not just you* – and walked off towards the sign that said 'Cloakrooms'. She checked her bag, and, pleased to be rid of its weight, returned to the foyer where she sat and sat, and eventually wondered if anyone wanted to see her at all.

And then, when she had almost given up hope, a young man in RAF uniform came down one of the branching corridors and said, 'Miss Petrie? So sorry to have kept you. I do hope you had time for a cup of tea.'

Obviously he did not expect an answer and merely ushered her down the corridor to an imposing, highly polished double door. He knocked, opened the door, said, 'Miss Petrie, Commander,' and stood back to allow Rose to enter.

There were four people, one woman and three men, sitting round a table. The one addressed as 'Commander' stood up and said, 'Do come in, Miss Petrie. It's good of you to come.'

The commander was the man whom Rose had been thinking of for a year as 'the butler'.

How polite he was. How good of her to come, indeed. He knew perfectly well she could do nothing else.

'Sir,' she said, and sat down in the chair at which he'd pointed.

Two hours later, a passenger in a military vehicle, Rose was on her way to the house in Bayswater where she was to be based for as long as 'the butler' felt she was needed.

The landlady of the pleasant house to which she was driven, Mrs Bamber, was obviously very used to residents who came for short stays. She showed Rose into a bright airy bedroom that smelled a little of lavender.

'Bathroom's just down the 'all and the yellow towels is yours. Make yourself comfy and I'll bring you up a nice cuppa. Evening meal at seven. Me and my daughter'll eat with you; she's a nurse at St Thomas's and won't ask you no questions. If, God 'elp us, there's an air raid, and God knows there shouldn't be, we 'as a shelter in the garden.'

Rose sat on the pretty, spotlessly clean bedspread and listened to Mrs Bamber's muffled tread on the carpeted stairs. London. She was actually in London and somewhere in this magnificent city lived Cleo. If only there had been time to let her old friend know that she was coming. Still, according to the commander, there would be no time to socialise. Next time – if there was a next time.

She knew very little of her assignment. She was to

be a driver. A certain very important person was to be driven to various locations, the first one being Brighton.

'Have you visited Brighton Pavilion, Miss Petrie?'

'Afraid not, sir.'

'Well worth a visit, for its sheer extravagance, if nothing else. Your passenger expressed a fondness for it. He may – or then again he may not – decide to go. Perhaps a pleasant drive along the front. There are several splendid hotels where he might, or again might not, choose to lunch with local dignitaries.'

Rose sat on the bed and wondered who her passenger might be. A wealthy foreigner whom someone wanted to keep happy? A foreign dignitary? An American? That was it. Americans loved English eccentricities.

The steps were heavier on the stairs and Rose could also hear deep breathing. She ran to open the door and there, two steps from the top, was Mrs Bamber carrying a tray.

Rose hurried forward and took the tray from her. 'I'm sorry, Mrs Bamber. You don't have to wait on me. You really shouldn't carry trays like that.'

'Oh, I like to make my ladies welcome, Miss Petrie. I've been a landlady since 1920. My man died in the first war – gas poisoning, awful it was – but I 'ad my daughter and my 'ouse, and it's kept us fed, warm and dry, so can't complain. Now you 'ave a cuppa and then a bath, or 'ave a bath after supper. Water won't be warm enough till gone 'alf six but it'll stay warm.'

'It would be lovely to have a bath after supper, Mrs Bamber.'

'That's settled then, but not too late, mind. We all 'as to be up early. Dining room's bottom of the stairs, first door.'

Rose said thank you, closed the door behind her land-lady and walked over to the dressing table where she had put the tray. There was a beautifully ironed, embroidered linen tray cloth that spoke so eloquently of her mother that Rose almost cried. A small pot of tea, a china cup and saucer with bluebells painted around the rims, and a matching plate that held two home-baked biscuits. They smelled of home.

Be strong. Rose, you're in the army and have a job to do. Do it properly.

No one was harder on the Petrie women than the Petrie women themselves.

At seven o'clock, Rose, carrying the much lighter tray, walked down to the dining room and entered.

Mrs Bamber and a young woman were already in the room.

'This is Iris, my daughter,' said Mrs Bamber proudly, and Rose could see why she was proud. Iris was beautiful. She had natural blonde curly hair, the bluest of blue eyes and a beautiful, curvaceous, feminine figure; in fact, Iris looked like Rose's idea of a film star.

'She takes after my Albert,' said her mother, who was putting the final adjustments to the table.

After the comparison she had just made, this comment made Rose smile.

Iris put out her hand and shook Rose's. Hers was a strong handshake and Rose found herself smiling at the slightly older young woman.

'Hello, I'm Rose.'

'Iris. Do sit down. The soup's ready.'

Mrs Bamber was right. Iris would not ask Rose about her assignment. In fact, she would not speak to her at all, apart from the few words and phrases that civility demanded.

In silence they had potato soup, followed by Spam fritters, mashed potatoes and green beans.

'We'll finish with a nice pot of tea and an oatcake with a slice of cheese.'

'I have to iron a uniform for tomorrow,' said Iris, getting to her feet. 'Enjoy your bath, Miss Petrie, Rose, but I have a very early shift and would like to be in bed . . .' she looked at her tiny watch, 'before nine.' She nodded to Rose and left the dining room.

'The hours she works would amaze you, Miss Petrie. Slave labour is what goes on in 'ospitals, and every day a clean uniform. Poor lamb comes 'ome, eats, irons and goes to bed.'

'Yes, I think everyone works really long hours these days, and nurses, well, all medical personnel, really, are needed all hours of the day and night.'

Frankly, Rose felt that everyone in the Forces worked long hours but, remembering her few days in the hospital in Dartford when her munitions factory had been hit, she decided not to find Nurse Iris Bamber too grumpy.

Could I be a nurse? she asked herself, and answered immediately: not in a million years.

Quickly she ate her oatcake, leaving the cheese so that it could be used for something else, drank a cup of tea, really because Mrs Bamber had gone to the trouble of making it, and went upstairs to have her bath.

Next morning she was up and out before seven. She recognised the vehicle that had driven her to Mrs Bamber's, and the driver too was the same.

He said, 'Good morning,' as Rose got into the front beside him.

'You'll use public transport from now on, Miss Petrie. Here's the bus timetable and they're mostly on time.'

He said nothing else and Rose sat quietly, looking at the scenery in Whitehall as it became more austere, until they arrived at the important building. The commander was waiting. He looked her over and seemed happy with what he saw.

'Right, follow me.'

Rose followed him through the building to the back entrance. A lovely mews stretched before them and one of the garages was open.

'There's your car, Rose. You know your assignment. Good luck.'

Rose walked over to the garage and slid into the soft leather-upholstered driver's seat. It was the car they had given her before, but still she took a second to marvel at the sheer beauty of it before starting it, and then she drove, as carefully as traffic allowed, to her destination.

She drew up at a door she had seen only in photographs or on a newsreel, and before turning off the engine she glanced at the window beside the door. No, not yet, and so she turned off the engine and waited.

She did not have to wait long. A few minutes later the door opened and a tall, burly man came out, looked around carefully, and nodded. Behind him appeared a familiar figure and, in spite of her knowledge, Rose's heart skipped a beat. He was so recognisable, almost a caricature of himself. But she obeyed her instructions: 'Your job is to drive them wherever he wants to go and to bring them back, preferably in one piece.'

She heard the word 'Brighton'. Answered, 'Sir', started the engine and eased the beautiful car into the road. She stole a quick look in her rear-view mirror, not only to make sure nothing was behind her, but also to look once more at that enigmatic figure. He was smoking a cigar while he read a document.

Rose's blood, which had been galloping madly around her body, gradually slowed down to a relatively normal pace and her breathing quietened. *Who is ever going to believe this – when I get to tell them?*

She concentrated on her driving. She drove down a street that not so long ago would have been filled with nose-to-tail traffic: buses, lorries, ambulances, taxis, private cars. Today she saw two buses on the other side of the road, one delivery lorry parked in front of a small grocery shop, and a bicycle. Well-wrapped people stood at bus stops, stamping their feet to keep them warm. Had there been no petrol rationing, Rose was convinced that most of the well-dressed pedestrians would have been vying with her for road space. She smiled to see a surprised look of recognition, fevered pointing, waving, saluting.

'Slow.'

She obeyed the curt command.

'Drive on.'

And so went the journey out of London. It seemed to Rose that her passengers wanted to be seen, wanted to be recognised.

They were out of the city and the speed increased. Few private cars passed them, or drove alongside, but there were military vehicles, small and large, coming and going, brave flags of Allied countries flying in the stream of air caused by their speed. Again it seemed that her passengers courted recognition, and she saw his hands being raised in salute as burly, ill-shaven men leaned out from under the canvas of army trucks and waved.

The last hour or so was peaceful, the car purring along like a contented kitten, the passengers totally involved, one with the day's *Times*, the other with folders of paper.

They reached Brighton and Rose drove to the Pavilion, once the favourite home of the flamboyant Prince Regent, but before she could slow to a halt a voice that she had heard often on the wireless said, 'Drive down the front, Lance Corporal.'

Rose strove to remain detached, professional. The voice. The world could recognise that voice. It made the wisps of hair on the back of her neck stand up.

'Sir.' *This is my job. Just do it, Rose, do it.*

The sea was stormy, throwing itself angrily against the shore.

'Pull over.'

Rose obeyed. Only a few stalwarts braved the cold to walk along the front, woollen hats pulled down around their ears, thick scarves wound around thin, wrinkled necks.

'The door,' said the other voice, and Rose almost jumped out and hurried round the car to open the door. Out stepped Winston Churchill, followed immediately by the taller man. The Prime Minister took a few breaths of good sea air, waved to three old men who were shuffling along against the wind. 'Best air in the world,' he called to them, 'English air.'

A moment later he was back in the car and three elderly men were looking after him in excitement and disbelief.

'I think we've done enough, Petrie,' said the other voice. 'The War Office.'

'Sir.'

Rose drove back to London; when they reached the War Office, her two passengers left the car and hurried inside the building and she drove the car back to the depot.

'A job well done,' said the officer in charge of vehicles. 'Discretion at all times. Be here tomorrow at ten and you'll find out where you are to take them.'

'Sir.'

Rose felt that she had said nothing but 'sir' for days. She took her bus timetable out of her pocket and began to work out the best way to get to her digs. But first, a cup of tea and a roll or a bun. She made her way to the Strand and went into the Lyons Corner House. As usual it was packed, but Rose bought a pot of tea and a cheese roll. That reminded her of Brad; he had simply not understood an English cheese and pickle sandwich. She sat down in a corner, poured a cup of tea and relaxed.

Her mind went over her original instructions again and again, and the more she repeated them the more excited and terrified she became. Never would she have envisaged this. Transporting a senior army officer, even the documents needed by an officer, would have made her feel useful and proud but this . . . even her parents would find it difficult to believe when she was eventually allowed to tell them.

'We're rather short of drivers at this time, Lance Corporal, but we heard about you from an important official. He says you have all the qualities required. There are times when it's necessary that no one knows exactly where a vitally important official is. We set up decoys, doubles, using official cars, official drivers and, make no mistake about this, bodyguards. For the next three days you will be driving the Prime Minister around London and the south coast.'

Rose remembered how her heart had skipped a beat – in fact, almost stopped at that news. She hoped she had managed to hide her shock.

'You will, of course, be driving a double, but the bodyguard will be very real and very necessary. Do you understand?'

'Yes, sir.' She was pleased at how calm and professional she had sounded when every instinct had made her want to jump in the air and shout with excitement. *It's an assignment, that's all, a professional assignment, and I will stay calm and carry out my duties.*

'Good. The commander was sure you would not let us down.'

She could tell no one of her assignment, not her parents, her friends, and not Brad. She bit into the cheese sandwich, which was delicious – perhaps because she was so hungry – and found herself wishing that he was sitting there across from her. She could almost feel his presence, hear his voice. How had he become so important to her? What was it that suddenly appeared, as though from nowhere, and bound two people together with an invisible but unbreakable cord?

I haven't been hit by a Spitfire, Daisy, she sent a mental message to her twin sister. *I've been run down by a Matador lorry.*

She finished her cup and poured another one. Rose, the lance corporal in the ATS, was absolutely delighted to have been chosen for this assignment, but Rose Petrie, the woman, was unhappily conscious of unbelievably bad timing. She relived those moments standing with Brad at the door of her billet. She felt his hands on her, saw his eyes that asked so many gentle questions, felt his lips . . .

Had he tried to contact her? Two or three more days before she would find out. What if he had not, what if . . . ?

No. Rose dismissed negative thoughts. Brad had said he would call; if he had not, then it was because he was a soldier and was busy somewhere else.

The third cup of tea was cold. Rose looked at her watch and had a truly lovely idea. Her landlady would not expect her before seven and so she was free to do whatever she wanted.

Cleo.

She would go to Cleo's office building – luckily Cleo's last short note had given the address – and ask if it was possible to see Miss Fitzpatrick.

The office, a stone's throw from the Admiralty, was in a building just as overwhelming as the one in which Rose had been interviewed.

The receptionist here was approachable and quite happy to ring through to see if Miss Fitzpatrick was available to see a Miss Petrie.

A few minutes later, the elegant, trim Cleo arrived, breathless. 'Rose, my very dear Rose,' she said.

The girls looked at each other, assessing how the year since they had last been together had affected them, and then, naturally, they hugged.

'Now, tell me, what on earth are you doing in town? You're in uniform and so you're working. Come along,

I've taken five minutes and we can walk up and down outside, or there's a canteen, but the food's dire.'

They opted for outside where a frail sun was doing its best to warm up the cold air.

'It's lovely to see you, Cleo. I'm in London, working, but I wasn't needed this afternoon and so – here I am.'

'You didn't have time to ring me? Remember my teeny, weeny guestroom.'

Rose explained that there had been no time to do anything, and told Cleo that she had been billeted by the army.

'Terrif. You can have dinner with me tonight. Not much, home-made vegetable soup, followed by, wait for it, a real boiled egg – I have two fresh ones from never mind where – and, for pudding, a tin of pears.'

'I'd love to, Cleo, but my landlady expects me.'

'And will be absolutely delighted not to have to use her extra rations. I'll ring her – we're bound to have her on our list. We haven't seen each other for ages and we can talk our heads off and then I'll put you on the right bus. What do you say?'

What could Rose say but yes?

She walked around London, seeing for the first time signs of the devastation with which every Londoner was only too familiar. She gazed at the magnificence of the Parliament building and then at the damaged St Thomas's Hospital, which stood directly opposite on the other bank of the Thames. For a moment she wondered if the poor light was playing tricks with her eyes. There did not seem to be any windows. She gazed and realised, to her horror, that the windows – or where she thought

205

windows might have been – had been completely bricked up. She knew the sprawl of the famous hospital had been severely damaged earlier in the war. Had every window been blown out, causing who-knew-what appalling injury to life and supplies?

How do they work? How do surgeons operate? Artificial light? Those poor nurses and doctors, they must feel like moles. So help me, I will never complain again – about anything.

She climbed the steps of the National Gallery at Trafalgar Square and was disappointed to find that the building was empty, not just of people, but of paintings.

'Don't you read the papers, love? They've all been buried for the duration. We don't want no more of our 'eritage bombed to bits, do we? There's been such a moan, though, that one picture gets brought in now and again for a little exhibition. We even has piano players like . . . now what was 'er name? Hess, that was it. Very German sound, that, but the punters seemed to love 'er. Some was crying, would you believe? You stationed here, then read the papers and come another day.'

Not a terribly exciting visit to the great gallery. I'll come back when the war is over, Rose promised herself, and then, since it was too dark and cold to do anything else, she walked back to Cleo's office and waited for her.

Cleo's little flat, the basement of a charming house in Chelsea, was a delight. 'And all this is yours? How amazing to have your own flat.'

'Even though we're in Chelsea, which is quite upmarket, Mummy thinks I'm living in semi-squalor. She hasn't visited. She's afraid of London, afraid of everything, poor old thing, especially with this break in the lull or, who knows, maybe the end of it. We keep telling her how well the barrage balloons work and we tell her the RAF is too good for what's left of the German air force, but she just can't handle it. Cries all over me, "Come home, darling." But I love my work; love doing something useful, as you do. Dad pops in from time to time. He brought me the eggs, very naughty, from a local farm. There were three, but I ate one yesterday and thought two would make a nice omelette, but doesn't the thought of a soft-boiled egg with toast soldiers make you feel all safe?'

'Not sure if I feel nostalgic, but it does definitely say Sunday supper before the war.'

'That's nostalgia talking. Here, have a sherry. Pa brought it up on Sunday but he drank some and then, well, I'm not living like a nun; Arthur had some the other night after the cinema.'

'Arthur?' asked Rose as she accepted a small glassful of a golden liquid.

'Just a chum. He works with me, or really I work with him. We're encryptors.' She looked at Rose, who appeared unsure. 'We take a message and put it into a special code; sometimes it's the other way around. But you're driving. Didn't I tell you that you would be?'

'Yes, you did. This is only my second assignment. Usually I drive military vehicles full of personnel and/ or equipment.'

'Hold on.' Cleo went into her tiny kitchen and came out with the soup tureen. 'A different job every day?'

'Today a posh car, tomorrow an ambulance. The next day I might have to take an engine apart.'

'Your poor nails.'

They both laughed at that. What a Sally-like remark. Rose felt sixteen again. 'Tell me about Arthur.'

'Luckily he doesn't set any bells ringing. I'm not completely sure, but I don't think he's really into girls, if you know what I mean. Awfully kind, though, and manages to get into decent restaurants. There are one or two old "squeezes", but one's in India and God knows where the other one is. Now you tell me everything about your love life. The ATS – there must be a thousand gorgeous men lining up.'

Rose smiled. 'Possibly, but they're usually covered in oil or they haven't had a shave for a week, and all they beg me to do is, "Fix it, Gorgeous."'

'And apart from the great unwashed?'

'There's Brad.'

'Your face and voice said it all, Rose. Tell me. Brad? Unusual Christian name.'

'It's Bradley, Bradley Hastings. He's the American who rescued us when I had the blow-out. But I've only seen him a few times.'

'That's all it takes. He sounds like an officer. Tall, handsome, rich?'

With a shriek Cleo jumped up and ran into the kitchen. 'I forgot the eggs. Oh, they'll be like rocks.'

They were not runny but neither were they hard.

'They've survived. That's your Bradley's fault. Bradley. I've heard that name recently – or read it. *Is* he an officer?'

'No, a sergeant.'

'I don't suppose he's an oil millionaire from Oklahoma. If he is, does he have a brother?'

'He's East Coast and is an only child. That egg was absolutely delicious. We get powdered these days.'

The grandmother clock in the hallway began to chime and automatically Rose counted. 'Oh Lord, Cleo. It's nine o'clock. I'll have to dash. I'm so sorry.'

In her head she could hear Iris Bamber reminding her that she liked to be in bed before nine.

I'll creep in.

Cleo looked at her own watch as if she too could not believe how long they had been eating and chatting. 'Come on, grab your coat. The bus stop is just round the corner on the King's Road.' She was tying the belt of her own coat as she spoke. 'Oh, Rose, I wish you could stay here tonight, but it would lead to problems. Next time just tell them and it will be fine.'

They hurried out. The night was dark but there was a sliver of a moon and some stars helped. They almost bumped into someone walking a dog and he swore at them. 'What are you doing out at this time? Get yourselves off home.'

'Our local arbiter of morals. Don't worry. He would have yelled just as loudly at seven, and I'm sure he peers through his curtains – looking for spies, says Arthur, or anyone else being naughty.'

They turned the corner onto the main road and were just in time for Rose to catch her first bus. 'Just tell the driver which bus you need next and he'll let you off. It's been wonderful. Let me know when you're coming back.'

Rose jumped on the bus; as it trundled off, she looked back and, through the crisscrossed tapes on the windows, saw Cleo turning the corner. She would be inside her lovely little flat long before Rose arrived at her digs.

How quickly the time had passed and what a lovely evening they had shared. It had been as if they'd never been separated. Rose smiled happily as the bus travelled slowly out of Chelsea and into South Kensington. Even though it was almost impossible to see clearly, she tried to guess more or less what she was passing: the Victoria and Albert Museum, Brompton Oratory, eventually the Royal Albert Hall. She vowed that, as soon as the war was over, she would actually visit some of them. Another bus with blue-painted windows took her close to Kensington Gardens, and she tried in vain to look for lights that might come from Kensington Palace, which she thought must be close.

She got off the bus on the Bayswater Road and, a few minutes later, was at her lodgings. Mrs Bamber was sitting in the hall with a lighted candle, wearing her nightclothes, her hair excruciatingly rolled into a tortured mass of metal curlers.

'I'm so sorry,' whispered Rose. 'I hadn't seen my friend for a year.'

'All right, love, and there's cocoa on the 'ob, if you want to 'elp yourself. My Iris is at the pictures with 'er mates. 'Ope she doesn't wake you.'

Since Rose had had no time for a cup of tea, she did indeed pour herself a cup of Mrs Bamber's cocoa. She whispered 'Good night' as she passed her.

When she had washed and was ready for bed, she saw her landlady still sitting on the bottom stair, waiting to hear her daughter's footsteps, just as her own parents had done in the past, and no doubt still would.

FIFTEEN

Next morning, Rose and Iris were both awake with the larks. The smell of frying bacon filled every corner of the comfortable house, and Rose, very surprised but delighted, was given three slices of bacon with her toast.

'That's too generous, Mrs Bamber,' she said, unable to bring herself to breakfast on lovely bacon while the others were eating porridge.

'Nonsense, it's yours lawful. If you 'adn't been out last night, it would 'ave been your supper.'

'If you're sure . . . Thanks very much.'

'Iris saw a lovely picture last night, didn't you, Iris? *Mrs. Miniver*, it was called, with Walter Pidgeon; 'e's ever such a lovely man. I always believe 'e is the person 'e's pretending to be.'

'I know just what you mean,' agreed Rose, 'and I bet Greer Garson was lovely. Even her name is pretty.'

Iris stopped eating for a moment, then said, 'Go and see it for yourselves. I think they're only allowed two or three showings before it has to go somewhere else, but don't watch it if you cry easily, like Mum. Your ninepence would be wasted, Mum.' Iris got up, taking

211

a cup of tea with her, and went upstairs to get ready for her shift.

'She does love to tease me; knows perfectly well I'll love every minute, even if they all get killed. And they will, won't they, since it's about the war?'

'I shouldn't think so. People would be furious if Greer Garson was to be killed and my mum would be livid if they did anything bad to Walter.' Rose put her napkin down and stood up. 'I have no plans for this evening, Mrs Bamber, so I'll come back here when my shift's finished.'

'All right, love. If I'm not in, there's a spare key under the middle plant pot on the top step.'

Rose thanked her and went off to get ready, all the time wondering where she would be driving today.

'Worked beautifully, Rose; take a look at that.' The commander handed Rose a large-circulation Brighton newspaper.

On the front page was a picture headed 'Prime Minister takes the air'. There was the seafront. There in the background were the windblown old men, and waving to them enthusiastically was none other than the Prime Minister, Winston Churchill.

'When was that taken?'

'I wasn't there, Miss Petrie. You know more than I.'

'But I didn't see anyone with a camera or even see a flash, and there's bound to have been a flash, isn't there, sir?'

'Obviously I know as much about the art of photography as you do, but frankly, I don't care, the photograph was taken. There it is in the paper. No doubt other papers will pick it up. Newspapers never lie, Miss Petrie. Yesterday the Prime Minister was in Brighton. You see his picture there in black and white. Have a good day, Miss Petrie, wherever you go.'

He was gone before she could say anything. She wondered what his name was. She still thought of him as 'the butler', but here he was addressed as 'Commander'. She should have asked her parents the name of the owner of the great house, Silvertides, where she had met him first. Was he the owner, or an important visitor? Surely important visitors did not answer doorbells. Next time she was at home, or when she wrote, she would ask, definitely.

'Lance Corporal Petrie.' The quiet voice came from the corridor down which the commander had disappeared. 'Your car is in the mews. Your passenger will tell you where you are to drive him. Please go to the canteen and ask for a Thermos flask of tea or coffee and a sandwich. One never knows in our line of work when one will be fed, or even when one might make oneself comfortable, may I say. Take advantage of the building's facilities, Miss Petrie. It may be a long day.'

The uniformed man, whoever he was, turned and walked back down the corridor. A door opened and he disappeared inside.

'Very Penny Dreadful,' said Rose to herself, quoting something she had heard her father and eldest brother say. They meant that whatever was happening was like the tales of espionage or derring-do that appeared in the inexpensive magazines that were very popular in the United States. She decided to take the unknown man's advice, so hurried off to the canteen, where a reluctant assistant

213

eventually allowed her to borrow a small Thermos flask. She looked at the food selection and, conscious of her coupons and what her mother would say about her choices, she bought a small bar of chocolate and a bread roll. A chocolate sandwich would make, she decided happily, the perfect lunch, especially after a hearty breakfast of toast and grilled bacon.

Once ready she went out to the mews, put her lunch in the car, and, again thrilled by the sheer joy of being allowed to drive such a luxury vehicle, moved it to the back door, where a very large London policeman stood watching the human traffic.

'Waiting for a passenger, miss?'

'Yes, Officer, my orders are to wait for them almost on the very spot where you're standing.'

He laughed. 'Then I'll move myself back a step against the door, miss. This door isn't easily overlooked, and if anyone was on a roof over there, or up one of them trees – and seems they'd have to be monkeys to get there – and they was curious, like, and wanted a peek at anyone coming in or going out, I doubt they'd see through a delicate little lad like me.'

'Perhaps that's why you're here this morning, Officer.'

'Move your car, love. They'll be here in a tick.'

Rose smiled at him. 'Yes, Officer.'

She had no sooner repositioned the car and opened the passenger door when her passengers, hidden from the view of any monkeys in the trees by the large policeman, came out of the office building, bent down and got into the car. The policeman saluted and closed the door.

Rose heard a voice that she knew well say, 'Buckingham Palace.'

'Yes, sir,' she said, trying to keep a tiny shake from attacking her vocal cords. She turned on the engine and eased the car away from the door and out into the road.

It would have been quicker for them to walk, since the roads were busy with mid-morning traffic, but eventually Rose reached the magnificent gates and halted. The policeman at the gate saluted and waved the car forward.

'Follow the driveway,' said the voice, and Rose obeyed.

I am in the grounds of the King's palace. Wait till I tell Mum.

She followed the road, looking hopefully for a covered entrance, where it would be easy, in any type of weather, to leave a vehicle, a car, even a coach, or dismount from a horse, without getting wet. She taxied the car to a halt exactly at the foot of a flight of stone stairs and had time to notice the two men who had hurried out of the door at the top of the stairs. One opened the passenger door and stood back to allow her VIP to get out. He did. Ignoring everyone, he walked up two stairs before turning as if to return to the car. There was a blinding flash of light, so unexpected that Rose jumped. She heard a laugh behind her where her second passenger still sat.

'The press, my dear Miss Petrie. The Prime Minister has an urgent meeting this morning with His Majesty. Stay with the car until we're inside and then you'll be told where to park. Hope you brought a good book. If not, borrow my *Times*; it's on the back seat.'

The men disappeared inside the building and Rose sat, as she had been ordered. While she waited she tried to imagine where they were and what they were doing. Were there opulent red carpets on all the stairs, sparkling chandeliers hanging from every ceiling? Oh, just to have had the tiniest peek inside. She was trying to work out what would really happen if the King were to meet Mr Churchill inside. Did Mr Churchill bow or did the King say, 'Good morning, Winston, do sit down'?

A rap on her window startled her. 'Shift it round the back, love. Don't have to back up, just follow your nose.'

The footman, or whatever, whoever he was, had an accent that came straight out of the East End.

Rose laughed at herself as she 'shifted it'. She had thought every accent heard in this historic, magnificent building would have been fashioned out of cut glass, and was at first disappointed and then delighted by democracy in action.

She parked where she was directed and then, as the cold March winds caused the temperature inside the car to drop, she got out, removed a tartan rug from the boot, and wrapped herself in it before returning to her seat. She sat watching what she could see of buildings, trees, and beautifully intricate wrought-iron gates that looked more like works of art than mere gates, until the windscreen had completely frosted over. She poured herself a small cup of the coffee she had brought with her – she had no idea how long she would be and so judged it better to save some for later – and sipped it slowly. Probably because she was cold, she thought it tasted better than any coffee she had ever had. She got out, stamped her feet to get her circulation moving again, reached into the back seat for *The Times*, returned to the driver's seat and began to read, from cover to cover.

What price the glamorous job of driver for VIPs now? Why, oh why, had she not worn trousers?

Suddenly the window was dark beside her and then the door opened. 'Lord above, girl, stay in there much longer and they'll have to chip you out.' A uniformed policeman bent over and took her hand. 'Did no one tell you to take a pew in the sentry box? Come on, they've got a little heater in there, an' all.'

He had given her no opportunity to answer him, though she began to say, 'But my boss—'

'Will expect to find you warm and snug instead of catching your death in the car. Come on.'

Rose stumbled as she got out. He caught her and it was only then that she realised how cold she was. 'Please don't . . .'

'We looks after one another, love. It was young Archie, came out for a smoke, and asked where you was.'

'Sorry to have been so stupid, Constable.'

'I'm a sergeant, love, but no offence taken. Just be glad I found you. There's some real bigwigs in there today. Wouldn't do at all for them to go looking for you.'

Rose said nothing but, as she began to thaw, she felt herself get a little cross. Shouldn't her instructions cover things like where and how to make oneself invisible when waiting at palaces? But perhaps a driver who had gone through the entire gamut of driver training would have absorbed all the peripheral details.

She was in the sentry box and a seat right beside the little heater was made ready for her by the guards on duty. 'And there's char here as would put hairs on yer chest, as the saying goes, miss, no offence meant.'

'Sounds perfect,' said Rose with a dazzling smile.

She sat with her new acquaintances for another ninety minutes, watched them perform their duties, shared their sandwiches, and marvelled at their sense of fun as well as their deep respect for the work they were all doing.

Policemen, soldiers, ATS driver, they were all in this together and, for Rose, it was a day to remember. It was to become even more memorable.

At quarter past two, over three hours after she had arrived at the palace, a call to the sentry box informed her that Lance Corporal Petrie's passengers were leaving.

'That means you have time to put on your coat and hat and get round there to fetch the motor.'

She thanked the soldiers and police for their kindness.

'You're welcome, love. Pop in any time you're passing.'

She waved, and hurried round to where she had parked the car, turned on the engine, frantically rubbed the windscreen and got in, hoping that she would be able to see out of it by the time she reached the steps.

She drew up, left the engine idling, and waited. A few minutes later a group of men appeared in the doorway and Rose's passengers, accompanied by a senior naval officer, came down the stairs. All three got into the car.

'Admiralty House, driver,' said a voice.

'Sir,' said Rose, and drove majestically to the gates of Buckingham Palace and then out onto the busy road. Admiralty House was one of the many addresses that Rose had memorised, but she had never expected to be driving to it from Buckingham Palace and was relieved when the same calm voice issued directions. They reached their first destination, the extra passenger got out, and by the time he had disappeared inside the Admiralty, Rose had been given her next order.

'Victoria Station.'

Why was she taking them to Victoria Station? To pick up a passenger who was returning – from a well-deserved holiday, perhaps. Or was the quiet man behind her, who was once again smoking a cigar, taking the boat train to Dover so as to sail to . . . a secret destination, not for a holiday but for a meeting? It was very dangerous to go to Europe, but Tomas and pilots like him flew there often on missions of mercy.

She disciplined her wild imaginings, telling herself that she should be doing her job and not wallowing in flights of fancy. Her passengers, or the special passenger, were making no effort to hide. They sat straight up, the instantly recognisable homburg hat placed squarely on the well-known head.

He needs people to see him. Why? Because the real man is somewhere else, involved in something terribly vital to the war effort, and he wants no one to know he's there.

Just then, a car pulled up almost parallel in the lane beside her.

'Stupid ass,' muttered Rose under her breath. The car had come much too close, but the driver seemed to be a tad ashamed of himself, for he lifted a hand in a short salute as his car slipped back until it was no longer alongside.

'Change lanes at the earliest opportunity, Petrie.' The calm voice spoke in her ear. 'That car got much too close.'

'I thought I'd try to move over, take the next right. We make a little circle and we're back on the road.'

'Excellent. Do that.'

Rose glanced across. The small, undistinguished black car was once more right beside them, a figure in the back seat looking directly into the passenger seat. He raised his arm.

'God damn it, accelerate, girl, accelerate.'

That command was almost lost in the sound of a gunshot, but Rose had heard the order and had acted instinctively. Instead of accelerating, with all her strength she had slammed on the brake, causing the car to stop, practically on its nose, sending both her passengers flying. They landed heavily, in an uncomfortable heap on the floor. The driver of the car in the next lane, obviously expecting Rose to speed up in a desperate but futile attempt to escape the would-be assassin, had himself accelerated and was now some distance ahead, weaving and dodging as he tried to escape determined pursuers.

They had come out of nowhere. Lights blazed, sirens sounded and Rose's car sat, as if on a guarded island, while they hurtled past.

Drivers in cars behind, and Rose, quietly thanked any power that had been watching over them, slowed and pulled over, white, shocked faces glancing at Rose or into the back seat. But the passengers were still on the floor, the taller, heavier man protecting the body of the other man with his own.

What seemed like an eternity had taken seconds and, as realisation dawned on Rose, she began to tremble.

'Rose,' the man behind said quietly, 'start the engine and wait for your escort. They're coming now. Follow the two leading bikes. Everything is under control.'

Would she talk about it one day? Would she laugh as she told of her Very Important Persons being thrown in a heap on the floor? Would she remember that during the incident she had felt nothing but determination to do her job, coupled with anger that *he* should be subjected to this? She did not know.

She obeyed her orders and drove through London surrounded by motorcycle police.

'Clever move to brake, Lance Corporal.' The well-known voice again sent shivers up and down her spine.

It has to be him. It can't be a double. He's too good.

'Gave it some serious thought, lying on the floor there. Not my first indignity, and won't be my last.'

'Sir.'

She followed the leaders, as she had been ordered, but had no idea which seat of power she had reached. Before the outbreak of war she had rarely visited London and, although now and again she had recognised a statue or an arch or even the front of a great department store, without street signs in areas with which she had not become completely familiar, she felt lost.

The passenger door was opened and the two men got out. To Rose's surprise her door was opened by a soldier. She was even more surprised when he gestured to her to leave the car.

'A reviving cup of tea, Lance Corporal,' said the taller man.

'Don't be a bloody fool, man,' said the VIP as he walked into the foyer. 'She needs a brandy like the rest of us.'

Rose was trembling, reaction perhaps to having been in danger. But as her passenger reached the door he turned, smiled at her and said, 'Bloody quick thinking,' and the voice was not the voice she knew.

A marine brought her a chair with the brandy.

On the next day, Rose travelled by bus into London and was shown into a room where, she was told, she was to be debriefed.

The commander was there, the taller VIP who had been in the car with her, and several men, some in uniform, some not. The tall man, not named, was an experienced and highly skilled bodyguard, she was told.

'Everything worked beautifully, Lance Corporal, and we're quite happy with your work. No doubt we'll be calling on your services again. Anything you want to ask?'

Which of the many questions in her head should she put forward?

'The shooters, sir?'

'No, we haven't caught them, but have no doubt they'll be behind bars soon. Read the papers yet?'

'No, sir.'

'Nice picture of the PM going into Buck House. Excellent. And the *Evening Star* got rather a good shot of the actual incident: "ATS Driver's Quick Thinking Saves the Day".'

He walked across to the desk and picked up a copy of the newspaper. 'I know it seems fearfully *Boy's Own*, Miss Petrie, but there are evil forces alive in the world. While you were driving your gentlemen around, allowing them to be seen, the real PM was engaged in secret but vitally important talks . . . We won't play today; you are free to return to normal duties. You have time to catch the afternoon train.'

'But my things . . . ?' Rose began.

'Mrs Bamber is the essence of efficiency. Your kitbag is at Reception.'

It was over. She had been part of something for two days but was now surplus to requirements. She stood up, saluted, and walked out.

A Jeep was waiting outside and she was whisked to the station. Several hours later, space was found for her on a lorry that was heading to her base from York Station. Rose wondered whether she should laugh or cry. Neither, probably. She had been a small part of something she had to believe was important and now she was back at her camp, and could tell no one anything at all about where she had been and what she had been doing. Nor would anyone ask.

Brad? Just thinking his name conjured up his handsome face, his quiet but very masculine voice. He would not ask. She only hoped that he had tried to be in touch while she had been away.

'Rose, lovely. We weren't expecting you back until tomorrow.' It was Francesca.

'Job didn't take as long as they had first thought. Any messages, letters?'

'Were you painting the town red? You look jolly tired.'

'Messages?'

'Of course. He rang the public telephone. Aren't Yanks clever? How did he get the number?'

'Don't tease.'

Fran smiled, gave her a hug and a small piece of paper. 'He rang, a chap from the machine shop came down, I went up, and told him you'd been called away. His message is on . . .'

But Rose was reading the note. 'I don't believe it. London?'

'What kind of bad luck is that? But look on the bright side. He travelled down, military convoy, overnight. Impossible to meet, Rose, and he did say he'd be back in a couple of days. Now, can't you tell me anything about London?'

'It's big: fabulous buildings, huge department stores – some rather pompous, even intimidating. There are bombed-out buildings, holes in some roads, signs of fires, and a smell of smoke – and I don't want to think what else – hangs over everything and brings home just how bloody awful this war is. But my landlady was lovely, and her daughter, who's a nurse at St Thomas's Hospital, saw that film Terry wanted to take me to see, *Mrs. Miniver*, and she says it's a real weepie.'

'My kind of film. Now, put your coat on; it's teatime. Gladys'll have saved us seats.'

SIXTEEN

May 1943

The winter had been long and cold. A perfect English spring flooded in with almost daily showers that certainly brought the May flowers.

Off duty for the afternoon, Rose and Brad were walking towards the village of Long Marston: Brad was interested in English history and was determined to see the site of the battle of Marston Moor; he was also determined to find a pub with what he called 'real sandwiches'. Underfoot were carpets of tiny flowers and the sight had Rose humming an 'April Showers' song, which she was sure she had known for as long as she could remember.

'Absolutely, that song has to be the same age you are, Rose, and it's not British, it's Al Jolson in a Broadway show, '20s sometime.'

'I think you're confusing two songs, Bradley Hastings. The one I'm humming was in the film *Bambi* – "Little April Showers", I think it was called.'

He stopped striding across the moor and grabbed her, and Rose laughed and tried to escape, but of course she did not actually want to escape and he had no intention of letting go. They stood just looking at each other and then Brad pulled Rose against his chest and she remained there, perfectly happily, while he whispered nonsense about raindrops and baby animals and spring flowers into her ear. Rose listened to his voice and to his heart and wondered if it were possible to die from happiness. Never had she been in such a relationship. Being with him was exciting but it was also peaceful.

He had returned from London and hand-delivered the letter he had written to her while a train had carried him back to York.

Dear Rose,

    I miss you every second of every minute, and why? I don't understand it and yet, I'm a college man, supposed to have some kind of education. We only just met. It's not like we grew up in the same town, played tennis at the same club, went together to the prom. Nothing like this has ever happened to me before. I remember that ghastly night when we found you sinking into the ditch. A woman I had never seen before – why should her plight affect me the way it did? – but, somehow, the moment I looked in your beautiful eyes, I knew the world had changed for me.

    And then that Saturday night, I stood there outside the door of that damned Nissen hut and I kissed you, and, Rose, I wanted to stay there for ever.

    My father is here, not in Yorkshire, in London, and I was sent down to see him because when my dad speaks, people run to do what he says. He wants me to take a commission and he wants me in London. I

can fight him, Rose, but I can't fight the whole darned
army and I don't know what is going to happen. I
think I'm safe for the present and my plan is to do my
job the best I can and to get to know Rose Petrie, hey,
a real beautiful English rose.

Does any of this make any sense to you? If it does,
would you care to go into town with me Friday night?
There's a bus from the base, gets back 23.00 hrs.
We could

The letter stopped there, probably because the train had
reached York. He had signed it 'Brad'.

Rose had read the letter so often that she could have
recited it, and she had smiled, laughed a little, and cried
a little too. She had only just met him, but had never
known anyone quite like him, and life had changed for
her, too. Not on the night they met, but in the hour
before the hop at the American base, when he had tried
so hard to pretend he liked his cheese and pickle sandwich. A trivial little thing – but tiny things can be very
powerful, can they not? she thought.

Two days after the letter was delivered he telephoned,
and this time she was there, ready to run like a hare to
the call box, to stand in the cold, first to listen to his
voice and then to tell him that she would be free on the
Friday evening.

They had met as often as possible after that. When
they could not meet, he telephoned. Sometimes they
could not communicate at all. The war and their work
came before everything else. And there had been plenty
of both. Rose seemed to spend her working days either
covered in oil and dirt inside the 'working parts' – usually

non-working – of some military vehicle or, scrubbed and polished, driving a vehicle, delivering men, materials, medical aid; she never knew from one day to the next what her assignment would be. Brad never spoke of what he actually did all day, but when Rose mentioned the rumours about fights between black and white American soldiers that seemed to fly around day after day in the local newspapers, he did talk about it.

'Can't lie to you, Rose, and I hate even to talk about it because it's a very ugly part of our history. Yes, there are prejudiced people in the army. I pray I'm right in saying it's just a few who think one colour skin is better or worse than another. Most of the time, guys rub along together; everyone knows that the guy beside you, whatever colour he is, is the one you'll depend on in conflict. We've had some pub brawls – alcohol does inflame, I guess; even a few fights right on base, and we don't like it any more than you guys do. On the whole, England accepted our coloured soldiers as easily as it accepted the rest of us, and let's hope our misguided hotheads will learn from you.'

Rose thought for a moment. 'I'm glad we're nice.'

He had laughed then, his lovely warm laugh. 'Some of you are very, very nice, Miss Petrie.'

'C'mon,' Brad growled now, releasing her. 'I want to see this battlefield, brush up on my English history. We had a civil war, you guys had a civil war.'

'Can't see anything civil about a war,' said Rose, 'but all you'll see, Sergeant, is a field and a monument.'

'Exactly the same back home, a field and a monument. OK, history lessons over; let's find a pub.'

They found several pubs of various ages, hundreds of years old, new-built to look like hundreds of years old, and several in between. Eventually they decided on one called the Horse and Saddle, because Brad liked horses.

'Perfectly good reason for choosing a place to eat,' said Rose.

'Glad you agree,' Brad said as he put his arm around her slender waist, and, laughing, they bent almost in half to get in without knocking themselves out on the low doorjamb.

The menu was sparse, but when the cook discovered that his male customer was an American soldier, he suddenly remembered that there were some locally made sausages in his larder. 'I know you Yanks eat steaks all the time, but these sausages are delicious. I'll do you a nice plate of mash with them; a bit different, boiled potatoes mashed with some boiled parsnips, all out of my own garden.'

With the food he served them tankards of ale, and Rose and Brad sat in the inglenook and enjoyed every bite and every sip.

'Best sausages I ever tasted,' Brad congratulated the cook who had come to see how his American customer was faring, 'and I liked the mash too.'

'Then tell your mates, lad. We're a bit off the beaten track but I usually manage to have something – a rabbit, pigeons; sometimes even a nice fresh-caught trout.'

They promised to tell everyone they knew and, hand in hand, walked back across the moors. Every now and again they stopped just to look at each other and, of course, to kiss. It was always Brad who pulled away.

'You are irresistible, Lance Corporal, and I wouldn't be human if I didn't want to . . . Oh God, Rose, I wish

I could see the future. My platoon is here for a reason and none of us knows exactly what that purpose is.'

'Three years, Brad, we've been at war for three years, give or take a few months. It must be over soon, especially now that—'

'We're in,' he interrupted her.

'Yes. We must be positive.'

He started to laugh and, since they had grown so serious, Rose wondered what he found so amusing.

'Run,' he said, grabbing her hand and pulling her along. 'Here they come. "I'm always chasing rainbows",' he began to sing in a pleasant baritone, just as the heavens opened and an April shower that had saved itself up for a special occasion decided to fall. 'Race you,' he shouted.

They ran. He was marginally faster, but Rose was more used to running in such rough terrain and, both soaked to the skin, they were neck and neck as, exhausted, they left the moors. The bus driver who picked them up some minutes later was none too pleased as they dripped all over the seats, but he said nothing except 'Crazy Yanks' as he opened the door to let them alight when they reached Rose's base.

'When?' began Brad.

'When we can,' she said.

They did not kiss, not there beside the guardhouse.

'See you,' he said, his hand brushing her face.

'See you,' she replied, and watched him lope off.

Francesca met her almost at the door of their billet. 'You're soaked,' she exclaimed as if, possibly, Rose was unaware of the fact. 'Starling wants to see you. Not a problem, he says, but, if possible, as soon as you got back.'

230

'And it's not a problem. I suppose he wants me to drive the bride to the wedding. Have they set a date yet?'

'No, Mamma dreamt of having some of the family there but she's not having much luck. She expected communications to speed up once Italy joined the Allies, but they haven't . . . and, of course, no one in our Italian family has a telephone – awkward. I don't know why Starling needs to see you, Rose; you know he usually separates work and personal relationships.'

They had reached their billet. 'I'll get changed and go up to the depot, Francesca, and I do hope everything goes well with your mum's wedding plans.'

'Me, too. They took forever to admit to liking each other and, as for plans to marry . . . never mind, they've got there now. Go and dry your hair: you look a mess.'

'Thank you, my dear friend,' said Rose, affectionate sarcasm dripping from every word. 'I'm almost there.'

She hurried inside, decided against taking time to have a shower and merely changed her clothes, brushed out her hair and plaited it again.

Five minutes later she was knocking on the door of Warrant Officer Starling's office.

'Come in, Petrie.' Obviously no one else had been sent for.

'You sent for me, Warrant Officer.'

'Not exactly, Lance Corporal. You're still off duty, but I hoped you would – knew you would – come up. I'm sorry, but I've had a telephone call.' He stopped and looked at her. 'You're being transferred, Rose.'

His use of her Christian name alerted her. This was serious.

'Transferred?'

231

'To a depot in London, as a driver. Not all bad news; you'll be able to pop down to Dartford, see your parents, old friends.'

'Am I allowed to ask why?'

'You can ask me anything you want, Rose, and if the answer isn't an official secret, I'll tell you.' He looked directly at her and his face was serious. 'You saved my Chiara, I can never forget that. If I can ever do anything to help you in any way, I will. You're damned good at your job and you've been noticed: it's as simple as that. I know that maybe, personally, this isn't the best time, but everything that's real lasts, believe me. You have no choice here – but Chiara, Francesca and I want you back for the wedding. You'll do your best, won't you?'

'Yes, sir. When do I leave?' she asked mechanically, her mind racing.

'First train tomorrow morning.'

'No.' The word exploded from her. Tomorrow. How could she possibly move to London, to anywhere, so soon? 'It's impossible. I need to pack, to alert people, to do a million—' She stopped. He was looking at her, listening to her.

'Train's at 6.45 a.m. Dismissed.'

She jerked herself to attention. 'Sir,' she said as she saluted, then turned and walked out of the depot.

She had no thought for who had ordered her transfer. Her mind could think of nothing and no one but Brad Hastings. Good Lord, there were scarcely twelve hours left before she would be on a train trundling its smoky way south.

Pack. Her parents. Gladys, Francesca, Mildred. Chiara. Cleo. Chrissy. She could not forget Chrissy. Notes for her successor on the unfinished work on that engine. Starling, or Francesca, would tell Chiara. That left Brad. How sweet had been their time on the great moor. What if she never saw him again? Why were the Americans here? She wondered what their great plan was, and where it would take Brad. Would he be able to tell her? What if she never saw him again?

No, she would not think like that. Rose hurried back to her billet.

Anxious faces looked at her, from seats around the stove, from the edges of beds, from the hard chairs by the tables.

'I'm not being court-martialled, ladies. Afraid I've been transferred to a depot down south. London, actually, and now I have to pack.'

'You have to eat, Rose; we were waiting for you. We're just on our way.' Gladys was sounding quite cheerful and matter of fact, but her face was strained.

'Had a great late lunch, ladies. A cup of cocoa later will be fine. Really must keep my parents up to date.'

'You know I'll forward anything. Brad? Do you have a way of contacting him?'

'I know where he is, Gladys. Don't worry. I'll write a quick note and, if he asks for me before he gets it, then I hope you'll let him know.'

'A promotion, I suppose.'

A promotion. The thought had never occurred to her. 'No idea. Shouldn't think so. I haven't had time to read my orders. Don't really want to, which is rather childish, I expect.'

'London, you say?'

'Yes, and that's not too far from home. We'll keep in touch and I'll expect you to come down to Dartford.

Mum and Dad'll be thrilled to meet you and I won't miss Francesca's mum's wedding.'

Gladys smiled. 'Won't that be a day? We should form a guard of honour for the WO – or, wait, we could be flower girls. I'll talk to Fran.'

'Call her Francesca and you'll have a better chance.'

Gladys opened the door as if to go out and then pulled it to again. 'What time?'

'First train.'

'Damn. I'm on duty.'

'Hey, this isn't another Dunkirk. I'm only going to London. Now go away and let me get on.'

There really was not too much to pack: her uniforms, some sports clothes, night things, and one or two pieces of casual clothing. 'Be great to get home, even for a few hours, and get some lighter things.' But would she be in London long enough to earn some time off to get to Dartford?

Transferred. What was she thinking? She was being transferred; each time she had been transferred she had spent several months in the new billet. *Brad*. She relived their hours on the moor, felt his arms around her, and the feeling of utmost safety as he held her, heard his voice as he sang her favourite song. Were she and Brad merely 'chasing rainbows'? Surely not.

Why? The word seemed to echo around the Nissen hut. It wasn't fair; it just wasn't fair. Something very beautiful and sacred – yes, sacred, she could say that – had begun to grow, take shape, take root and . . . she had been transferred. Would she ever see him again? Why would he try to keep up a relationship with someone in London when the camp here was full of women, several of whom would be only too happy to take her place?

For a mad moment she allowed despair to overcome her. Only a few hours ago, she had been in his arms, and now . . . No, she would not give in. He was special; what had begun to grow between them was special. What was a few months, after all?

She had not packed her notepaper and so she sat down to write several quick notes. The first one was to Brad and, very carefully, she wrote her new address at the top of the page.

'Dear Brad, Thank you. I had such a lovely time today.' She tore up the paper and started again.

Dear Brad,

I loved every single moment of our time today. Orders were waiting for me, though, and tomorrow I will be on the early train to London. No idea if it's short or long term, but I will be a driver and, after all, that's what I always dreamed of being.

She stopped for a moment, wanting to write down how much he had come to mean to her but afraid to say too much too early. What could she say?

Eventually she added, 'I hope we can keep in touch.'

Again she struggled. Should she write 'Love, Rose', or was that too much, too soon? Too forward? No actual words of love had been spoken by either of them.

She decided on simply 'Rose'.

Before she could change her mind, she folded the sheet and put it in an envelope, which she sealed. Resolving not to look at it again, she got to work and wrote one short note after the other.

By the time the others returned she had a neat pile of stamped envelopes.

No one had heard from Phil in months, but there had been no terrifying communication from the War Office either, and so Rose had decided she would write to him, then to Sam, who would tell Grace, and lastly to Sally, who would tell Daisy. After all, she had written to Daisy recently and it was impossible to write to everyone. As it was, postage was costing her a fortune. When she got to London she could use the public call box to ring Cleo and bring her up to date.

What fun that would be, and somehow so sophisticated.

SEVENTEEN

London, September 1943

By the end of September, Rose felt that she was beginning to know every street, every alley, and every shortcut, not only in London but also in the entire south of England. She had, after all, driven up or down each and every one of them, and, in her own time, had walked many of them. She knew the great buildings and the not-so-great, the railway and bus stations, the hospitals, the theatres, the monuments, the hotels, the restaurants and the small cafés. Even in its war-ravaged state, the great city had cast its spell and Rose Petrie was captivated.

Her only problem with London was its distance from Yorkshire, where Sergeant Bradley Hastings was based. They had seen each other once since she had taken up her new appointment. Brad's father, whom she now knew to be a very important person indeed, seemed to fly back and forth across the Atlantic with more ease than Rose travelled to Dartford, but, when Senator Hastings was in London, he liked to see his son.

'Drives me crazy, Rose, politicians' maneuverings,' Brad had written,

> but if it gives me even half a chance to see you then I'll go along with it. And, to be fair to Dad, he only pulls strings attached to me once in a while. Besides, my boss isn't stupid and he's going to make sure I learn something of interest to him. Everybody wins.

They had met in Green Park, one long, hot, August afternoon, when foreign dignitaries were enjoying a garden party at a stately home. He had come up the steps from the Underground station and, at her first sight of him, her heart almost stopped. He was wearing civilian clothing: dark-blue cotton trousers and a white short-sleeved top; round his waist he had tied a dark-blue cardigan. He looked wonderful, clean and strong and healthy, and somehow very, very American.

'Boy, I've missed you,' he said, taking her in his arms.

All the way to Green Park Station, Rose had been worrying about how she should greet him, and yet how easy it had been. He held her and she stood close, looking up into his lilac-blue eyes. 'I've missed you too, Sergeant,' she said, and he bent down and kissed her.

People were milling around them, people entering or leaving the Ritz Hotel, or just rushing, as Londoners seemed always to do, but no one broke the invisible ring around their little island.

They seemed totally oblivious of anyone but themselves as, at last, they moved, holding hands and walking along past the world-famous hotel.

'I wanted to have afternoon tea in there, Rose: very British. Is that something you'd enjoy, or maybe you've done it?'

'The Ritz. Are you out of your mind? Have you the slightest idea what . . . ?' Rose stopped as, for the first time, she realised that Brad was the type of man who patronised the Ritz, who could easily afford it.

He seemed to read her mind. 'Not on a GI's salary,' he said, and laughed.

'GI? We hear that all the time.'

'General issue. The uniforms.'

She laughed. 'Your uniform wasn't general anything.'

For a moment a cloud passed across his face and his eyes darkened. 'No, it wasn't, Rose, and yes, my folks have money.' His voice was hard. 'Let's not make it an issue.' He looked at her lovely face and saw that she had grown very pale.

'Oh, Rose,' he said, as once more he took her in his arms and held her close to him; as if, with his body, he would protect her from anything. 'I'm sorry; let's go someplace and talk.'

They turned. He took her hand as if he feared that she would forbid him that intimacy and, when she let her hand rest in his, he tightened his grip. 'Sometimes I can be such a damn fool.'

She said nothing but squeezed his hand as they retraced their steps, and this time they walked through the gates of the park and began to stroll around the perimeter. On their left stood a line of imposing buildings. Most, with their no-doubt glorious gardens, were hidden from passers-by, while before them and to the right of them grass and trees stretched as far as the eye could see.

'Is it OK to walk on the grass?'

'If it's not, then all those people over there will be in a lot of trouble soon.'

'I seem to remember signs all over that said, "Do Not Walk on the Grass".'

'No idea,' Rose said, as she pulled him over onto the grass where a man in a non-military uniform was setting out deckchairs. 'I suppose they might say that if the grass was being reseeded.' She looked up into his eyes. 'Why are we talking about London parks?'

'I think it's called "Avoiding the issue".'

They had reached the bottom of the outside path. They had a choice of crossing the road towards Buckingham Palace or turning left. He gave her no choice but waited for a break in the unnaturally sparse and quiet traffic – no horns blaring, no brakes squealing – and escorted her across.

'Some building!'

'Issue,' murmured Rose.

He laughed. 'Let's go down Horse Guards; no, we might be seen. Better to turn back through the park; we can talk as we walk.'

'Who might see us? Is there something you're not telling me?'

They were silent for a few minutes and then Brad said, 'Like I told you, I have to meet my dad for dinner tonight and he thinks I'll arrive more or less on time. He's at a function. His life is regimented by functions, meetings. I told you he's a senator, Rose; pretty powerful stuff. His folks were, well, more than OK financially, but Mom's family are seriously wealthy. Does that bother you?'

'It has nothing to do with me.'

'But it does or, let's say, I want it to. I did go to college, Yale . . .'

She nodded. 'OK, you went to a great university.'

'Yale Law School.'

'You're a lawyer and you joined the army?'

He nodded.

'You had a good reason?'

'It wasn't to annoy my parents, although both of them believe that it was. I felt sure that war was coming, that it could not be avoided; many Americans did. Any idea of the number of Americans in the Canadian Air Force—?'

'Brad,' she interrupted him.

He stopped there, almost beneath the branches of a tall sycamore, and pulled her round so that they were face to face. 'I didn't want to be a lawyer, Rose, and I certainly never planned to go into the military. I studied law, OK, to get my folks off my back. Any idea what I really wanted, still want, to do?'

Rose looked at him, her eyes bright with unshed tears. She wanted to scream at him, to ask him why any of this was relevant to her, ask why he felt she needed to know. She did not scream but instead asked quietly, 'What did you want to do?'

'Teach history.'

She saw him on Marston Moor, reading the inscription on the memorial, showing that he knew something about English history too. She smiled. A teacher. She would never have guessed.

'Do it,' was all she said.

With a whoop of joy, which startled a few elderly walkers, as well as several pigeons and two squirrels rooting at the foot of a nearby tree, he put his arms around her and whirled her around.

'*Do it*, she says, *do it*.' He laughed with joy. 'So simple. Oh, Rose Petrie, I love you.' The grin left his face and he looked at her as if he had never really seen her before. 'I love you,' he shouted. 'That's what all this was leading to. I love you, Rose.'

'For Pete's sake, lad, kiss her and let us all have a bit of peace and quiet to read the paper.' An elderly man in one of the deckchairs looked from Brad to Rose, then continued, 'Go on, girl, answer him.'

'He hasn't asked me anything.'

'Oh, blimey, do you want a kiss or don't you?'

'Yes, Rose,' said Brad, striving to look very solemn and serious. 'Do you want a kiss or don't you?'

He did not wait for an answer.

When he released her she almost stumbled. Daisy was right, but Rose felt as if she had been flattened, not only by the Matador, but also by a Spitfire. It was rather a lovely feeling. 'Oh, Brad, dear, dear Brad.'

He kissed her again. 'Miss Petrie, do I ever like doing that. Let's go have tea. Not in the Ritz, I'm afraid. They have a beautiful private dining room where really important meetings are held. We can only guess at the participants but just in case someone drops in who knows . . .'

'There are lots of places on Piccadilly.'

'I'm sorry, Rose. Don't I sound like a little kid who doesn't want Daddy to know what he's doing?'

Once again they had reached the gates, and this time they turned left and walked away from the Ritz until they were able to cross the road in comparative safety.

They stopped at the first hotel where Brad chatted to the doorman. Rose could hear a recording of Noël Coward's soothing, honeyed tones coming from inside.

'Tea and scones,' Brad said as they were ushered in. 'I'd love tea and scones, wouldn't you, Lance Corporal?'

'Love it,' she said as brightly as she could, for she was feeling slightly guilty. Brad was not the only one keeping secrets. She had never told him about the assassination attempt on a man who was risking his life every day to protect that of the Prime Minister. She had not told him that she had once driven General Eisenhower to a secret meeting in a big house.

'Brad?'

'How neat is that?' He held up the menu card. 'With jam, or with cream and jam?'

'Don't they know there's rationing? Where are they getting jam or cream?'

'They have a cow on the back lawn, which is lined with jam bushes.'

She started to laugh. 'Sorry. Sounded like the poor cow was lined – and what is a jam bush?'

They sat, they laughed, they talked, they ate scones and they drank tea – which Brad especially enjoyed.

'Wait till you drink my mother's tea. Petrie's Groceries and Fine Teas is renowned . . .' She did not finish.

Brad looked at her and, leaning over, took her hand in his. He kissed the back of her hand as he looked into her eyes. 'One of these days I will sit down in your mom's front room and I will drink her "Fine Teas". Maybe it will be a while before we meet, but I meant what I said, Rose. I love you, and every time I even just think of you, I find I'm loving you more.'

243

He looked around the pretty English country house-style interior, as if memorising it. 'It's cosy,' he said, 'and I like cosy.' He gazed through the floor-to-ceiling windows, partially covered by their drawn blackout curtains. 'Look over there, in the park. I think that's my favourite tree. It's the tree that saw me try to find the courage to tell a girl I loved her. You haven't really said anything about that – my declaration. Maybe it was a shock. A girl goes out on a late summer afternoon for tea and scones and, wham, this guy suddenly tells her – and half of London – that he loves her. And he does, Rose, with every atom of his being. Do you love him, even a little bit?'

Rose began to laugh. 'If you would stop talking for a moment, I might get a chance.' She leaned over the table and put her free hand on his lips. 'Ssh.' And when they had stayed like that for a little, she withdrew her hand. 'That will always be my favourite tree too. Yes, Brad, I love you. It was wonderful news to me when I realised that I have loved you for a long time.'

There were several, mainly elderly people in the room, and each and every one was listening to and enjoying their conversation. Brad looked back at them, bringing his most devastating smile into play, no doubt causing one or two elderly hearts to flutter pleasantly. 'Lovely to have had tea with you, ladies and gentlemen. Come on, Rose, you go powder your nose while I pay the bill.'

He stood and bowed, and Rose could scarcely believe what she saw. With the exception of an elderly gentleman in a wheelchair, everyone else stood up too, and as Rose and Brad left the room, they clapped.

'And Mom says the Brits are stuffy.'

He found their waiter and, with many thanks and a generous tip, paid the bill. Rose was waiting for him on the pavement, the skirt of her yellow-and-white summer frock blowing in the breeze.

'That's a cute dress, Rose,' he began as he walked with her to her bus stop. 'Damn, how do I begin?'

'At the beginning is always good.'

'Oh, Rose, honey, this afternoon was meant just to be . . . perfect. You and me. I wanted to tell you that I love you, that I want to marry you, and oh how much I hoped you'd say you loved me too. And then orders came in. One of the things I need to tell you is that I'm going away for a while, a training exercise. Don't know how often I'll be able to contact you, if at all, but I'll try.'

He had just said that he loved her and with almost the same breath had said that he was going away? Surely not. 'Going away? Where?'

'If I knew I couldn't tell you. If I'm in Britain, I'll call you; if I'm not, I'll write. That's the best I can do, my darling.'

'Oh, Brad,' Rose said and, oblivious of the sensitivities of anyone near them, she threw her arms around him.

He held her tightly, murmuring words of love into her hair while she thought of Sam and Grace, Daisy and Tomas, and all the other lovers who found themselves being tossed hither and yon by the waves of war.

'It can't last for ever, Brad, and I'll be waiting. No, please, go and meet your father. You don't want to be late,' and she pulled out of his arms and hurried along the street, arriving at her bus stop just in time to catch the last bus that would get her back to base on time.

Every day she looked for a letter or a card, and from the time she got up in the morning until the moment she climbed, exhausted, into bed at night, she listened for someone calling her name. But no letters came from Brad and neither were there any telephone calls.

He loved her. He had said he loved her. She had witnesses, and she smiled tearfully as she remembered the faces of the elderly residents of the hotel where she and Brad had had tea. But she did not need witnesses because she believed in him implicitly. He was the man Stan had assured her was out there, the one who, according to Stan, would be in her 'league'. That league was to do with character, and personality, and had nothing at all to do with money and position.

She put herself, heart and soul, into her work.

In the weeks following that lovely, last meeting with Brad, it seemed to Rose that she had never worked so hard.

On her first morning in the vehicle depot she had had a pleasant surprise. There was a new mechanic in the huddle around an ambulance that was being readied for transfer abroad. It was a woman; Rose could not see her face, but then she heard the voice.

'Corporal Church?'

'It's Sergeant, thank you . . . Rose? Rose Petrie. How lovely. So this is where they sent you? I heard you were driving.'

'Yes, ma'am. On and off.'

'Let's have dinner together and we can catch up. Now, you lot, let's get this vehicle safe and secure for our wounded personnel.'

Sergeant Church was another of Rose's happy memories of her early training in Preston, and so far was the first member of the ATS to join Rose in London.

She remembered how patient the mechanic had been and how much she had been liked and respected by everyone, including male mechanics.

Rose could scarcely wait for the dinner bell to sound. She looked forward to catching up.

London was full of dignitaries from the Allied countries. Many, if not most of the 'top brass', as they were termed, really liked the beautiful Daimlers provided by the British Government, and Rose found herself driving American and French dignitaries to meetings in and around London. She surreptitiously examined every American of a certain age, wondering if he could possibly be Brad's father, but after a while, tall, well-built men with American accents and beautifully tailored suits began to resemble one another, and she felt that she was even in danger of not remembering what Brad looked like.

He had not telephoned and therefore it seemed that he must be overseas; otherwise he would have called her, as he had promised. But if he was in a theatre of war, where were his letters? And then, out of nowhere, arose rumours that the Americans were planning to bring the war to an end and, to do this, they were actually rehearsing the final blow somewhere in England.

To many it sounded insane, like a very bad Hollywood movie, but to members of the military – and certainly to Rose's platoon – it sounded like something guaranteed, the beginning of the end. And oh, how they longed for the end.

Vera Lynn's voice soared out of open windows, repeating her encouraging messages from wirelesses in every home throughout the land, assuring the military that when they heard Big Ben they would be safely home, or that one day soon returning servicemen would see bluebirds flying like little live Spitfires over Kent's magnificent stretches of white cliffs. Like thousands of other women who waited, Rose knew every word of every poignant song, but her question was never answered. Where was Bradley Hastings?

Autumn had blown in, carried by winds strong enough to strip the leaves from every tree in Green Park and elsewhere. Small branches and an occasional heavy bough followed the leaves and covered the usually immaculately tended greens with untidy piles.

Rose waited patiently to hear from Brad and from Chiara who had made no mention of the abdication of the King of Italy or the fall of the dictator, Mussolini.

'Italy's on our side now,' she told herself, 'and that's bound to please Francesca.'

So it did, and, at last Chiara found time to write.

Mamma is delirious with joy. She's hoping that now some of the family will be able to come to the wedding, even if it's only one or two. In Italy the whole village would come; they'd help with the food and the wine. There would be singing and dancing well into the next day but, don't worry, Rose, we'll have a wedding for Mamma that would please dear Nonno.

A few weeks later Daisy Petrie had a twenty-four-hour pass and, for once, was close enough to be able to visit her sister. 'The leaves did look rather pretty all over the parks and gardens but, believe you me, they are a dratted nuisance on an airfield,' said Daisy. 'They seem to come from miles away. As far as I remember, there are a few scraggy rose bushes on my base and a holly bush that somehow appeared outside the CO's billet.'

Rose tried to rustle up some interest in rose bushes and holly but could not manage.

The young women were having tea, courtesy of Daisy, in Fortnum and Mason's lovely store on Piccadilly. The tea itself, they agreed, was almost as good as the blend their parents ordered for a few special customers, like Rose's 'butler', who actually owned the great house to which Rose had once delivered a bloodstained dispatch.

'I never see him in uniform, Daisy, always very well-tailored civvies, but I suppose he's in the Forces. He's often referred to as "the commander".'

'Why? Maybe he's in the navy, or was in the navy. He could be a politician or an adviser, or even a boffin like our dear Dr Fischer.'

'Have you seen Mr . . . sorry. We spent years calling him Mr Fischer and it's hard for me to remember him as Dr Fischer.'

'Not recently, no, but I do know from Mum and Miss Partridge that his landlady is being paid to keep his room available for him. He wants to return to Dartford when the war's over.' Daisy cut a small piece from the cake she was eating and pushed her plate towards her sister. 'Try that. Tasty, and I swear it has to have real eggs in it.'

'So many things I want to know and will never be told about,' Rose said with a sigh as she sampled the small sponge square, 'including whether or not this cake has eggs in it.'

'So many things we have to take on faith, Rose. Tomas and I are never on the same station. He doesn't tell me about his sorties; I never tell him where I've dropped a parcel. Brad may even be back in the US. Who knows? You have to trust.' She twisted her beautiful engagement ring around on her finger as if just touching it gave her some strength. 'You're in love with him and you say he feels the same about you?'

'That was September.'

'Is he worth waiting for?'

Rose had actually never asked herself that question. She and Brad had admitted their love for each other. There had been no talk of plans, of possible – probable? – difficulties because she was a grocer's daughter from Dartford and he was the only son of a wealthy American politician. There had been no time. He had left her and, as far as she knew, had spent some time with his father before returning to his base in Yorkshire. She remembered him now: saw him standing under the tree in Green Park; bowing to the elderly people in the hotel; smiling, that beautiful open smile.

'Yes,' she said.

EIGHTEEN

Rose had enjoyed her dinner with Sergeant Church, whom she was to call Prue when they were together and Sergeant or Ma'am when anyone else was there.

'Prue?'

'Short for Prudence. I ask you, Rose, Prudence Church. Did my parents even say the two words together before they had me christened?'

'I like it.'

They had eaten their midday meal, chattering all the while as if they had always been friends. 'I think real friendship is like real love, Rose. Sometimes you meet someone and instinct tells you this person will mean something in your life. I liked you from the start.'

'Thank you, Prue.' Rose had been about to say 'Ma'am', but managed to stop in time. 'I took to you at once. You were so capable but so patient.'

'Poor me. What chance did I have with a name like Prudence Church?'

They laughed, looked at the Bakelite clock that hung on the ugly green wall near the kitchen, and went back to work.

'It's going to be such fun here,' said Prue. 'Now, let's lead by example and get back to the depot on time.

Not all non-commissioned officers were like Prue.

'Ever heard of an amphibious vehicle, Petrie?'

Motor Vehicle Warrant Officer Carter was leafing through some papers as he sat behind his desk. He looked up at her. 'Well?'

'Not that I can remember, sir. I have seen one or two films about waterproofing vehicles but, if they were serious, then it was only at the very earliest stage of development.'

'You have an American boyfriend. Has he mentioned them?' He waited for an answer and then said, 'Don't look so shocked, Lance Corporal, there are no secrets in the military. Has he? He drives a Jeep, doesn't he, a Willys Jeep, the MA model?'

Rose – thinking it possible that WO Carter might even know Brad's date of birth – said, 'He did drive one, yes.'

'And where is he stationed?'

'I don't know. Many of the American soldiers were transferred. We haven't been in touch for some time.'

'Better and better. Please let me know when you hear from him.'

Rose had no intention of promising any such thing. If, or when, Brad telephoned or wrote to her, much would depend on what he had to say. 'Is that all, sir?'

'Anyone else from your former station shacked up with one of the Yanks? Seemingly nylon stockings reel you women in like fish.'

Rose, who was at least two inches taller than the warrant officer and a great deal fitter, played with the dangerous thought of doing him some not-too – well, fairly – serious bodily harm. 'I wouldn't know, sir, but since I believe "shack up with" means to be living with another person, I can't see how that's possible.'

'Careful, Rose, careful. Just because Starling thinks the sun rises and sets on your head – it doesn't, by the way – and some ponce at the War Office seems to think likewise, don't think you can take liberties. Perhaps I could arrange for your mail to be opened.'

Rose took her courage in both capable hands. She was unsure if it was legal to open mail, especially if it came from a British ally. Sam's letters from his POW camp had been read by his captors and his letters from 'the field' had obviously been read, but that was in case, inadvertently or deliberately, a soldier had written something that would help the enemy. 'Maybe I should discuss this with my friend at the War Office, sir. And you do know, I'm sure, who Master Sergeant Hastings' father is?'

'Get out.'

'Sir.' Rose saluted and marched smartly from the room.

Where on earth did that come from? she asked herself as she almost ran back to her billet. You should have kept quiet, Rose, and if you have a chum at the War Office he's never introduced himself. And that smart remark about Brad's dad! I can't believe what you've just done. It doesn't matter that he had absolutely no right to talk to you like that.

She lay down on her bed when she returned to the billet and went over and over the interaction with the WO. What a difference between him and WO Starling, the absolute epitome of a good non-commissioned officer. Was there anyone she could ask for advice?

Oh, Brad, I hope I hear from you soon.

'Golly, that's not like you, Rose, flat out on your bed at three thirty in the afternoon.' Agatha Bird, one of the other motor-pool drivers, had come in to change her stockings, which sported a ladder almost wide enough to climb on, straight down the front of her leg. 'Twice worn, would you believe, and nothing, absolutely nothing I can do to repair it.'

'According to old Carter, all you need to do is meet a Yank, shack up with him – to use his delicate term – and live a life full of nylon stockings.'

'Oh, Rose, you are an innocent. Didn't you know ATS personnel are usually called "officers' groundsheets"?'

'What does that mean?' asked Rose, before she realised and blushed an unbecoming shade of red. In an attempt to recover she said that the warrant officer had asked what she knew about amphibious vehicles.

'Frogs.'

Rose glared at her roommate.

'Sorry, Rose, couldn't resist. Why did he want to know that, and do you know anything? I've never seen any vehicle that could travel over land and under water. Submarines aren't amphibious. Don't you think that's a bit like a Jules Verne story?'

'Didn't you get all those films about tanks and lorries and tractors? I saw one about early attempts at water-proofing but I can't remember a single thing about it.'

'It was so riveting.'

'Exactly. But why does he want to know? And does he think the Americans are a step ahead of us and he wants a slap on the back for finding out?'

'Yes, to both, I would say. And by the way, who's the sergeant you had dinner with?'

Rose told Agatha how she had met Corporal, now Sergeant, Church. 'You'll like her, and I'll introduce you the first chance I get. Probably you'll run into her anyway. She's the new chief mechanic.'

'Sergeant P. Church. I was expecting a man, but then I'm always expecting a man. She won't hobnob with a lowly lance corporal.'

'Lots of NCOs socialise, Agatha. Just remember to keep business and pleasure separate.'

'Right. So let's get back to frogs.'

'Very funny. I honestly don't know why the Americans – and Canadians, I seem to remember – are here. Rumours tend to fly around like dandelion seeds in a wind. No one knows where they come from, but they're there. If the Americans are rehearsing a manoeuvre then all I can say is good luck to them. They're a close ally. Doesn't that mean we shouldn't spy on them? Asking me to tell him what Brad and his platoon are doing is spying, in my book.'

'But if we're on the same side it's likely he wouldn't object to telling you.'

'Doesn't feel right,' said Rose, swinging her long thirty-denier-stocking-covered legs off the bed. 'Carter threatened to open my letters.'

'Ooh, not nice, but I think he's allowed, if a senior officer thinks there's grounds of some kind. Four years we've been at war, Rose. We're all at the end of our tethers. I have a feeling that almost anything goes. Talk to the CO. She'll set you straight. Or Sergeant Church – she'll sort him. I wouldn't want old Carter reading my Jeremy's letters: curl his hair if he had any.'

But Rose had no letters.

She wondered if Brad had changed his mind. Much can happen in two months. He could have met someone else. He could be in the States, deciding that a love affair, where the couple were at least three thousand miles apart, made no sense. Perhaps he was ill, had been injured, perhaps he was . . . No, she could not even think that word. She could bear no more.

Work. Work was the best defence against despair.

And so Rose worked.

Her best days were when she had passengers to transport. She had driven military sitting quietly in the back looking at the scenery, and she had foreign dignitaries who spoke in languages she did not recognise, which was hardly surprising as she had met very few people who spoke anything other than English. Dr Fischer, she now knew, was German, but he had only ever spoken perfect if heavily accented English; Tomas, her brother-in-law-to-be, spoke several languages fluently, according to Daisy, but he too spoke English and she had never heard Czech spoken. She would have recognised Italian at once since Nonno had occasionally spoken in his native language to Chiara. But she was quite sure that Italian was never spoken by any of her dignitaries.

One morning in early November she was told to drive to the American Embassy on Grosvenor Square to pick up two Americans, obviously extremely important ones, and take them to the Ritz Hotel. She was then to wait for as long as they were inside. Understanding that she might be there for hours and could, in no circumstance, leave her vehicle, Rose prepared in advance. She carried a book, *A Tree Grows in Brooklyn*, which she had been told by Sally that she must read – Sally read a lot while waiting backstage – and she had a fish-paste sandwich which, she told herself, was better than nothing, and a Thermos of tea.

Her passengers, a man and a woman, both extremely well dressed (surely clothes were rationed in the United States too?), chatted all the way from the embassy. Rose tried not to hear what they were saying. The woman's voice, however, was especially strident, and the conversation became less like chatting and more of a discussion, possibly the extension of a meeting they had already had. Rose tried to blot out the voices by humming or even singing under her breath until she heard, 'And where did you say your son was? Brad, isn't it?'

The man's voice was quieter and so Rose could not make out his answer, but she assured herself that there were hundreds of Americans named Bradley. She tried not to listen but she almost felt her ears straining to pick up any sound.

They were on Piccadilly. They passed Fortnum and Mason.

'Do I ever love that store, Anderson.'

Anderson. Was her passenger a Mr Anderson, or did Mr Whoever have a surname as a Christian name, just as Bradley had?

'Most women do,' the attractive voice replied, 'but it's not one of Mirabelle's haunts. Brad asked her about it and she advised him to check it out for himself.'

Rose drew up at the side door of the Ritz Hotel, and whatever the woman said in answer to that was lost for ever. She looked at her male passenger as carefully as she could, noting his height, his build, his facial features, and decided he looked American and nothing more. Was he Brad's father?

How stupid you are, she chided herself. He looks nothing like Brad and his name is Mr Anderson.

The uniformed doorman had opened the door for her passengers. They alighted. The woman walked straight into the hotel but Mr Anderson stopped as he passed Rose's window. 'Thank you. I hope we don't keep you too long,' he said, and followed his compatriot up the steps and into the hotel.

'And, like most Americans, he's very polite,' Rose added.

She moved the car to her designated parking place, poured herself a cup of tea and unwrapped her sandwich, trying to make herself believe it was filled with the finest line-caught Scottish salmon. She opened the book, which she had been told was a beautiful story about an Irish family living in Brooklyn in the first twenty years of the century, and began to read.

At any other time, the story would have captured her immediately, but she could not settle. Again she heard 'Mr Anderson' speaking both in rather hushed tones from the back of the car, and then in a clear voice as he bent to talk to her through the window. She was sure that she had heard that distinctive voice before. Common sense took over. She had never driven this particular VIP before – he was not the type of man who faded into the background or was indistinguishable in a group. But the voice? She told herself to stop being silly, to finish her sandwich and her drinkable tea and to start to read the book again.

She picked it up from the passenger seat and it fell open as if it was used to being open at that page.

'. . . something in the man reminds you of him.'

The words pierced her to the heart. She thought of Brad and the American called Anderson who spoke with Brad's voice, reminding her of him, and then she wondered why the book, Sally's book, had fallen open on that page. Was it an accident, or had Sally read it so often that the book automatically opened there? And if so, what did the passage mean to her old school friend? And then Rose laughed and relaxed. Surely if the book meant something special to Sally she would not, so easily, have given it away.

I'll write to her when I've finished it.

Her mind made up, Rose opened the book at the beginning and began again to read.

'Good story?' After the utter silence of she knew not how long, the voice beside her at the window made her jump. She had been quite lost in the tale.

'Sir. Sorry.' She reached for the handle to let herself out.

'No, don't worry. Look, we will be some time and that's a dreadful waste of your time and of this beautiful automobile. I called the boss and he OK'd it. You go on back to the depot and when – if – we ever get done, we'll get a cab. Heck, maybe they'll even let me ride a bus, a London bus.'

As quickly as he had come he was gone.

Two hours later, Rose was driving a renovated ambulance to a military hospital near Dover. She returned by train to London and got a lift to her depot in the rather badly aired cab of a truck whose driver was delivering sheep to an abattoir.

'Life's little tapestry,' she heard herself saying.

'What's that, lass?' asked the rather large woman who was driving the truck and who, from the whiffs from her underarms, had taken the advice to save water rather too seriously.

'Didn't know I was speaking. I was thinking about all the unexpected things that happen to us every day.'

'Aye, that's what my old man must have been thinking when he came out of the pub at dinner time and got hit by a bit of shrapnel as big as a bus.'

Rose felt terrible. 'I'm so sorry, that must have been dreadful for you.'

'It was him that got hit, love. The kids don't miss him neither.' Perhaps she too felt that she was sounding rather unfeeling, for she swiftly added, 'It was quick, and that's a blessing.'

The rest of the journey was spent in silence, but when they reached Rose's base, the woman surprised her again by wishing her luck.

'Think all you young girls is marvellous, driving ambulances and flying aeroplanes, would you believe? But more than time it were over. Thought them Yanks coming was supposed to fix everything. There's millions of 'em in Northern Ireland, on the south coast, everywhere. Can't pop in for a half without falling over one of 'em. Got to be on my way. Butcher's waiting. Flag me down anytime, love. Always got room for the army.'

Rose thanked her and waved as the great truck with its overcrowded passengers carried on its way. What a character the driver had been. Was that what was called Blitz spirit, this ability to be cheerful, no matter what?

She watched until the truck had disappeared around a bend and took several breaths of clean air. Body odour and sheep were not a good mix.

'Got a lift back then, Rose?' Corporal Sweet stated the obvious. 'I think his nibs – sorry, Warrant Officer Carter – has another job for you. He's still in the office.'

Another job? Rose looked at her watch in case her body clock wasn't functioning and she would discover that it was only early afternoon.

The watch read eight thirty. Rose shook her left wrist and listened to the steady ticking. The watch was working perfectly and so was her body clock, which was telling her that it was high time she had something to eat. 'Blast,' she said, and kicked a tuft of grass.

No point in delaying. She went straight to the depot office, knocked, and was told to enter.

'Glad you got back, Petrie. God, you smell. What did you come back in, a refuse bin?'

She was sure he did not expect an answer.

'You had better have a bath and then see if the kitchen can give you anything. I take it you haven't eaten?' He reached into a drawer and removed some papers. 'Couple of letters arrived for you. If there is something that you can share, it would be nice to have advance warning of what our allies are planning – only as it affects us, of course. Wouldn't want you snuggling up, even with an ally, just to get a little information. You've been asked for special, some American woman as "felt so safe in her hands" as she told her ambassador. Pack for an overnight; nice frock, if you've got one, and probably you'll need all your jumpers and some woolly pyjamas. You're driving to a country house – bound to be bloody freezing. Lots of foreigners are going, military, diplomatic. Keep your ears and your eyes open and bring your passengers back safe, Sunday lunchtime. All right?'

261

'You said a woman. The one I drove today?'

'Of course it's the woman you drove today, and she'll have someone with her. Could be de Gaulle, could be Eisenhower. You just do your job. Dismissed.'

Rose took the letters handed to her, saluted and hurried back to her billet where cries of 'Heavens above, Rose, have you been sleeping with wet dogs?' drove her to the showers before she tried to find a hot meal and peace to read her letters. It took an immense amount of willpower not to look at either of the two envelopes. She felt as she had long ago as a child when, with her twin sister and her brothers, she had waited sleeplessly to see if Father Christmas had visited.

She stood in the cubicle enjoying what was left of the now warmish water on her back and shoulders while her mind worked furiously.

She was much too junior to be ordered to drive either of the two generals in London; besides, each had his own dedicated driver. Carter was being, for him, amusing.

'Ha-ha,' she said as she tried to rub dry her hair, looking over longingly at her folded clean clothes. In the pocket of her jacket were the letters and she desperately wanted to read them.

She dragged a comb through her hair, plaited it, dressed and wrapped herself in her Teddy Bear coat.

Quickest shower ever, she thought, but how good cleanliness felt.

In the dining hall were several stragglers and a very tired kitchen assistant.

'Only hot plate is soup, barley,' offered the server.

'And it's thick enough to walk on,' called a disgruntled mechanic.

'Just the way I like it,' said Rose, and was given a large bowl of steaming hot thick soup, a rather tired morning roll and an even more exhausted apple.

'Happy Hallowe'en.'

'It's November.'

'Apple's left over from Hallowe'en but there must be a little bit of goodness in it.'

Rose looked at the apple. 'Pre-war Hallowe'en?'

'Very funny. There's cocoa.'

She took some cocoa, her soup and her roll and went to an empty table, so that she could read her letters in peace.

She smiled, a broad, happy smile. A letter from Brad – she was almost sure that was his writing on the blue envelope – and one from her mum. She was more than happy to see the face of the reigning monarch, George VI, on the stamps on both letters. Brad was in Britain somewhere.

Dear Rose,

   I love you. I hope you still love me. I know I
haven't written and I'm sorry but, believe me, my
beautiful girl, I have never been worked so hard in my
entire life. Several times I started a letter and fell
asleep over it. Can't say what we're doing or where
we are, not that I'm absolutely sure where we are
myself, since there are no road signs of any kind
around here and nothing that helps. One hill looks
much like another hill, and one tree like another. I can
tell the difference between, no, they'd scrub out what I
was going to write there so I'll write this. I love you
with all my heart and that Saturday was the happiest
day of my entire life bar none.

263

Do you feel even a little bit the same? Oh, honey, I dream of holding you. Please write. It'll take a while but they swear mail will reach us.

Brad

Rose read it until she had memorised every word – and her hot soup was cold – but she ate it and decided it was absolutely delicious, as was the roll and the cocoa which, sensibly, she had been drinking while she was reading.

Very carefully she folded the sheet of paper, admiring his firm, strong handwriting as she did so, and returned it to its envelope, which she put in her bag. She took the second letter and opened it.

Dear Rose,

Now try not to be upset and worry but Phil has been injured in . . . an incident, they called it in the telegram. A magazine exploded and I couldn't understand that but Daddy told me what it is. Phil got hit by bits of metal and is in a hospital, not on the ship, but somewhere they won't tell us but it's not England, it's in the Mediterranean. Daddy said we would take our savings and go but they say we're not allowed and they'll keep us informed and when he's well enough to travel, he'll be brought back to England. Daddy says I have to tell my girls the truth and so my Phil has lost his left arm and there's something wrong with his left ear. He hasn't got one and can't hear on that side but he's alive, Rose, and that's all I [she had put a line through 'I' and had written 'we' so that the sentence finished] and that's all we care about, isn't it?

I want him home here where I can look after him. Dad says I shouldn't ask but I'm going to ask them to send him home in plenty of time for Christmas. He hasn't had Christmas at home for years and the doctors here are better than in the Mediterranean. Everybody knows a person gets well quicker at home.

Miss Partridge is a wonderful help and young George is ever such a good boy. He's grown a lot since you was last home, seemed just to spurt. He says, apart from his black hair he's getting to look more like a Petrie. Good laddie, isn't he?

Come home when you can and maybe they'll give you a pass when our Phil comes home. He'll feel better seeing his sisters.

She finished by sending Rose all her love. Rose smiled through the tears that had begun to spill. 'All her love' had been sent to Daisy and to Sam and probably on to poor injured Phil himself.

The family had worried about their sailor son for a long time. They were used to not hearing from him for months and then getting four, five or even more letters on the same day. No letters but a telegram had come, and Flora, who had received two before during the course of this terrible war, had, as always, feared the worst. But he was not dead. Her son was injured, maimed even, but she would love him and care for him for as long as he needed her.

Rose knew that as well as she knew her own name. Phil had been injured but the injuries were not life-threatening, and Brad Hastings was somewhere in Britain and he loved her. Life could not get better.

She returned to her billet to write to her parents, assuring them that she was well, enjoying her work, and that she would come home as soon as she possibly could to see Phil. In the meantime she would write to him. She reminded her mother that she had had leave the Christmas before, and so it was unlikely that she would be given Christmas leave two years in a row. And then she wrote to Brad, a letter that she sent to the strange address he'd given, praying that those seemingly odd letters and numbers would make sense to the Post Office.

Looking round the billet, she saw that most heads were already on the pillows. Before she sealed the envelope, she kissed it, wondering how long it would be before she saw Brad again and felt his lips on hers.

NINETEEN

Rose was absolutely stunned. She had packed her kitbag for her overnight stay, put it in the car and made her way to the depot to sign out the gorgeous Daimler, her favourite car. She had been given her instructions and almost gasped with surprise. Lance Corporal Petrie was ordered to drive Senator Jarrold and possibly a second dignitary to Silvertides Estate, Dartford, Kent.

How frustrating, thought Rose, that she would be on duty within walking distance of her own home, and unable to pop in to see them. What a beautiful surprise that would have been for Mum. Nothing could make up for Phil's injuries, but having one of her children home, even for half an hour, would have cheered Flora.

Senator Jarrold was staying at the American ambassador's residence and Rose drove there first. The senator certainly packed quite a few clothes for a one-night stay, Rose decided, seeing various items of luggage being loaded into the car. What on earth had been planned by the commander, if indeed it was he who had organised the house party? Thankfully, the Daimler was a large, roomy vehicle and there was more than enough room for the French officer, whom she picked up at his hotel. Rose had expected to see someone in the style of General de Gaulle, an exceptionally tall man, but her passenger was of average height and very slender.

If her passengers had never met or even communicated with each other before, they had no trouble at all in chatting together. The language used was French, and Rose envied Senator Jarrold her fluency. Idly she wondered if the French officer spoke no English, or perhaps their conversation was so important that they wanted to ensure that Rose did not understand them.

The Frenchman spoke perfect English, as Rose discovered when they reached Silvertides Estate. The man addressed as 'Commander' in the office, but whom Rose preferred to think of as 'the butler', came down the steps of the house to greet them.

'Lord Silvertide, it is very kind of you to host this meeting,' said the French officer. Senator Jarrold added her thanks.

'London is lovely, but what a joy to be in a glorious private home where we can pretend for a few hours that we're simply guests of the family.'

'The family is delighted to have you here as a guest, Senator. My wife suggested coffee in the drawing room and you'll be glad to know she ordered a roaring fire.'

He nodded politely to Rose and walked up the steps with his guests.

A member of staff, an elderly civilian, then directed Rose to where she should park the car. When she had done that, a housemaid came out to take her to her quarters for the weekend. These consisted of a small sitting room, a smaller bedroom and a nicely appointed bathroom. Rose, who had never in her entire life enjoyed the luxury of a private bathroom, her own bedroom and, wonder of wonders, a sitting room, thought it all quite marvellous.

'Used to be the governess's rooms,' the housemaid informed her. 'I suppose it'll do for you. It's better than being up on the servants' floor. The wind comes right off the river, perishing sometimes.' She turned to leave and then turned back, 'Not sure whether you're them or us, but lunch is at one and dinner's at eight.' She looked unsure. 'Or maybe it'll be later as there's guests.'

With that rather unsatisfactory information she left, and Rose, quite sure that she was not one of 'them' but more probably one of 'us', found herself hoping that she would be told for sure before she had missed too many meals. Her duties, as far as she knew, were to drive Senator Jarrold and possibly the French officer wherever they wanted to go at whatever time they decided. But, in the meantime, she had her own sitting room and so she decided to sit in one of the very lovely chairs and read more of Sally's book.

She was totally involved when she was disturbed by a knock on the door, which opened to admit a woman who was, at one and the same time, familiar and yet a complete stranger.

'Forgive me for disturbing you, Miss Petrie. I'm Mrs Brown, the housekeeper. You probably don't remember me but I helped look after you and the poor young gentleman as died trying to do his duty. A beautiful spring day, it was. Dreadful sad.'

'Of course I remember, Mrs Brown, and yes, it was quite dreadful. You made me tea. I hope I thanked you.'

'You're welcome, I'm sure, but I'd like to know your preferences for meals. Mr Cornelius thinks you might prefer to dine alone and, of course, we're most willing to arrange things as you wish, but I wondered if a young lady like yourself might not be happier having meals with senior staff – only three of us these days, I'm afraid.'

'Whichever would be easier, Mrs Brown,' said Rose, who had fully expected to be grabbing a sandwich and a cuppa in the kitchen.

'Thank you, miss. With so many house guests and a depleted staff, having you join us would free up a housemaid. We set a good table here. Her ladyship is very strict over rationing – nothing under the counter comes to this house – but it's amazing what a good cook can do when she puts her mind to it.'

Immediately Rose thought of her mother, who had lost one son, had a second injured and then imprisoned, and who was now dealing with worry over yet another seriously injured son. How hard she worked to make her family's meals as tasty and nourishing as possible. Now it seemed that even the great houses like this one had to make do and mend and squirrel away a few ounces here and there so that one day there would be something really delicious for the family.

At lunch she discovered that there were dignitaries from each and every Allied country spending the weekend at Silvertides.

'All these very important men, all speaking several languages. Oh, and the lady politician too. Changed days, but it's the ideal house, don't you think, Miss Petrie? It's not too far from London, but far enough away to be well off the radar.'

Rose smiled at the butler, Mr Cornelius, who, being round and rather wobbly, certainly looked less like the

Hollywood idea of a butler than did Lord Silvertide, who was tall, slender and stately.

'Perfect seclusion, Mr Cornelius. I imagine there will be lots of meetings.'

'I have no idea what his lordship's guests will be doing, Miss Petrie,' said Mr Cornelius, in a tone that implied he knew perfectly well but a mere driver had no business asking what the host's guests were doing, 'since the gentlemen plan, and the lady, of course, they plan to be sequestered in the blue drawing room this afternoon and in the library after breakfast tomorrow morning. This evening everyone will attend a cocktail party – I think that's what the Americans call it – at a neighbouring estate, returning for dinner at nine. I would assume you will be driving your lady.'

Rose nodded and said that she was supposed to drive the American senator wherever she wanted to go. She was rather ashamed to realise that she was looking forward to seeing Senator Jarrold's cocktail dress. She sighed. The senator had worn the most incredible grey full-length fur coat on the journey from London. No doubt the magnificent coat would be worn again this evening, and thus the dress would be hidden. She had been looking forward to telling her mum and her sister about the fur, which was so like the coats worn by American ladies in glamorous films, and a fabulous evening dress would be something else to talk about.

'I don't suppose I could walk a little in the grounds, since I won't be needed until the evening?'

'Walk in the gardens by all means, but don't go off through any gates. Wouldn't want the security men jumping out at you.'

'Perhaps I'll just stay inside and read,' said Rose, who found the thought of being accosted by 'security men', possibly aided by large dogs with very large teeth, rather disconcerting.

'Go and get some fresh air afore it gets dark, lass. Even this late the gardens are lovely. You'll have them all to yourself.' Mrs Brown waited until the butler was out of earshot. 'He sees spies everywhere. Saw two nuns collecting for refugees in Dartford the other day and was sure they was German paratroopers.'

Spies? Mrs Brown's tale triggered a memory. Rose remembered a cold Saturday evening a year or so before the war when she, her sister, and some friends had gone looking for spies on the nearby salt flats. They had caught nothing but bad colds.

'I'll wrap up and walk around the garden, Mrs Brown,' said Rose, and went to fetch her coat.

Out in the garden she wished that she had rammed on a hat. She pushed her hands as deep into the pockets of her greatcoat as they would go and cursed herself for allowing conceit to win over common sense. Her Teddy Bear coat would have been a better protection against the biting wind. She walked quickly; this was no time to stroll around admiring plantings. She found a pond that she was quite sure would be frozen over by morning and wondered what would happen to any fish, if indeed it contained fish, if the water froze. But it was too cold to stay gazing at the statue that portrayed a rather handsome, scantily clothed young man with wings on his heels. His name hovered on the tip of her tongue but refused, probably because of the extreme cold, thought Rose, to jump off into the world. The next architectural point was a wrought-iron archway over which twined leaf-less tendrils. Even to Rose's unskilled eye, the ironwork showed the hand of a master. She imagined it with white roses tumbling over it in high summer. How lovely it must be and, naturally, the roses would be highly scented, and their perfume would drift all over the garden. 'Lovely.'

'Yes, it is, even in winter. Honeysuckle. I love it,' an almost familiar voice agreed with her. 'Sorry if I startled you, Lance Corporal, but sometimes I find it's better for international relations if I leave a discussion before I lose control and knock a few heads together.'

Rose had indeed been startled. Standing on the path beyond the archway, but facing it, was the American whom she had driven to the Ritz Hotel. Was it the dark-ness of the secluded garden or the frivolity of his remark, but Rose heard her voice saying, 'Maybe knocking a few selected heads together might be a good idea.'

He laughed and again she thought the sound familiar, but she told herself that all Americans from his part of the United States probably sounded the same. He moved closer to her and instinctively she moved back a step and he stopped. 'I do believe you're right, Lance Corporal, but, I assure you, such an action would not augur well for, what shall we say, friendly interchanges among peoples.'

'Perhaps not, sir, especially since there's too much violence in the world at the moment.'

He looked up at the sky where a sprinkling of stars was shining bravely. 'Again, you're right,' he said. 'Guess the air will have cleared and so I'd best get back inside. Don't stay out here too long: you'll freeze.'

He walked back towards the drawing room's curtained French doors and disappeared inside, and Rose, suddenly aware of exactly how cold she was, hurried back to the kitchen door, appreciating the wall of heat that enveloped her as she opened it.

'His lordship's chauffeur was looking for you, Miss Petrie. He wants you to help him warm up the cars.'

'Of course, I'll go right away.' Rose had scarcely had time to warm up herself, but the chauffeur wasn't to know that she'd been chatting to . . . whoever he was in the garden. Warming up the cars was bound to help her too.

The chauffeur, Ingram, saw Rose approaching and an angry look crossed his face. 'I thought you was supposed to change.'

'Change? Change what?'

'They did tell you to bring a smart frock?'

Rose had completely forgotten that command, especially since she could see no reason for her to be out of uniform.

'You do have one?'

Rose had packed a dress her mother referred to as a 'dress up or dress down' dress. It was lightweight black wool with three-quarter-length sleeves, a kick-pleat at the back and a relatively modest sweetheart neckline. Unfortunately Rose had nothing but a string of faux pearls with which to dress it up, and so she had decided, should she need to look smart, to weave these, rather cunningly, through her hair. She would, she decided after much debate, look presentable.

'Look at me, Petrie. Do you think I usually drive 'is nibs wearing black tie?'

'Sorry, I hadn't noticed, I was thinking about something.'

'Then think about getting yourself ready.' He looked down at her legs. 'Please say you have finer stockings than those. For heaven's sake, girl, you and I are to mingle, champagne in hand, with our little ears wide open, just in case someone drops a little pearl.'

'A pearl. What kind of pearl?'

'A word or ten to tell us what any one of our Allies is planning. Now move, and heavy on the perfume.'

'Allies, Ingram, you do know what that means?'

'You're getting above yourself, girl. Knowledge is power. Don't forget the scent.'

Rose had no perfume at all but, if anyone noticed, nothing was said. She did worry that her coat certainly did not look like the coat of a woman used to 'mingling' with champagne in hand.

Her passengers were already at the car and the male dignitary was not the very correct French officer, but the man who had chatted to her in the garden. Senator Jarrold frowned when she saw Rose's coat but, to Rose's surprise, it was because the senator thought the coat too thin to be of any use in cold weather. She shrugged herself out of her fur coat and handed it to Rose. 'Take it, girl, I'll wear my stole.'

She ignored Rose's stuttering attempt at a refusal of the very kind offer. 'Wear it with panache; you're exactly the right height for it – and weight,' she added rather sadly.

A few minutes were lost while the fur stole was brought down from the guest's bedroom, but it gave Rose an opportunity to admire the truly beautiful designer dress. Senator Jarrold shimmered from the diamonds at her ears and her throat all the way down to her knees. Below them Rose saw the finest of silk stockings and handmade black shoes. She could hardly wait to describe the outfit to Daisy and their friends.

'Oh, you look stunning,' she said before she could stop herself, and Senator Jarrold smiled her thanks. 'Why, thank you, honey. I do take that for a genuine compliment.'

The senator wrapped her silver stole around her shoulders and they were on their way, Rose and her very important passengers in the second car of a fleet of three.

Less than thirty minutes later, Lance Corporal Rose Petrie drove up to the great stone steps of a country house even more imposing than Silvertides, wearing a coat that she was sure had cost more than every penny she had ever earned or would ever earn. If the butler thought it odd that a chauffeur was wearing fur, his well-schooled face gave nothing away. The coat, far heavier than Rose's kitbag, was lifted from her shoulders and spirited away. She found herself praying that it would be found again at the end of the evening.

Rose was completely out of her depth. How was she to find Ingram, the commander's chauffeur, and what exactly did 'mingling' mean?

'You don't look half bad when you're dolled up,' said a voice, and her partner for the evening appeared from the direction of the hall. 'Like the way you've coiled your hair, very feminine.'

Rose said nothing.

He sniffed. 'I smell soap.'

'It's what my mother taught me to wash with. Palmolive, it's called.'

'Very funny, Petrie, but you're supposed to be one of them. Where's the perfume?'

'I don't have any,' said Rose, who had detected the faintest, most enchanting smell when Senator Jarrold had handed over the coat. That was perfume, she thought, and nothing she could afford could possibly compete.

While they talked, Ingram had gently guided her, his hand cupped under her elbow, along a carpeted corridor where gold-framed paintings adorned the walls and several small but extremely elegant pieces of furniture were positioned under them. Music and voices competed for air room and Rose relaxed. She was a guest in a beautiful house; she expected that she would never be in this position again and so she would make the most of it. How her mother would enjoy the descriptions of furniture and clothes – if Rose was ever allowed to tell her of the evening.

Where did they find all those magnificent flowers? They were at the open doors of a crowded reception room in which vases of exotic flowers had been arranged on almost every surface. A glass of golden liquid was put into Rose's hand and she and her partner moved on into the room.

'It's real champagne, Rose. Enjoy that glass, but be careful with it; it'll go straight to your head.'

Rose laughed. She knew it was unkind – no doubt he was trying to be helpful – but had he the faintest idea of how patronising he sounded?

He did not. 'Laughter's good,' he said. 'You've got a nice laugh. Last woman I had to take to a party laughed like a braying mule.'

Rose wondered if she would face a court martial if she picked up Ingram and disposed of him somewhere. There was, though, the slight possibility that the smart dinner jacket hid the body of a martial arts champion who could take care of himself. Just thinking of it, though, had made her smile, and that smile was noticed by Senator Jarrold and her companions from across the room.

'Glad you loaned the Petrie girl your coat, Araminta,' said the other American. 'I came upon her by the fish pond and thought she'd catch cold then.'

'What was she doing out in the garden?'

'Taking some exercise, I suppose – or maybe blowing off steam, like me.'

'Why has Silvertide planted her here? Her body language tells me she's just this much short of socking her escort.'

He laughed, and Rose heard the sound and thought of Brad. She pushed the thought from her mind. 'Shall we split up? I'll go off to powder my nose and I'll listen to the conversations.'

'Good idea. The guests have all been vetted and likely they are one hundred per cent on our side, but one never knows. I'll catch up with you later.'

Rose looked around the room at the men and women either deep in serious conversation or laughing together at someone's joke or tale. She put her half-finished glass on a convenient table and began to make her way through wall-to-wall people, all seemingly determined to enjoy themselves. She saw two women walking purposefully towards one of the many doors, and decided to follow them. Then she too would look as if she knew where she was going.

One had disappeared into the cubicle by the time Rose caught up with them and the other was very carefully examining her teeth in the mirror that hung above a painted porcelain basin. She saw Rose in the mirror and said something, but between her heavily accented English and the fact that she was holding her mouth open with her fingers, Rose had no idea what she was saying.

'. . . don't you agree?' finished the woman, having removed her hands from her mouth.

Rose made a sound that could have been taken for anything and the woman smiled. 'Exactly,' she said, just as the door opened and her companion came out.

They exchanged places after the woman had politely indicated to Rose that she was welcome to make use of the facilities first, if her need were greater.

'Your head, it is real?'

Assuming that she was asking about her hair, Rose touched the beautiful coil at the back of her neck and said yes.

The woman looked at Rose's 'dress it up or down' dress and said, 'You can sell for much money.'

Is it likely that this woman might say anything the commander would want to hear? thought Rose, as she tried to smile while edging away. The opening of the cubicle saved her and so she took her place inside. When she came out after a few minutes, both women were gone.

Rose made her way back to the party. Ingram was waiting for her. She expected him to ask if she had learned anything in the ladies' room. Instead he asked her how well she knew Senator Hastings.

'Never heard of him,' said Rose, who was already beginning to put two and two together. A rich father who had meetings with important people in places like the Ritz Hotel.

'Hastings, your friendly American. You drove him a few times and you were in the garden with him. What did you talk about?'

This could not be happening. Hastings? She did not want the American's name to be Hastings. His name was definitely Anderson. He could not be Brad's father. 'I have no idea what you're talking about, Ingram.'

'Over by the fireplace, talking to the commander. Who is that?'

She turned her head but she did not look because a stone in the pit of her stomach was telling her who was chatting by the fire. 'I'm just the driver; we weren't introduced.'

He looked at her and then decided that she was telling the truth. Drivers did not expect to be formally introduced to the packages they delivered. 'His name is Anderson Hastings. Job? United States senator. One wife, Mirabelle Bradley Hastings, swimming in oil and everything else. One son, Master Sergeant Bradley Hastings. Need I go on?'

'I didn't know any of that, and it's none of my business. What difference does it make who he is? You didn't expect me to listen in to his conversations.'

'That would be quite nice.'

'I listened to the two women I followed to the loo. Riveting. One mangled the King's English and the other spoke very little. She obviously thought my dress disgustingly inexpensive and dropped a hint that, in order to salvage my wardrobe, I could sell my hair. I got out before she reached for scissors.'

'And Bradley?'

'I've already told those who needed to know that we haven't been in contact for some time. You surely can't think his father, if that is his father, is not on our side?'

'Of course not. The family foundations have put millions into aiding the war effort, and they are amazingly generous with the Bundles for Britain scheme some other rich American woman set up. Odd that the only child is a non-commissioned officer. They could have bought him a commission if his degree from Yale hadn't got him one on a silver salver.'

'Haven't you ever heard of principles, Ingram? Now, if you'll excuse me, I'll go to the table over there and listen in to lots of conversations. What's the betting that most of them are talking about the ridiculous price of caviar, or the appallingly badly trained staff one gets these days?' And with that nasty little dig, Rose turned and left him.

She walked with unseeing eyes across the luxurious carpet. Of course she had known that Brad's father was a senator, but she had stupidly fought tooth and nail against admitting that the friendly American she had driven around London and talked to in the commander's starlit garden was Senator Hastings. Had Brad told his father about her? Had he said, 'I'm in love with a girl whose dad has a grocery shop?' Had he told him that Rose had left school at fourteen with no qualifications at all? Wow, how beautifully she would slot into this family.

Slot into the family! What on earth was she thinking? Brad had said he loved her. A few days later he had disappeared out of her life without a word. She would not think of him, even though he had whispered that he wanted to marry her.

Even in a time of war, of rationings, of short supplies, of shipping difficulties, to her untrained eyes there seemed to be plenty of luxury items available for those who had the funds to pay for them. Not all the guests agreed with her, as she heard one or two of those gathered around the long table, men and women, talking of 'the good old days' when one could really 'set a decent table'. She strove to remember that each and every person here represented his or her country in some way, and perhaps had made sacrifices that she would never be called upon to make.

Rose picked up a small plate and helped herself to half a boiled egg. The yolk had been taken out, mixed with all manner of things she did not recognise, and pushed back in. Rose wondered how she was supposed to eat it and what she would do if it tasted horrible. Was there some way of disposing of it? She looked back at the large oval plate on which sat at least twenty of the eggs and reminded herself that eggs were scarce. She could not possibly waste food.

'Finger food, honey,' whispered Senator Jarrold, who had moved so quietly that Rose had not noticed her arrival. 'Devilled eggs, and almost as good as my recipe. Enjoy,' she whispered as she moved away, her diamonds glittering in the candlelight.

Rose enjoyed, and stood for a moment trying to list the ingredients. Mum would love to try that.

'Couldn't believe it, the bottom half resembled a boat, and the top looked like a tank.' The accent was English and the dinner-suited man was standing a few yards away from Rose and was chatting to a man in uniform.

'An amphibious vehicle. There is nothing new about trying to design a vehicle that can move safely through water and on solid ground too. You really must bone up on naval history, old chap. Fascinating. Everything from coracles to mulberries. Didn't that Leonardo chappie draw models, or was that only of aircraft?'

The uniformed man was looking directly at Rose as he spoke. She put down her plate, as if that was what she had intended to do all along, and moved away from the table.

The conversation carried on but the sense of it did not reach Rose. She wondered if what she had overheard was the type of party chitchat she was supposed to report. She could see no value in it. WO Carter had brought the subject up first, though, and here were two men – one a sailor, if she had read his uniform correctly, and the other a civilian, possibly a government officer – saying there was nothing new in amphibious vehicles; or was that what they had been saying? How could a spy learn anything from the tail end of a conversation? Two grown men, each of whom had, no doubt, spent part of his childhood sailing boats on a pond, were simply talking about boats – and fruit. She hummed the old nursery rhyme 'Here We Go Round the Mulberry Bush'.

'Nothing to report, sir,' was what she would say if questioned.

Rose was hungry and thirsty. She had eaten half of a mucked-about-with egg and had enjoyed almost half a glass of what she had been assured was first-class champagne. She would rather like to finish the drink if it was still where she had left it.

The domestic staff members were much too well trained and her glass had been removed long before it could possibly have marked the polished wood on which it had sat.

She almost said hurrah for well-trained staff since, almost immediately, a young man with a tray approached and offered her a second glass. It was cold and delicious, and she was enjoying it very much when another snippet of conversation made its way to her from behind a large bank of plants.

'Pontoons, flat-bodied boats, very uncomfortable in rough weather.'

A woman's voice this time, but not a familiar one, and each word more difficult to hear than the word before as the talkers moved away from the area. Rose, glass in hand, made her way around the flower barrier as quickly but as subtly as she could.

Impossible to know which member of which group had been speaking. Several groups of people were obviously making their way to the cloakrooms. The party was coming to an end.

Rose followed on; it had been an experience but she was quite glad it was over.

TWENTY

'And what precious gems did you pick up on your little visit with those and such as those, Petrie?'

Once again Rose wondered just what Carter thought she might have overheard. The guests in both great houses were Allies. She decided to see how he would deal with the unvarnished truth. 'Should I ever need money in a hurry, Warrant Officer, I can sell my hair for "much money".'

'Very useful, I'm sure. And as to the war?'

'The only time I heard anyone mention the war, sir, was when someone complained that shortages were ruining parties. They did hold meetings but I wasn't near any of those. Sorry, sir, but surely you didn't expect someone like me to be able to nose out a spy or a traitor?'

'You watching too many spy films, Petrie? You're not bright enough to make a spy, but you've got a Yankee boyfriend. They're planning something and, yes, they'll tell us when they're good and ready, but wouldn't it be nice to know now? Promotion, Petrie, the ladder of success; are you climbing it or not?'

Rose had never given much thought to promotion, being more interested in doing her duty as faithfully and as thoroughly as she could. She answered truthfully, 'Never give it much thought, sir.'

'Some of us don't think of anything else; that next stripe tantalises, staying just out of reach. Now, say you was to have a golden nugget that I could pass on to . . . someone, then maybe I could put something extra in your way.'

'Master Sergeant Hastings wouldn't tell me anything, even if he knew it, sir.' The word 'sir' seemed to stick in her throat.

'How would you like to spend the rest of this bloody war driving vehicles the scrap yards would refuse?'

What was she to answer? Tell the truth: I would prefer to drive the latest Daimler? Tell him that somebody had to drive them – or would that be judged colossal cheek? She said nothing.

'Seems you're so pally with the Yanks, you walked into that posh place wearing a fortune in mink. I have eyes and ears everywhere, Petrie. Belonged to the woman who says she feels so safe in your little hands.'

'Senator Jarrold is an extremely thoughtful woman.'

'And Senator Hastings?'

'I wouldn't know how thoughtful he is.'

'And what did you talk about during your little tête-à-tête by the goldfish pond? You look startled, Lance Corporal. A friend told me.'

Rose took her courage and her growing anger in both hands and held tightly. 'International relations.'

Warrant Officer Carter grinned just like a cat that has finally found an available dish of cream. 'In particular?'

'Well, sir, we discovered that occasionally each of us would like to punch someone right in the nose, but, because of the same international relations, we take a walk instead. Now, if that's all, sir, I need to iron my uniform for tomorrow.' Rose did not wait to be dismissed but saluted smartly, turned on her heel and left the office.

'I think the phrase is "professional suicide",' said Agatha, when Rose told her of the conversation with WO Carter. 'He's been passed over for promotion so often and can't bring himself to believe that it has anything to do with his less-than-riveting personality. Possibly a little late to warn you, but the less interaction with him the better – strictly business; no personal conversations at all.'

'Thanks a lot.'

'Anyone seen a Rose Petrie?' yelled a voice from the door, and Rose called, 'Here,' almost as loudly.

'Phone call.'

The first terrifying thought was that something had happened to Phil. Mr Tiverton would ring. So afraid was she that it never occurred to her that it would be very difficult for the vicar to discover the number of that one public telephone box out of so many. She ran to it. 'Hello,' she gasped.

'Rose? Gosh, honey, you didn't need to run. I have a whole bucket of those pennies.'

'Brad?'

'How many guys are you expecting to call, Miss Petrie? Yes, ma'am, it's Brad, and I wanted to apologise on behalf of the US of A for keeping me God alone knows where for all this time. Say Brad again,' he whispered, his voice deep with rich meanings. 'Just hearing you say my name is a joy.'

'Brad,' she said. 'Brad?'

'Great, your voice saying my name is in my head now and I have a feeling that I'll need to listen to it over and over in the months ahead.'

'Is something happening?' She was asking the very question that Carter wanted her to ask, but not for Carter, for herself. 'Sorry, Brad, I didn't mean to ask like that but . . . but . . . oh, Brad, I do love you and I worry.'

Oh, why did I say that?

'Brad, forget everything I've said.'

'No way. I will remember "Brad, I love you" for ever. But, honey, I don't have much time and I needed to tell you my dad called a while ago. He says he's met a really beautiful English girl who's an ATS driver, a Lance Corporal Petrie.'

Rose waited a moment or so for him to continue, but when he stayed quiet, she spoke. 'Seems I've driven him a few times before last weekend. I thought he was Senator Anderson. I forgot what a bad habit you Americans have of using surnames as Christian names – very confusing. On Saturday evening I met him by a fish pond, and later drove him and another American senator to a country-house party. Is that what you wanted to know?'

He laughed. 'He never lies to me, Rose. Sometimes he omits to tell me something he thinks I don't need to know, like whether or not he introduced himself, and whether or not the lovely English girl told him his son is crazy for her.'

'I liked him, Brad. He said nothing about his son and he asked me nothing. Well, he did.' She stopped without telling him what his father had asked.

'Don't tease, sweetest Rose. I didn't react; at least I don't think I reacted when he said your name. As soon as I can, I want to tell him – and Mom. I want to walk up to them, with you beside me, and say, this is Rose, the woman I love and want to marry. It's amazing, I'll tell them, what a lucky guy can fish out of an English ditch.'

She thought she might explode with joy. Surely this happiness was too big for a mere human body to contain. 'He asked nothing, Brad. He was sweet, told me I'd freeze if I stayed out any longer. But I can't think why he'd ever put the two of us together.'

She heard him groan. 'Me. I did it, that day we walked in Green Park. I was high as a kite with happiness when I met up with him and he guessed it had to be a girl.'

'You told him my name?'

'No, if I had, he would have introduced himself to you. I said I met a fabulous English girl who's in the ATS; he was impressed, hoped we'd see more of each other. I told him I sure would be working on that. Mom has a goddaughter she would quite like to welcome into the family, and she has a couple of golfing buddies with daughters. Poor girls are as tired of being pushed at me as I am of being offered up to them.'

Rose smiled. Could life and love, which had always confused her, be so simple? All her life she had had friends who were male. Only with Stan had it been a bit different, she supposed, and with the awful Terry. But now it seemed possible that two people might meet, sometimes in extraordinary circumstances, and then meet again and talk, and somehow they're in love. Such a beautiful, miraculous and thrilling realisation. Rose Petrie was in love with Bradley Hastings and he was in love with her. She said nothing of this. Instead she said, 'There are three people waiting outside in the cold, Brad.'

'OK, I'll be real quick. I'm busy, we're playing soldier. Things are being thrown at us or dropped on us and most of the time I am cold, tired and very, very wet. When this is all over, let's get married and go somewhere very hot and dry.'

The line went dead. Had he run out of coins or had he said too much? Seemed to Rose that Sam had told his family exactly the same about his military training; things were always being thrown at him or dropped on him, and by this she had supposed he meant ammunition – surely not live – and he was always crawling through ponds. Possibly that was an integral part of every infantryman's training. She would not allow herself to worry, and neither would she worry about goddaughters or golfing buddies.

'I get pneumonia and I'll sue you, Petrie,' said the first person in the queue for the telephone, and the others nodded in agreement.

'Sorry, sorry, sorry,' said Rose as she hurried past them and back to the warmth of her billet.

During the days that followed, those who were lucky enough to have Christmas leave packed their bags and made their separate ways across the United Kingdom. The others, like Rose, continued to work. There was no shortage of projects. The short December days, no matter how cold or bleak as they rushed headlong towards the fifth year of this war, were always cheered by the arrival of the post. For months the Government had had posters strategically placed, telling everyone, everywhere, from the North of Scotland to the tip of Land's End, to remember service personnel at Christmas. Rose was heartened to receive cards from ATS personnel with whom she had trained, from former school friends, from Mr Tiverton, the vicar, and was especially touched – and embarrassed – to receive a card and a beautiful hand-knitted scarf from Stan's grandmother. Her heart went out to that old lady who, for the second year running, was sitting alone, knitting for everyone but the person she had loved more than anyone else in the world. Rose had never been in the habit of exchanging gifts with Mrs Crisp, but she vowed to begin this year. If she sent a card as soon as she could find one, Mrs Crisp would be bound to receive it before Christmas. She remembered that Stan had always bought angels, shepherds or a Robin Redbreast, preferably with at least a twig of holly and fat red berries, for his gran's card, and so Rose would take up that tradition now; she vowed to continue it year after year.

Francesca and Chiara wrote bringing Rose up to date with their plans.

It will be a small wedding, Rose, as small as my
Italian relatives will allow, but it would make us all
very happy if you could be here too. You saved my life
and you tried so hard to save Nonno's. How happy he
would be to see you with us, a very special member of
our family. I will let you know as soon as I know the
date, or maybe Enrico will know a way that is faster
than the post.

Rose felt Chiara's happiness jump from the page. I'll certainly try, Rose decided, even if I am almost the only one there who doesn't speak Italian.

But for the moment she was determined to enjoy Christmas Day, even though she was on maintenance duty. Together with another driver, she cycled to a farm where they bought – 'at a special price for the ATS' – a small tree. The farmer threw in a few sprigs of holly and cut-off branch ends from bigger trees, and the two young women managed to get all their purchases into their bags and transported, without too much difficulty, back to the station. They sang Christmas songs and, when they ran out of songs and carols that they both knew, they changed to favourite songs of the year.

'"In the shade of the old apple tree",' sang Rose at the top of her voice as she tried to remember every detail of London's Green Park and Yorkshire's Marston Moor.

'"I'm always chasing rainbows",' her companion sang, unaware or uncaring that she was completely out of tune.

They reached the gates and, singing last Christmas's classic, 'White Christmas', sailed through, holding their twigs of holly aloft as if they were regimental standards.

'Right, we've done the hard work; let the others decorate our little home from home.'

Decorations were unearthed from a cupboard in one of the offices, but before they were arranged on table-tops or tied to bedsteads, the two stalwarts, who had made much of the fact that they had gone bravely out into the cold to find the tree, were as involved as anyone else.

Rose recalled Christmases at home with her family and was sure that most of the others did too. Occasionally a tear was shed as the ATS women felt homesick or, in spite of the friendly group around them, lonely. They watched as the fittest, most agile and tallest balanced on a ladder as she attached all the Christmas cards to strings, which had been saved from the year before and probably the year before that.

Warnings accompanied the decorating. 'Watch that string, it's pre-war – you can't get string like that these days. I'll want every inch of it back, and if anyone gets some on a parcel, donate it, please.'

On Christmas Eve almost everyone who was off duty attended the multi-denominational carol service.

'My fifth carol service of this damned war,' said more than one woman, 'but somehow, and I don't know how, I found this one really inspiring.'

Rose agreed, for as she had listened to the readings or joined in the singing, she could see four girls, arm in arm, walking down a dark street to an ancient church lit only by candles. They would do it again, she vowed. Not this year, maybe not the next, but they would do it and the church would be ablaze with lights and the church bells would peal out the message of goodwill to all men.

Despite rationing and shortages, the cooks were working hard to make the meals not only nourishing, but also mouth-watering. On Christmas Day, Rose was working on the rather tired engine of a Morris Reconnaissance car and therefore was not too concerned about the menu for Christmas dinner. No matter how tasty it was, it was not cooked in that cosy flat above the grocery shop in Dartford. She was completely involved in her work; her hands – and even her nose where she had rubbed it – were covered in dirt and oil. She had decided to bury herself in hard physical labour so as to drown out the reality that she was not very far from home and all those she loved. For the first time, however, her thoughts and dreams and memories were not all about family but about a beautiful man who had come into her life such a short time ago. Yes, she admitted to herself,

Stan had been right all along when he had said that one day she would meet a man who would be right for her, who would be in her league.

'Is Brad in my league, Stan, my old friend,' she said now, 'or more importantly, am I in his?'

Stan's grandmother was not the only one who had sent Rose a Christmas gift, and like many of the other lucky ones who received presents from home, Rose had shared her treats with the others in her billet. Now she worked on the engine until she knew it would be foolish to work any more, hungry, tired and in rapidly fading light.

A hot shower. That was what she wanted. That would be the best Christmas present. She tidied her station, cleaning every tool before putting it away in its proper place, cleaned her hands as well as she could, pulled off her overalls and put them in the laundry hamper, turned off the lights, and walked out, locking the door behind her. Since there were no mirrors, apart from those on vehicles, she had no idea how dirty her face was.

'In disguise, Rose?' asked the first person who passed her.

Rose put the remark down to Christmas spirit, perhaps the glass of wine the cook had promised to find for everyone in the decorated dining hall.

Some runners laughed as they passed her and one called, 'Merry Christmas, Cinderella.'

Rose looked down at the uniform. Well pressed and perfectly clean. Cinderella surely had worn rags.

She reached her hut and went in.

'Surprise,' yelled the women who were there. 'Quick, Rose, before he goes. Poor man only has twenty minutes before he has to leave.'

Rose was confused by the silly remarks about Cinderella. 'What's wrong with all of you? What man? Where?'

'Quick, this is my last half-inch of cleansing cream. Use it to clean your face and never forget who cleaned you up on Christmas Day.'

'The CO's office, Rose. Run, and wipe your face on the way. And wish him Happy Christmas from us too.'

She hesitated. 'Brad? Is it Brad? It can't be Brad,' but, without stopping to clean her face, she ran back out into the cold December day and up the hill to the office block. Standing outside was . . .

'Brad.'

She ran to him and he held out his arms and closed them round her as if he would never let her go. 'Merry Christmas, Rose,' he said, and bent down to kiss her. 'Happy, Happy Christmas, my beautiful, wonderful Rose.'

How lovely it would be to stand like that for ever, held against his chest, watching perfect white flakes of snow drift down out of the grey sky onto his dark hair, but she could not. He was a soldier and must be back on his base.

'I have to go, sweetheart, but just seeing you has made my Christmas. I've left a box for you and the girls; oh, and Arvizo says *Feliz Navidad*. He hitchhiked clear across country to say that to Gladys.'

Rose had known that her friend Gladys was writing to the American soldier, but not that they were so close that he would go to such lengths to see her. 'I'm glad they're still in touch. She worries because she's older.'

'Tell her not to worry. He's been in the military since he was sixteen years old and we soldiers age fast. Now, enough of them. I'll walk you back to your billet, and then, oh, Rose, Rose, my so special Rose, I don't know when I'll see you again. I'm moving again but that's all I can say. Possibly I'll be overseas. When I get back, will you marry me?'

'Yes, Brad, I will.'

'So we're engaged, more or less?'

'I think so, Brad,' Rose whispered, her whole body quivering, not with cold, but with joy.

'I didn't have time to look for a ring.'

'I don't need a ring; it's more than enough to see you and hear your voice.'

He let her go. 'Wait,' he said, and he held out his hand. 'This is my class ring from Yale. Way too big for your fingers, but maybe if you wore it round your neck . . .' He slipped the heavy gold ring into her hand. 'Will you take it, honey?'

'I'll find a chain and I'll wear it always – until you come back from wherever you are going.'

He reached up and she saw that he wore a chain around his neck. Little metal tags hung from it and he took them off. 'Dog tags,' he laughed, 'and I can get another chain easy.'

He slipped the chain through the ring and lowered it over her head. 'Wear my ring, my Rose, because it says, Bradley Anderson Hastings loves you and will love you for ever.'

Rose struggled to hold back the tears. She felt the weight of the ring against her skin; she would always be able to feel it. There would be time enough to worry about what her parents might say concerning her plan to marry an American and probably going with him to that town in Connecticut. There would be time enough to worry about his mother and her hopes and plans for her only son, time enough to worry about so many things, like whether his father, who had been so friendly and kind when he saw her only as an ATS driver, would be just as courteous when he realised that she was the girl with whom his son had fallen in love. But now there was only Brad who was going into danger. He was a soldier and would do what he had to do as professionally as he could.

'Come back to me, Brad, some day.'

He kissed her again until they were both breathless, and then he took her hand, but not before she saw the tears in his eyes, and he ran with her down the hill.

They did not speak again. Rose stood at the door of her quarters and watched him race to where a Willys Jeep sat, the engine already running. He jumped in, the driver accelerated away.

A moment later, Rose was alone in the snow.

TWENTY-ONE

February 1944

The year began badly. What was left of the German air force threw itself into more attempts to bomb Britain into submission. Unfortunately for Germany, they could not outfly the more manoeuvrable Royal Air Force planes, or match the skill of the night fighters, and so they did not succeed. They did, however, cause some damage and there were casualties. One night a stray bomb hit Mrs Bamber's house while she sat, as always, on the bottom stair, waiting for her daughter to come home from another exhausting shift at the hospital.

Iris, forced to seek refuge in a shelter, worried about her mother as she sat there. The unknown woman beside her started a conversation. Such conversations were one of the few compensations for being forced, tired, worried and frightened, into the shelters. Strangers would chat, sometimes for a few minutes, often for hours as they sat waiting for it all to be over. 'Bloody Jerry. Just as we was beginning to think there wouldn't be no more – bang. You a nurse, pet? Gawd, you girls is something else, the way you cope. Hubby waiting up?'

'My mother. We've been lucky so far,' Iris said as she tried hard to remain calm. 'We made it through the Blitz, not a scratch, and this is nothing, nothing at all like it was then.' She tried to send thought messages to her mother. *Go to the shelter, Mum. There's not many of them; it'll only last a . . .*

The all clear sounded then and – with the other Londoners who had found themselves together, including her new friend, whom in all probability she would never see again – Iris left the shelter as quickly as possible. She hurried on towards a bus stop, hoping against hope that a bus was running that was going her way. She had a little luck. A night bus, whose route took it not too far from the street, stopped for her, and she stood with the conductor and looked out towards the area where her home stood.

She saw the flames first. She heard the crash of falling masonry, of shattered windows. She smelled cordite.

The commander alerted Rose.

On a cold, grey afternoon, Rose – who for once had a free half-day – made her way to the little church where the funeral service was already in progress. Iris, in uniform, stood with one elderly man and two middle-aged women at the front of the church. There were one or two rather distinguished-looking men and women at the back and a few people, possibly neighbours and friends, in other pews.

Rose found herself remembering Mrs Bamber's kindness, and then she thought of Stan and of her brother Ron. One day I'll visit your graves, she assured them.

The sad little family group stood outside the church and thanked everyone for making the effort to attend on such a dismal day. To Rose's surprise, Iris, who looked pale and tired, but somehow even more beautiful than she had when they first met, brightened when she saw her.

'Oh, Rose, thank you so much for coming. Mum would be so pleased to see you here. Her boss came, which I hadn't expected, the neighbours, and my uncle and my aunts.'

The two young women hugged. 'Your mum made me feel so welcome, Iris. I'm very sorry.'

How do you ask someone you hardly know if they have somewhere to live and how do you help if they haven't? Rose asked herself.

'I'm living in the nurses' hostel, Rose.' It was almost as if Iris knew what Rose was thinking. 'And there's room at my auntie's when I'm off duty.'

They did not make promises to stay in touch. The war had brought them together for a moment. Now each girl would carry on doing the job that she had been trained to do. They might never meet again – that was the nature of war – but if they did, they would be happy to see each other.

Not long into the New Year, Rose was given a week's leave and was able to go home to be with her family. They planned to visit Phil, who was, at long last, back in England, although still in hospital. Fred had written to his other children with the news, explaining that their mother was so happy at the thought of seeing her son that she could not stop her hands from shaking and was unable to use a pen.

'Dear Sam, Rose and Daisy,' he had written.

Mum and me is over the moon and we know you will be too. Our Phil is come home and is being transferred to a special hospital for wounded servicemen just a few miles from – would you believe, Dartford, on our very doorstep. We can see him as soon as they tell us he's settled in, whatever that means. The waiting is hard as all Mum wants to do is see him, touch him, feed him o' course, but we're trying to be patient, the doctors knows what's best. And yes, your mum is managing to bake, although the pints of salty tears as goes into them scones is something awful. George has decided that he will be 'the runner'. Sally's dad had him at the pictures and there was something about a boy doing all the carrying of letters, spying or something, and our George is going to keep track of messages between you lot and our Phil.
Can't remember as Phil ever met the boy and Mum was worried as how he might be a bit too much for Phil in his condition but he done really well with you, didn't he, Sam, and I think he'll make Phil laugh, Phil not ever being used to having someone waiting on him hand and foot.

Rose read her letter over and over, and pictured her brother and sister reading their identical letters at the same time. It was almost like being in the kitchen with them, the wireless and a mug of cocoa.

A familiar ache struck her. Thinking of poor, wounded Phil had served to remind her of Ron, and memories of Stan were never far behind. Would she ever be able to think of them without pain? But eventually her stomach churned with excitement as she thought that there was always the chance that she might see other family members during her week's leave. According to Mum's Christmas letter, Daisy and Tomas visited Dartford as often as possible as they tried to arrange their wedding. Sam was once again 'with his regiment', but neither his fiancée, Grace, nor his parents had any idea where he was. What if he were near Brad? What if they were to meet? Possibilities for happiness were endless.

As always when one of her children was coming home, Flora tried to prepare all their favourite dishes. 'I had five children, but I pride myself on knowing all the favourite meals,' she told Miss Partridge, who had come into the shop for an extra morning so as to give Flora a chance to prepare her equivalent of the fatted calf. 'And I need to give the girls' room a good going-over.'

Miss Partridge smelled beeswax polish, something cooking – possibly home-made stock for the hot soup that would be cooked all afternoon to nourish Flora's returning child, and smiled. 'Flora Petrie, the whole of Dartford knows perfectly well that one could eat a meal off the floor in any of your rooms at any time.'

Flora blushed with pleasure at the unaccustomed praise. 'You're kind to say so, and I do try to keep up standards – slipping would be letting the enemy win, wouldn't it? – but I just don't seem to have the same energy these days.'

'When did you and Mr Petrie last have a holiday?' asked Miss Partridge.

'A holiday?' Flora repeated the word as if it was new to her. 'We had a day out here and there every summer when the children were small. The beach; they always liked the beach and the donkey rides, or we'd take a picnic on our bicycles – some lovely picnic spots around Dartford, you know. We had a nice cup of tea at a café after our first visit with our Phil.'

'I know you did, and I think you should have a whole day out while Rose is at home. I'll take care of the shop and young George.'

'You're very kind, Miss Partridge, but we'll have a visit with Phil on Sunday. George will go too. He plans to chat to Phil about how the war's going, especially anything that involves Phil's precious Royal Navy, and then he'll write to our Sam about the conversation. Do you know, the longer George lives with us, the more I wonder what his father was thinking of, abandoning a family like that.'

'Being sent to prison isn't exactly abandoning one's family, Flora dear, but . . .'

Whatever Miss Partridge had been going to say was lost for ever as there came a bang on the door and a voice calling, 'Hello, the house,' and Flora and Miss Partridge ran to meet Rose, who had walked up from the station.

Miss Partridge hugged Rose, extracted a promise of a chat, and then diplomatically took herself off to leave mother and daughter together.

In no time at all, the kettle was boiling for tea and a plate of fresh scones was warming in the oven.

'My scones aren't the same these days, pet,' said Flora as they settled down. 'Nothing is, come to that, but we manage. Now, tell me all about your Italian friend and this young man you mentioned and all your driving. Rose Petrie, we are so proud of you.'

Rose reached for a second scone, which she did not really want, but she intended to show her mother that her baking was as good as ever.

'You have to tell me the absolute truth about Phil's injuries, Mum,' she said as she helped herself to a tiny spoonful of the final jar of last year's raspberry jam.

Tears welled up in Flora's eyes and she shook her head as if to clear it of all negative thoughts. 'We told you he lost his left arm. So, you're right, Rose, it's better that you're prepared; there's nothing left of it at all and there was some damage to his shoulder. He's had surgery on that and it's healing nicely, the surgeon told us.'

'His hearing, Mum?'

'There's nothing they can do about the left ear, and there's still ringing – whatever that means – in his right ear, but once that's over his hearing will be perfect.'

'That's a blessing, Mum.'

They were still talking two hours later when Fred and the Petrie foster son, George, arrived home from the warehouse, having gone there to pick up rationed supplies for Fred's customers. Rose, who hadn't talked so much for some time, was expected to tell her stories all over again. But she wanted to talk about Phil and about young George's plans for his future. After all, he was seventeen now . . . She decided to leave discussions on George's future until later.

'Phil's finished in the navy, and he's right sad about that, but there's a job for him here – if he wants it, that is; someone has to take over the shop some day,' said Fred.

'I won't have my poor boy think he has to work for a living, Fred. He can stay here and when he's strong enough, he can help out in the shop if he wants to, but no one's going to force him to do anything he doesn't want to do.'

Fred looked somewhat stunned by this outburst and Rose stretched while she tried to think of anything encouraging that she could say. She tried to remember if Phil had ever worked in the shop, after school, on Saturdays, during school holidays. She knew that he had driven the van sometimes, and that, like their two other brothers, he had been useful in carrying heavy boxes or tea chests, but had he ever worked behind the counter, as she had done sometimes, and as Daisy had done, day in and day out, for years?

'I suppose the doctors will suggest that he moves slowly, Mum.'

'One of my boys? Move slowly?'

'I meant as far as making a decision.' Rose looked over at her father. 'Have they talked about a discharge date, Dad?'

'It'll be a while, love. Mum wants him home, thinks she's the best one to look after him, and that's true,' he added quickly as he saw the expression on his wife's face, 'but our lad needs physio and specialised medical care at this point, and we can't do that.'

'He won't be able to work at all for a while.' Young George decided it was time he added to the conversation. 'Adjustments have to be made.'

All three adults looked at the boy as if he had suddenly spoken in an unknown language.

'Adjustments?' Flora asked.

'They didn't pay much attention to me when I was in there, and so I heard everything they said.'

Rose looked at George, whom she had tended to remember only as the young troubled boy who had been taken in by her parents after the death of his mother and brother in an air raid. She saw now that, while she had been away, George had grown and developed until he was almost a man. Fear for him clutched her stomach. He had lived through too much already, but if this dreadful war went on much longer, he would be expected to serve in the armed forces.

'George, do you mean the doctors say things to one another when there is just you there with Phil, but they don't say them when Mum and Dad are there?'

'I don't know what they say when Mum and Dad Petrie are alone with Phil, Rose, but when I was keeping him company, telling him what Sam's been doing and Miss Partridge and that, they talked about future surgery and therapy and getting over shock. Seems Phil still has night-mares where he thinks he's on the ship and he can't get away.'

'It's all right, George, lad. They do tell us what still needs to be done, and Mum and me know about the dreams,' said Fred. 'Rose'll come with us on Sunday. We'll make a nice day of it. A nice visit with our Phil and then a late meal in a pub. One of these days the nurse said they'll let us take Phil out with us.' Fred turned to Rose. 'The doctors do try to tell us everything that's happening, and his condition changes day to day, good days and bad days. We'll tell them we want to know if Phil will be strong enough to be at Sam's wedding; Sam wants him as best man.'

Rose was delighted that the conversation had moved away from the emotive subject of Phil's future to the happier topic of Sam's. At this point all the family knew about their elder son's wedding was that he fully intended to marry his sweetheart, Grace Paterson, just as soon as it could be arranged.

'And what about Daisy?'

'How can there be a wedding until this damned war is over? They're never in the same place for more than two minutes at a time.' As usual, Flora exaggerated.

Rose felt the warm weight of Brad's class ring against her skin. Was this a perfect time to show it to her parents, to explain the significance? If only there had been a recent communication from Brad. Daisy and Tomas had two-minute meetings; she and Brad were never in the same place. How she wished that he were here; that she could prepare a sandwich – a decent, delicious Brad-sized sandwich – and go off for a lovely long walk in the beautiful Kent countryside.

'You've gone all funny, Rose.' George brought her mind back into the room.

She forced herself to smile. 'I was just wondering whether or not to tell you all about someone very special.'

Flora jumped up. 'Not a word till I get back. I'll just light a match under the soup.'

Fred watched his wife, all gloom evaporated, hurry into the kitchen before leaning over and squeezing his daughter's knee. 'Two weddings or, who knows, even three, would be a right nice way to celebrate the end of this bloody war.'

'Dad, language,' said Rose, adding quickly, 'but it's not nearly ended,' as she heard her mother hurry back. 'Let's try to be positive.'

Flora, her smile lighting up her face, plopped down in her armchair. 'There, we can have a nice chat. Tell us all about your chap, Rose, love.'

'All right. There is a very, very special man. He's a soldier, a sergeant—'

'Oh, nice, like our Sam,' broke in Flora.

'He and some of his men pulled me and Gladys – you remember my old friend Gladys – out of a type of ditch at the beginning of last year . . .'

'Last winter, and we're hearing about him now?'

'Give 'er a chance to tell us, love.'

Rose smiled at her father, all the time wondering if he would be quite so understanding when he heard the whole story. 'It was nothing but a slight accident, Mum, a skid on some ice and we overturned, but no one was hurt. In fact the girls were quite pleased.'

'Pleased? They're in an accident and you say they're pleased. Oh, Rose, love, were you driving?'

'Yes, Mum, but no problems. I was exonerated; it was winter conditions, more or less unavoidable.'

'Why were the girls happy?' began George, and then, as a thought came to him, he grinned from ear to ear. 'Because they were rescued by big handsome men, weren't they, and those men were Yanks? Bet they were.'

Rose could see realisation dawning on her mother's face and the beginning of a frown but, before Flora could say anything, Fred broke in, 'That's nice. We read as there were Americans in the north, Rose, in Northern Ireland and the Midlands too, I believe. Seem to be nice lads, from what we hear, and ready to do their bit. Maybe I shouldn't say, but there's rumours that the Yanks is planning to invade Europe – they've got thousands of men and machines all over the place. Seems they made arrangements to come over here and work out all their manoeuvres on friendly soil. When I went to the pub last Saturday afternoon with my ARP shift, we heard stories, probably a bit exaggerated, about huge tanks the Americans were trying to hide or camouflage.'

Flora stood up and walked over to the fireplace where one of Sally's silver links from the Christmas decorations still sat on a candlestick. She kept her back to the others. 'I don't want to hear about invasions. My boy already invaded and ended up a prisoner. What makes the Americans think they can do better?' Her colour heightened by her unusual ill temper, Flora turned to Rose. 'So this lad's an American, our Rose. You didn't think you could tell us?'

Rose put her hand up to touch the ring through her jumper. 'There wasn't anything to tell, Mum, not for a long time.'

Flora removed the broken decoration and returned to her chair. 'Well, tell us now, love, especially if he's very important to you.'

Rose smiled at her mother, who tried bravely to smile back. 'His name is Brad, Brad Hastings, and he's tall, and I suppose he's good-looking. Yes, he's very good-looking: lovely eyes, and he has a nice voice; not loud, not soft, a manly voice. He's beautiful, Mum, just beautiful, inside and out.'

'Oh yuck!' exploded young George. 'Is he a cowboy? Does he wear a cowboy hat and fancy boots like in the pictures? Does he say "pardner" and "yes, ma'am" all the time, and chew gum or tobacco?' He gave Rose no time to speak but answered himself. 'Fantastic. When is he coming to see us? I've never met an American.'

'And you never will, lad, if you don't let Rose talk,' said Fred firmly. 'You're behaving like a four-year-old instead of a lad almost grown to a man.'

'Only teasing,' said George.

'How long have you been seeing him, Rose?' asked Flora, her voice still showing her hurt.

Rose considered the question. 'It's so hard to say, Mum. We met and then his CO invited everyone to a dance at their base. I told you about that.' Surely she had said that the dance was on an American base?

Her parents nodded.

'Brad drove me to the dance—'

'Wow, in a Jeep, Rose, did you get to be in a Jeep?'

Rose nodded. 'I saw him once or twice. Once we walked on the moors and had lunch in a pub. He knows a lot about English history and so he was really fascinated by old pubs and old villages. But we couldn't meet regularly because of our jobs. I was transferred but we wrote to each other and sometimes Brad telephoned and once we were able to meet in London.' She decided this was not the time to mention his father or the fact that, without knowing who or what Brad's father was, she had actually been the American senator's driver. 'He was transferred and I don't know where he is exactly, but he's somewhere in the south of England because he came to see me on Christmas Day. Would you believe, somehow he got to my base, waited for me to finish my shift and then we met for a few minutes.' She relived the moments: the snow in his hair, the love in his eyes, the touch of his lips, his question and her answer. 'He brought a lovely hamper of food for me to share with my roommates. From Fortnum and Mason, Mum, like your special honey. Do you remember that?'

''Course, I do. Got the jar on the counter in the shop – ever so lovely it is.'

'What was in the hamper, Rose?'

'Chocolates, Georgie Porgie, and smoked salmon, lovely things. Even a bottle of champagne.'

'So he's rich.' George decided that being able to assess Brad's financial status was worth putting up with silly old nicknames.

'Not necessarily.' Fred decided to answer for his daughter. 'They say Americans are very generous. He got a lift from his base to yours on Christmas Day, Rose, to see you for a few minutes?'

Rose nodded.

'Nice lad, don't you agree, Flora? Here were you last year asking for a nice lad for our Rose, and along came Brad Hastings.'

'With a name like that he has to be a cowboy,' said George.

'The soup's ready,' said Flora, leading them into the kitchen. 'I'm glad you told us, pet. I suppose our Daisy has known all along.'

Daisy had no knowledge of the heavy golden ring that nestled inside her sister's bra. 'More or less, Mum. We haven't talked much. We're both very busy.'

How could she explain that the dawning realisation that she loved and was loved in return was much too precious to discuss with anyone? It had been enough for a time merely to experience, to feel.

'Gosh, I've missed your soup,' she said as she sat down between her father and her foster brother at the same table with the same blue-and-white checked cloth, and was passed a bowl, the one with the tiny chip out of the rim, a chip that was deemed too small and insignificant to be a cause for throwing it away.

'I've always loved this bowl,' she said as they began to eat.

They took the bus the few miles to the hospital. The weather refused to be obliging; it was very cold and the mist that hung over everything seemed to have frozen, completely blocking out what might have been pleasant views from the bus windows. Not that anyone could see anything, since the windows had been taped over to avoid the possibility of a passenger being struck by shattered glass should there be an air raid. With such reminders around them, it was almost impossible to be cheerful, but they tried. Rose was going to see her brother for the first time in years, and that fact outweighed the knowledge that he was not physically the same Phil that she had seen on that long-ago Christmas.

'I'm so glad I got leave, Mum, and I'll tell him about the cars I've been driving.'

'I want to hear about the cars too,' Fred and George said together, and the women laughed. Rose had saved some of the chocolate that had been in Brad's Christmas hamper; Flora had baked a honey-and-walnut pudding, which she hoped the nurses would allow Phil to share with other injured soldiers in the same room. Since it was mainly stale breadcrumbs, flour and chopped walnuts – generously given to her by the Humbles at Old Manor Farm – she had used fresh eggs and sweetened it with honey, and then baked it in a pie dish.

'It'll be easy for him to cut up, but I do wish I had more honey to drizzle over.'

'The men will love it, Mum Petrie,' George assured her. 'Alf selected the walnuts special.'

The ever-doubtful Flora smiled at the boy. 'You're right, George. A bit of home cooking always goes down well, and with our Rose's posh chocolate . . . I've never seen this make, Rose.'

'It's American, Mum. Almost everything on the base is shipped over from the States.'

'On ships?' George's surprised shout must have been heard by almost everyone on the bus.

'Never thought to ask, George. I assume shipped means shipped in ships.'

'That's terrible,' protested young George. 'I thought ships were needed for the war effort, not to bring posh chocolate. Wish I hadn't eaten it now.'

'Maybe it was flown in, lad. I mean to say, how long does a ship take to get all the way from America?'

'Wait a minute, Dad.' Rose had no idea how the American forces brought in their supplies but there was one thing she did know and she repeated it now to her belligerent young foster brother. 'George, there are thousands of American servicemen here. Where should they get their food? Talk to Grace when she's here next and she'll tell you how hard she and all the other Land Girls have to work to grow food for us – and there still isn't enough. Do you want to share yours with the Americans? They have thought it all over very carefully and someone, their president perhaps, said it was better to have their own supplies. And, George, they share. I'm not talking about bars of chocolate – maybe Brad's father brought them . . .' Too late she remembered that she had never mentioned Brad's father to her family. She decided to carry on and brave it out. 'When they come to our base, they bring food, lots of tinned goods, fruit, ham,

313

that sort of thing. Some lovely people in the area where I met Brad ask American soldiers to Sunday dinner. That is a kind gesture to men who are sometimes thousands of miles away from their families and very, very lonely. I never heard of any American who doesn't take gifts with him for the British family.'

'Why don't they go where the fighting is, if they're so wonderful? No one is fighting here.'

'Happen they're practising for something, George.' Fred had had enough squabbling. 'We'll find out what they're doing when it's time for us to know. You can't think Mr Churchill doesn't know they're here.'

''Course he knows. He's the Prime Minister.'

'Right, so let him get on with it. And we'll get on with visiting our Phil and we'll have no argy-bargy or glum faces.'

No one uttered a sound until they reached the hospital. Fred seldom put his foot down, but when he did he set it down firmly and the wise did not argue.

On a better day, a walk in the grounds would have been pleasant as they had been well set out by the original owners and were still reasonably well kept. Most flower-beds had gone, and much of what must once have been a magnificent lawn was now a vegetable garden, but there were still some trees that would soon bear the green of early spring and several showed promise of future blossom.

'Wouldn't it be nice if there was snowdrops and crocuses under them trees?' said Flora in an attempt to lighten the heavy atmosphere.

'I'm sure there will be, Mum, and daffodils,' said Rose, and she took her mother's hand as they walked into the hospital.

Their parents stopped to talk to the sister on duty and Rose and George walked on into the ward.

Nothing she had been told had prepared her for her first sight of her handsome brother. Once tall, broad-shouldered and slender, he was now barely recognisable. Even his face had shrunk; the skin, bruised and discoloured, now stretched across his cheekbones, and bandages still hid the damage the explosion had done to the left side of his face. She could make out the long thin lines of his body under the utilitarian blanket. How many of his mother's nourishing meals would it take to return Phil to the young man he had been? No matter how many, he would never look as he had looked – for how could an ear be replaced, or an arm? She saw the pyjama sleeve pinned to the chest of his jacket and faced reality.

'Hello, Rose.' His voice was a whisper.

She bent down and kissed his undamaged cheek. 'Dear Phil, I'm sorry I couldn't get here before.'

'There's a war on, love,' he said, and twisted the stretched skin into what passed for a smile. Bravely she tried to return it.

'Bit of a shock for you, Rose. Sorry, love.'

She took his hand. 'No, I'm sorry.'

'Me too. I really wanted to finish the war an admiral. Our navy has no idea what it's missed.'

''Course it has, Phil.'

'Our Rose has a Yank for a boyfriend, Phil. What do you think of that?'

Rose was astonished. Had the child George ever met Phil before the war? If he had, it was likely that Phil had

315

chased him off for being cheeky. Here they were now, talking and joking . . . like brothers.

'Tell me everything you haven't told Mum,' said Phil as he squeezed her hand.

'George.'

'I can keep my mouth shut.'

'He grew up in Washington DC and spent the summers in a place called Cos Cob, which is in Connecticut.'

'And? George, give Rose a hand to get me sitting up.'

'Can't, Phil. The old dragon's prowling. We'll have to wait for Mum and Dad Petrie. Here they come – and the dragon's with them.'

The dragon? Rose smiled. Nothing changed. She had had a teacher whom they called the Dartford Dragon. And now George had created a dragon. She was surprised to see that 'the dragon' was a nurse who was no more than five feet in height and with a very pretty face, set off, like a priceless cameo in a perfect frame, by her severely tied-back red hair. She ignored Rose.

'Let's get you up for your visitors, Phil. Your sister,' she said, nodding over at Rose, 'will give me a hand to lift you. He's heavier than he looks,' she said to Rose, 'and aren't we all since your mam keeps bringing in these delicious tarts?'

A few minutes later, Phil was sitting up against a bank of blindingly white pillows.

'Don't stay too long today, please. I don't want him disturbed or tired out. We've got a very special man coming in to see him; some of the other lads too, of course. He's called a plastic surgeon and Doctor thinks he'll be able to help Phil.' She smiled at Phil and her face softened dramatically. 'You can tell the family about new strides in medicine, can't you, Phil?' She nodded and moved off down the ward.

'As if I'd exhaust my own son,' said Flora huffily.

'What's this about a surgeon, lad? Haven't you had all the surgery you need?'

'This is different, Dad; it's a bit of a new . . . well, not exactly new, but there's been great strides in surgery because of this war. It was the poor air force lads; so many of them got horrifically burned when their planes went down. Some very clever doctor – a New Zealander, I think, but he's working over here now – Dr Archibald McIndoe, I think, and other doctors have been working out how to repair burned faces . . . other bits too. The consultant here has asked this man to take a look at my face.' He saw the expression of hope and joy flash across his mother's face. 'Mum, no. He can't work miracles. Maybe he'll decide he can't do anything that'll make a difference. But maybe he can make me an artificial ear; maybe he can remove some of these bloody awful scars. They graft undamaged skin from other parts of the body, very skilful. That'll be miracle enough for me.' He relaxed against the pillows, as if talking so much had tired him, and closed his eyes.

'Can he make you an arm, Phil?'

Phil opened his eyes and smiled at George. 'Wouldn't that be something, George? But no, that's a miracle too much at the moment, although these docs are working on creating limbs. You'll see, but in the meantime you'll have to be my helper.'

'I will. I'll be your left hand and your left ear, and maybe I could join the navy and finish your work for you—'

'Time for a cup of tea, Phil,' Fred interrupted their conversation as he saw that, although Phil was smiling at the young hero worshipper's enthusiasm, Flora was becoming upset. 'Rose, love, why don't you and Mum go and have a cuppa, and when you come back, me and George'll go?'

Rose stood up. 'Great idea, Dad. Are we allowed to bring Phil one?'

'A beautiful nurse'll bring me one soon, Rose, and with a slice of Mum's tart. Go on, you two. The men need to talk football.'

It was obvious that Flora wanted to stay beside her son. 'Come on, Mum, if we go, we can have Phil all to ourselves when we send Dad and George away.'

'It should never have happened. My boy, my lovely boy.'

To Rose it seemed that the more casual Phil was about his injuries, the more their mother became concerned. Sam had written to Rose a few weeks after they had heard of Phil's injury and had told her that Phil was lucky to be alive, so close had he been to the magazine that had exploded.

His injuries are pretty awful, Rose, and it will take a long time for him to recover enough to handle any type of work. But, to be frank, I'm gratefully amazed that he's alive. The other two sailors near him were blown to bits, poor sods. We'll try to keep that from Mum.

Rose was more and more of the opinion that it would be far better for her mother to be told of the deaths. Her son was alive. Injured, but alive.

'I never thought I'd get angry with George,' Flora admitted when she and Rose were sitting down in the hospital canteen. 'He was wonderful with my Sam, followed him everywhere like a puppy, fetching and carrying, but Sam has both arms.'

'So George will be even more help to Phil, Mum.'

'I'm all the help my son needs. Who's better to look after a child than his mother? No one.'

'This tea isn't too bad.' Rose looked around the canteen: basic chairs, basic tables, posters on the walls, some concerned with hygiene, but many exhorting people to save food, mend their clothes, and to be especially careful when talking to strangers. Not too unlike any military canteen she had ever been in.

'What does George want to do, Mum?' Better perhaps to change the subject.

'He's working a few days for us and a day and a half or more on the farm with Alf. Miss Partridge would like him to take some exams. You know she's been giving him lessons since he left school and she thinks he could get passes in English and arithmetic and stuff. If he got these certificates, she says he could get into a college of some kind.'

'And what do you and Dad think?'

'He's part of our family, Rose, a very special part, and we'll do our best for him.'

'You and Dad are absolutely wonderful. Does Miss Partridge think George is clever enough to go to a university?'

'She wants to help him do something. Seems she wanted to go to a university but her father said that it was too unfeminine. Can you imagine, education unfeminine? I just hope she's not living her life through George, but if

319

he's as bright as she says . . . Daisy says Tomas could talk to him, or Dr Fischer – if he ever gets to come home. Now we'd best get back, just in case that doctor person comes.'

'Just a second, Mum. I'm sorry I didn't tell you about Brad earlier; there really wasn't anything to tell. I'm still wondering how I could be in love with someone I hardly ever see. It was so unexpected.'

Flora smiled and it was a really warm Mum smile. 'That's what love does, pet, creeps up on you.'

'You don't mind that he's an American, Mum?'

''Course I do. I wanted you and Daisy to find nice husbands here in Dartford, but the world is a different place these days.' Flora looked over at the long counter on which were placed breads, scones, small slices of cheese and carefully measured servings of tart or cake, but they were of no interest to her. 'This damned, damned war,' she said. 'It's changed everything, and I have to accept the changes. My Ron dead; Sam – well, look at everything that happened to my Sam; and now my Phil is disabled.'

'He could have been killed, Mum. He was so lucky.'

'Lucky?' Flora almost gasped. 'How can you say that he's lucky? He's deaf and has only one arm. The pain my son has suffered.'

'But two lads who were standing beside him are dead, Mum.'

Flora covered her mouth with both hands, turned and almost ran from the canteen. Rose followed her.

Damn, damn, damn. Why did I say that? Because she should know, because she should be grateful, accept what's happened – and deal with it.

320

Fred and George realised that the cup of tea had solved nothing. Painfully aware of that, Rose hoped that Phil had noticed nothing of the troubled atmosphere.

'Off you go for a nice cup, Fred, George. They have some fairly fresh-looking pieces of fruitcake.'

'No, thanks, love, don't fancy hospital baking. George and me are looking forward to our pub meal, isn't that right, George?'

'Right,' agreed George at once.

'What's up, you two? You've both got faces that would frighten babies.' The low voice came from the wounded man on the bed.

Flora moved her chair closer to her son and took his hand. 'Thanks very much, Philip Petrie. Your mum and your sister were just agreeing that we are very lucky to have you back with us. Other families have not been so lucky.' Her eyes sparkling with held-back tears, Flora tried to smile across the bed to where her daughter sat.

The sharp sound of leather-soled shoes on the corridor floor alerted the family to the arrival of more than one person.

The dragon opened the door and followed a man into the ward.

'Mr and Mrs Petrie, I'd like to have a look at this young man here.' The man who spoke was about Rose's height but, since he had a natural stoop, he seemed shorter. He had very little hair, a large nose and round, friendly eyes. He held out his hand to Flora. 'Miles Hart,' he said, 'I'll take great care of your lad, Mrs Petrie, if you'd all take a seat in the corridor for a few minutes . . . Mr Petrie . . .' and he shook hands with Fred too.

The family walked to the door and Rose clearly heard, 'Well, haven't you got a beautiful sister,' before the swing door closed behind them.

'Beautiful,' said George as he scrutinised his foster sister. 'Well, I've never thought of it, but I suppose he's right, Rose.'

'Of course he's right,' said Fred, 'but what's important is what he's doing to our Phil.'

'Just an examination of his injuries, I would think, Dad.'

'Nice man,' said Flora. 'He's the first one ever to tell me his name, or shake hands with me. What do you think, Fred?'

'He knows how to put folk at their ease, love. What's important is – how good is he at his job?'

'. . . *something in the man reminds you of him.*'

'I'd trust him anywhere,' said Rose quietly.

Miles Hart did not keep the family waiting long. Less than fifteen minutes later the dragon ushered them back into the ward.

'We can repair a bit of the damage,' Mr Hart told them. 'It will take some time. It's rather delicate surgery and Phil has some healing to do before we can start, but we're going to work together, right, Phil?'

Phil held out his hand and the surgeon grasped it. 'I'd like to have a look at a few other lads in this ward but I'll be back, Phil. Mr and Mrs Petrie, Miss Petrie, George.' He nodded to them and, accompanied by the smiling dragon, walked off down the ward to disappear behind some screens around a bed.

'Repair? What does he mean repair, Phil?' asked Flora, as George was trying to come to terms with hearing a real live surgeon call him by his name.

'He didn't tell me what he can do, Mum; he's going to talk to another surgeon, maybe even this really famous chap, and he has preparatory work to do. I don't know what that means but I'm prepared to trust him. The boy in that bed is in a really bad way; he was a pilot. Believe me, I am very lucky compared to him.'

Flora sank back into her chair; when Rose went over and took her hand, Flora held on to her daughter as if to a lifeline.

'It'll be a while then, lad?'

'I think so, Dad.'

'And if you don't mind, my patient needs to rest now. He's had a very busy morning.'

George's 'dragon', as always, had the last word.

TWENTY-TWO

Rose, honey, the 4th Armored Division has arrived.
We've been waiting for them for some time but now
we'll get moving. Moving, as in going to the place
where we can do what we've been trained to do. Right
now it must seem to the nice people of this very lovely
corner of your 'green and pleasant land' that the entire
military population of the United States is coming to
visit. Farmers complain that we requisition their land,
and if we don't do that, they can't drive a truckload of
potatoes or cattle anyplace but 'those damned Yanks'
hold them up. Can't say I blame them, but I know
they'll forgive us for ploughing up their fields when
. . . we succeed in what we came to do.

I remember you said you were hoping to visit with
your folks for a few days and so I hope that, by now,
you're back in the London area and maybe we can get
a few hours together. Surely there must be one day
when we can steal a little time, not to stroll in our
lovely park – too cold!!! – but maybe to have a meal
together, go to a tea dance somewhere. The Ritz? Dad's
back in DC and so we wouldn't run into him although

a big part of me wants to walk right up to their front door and yell, 'Hey, Mom, Dad, I want you to meet the most beautiful girl in the world.' One day soon? You haven't changed your mind? You're still wearing the ring? Forgive me, but I so envy that little chunk of gold.

I had a call from my folks Christmas Day and I was going to tell them, got myself all primed and then Mom started to sniffle a little and then did that: 'Oh why isn't my only child here at home with his mother on Christmas Day?'

I want a picture of you, dearest Rose. I have you in my head and in my heart but it's nice for a guy to pull out his billfold and see the girl of his dreams in there. That reminds me, Arvizo sends his love. Gladys wrote that she feels she's too old for him. Threw him for a loop. To be honest, he's been in love at least ten times since the first day I met him, but Gladys was different. Any thoughts?

He finished by writing the dates when he thought he was free to travel up to London, adding that he hoped Rose would be free on at least one.

Rose made a conscious effort to hear his voice as she read, and so, when she finally folded up the letter and put it away, his deep, soft voice still echoed in her head.

The crushed might of Germany was still trying to prove world superiority and, while on duty, Rose had twice had to take refuge with her passengers in a shelter as the droning of approaching bombers could be heard. Once she was taken completely by surprise.

She was driving a British politician and a Polish army officer to a meeting and no one heard the approaching plane or even the air-raid warning. The car, a Wolseley, seemed to lift completely off the ground, shuddered a little, and then skidded to a halt, half on, half off the pavement of a side street leading from the King's Road.

My passengers, was Rose's first thought. 'Get down on the floor,' she shouted, as a hail of bricks and slates rained down on the car, smashing the windscreen. Shattered glass embedded itself everywhere. Some pieces cut through Rose's driving gloves and stuck in her hands, and she recoiled instinctively as a heavier stone hit her face. She threw open the driver's door, got out, and pulled open the passenger door. The Polish officer was beside his companion, wiping blood from the politician's forehead.

'Are you all right, sir?'

'A scratch, my dear,' said the soldier. 'We should be taking care of you. You are unhurt?' He saw her face and then her gloves. 'No, you are not.' He helped his companion up. 'Better to leave the car, old chap, in case more of the building falls on us. And you, Miss Driver, let me.' He took out a clean handkerchief and gently wiped blood away from her cheek. 'Lucky girl; a glancing blow, I think, and it will hurt for a time, but no real damage. Now let me see your hands. Come on, child. I am an army surgeon. I think I can mend a broken nose,' he gestured to the politician, 'and . . .'

Rose winced as he removed first the glass and then, very gently, what was left of her gloves.

He wrapped her left hand in a clean handkerchief. 'This one will need a few stitches, but first, see, here is the wonderful Red Cross. Sit down, child, here on the pavement.'

'My passengers?'

'Both outrank you.' The politician, his handkerchief still held to his nose, gestured to Rose to sit beside him on the pavement. 'This is the first time I've been caught up in an . . . incident. Now I know what it is really like. Thank you. You are a remarkable young woman. My daughter would be in tears.'

'I'm in the ATS, sir,' said Rose, as if that explained her stoicism.

'And so will have a little cry later, doctor's orders.' The doctor had been talking to the rescue services and had returned with two cups of sweet tea and a blanket that he wrapped around Rose's shoulders. 'The building, *Deo gratias*, was empty, but there are one or two casualties – unfortunate shoppers – and I will help there. No meeting for us today, Charles. The police will take you both home, but our so-clever driver first to a hospital for the little repair.'

Rose said goodbye and, aware that she was now reacting to the shock and emotion, sat quietly beside the politician as they drank the very sweet tea.

'What will I do about the car?' she heard herself say.

'Don't worry, Miss . . . what is your name?'

'Petrie, sir. Corporal Petrie, Rose.'

'It will be taken back to your base, Rose. I may call you Rose?'

'Yes, sir.'

'The surgeon general and I think you did an absolutely splendid job and we'll say so. You remained remarkably calm, especially when you found us rolling around on the floor bleeding. I think I'd have laughed. Hope I would have – pillars of the establishment, ends up.'

Rose wanted to smile but her skin hurt. 'One day, maybe,' she said.

'Good girl. Now here's a nice fellow come to take you to the hospital. Take care of yourself.'

The policeman helped Rose to her feet and, wrapped in her blanket, she was taken to the nearest hospital where her hands were treated. As the Polish doctor had said, only one cut needed a stitch; the others were properly cleaned and bandaged.

'In a day or two, you may drive if it's absolutely necessary,' said the emergency-department doctor, 'but no fixing engines, changing tyres. All right?'

As Rose thanked him and left, she wondered how she was to get back to base. A car was drawn up at the front of the hospital.

Good Lord, Carter.

The warrant officer strode up to the door. 'Well, Petrie, another of the Government's fleet of cars out of action, thanks to your driving. Well, come on, girl, get in the car.'

Rose, tired and still in some pain, was speechless. Of all the knights in shining armour she had conjured up out of her imagination, WO Carter was the last on a long list. She was even more stunned when he opened the door for her. 'Thank you, sir,' she managed.

'My first thought was to tell them to send you home – as far as possible, on the Underground. Nice and safe, that is, the deeper you go down, but we'd still have had to fetch you from the station.'

Still Rose stayed silent.

'Cheer up, Petrie, I'm only joking. The commander rang us – does that bloke ever sleep, I ask myself – but he said, "Fetch her, Carter; she's worth the petrol." You're not going to be sick on me, are you? You've gone all peculiar.'

328

Rose shook her head.

'Delayed shock, I expect. A few days in sick bay'll do you the world of good.'

'But I—' Rose began to protest.

'Doctor's orders – from the hospital.'

Rose had to admit that lying down in a quiet room for two days was a welcome experience. Girls from her billet were allowed to make short visits and each one came carrying a small gift. Even, on one occasion, Agatha brought a rather wizened orange. 'I think it's for marmalade, Rose, so maybe a bit sour. Put some sugar on it.'

But the best offering of all was a postcard from Taunton in Devon.

Hi, honey, checked your schedule yet? Guess what, we just discovered this stuff called ginger beer. I could become addicted – but not as much as I am to you.

As always, B

Rose held the postcard close, so that it touched the place where Brad's class ring was hidden. From feeling definitely groggy and weak, she became invigorated. What a joy to be loved. She had some suitable dates and she would write to Brad immediately.

What should she wear? It was still winter and so a new spring frock, which she did not have but would enjoy finding, was out of the question. Should she wear her dress uniform? Would Brad be in uniform? She could wear uniform with a civilian coat. Which coat? Certainly not the Teddy Bear. Mum had not needed her coupons to buy clothes for the sprouting George and so she would have plenty for a new coat. For a new coat she would need new shoes.

Rose looked at her face in the mirror. She was pale and her eyes seemed to have sunk deeper into her head, but at least there were no bad cuts or ugly bruises still showing from the accident. She would tell Brad about it when they met; for he would, of course, see her bandaged left hand, the same hand that had been injured in the bombing of the Vickers munitions factory early in the war.

'I'm feeling so much better, Nurse,' she told the army nurse who was taking her temperature a few hours later.

'Good. That's what we like to hear.'

'I'm sure I'm perfectly capable of going back on duty. We're understaffed, Nurse, and there is so much to do.'

The nurse laughed. 'Take your place at the end of the queue, Rose. We're all overworked and understaffed. Now, be a good girl and stick to fixing broken-down cars, and I'll be a good nurse and stick to fixing broken-down ATS girls.'

'But I really need to buy new shoes. My boyfriend's coming up to see me in a week or two and I haven't a thing to wear.' And then Rose remembered that Brad wanted her to have a photograph taken. How wonderful it would be to have one of him too. She sighed. 'And do I want to have my picture taken in uniform? I'd love to have a new frock for spring, and he mentioned a tea dance. Is it acceptable to wear uniform to a tea dance?'

'Considering a stray bomb did its best to kill you, I'm sure soldier-boy won't care what you're wearing in the picture. And, in case you haven't noticed, there's a bloody war on, so anything decent is acceptable – even in posh places like the Ritz.'

Rose looked at the nurse in astonishment. 'How did you know he's a soldier?'

'War, love. Everybody's boyfriend's in uniform. I thought RAF for yours.'

'That's my twin sister. Brad's American infantry.'

'Some people have all the luck. Got any chums, your Yank?'

'I'm sure he has, but he's nowhere near London.'

'But he's coming to London. Maybe he could bring a friend? Only joking. Besides, my last three afternoons off were cancelled at the last minute. I swear if the commander-in-chief himself was to ask me to lunch, there would be a blinking emergency.'

'Would you want to have lunch with the C-in-C?'

'No, I'd be petrified, but I bet the food would be good.'

'I don't know when my friend is coming. I have to write to tell him when I'm free, but I'll ask.'

'I'm no longer fussy. Male. Yes, that's about it. Male. Unmarried, preferably.' She looked at the watch pinned to her blouse. 'Got to go. Get back into bed and enjoy being waited on. I'll talk to the doctor about discharge tomorrow.' She whisked round and was gone.

Rose spent the evening writing letters; the first one was to Brad. She told him about the incident but made light of it, taking more time to tell him about her two passengers.

'They weren't at all pompous, Brad,' she wrote, thinking that was exactly what she had thought about Brad's own father: 'not at all pompous'. She told him about Nurse Colner, who had had no leave for weeks because of emergencies and added, 'Maybe Arvizo is coming to London with you.' That reminded her that Gladys had not answered her last letter, and so she asked if Arvizo had heard from her, and then she told him about Phil's progress and filled the rest of the page with telling him how much she missed him and longed to see him.

Writing had cleared her mind too over the question of new clothes. She would write to Cleo and suggest that they meet for shopping and, if London prices were not too prohibitive, she would buy a spring-weight two-piece costume, a pretty blouse and the world's most beautiful shoes – if they were not too expensive.

Agatha popped in on her way to tea later. 'You look much better, Rose. I wish I could say it was the orange that did it, but what's the secret? A man? You've heard from Brad?'

Rose laughed. 'Time, I think, Agatha, and being waited on hand and foot. You should try it some time. I wrote some letters, and I made plans to go shopping.'

'Oxford Street's the place, if it's still standing. I haven't been up to town in ages. Last time I was there, there was so much smoke and dust, I couldn't see a thing. Grey air always makes me ever so depressed. What's it like, driving?'

'There are pros and cons. There's much less traffic. Hardly any private cars and that's a blessing; some buses, trams, sometimes a few delivery vans but nothing like it used to be. Some pavements are busy in the city, where there are shops still open for business. Shopkeepers are wonderful, though. Even when the shop's been damaged, had the windows blown out no matter how well they were taped up, there they are, trying to keep everything clean and tidy. I am so grateful I never saw the aftermath of the Blitz.'

'I did, and that's why I can't bring myself to visit. I went up on a school trip when I was sixteen and I fell in love with London. Glorious buildings, beautiful parks, wide roads, sometimes with beautiful soldiers on beautiful horses, the river running so wide and slow through it, and all those bridges; it has to be, I mean, it *was* the most beautiful city in the world.'

'They'll rebuild it, Agatha. After all, it got burned down once before, didn't it?'

'I suppose so. Wish I hadn't remembered the soldiers. A lot of them will be dead now.'

Rose looked at her friend closely. There were tears sparkling in her eyes, which had dark circles under them. She was pale and looked tired. 'When did you last have some leave, Agatha? This isn't like you; it's exhaustion talking. What can we do to cheer you up?'

Jeremy? Like an arrow from a bow, a thought flew into Rose's memory – from weeks ago, when Agatha had said that she would not like Warrant Officer Carter to open 'Jeremy's' letters. But that was all she had said and Jeremy had never been mentioned since.

'I'm sorry, Rose. I knew I was a misery and I thought: I'll go to see Rose; she'll cheer me up, and now I've depressed both of us. The vicar at the service I went to last Sunday said the end is in sight. Some people started to cry, thinking he meant the end of the world – and sometimes it looks like that, doesn't it, all the big holes where houses used to be? – but he meant that the war will soon be over. Do you think he's right, that it will soon be over?'

'Yes. Look at this bombing; nothing like the Blitz. In Dartford, it was almost every day and night for months. My brother says the enemy has hardly any planes left.'

She smiled, her thoughts turning again to Brad and the other American and Canadian soldiers who were in the country. 'We're not alone, Agatha. My sister's fiancé is a Czechoslovakian pilot and he's with the RAF, and there are lots of others. My brother's fiancée, a Land Girl, knows Polish pilots, all fighting with us.' She blushed. 'And there are the Americans and Canadians, Australians and New Zealanders. They haven't invaded us; they're here to help.'

'But what are they doing?'

'I don't know. Brad doesn't say and I don't ask. But we have to trust our Government, Mr Churchill and the others. They won't let us down, Agatha. You'll see. I hope they'll let me go back to work tomorrow, and if they do I've got Saturday afternoon off. I plan to meet my friend Cleo. We met in basic training and she works right in London. Come with us. We'll go shopping and maybe have tea in a restaurant; doesn't that sound nice?'

'London isn't the same, Rose.'

'Of course it is, under all the dirt. The real London's still there. Maybe Prue will be free too. We could have a girls' day out. And when we get back in we can write and tell the lads what fun we've had without them. Brad and . . . Jeremy.'

Agatha put her head down on the rough hospital blanket on Rose's bed and promptly burst into tears. Rose, who was, sadly, too familiar with loved ones in distress, had never before dealt with someone she did not know well but who was obviously unhappy, patted her back and tried to make soothing noises, until eventually Agatha gulped in air, blew her nose and asked, 'Who told you about Jeremy?'

'You mentioned him, don't you remember, when I told you old Carter was threatening to read my letters? You said—'

Agatha did not let her finish. 'No, no, I made that up. I wish Jeremy would write loving letters. He's in North Africa. He hasn't written for ages and so it's impossible to know what's going on. I don't know where they are, what they're doing, or what I can do to help him.'

'Is he your boyfriend, Agatha?'

Agatha laughed, a harsh, horrid sound. 'No, he's not my boyfriend; he's my husband, and he thinks it was all a mistake.' She put her head down again and started sobbing.

Rose was stunned. *He could not mean his marriage was a mistake, or could he?*

Before she had a chance to ask, Nurse Colner returned to do her evening checks. She looked at the prostrate Agatha. 'Oh dear, and what do we have here?'

'My friend Agatha. She's a little upset.'

'Sit up, Agatha. Burying your head in the blanket won't solve anything. I know what will, though. How about a cup of cocoa, just this once, for you and Rose here?'

'Thank you, Nurse,' said Rose over the sobbing Agatha's supine form.

'Come on, Agatha, sit up. We're being treated like princesses here, so show Nurse you appreciate her efforts.'

Agatha gulped, blew her nose very loudly and sat down in the chair beside Rose's iron bed. 'I'm sorry, Rose, but I've really, really tried.'

'Can you tell me anything? I have no idea whether or not I can help, but I'll try. You're married?'

Agatha sniffed loudly, dried her eyes, and admitted that she had been married for almost a year, and had been with her new husband for only two days of all that time.

'We had a lovely wedding. Church was bombed out but we still wanted to get married there. We were both baptised there. Fire Brigade said nothing more was going to fall off, if we were quick, and we were. It was me and Jeremy, his mum, my mum and dad, and my cousin Lucy was bridesmaid. Some soldier who was passing was roped in as best man, since Guy, Jeremy's brother, was posted two days before the wedding.'

'That's dreadfully sad, Agatha.'

'It was lovely in a way. We had candles for light and the vicar's son played ever so lovely music on his violin. Bach, I think he said it was. Beautiful. Then we went to the hotel and had a meal, and the cake was fabulous. I should show you the pictures; you'd think it cost the earth and a whole town's coupons, but it was only a little sponge on the bottom, very nice. Everything else was cardboard and rice paper, painted to look like roses and such. The baker was a genius; looked like I'd got three tiers with ever such lovely decorations.' She was quiet, lost in happy memories, and the nurse chose that moment to walk in with the cocoa.

'Here you go, girls; it's Bournville, the real thing, so don't waste it. Feeling better?' she finished by asking Agatha, who thanked her for the cocoa and said that she was fine.

Rose waited until the nurse went off on her rounds and then asked Agatha if she wanted to talk about her marriage or go and have her tea.

Agatha needed to talk, to tell someone friendly about how unhappy she was. 'We had one day together and it was wonderful, and then Jeremy joined his regiment and I went back to my unit. That was what we'd agreed and it was fine for a few months although I missed him terribly. I waited for his letters, and when a letter didn't come, oh God, Rose you can't believe what I went through, wondering if he was dead or horribly wounded or captured.'

'Must have been dreadful.'

'Oh, an unmarried girl can't begin to know what it's like when the person you love more than anyone or anything in the world isn't in touch. I couldn't sleep, I couldn't eat.'

'But he has been writing?'

'Oh, yes, he writes, but it's weeks and weeks between and they're so miserable. He says it was wrong for us to marry when he was going off to war. Selfish of him, he says, because he's tied me up and now he's worrying about me and before he only had to worry about his mum. What will happen to us if he's killed, he asks. In his last letter he said it would be worse if he's terribly injured. He's seen soldiers with no legs, and blind ones, and oh, I just can't bear any more.'

Rose was appalled and the worst part was that she had no idea what to say. 'Does he want to end your marriage, Agatha?' she managed at last. 'Drink up Nurse Colner's lovely cocoa. Goodness, we've let it get cold.'

Agatha drank her cocoa and stood up. 'I'm sorry,' she said. 'I shouldn't have said anything . . .' She burst into tears again. 'But I had to tell somebody.'

'You'll have to leave, miss. I can't have you upsetting my patients.'

'It's all right, Nurse Colner, really. I'm fine. It's poor Agatha I'm worried about. Her husband's having a really hard time.'

337

'Everybody's having a hard time, love, and we all have to make the best of it. Some of us get it worse than others.'

'Agatha, tell Nurse, maybe she'll know what you should say to your Jeremy.'

'I've heard most of it already, Rose. How old's your bloke, pet?'

'Twenty-two.'

'Well, that's your answer; he's young. If you want him, tell him you do, no matter how he comes back, just as long as he comes back. He's scared. Everybody's scared. Mind you, he sounds like a nice lad, if he feels he shouldn't have tied you to him while there was a war on.'

'But I wanted to get married. I love him.'

'Then sit down and write to tell him that. Tell him you love him, you're glad every minute of every day that you married him and you'll wait for him, no matter how long you have to wait till you're together. Tomorrow, write the same letter, and on the tomorrow after that. Men are little kids really. Go on, go and write a letter and don't come back tomorrow if you haven't written it.'

Agatha smiled, a fairly tentative smile, thanked them, and hurried off.

'You're a wonder, Nurse,' said Rose. 'I hope you're right, but I'm not going to be here tomorrow, am I?'

'We're giving you one more night of bed and breakfast, and then you'll be discharged.'

When she had gone, Rose lay quietly for a time, feeling the mostly unoccupied ward settling down for the night around her, and it was not Agatha she was thinking about but Nurse Colner. Was she speaking as one who

338

had done exactly as she had ordered Agatha to do, or was she, unhappily, one who had not?

Should I ask her? No: much too intimate and delicate a question. I don't know her well enough. Maybe someday.

TWENTY-THREE

London, February–March 1944

Already, in late February, the March winds were practising for their annual thirty-one days of blowing. Since it was a leap year, the winds had an extra day of practice – and they used it – and Rose, tall as she was, was often bowled around the base. Small women, like Prue Church, had a much easier time. Rose and Brad, desperate to see each other, twice arranged to meet towards the end of February, but twice they had to rearrange. Whatever Brad was doing, it was taking up much of his time. Rose's shopping trip had been postponed three times and she was ready to accept that no flattering new clothes or perfect shoes would be found. And then Cleo phoned the public call box. She was free on the last Saturday afternoon. Could Rose and her friends meet her at Selfridges?

In the end, only Prue Church and Rose met Cleo. Nurse Colner seemed never to be off duty, and it appeared that Agatha now spent any free time writing to Jeremy. So far Rose had not heard that there had been a reply, but Agatha looked and sounded happier.

The three who did get together enjoyed themselves immensely. They chatted so long over their tea and scones that there was barely time left for Rose to find shoes, but in the end, with two 'fashion connoisseurs' to help, she found the perfect pair. They were available in black and beige, had heels that were almost three inches high and, because of the clever use of decorative leather straps instead of a solid top, could be either formal or semi-formal.

'I'd buy both colours if I didn't have the widest ankles in the entire ATS,' moaned Prue.

'They're designed to make your legs and ankles look thinner,' Cleo assured her. 'You have to take a pair, Rose. Depending on the weather or the occasion, they can be formal shoe or casual sandal. The designer's a genius, and he's used so little leather he's probably got two pairs out of leather for one more usual pair.'

'Then he's a she,' said Prue, which made them and the shop assistant laugh.

'Black, please,' Rose decided. 'More useful.'

'Wouldn't it be lovely not to have to choose between more useful and just heavenly?'

'And even with such a high heel, they're madly comfortable,' said Rose as she waited for her parcel to be wrapped.

'Oh dear,' said Prue, and the others looked at her.

'What is it, Prue? Are you all right?'

'Height, Rose, height. You'll tower over the man.'

'No, that's also heavenly, Prue. With the man I'm meeting, he'll still have to look down, while I look up.'

'Some women have all the luck.' Prue called the assistant back. 'I don't suppose you have those in a three, do you?'

Cleo had to leave them then as she had an afternoon meeting, but she reminded Rose of her tailoring skills. 'Pick up a bargain, Rose dear, and I'll tailor it to fit. It would be nice to have nothing but a lovely party frock to work on.'

Rose thanked her and promised to look, and then she and Prue spent the rest of their time walking around central London, a much better way for Rose to see how the city had fared than while driving her rather limited routes. Only one purchase had been made, but they had spent time with a friend, and, for all three of them, it had been a lovely break.

They stood on a bridge, watching the great River Thames slide slowly past under them. The Houses of Parliament, bruised and battered, still looked magnificent, as if, despite bomb and fire damage, they would stand there, proud against the skyline for ever.

'Do you think the bombing raids are finally over, Prue?' Rose asked as they leaned their elbows on the bridge and filled their eyes with wonder. 'Will we soon be completely relaxed as we shop or have tea with a friend? When will we stop straining our ears to hear approaching enemy aircraft?'

'Don't know when, but it has to be soon. As to relaxing, you've seen a wounded soldier, Rose. They're as safe as they can be in a hospital, but they still strain to hear. Even when the Prime Minister or the King or whoever says the war is over, even when we hear that, it'll take time for us to relax. But at least one of us has beautiful shoes to relax in.'

They walked to the Westminster Tube Station, two minutes or so away.

'Talk about relaxing, I hate the Underground.'

Rose patted Prue on the shoulder. 'They say it's much safer down here and we don't have time to walk back to camp.'

'Just tell me when we're there.'

There were no problems, no alerts, no delays. 'You can open your eyes, Prue; we're here.'

Even better was the message waiting for Rose when she got back to her hut.

'Brad telephoned. He'll ring back at nine.'

The note was in Agatha's writing.

Rose went up to the vehicle depot in a very happy state of mind. There was the never-ending paperwork to keep her busy. Glad that WO Carter was absent, Rose worked quietly until it was time for the evening meal, which she had with Agatha and Prue. More paperwork kept her occupied until just before nine. She closed up and hurried to the telephone box. A girl was already there in animated conversation. Nine o'clock came and, as if to mark the moment, the girl fed more pennies into the machine.

Rose tried to stay calm. If it were me and I was talking to Brad, I'd hate to be interrupted. So that's how she and the boy on the other end feel, so be patient.

At ten minutes past nine, her patience left her, and she rapped on the glass. To her surprise the girl turned and stuck out her tongue. Rose watched a horrified expression cross the young private's face when she saw that the impatient woman outside in the cold was a corporal. Still clutching the receiver, the girl opened the door. She was in floods of tears. 'I'm sorry, I'm so sorry, I didn't mean to—'

'Calm down and I'll pretend I didn't see. Now, say good night to your friend, and give me a chance to talk to mine.'

Please, please, let him still be there.

The door opened. The girl came out. 'Corporal . . .' she began.

'Chilly evening, Private. Better hurry to your billet,' she added as she went into the box – and waited – and waited.

How long can I possibly stay here, if someone else . . .? she was thinking as the telephone rang. *Please let it be Brad, please let . . .*

'Honey, are you there, Rose? I'm so sorry. I got held up. I hope you haven't been waiting long.'

'No, of course not,' she said. The truth was that she had been prepared to wait for ever. And if Brad had made the call later than he had expected, she had disturbed that poor little private for nothing.

'Next Saturday, the fourth, are you free, say from two?'

'I should be.'

'Meet me at Green Park. We'll have tea at—' The line went dead.

On the following Saturday, Rose seriously considered wearing her warm but not-too-flattering Teddy Coat when she set out to meet Brad. She had had no further word from him, but she decided to have faith that they would meet, even for an hour. At the last minute she put glamour before comfort and wore her tailored uniform coat over a two-year-old two-piece costume. She wore her finest stockings – having put on thin gloves in an attempt to prevent snagging – and, of course, the elegant and much-admired new shoes.

The wind propelled her along Piccadilly like an autumn leaf.

Green Park Station. If she stayed down she would be out of the wind but she would see nothing, and if she went out onto Piccadilly, she risked being blown over. She decided to go up into what now passed in London for fresh air. She would walk to the Ritz as there was shelter there. Heart in mouth, she arrived at the corner of Arlington Street and Piccadilly, just as a taxi drew up and disgorged its passenger. She saw him unbend himself from the taxi, stop to pay with a smile and a quip, and then straighten up and turn around to look anxiously in her direction. His eyes brightened and a smile lit up the dull March afternoon.

Rose was overcome by a wave of . . . a wave of what? Never had she experienced a feeling like this. Every nerve ending was jumping, as if touched by an electric shock. Her very fingertips tingled and every bone in her body was suffused with longing . . . But longing for what?

'Rose.' He said her name as if he was reciting a prayer. 'Rose.'

'Brad,' she breathed, and the next moment they were in each other's arms and she knew what she longed for. This: Rose and Brad together. 'Oh, Brad, I love you.'

He looked down into her blue eyes and kissed her. 'And I love you, my dearest Rose.'

'Now you've got that said, lad, can those of us what have trains to catch get past you? A better door than a window you'd make, lad.'

Brad apologised and drew Rose closer to the wall of the luxury hotel. 'Better door than window? What did he mean, honey?'

'You're so tall, he couldn't see around you or past you, I think, and certainly not through you.'

Brad was still confused. 'I get it, I think.'

'Doesn't matter, nothing matters.'

'Absolutely. Hey, you're up to my nose. New shoes. Elegant.'

'Thank you.'

'They need to be taken some place nice for very British afternoon tea. I don't have too much time, my darling, and so dancing in those cute shoes is out, although two hours of having you in my arms is hard to give up. We'll go to the Goring. Been there?'

'No. I'm a Lyons Corner House girl.'

'Excellent value and service, but today I feel needs some place special. Being with my girl makes it special.'

The Goring, when they eventually got there, enchanted Rose.

'Oh, it's absolutely beautiful, Brad. Does that make me sound unsophisticated?'

'I'm never perfectly sure what folk mean when they say sophisticated or unsophisticated. I guess my mother is sophisticated. She would say, "Anderson, this is a lovely room."'

Rose laughed. 'Bradley, this is a lovely room.'

'Why, you sophisticated . . .' He did not finish, but bent down and kissed her lightly.

They walked through the elegantly appointed entrance hall to a welcoming sitting room or lounge. In a large and beautiful fireplace a log fire was burning. Carefully arranged around the spacious room were small square tables with a gleaming leather armchair on each side.

'Cards, possibly,' said Brad. 'Let's take one of the little ones nearer the fire. I like a fabric cover for relaxing, don't you?'

They sat down and Rose looked up. 'Gosh, Brad, just look at that.'

A sparkling chandelier hung from the ceiling, and the firelight danced off every crystal.

'The light fixture? My mom would have noticed that too. I notice temperature, comfort and food. Two get gold stars. Now we'll check out number three.'

Rose laughed at him and continued to gaze in awe around the room.

There were uniforms from, it seemed, every branch of every service and every country. 'Look at these servicemen, Brad: Poles, Czechs, French, Norwegians, Canadians, and I think that shorter man hogging the fire is a New Zealander. Surely you're not the only American?'

'No way. I recognise some of the civvies, and that's a Marine Corps officer standing under that portrait over there. We have dedicated clubs: one for officers, one for other ranks. There's one does all ranks, Rainbow Corner, on Piccadilly. Coffee and doughnuts twenty-four hours a day in the basement. I haven't been yet, but I'm told there's great music for dancing . . . Artie Shaw, The Flying Yanks. Arvizo says he saw Jimmy Stewart, the film actor, in there, and a favourite of mine, Glenn Miller. He has an orchestra, plays the saxophone, have you heard of him?'

'James Stewart and Glenn Miller? Oh, we love James Stewart. My friend Sally's dad is a projectionist in a cinema, and he used to let us in to see all the films; and of course we hear Glenn Miller on the wireless.'

'Arvizo says most of the men like to go to American clubs, but I'm sure there are just as many of us who like to learn about the country we're in. When I was a kid . . .' He stopped, as if embarrassed to talk about expensive foreign holidays.

'Where did you go? I want to know everything.'

'And I'll tell you, my darling, but right now we need to talk about right now.'

He was leaving again. She could feel it. Her blood seemed to run cold, as if an icy wind had come in through an ill-fitting window and chilled her to the core.

The waiter arrived and personal conversation stopped while he fussed around making sure that everything was perfect.

'Sure beats the canteen,' Brad teased.

'There definitely is at least one artist at work here,' agreed Rose as she looked at the tiny but exquisite offerings placed on the table. 'It does look so appetising, doesn't it?' She admired the selection of tiny cakes, a swirl of cream or chocolate here, a hazelnut or a fresh raspberry there.

'Looks great,' said Brad.

'Then let's taste to see if it's as good as it looks.'

The chef was given maximum points.

'Sitting in a beautiful room like this with an even more beautiful girl, a guy might forget there's a war on.'

'And does he?'

'No, but it sure makes him long for it all to be over. I love you, Rose, and my God, I want you with every fibre of my being but . . .' He stopped talking and looked for some time at the markings on the silver pot on the table.

Rose took her courage in both hands and touched his hand. 'Brad.'

He looked up and smiled at her and she could almost think there were tears in his eyes.

'Every day for weeks, I debated with myself. Will I ask her to . . . ?'

'Ask her to what, Brad?' Strange, unfamiliar feelings were racing around inside Rose. Is he going to ask me to sleep with him? What will I say? I want to be with him but . . .

'Honey, I want to marry you. I want to marry you right now, this minute. That's what I had decided. I was thinking and planning and, damn but I'm ashamed of myself; I was going to ask you to marry me today, if we could get a special licence, but I won't. It would kill my mother and I guess yours wouldn't be too happy either.'

Rose felt that she could hardly breathe, so unexpected was the conversation. She gulped. 'No, my mum wants pretty dresses, bridesmaids, flowers.'

He smiled and then he said, 'Rose, will you give me back my class ring?'

One moment she had been on fire with love and longing, and now she could feel ice form in the pit of her stomach. His ring, she could feel it nestling there between her breasts. For weeks, months, she had kissed it morning and night, and now he wanted it back. The lovely dream was over.

'Of course,' she said as she tried not to sob. She tried to show, to say nothing, but finally gasped, 'I don't understand.'

He got to his feet and hurried round the table to sit on the well-upholstered arm of her chair and fold her in his arms. 'No, no, it's not like that, darling Rose. I wanted to ask you to exchange it for this one,' and he took a small box from his pocket. 'I'd get down on my knees but figure you'd be embarrassed to have all these people looking at you – or do you want me on my knees?'

She smiled through her tears. 'You're too tall, you would look a bit silly.'

'I know, but I'd do more than that for you, sweet Rose. Honey, I have to tell you, I'm going away, and I'll be gone for some time. We should have been gone by now but there have been delays, loads of reasons, but this is it. There's no leave until our job is done. It will take months, Rose, maybe more, but if we're successful – and we have to be, I guess; what with all the planning and manoeuvres we just can't fail – then this war will end. There will be dancing in the streets and all the bells of London town will ring out. Trust me in that. I promise by this ring that we will not fail. I'll come back and we'll begin our life together with your family side by side with my mom and dad – among all the flowers and bridesmaids.' He held the red velvet box out to her. 'This was my gran's engagement ring; I loved her to bits and she left this for me to give to the woman I wanted to marry. Darling Rose, will you take this ring?'

He opened the box and Rose saw the most magnificent diamond ring she had ever seen, the kind of ring that she had never dreamed she would ever see.

'Rose?'

'It's stunning, but I can't possibly have a ring like that; it's much too valuable.'

'You're worth much more to me than this diamond, Rose. Gran would have loved you. Maybe she foresaw you when she wrote her will.' He lifted her left hand. 'Please?'

Eyes brimming with tears, she nodded, and Brad slipped the ring onto the fourth finger of her left hand.

'Hey, look at that, a perfect fit.'

He kissed her then, oblivious of the other customers, some of whom pretended not to see.

Rose blushed as she saw the happy smiles, the occasional disapproving look. 'It is so lovely. But, Brad, I have to ask. Did you bring this glorious ring to England before you met me? Were you looking for a wife?'

He laughed, a happy, relaxed sound. 'No, although I guess every red-blooded male is always looking for a wife. When I talked to Dad a while back, he said he was sailing back to England. I told him more than I told him at Christmas; said you had my class ring but that I wanted you to have Granny's ring. I've had it in my pocket for two weeks.'

Rose looked at the ring and at Brad. For a few minutes she stayed silent, bewitched by the ring as it rivalled the chandelier above them in brilliance. 'And does your mother know?'

'Not yet, honey. Figured we'd tell our moms when I get back.'

'Good thinking. It is beautiful and I love that it was your grandmother's, but will you be terribly upset if I don't wear it until after my sister's wedding, and my brother's too?'

'No, I kinda like the idea of it nestling right there where my class ring is. Do you want to go to the powder room and change them over? Or keep them both.'

Rose stood up. 'Too embarrassing. I'd clink when I walked.'

When she returned holding the beautiful golden ring, he had paid the bill. 'Let's go get our pictures taken. Could you wear it for that, in a picture just for me?'

351

'I'd love a picture of this room, my favourite room in the whole of London.'

'We'll have a party here to celebrate when I get back.'

With a last backward glance, Rose walked with him out of the hotel. The photographs were taken and then they walked for a while, loath to say goodbye. Despite the chill winds, they sat on a bench in Hyde Park, held hands, and talked.

'I'll write whenever I get the chance, honey, but if you don't hear, know it's difficulty with the mail. I've bought loads of picture postcards of Merrie Olde England, and I'll send those. Can only get a few words on each but I'll fill the mailbags with them.' He saw sadness on her face and carried on, 'But I'll write real letters when I have more than a minute – and you'll write to me too, won't you?'

'Every day, every single day until you get back.'

'I'll carry your picture near my heart. The baser part of me wishes I'd asked you to marry me yesterday, a month ago; I thought about it a lot, Rose, but it would have been a base, selfish act. Our wedding day will be real special; not a hurried, what do they say, "hole in the corner" affair, and we'll take a honeymoon wherever in the world you want to go and then we'll decide what I'm to do to earn our keep and, even more important, where we're going to live. Connecticut is a long way from Dartford.'

'Someone will be unhappy whatever we do.'

'Maybe our moms will surprise us.'

'You can't tell me any more about where you are and what you're doing?'

'Heck, the entire population of the south coast of England knows where we are, honey, and no doubt guesses where we're going. I can't think why I never told you right at the start but the orders were hush-hush. What we've done is prepare the final push to end hostilities. We're ready to go, Rose. I wish I could tell you more because it's real exciting, a grand idea, a really big idea with input from some real boffins. I've got some newspaper clippings here . . .'

He pulled out an envelope and Rose looked through them as well as she could.

'What on earth is that? We have nothing like that in our depots.' Rose pointed out what appeared to be a large six-wheeled truck, but she could see rather peculiar appendages underneath the body.

'It's an actual amphibious vehicle, sweetheart; it really works both on land and in water. That's a propeller and a propeller shaft. It's an early model.'

'You plan to drive through rivers or lakes? We have bridges in this antiquated old country, Bradley Hastings; some built – would you believe? – by the Romans. They invaded us, just like you.'

'We're not invading Britain, sweetheart. We're Allies, here to help.' He scooped up the slips of paper and Rose clutched his arm, suddenly anxious to feel his warmth, his strength.

'Then?' She could say no more.

'Yes,' he said. 'Darling, I have to go or I'll miss the last train. Let me get you a cab?'

She tried to smile. 'Even if you could find one, the poor driver wouldn't have the petrol. I'll be fine. Come on, I'll walk with you to the station.'

Hand in hand they hurried along. In Victoria Station, Brad pulled Rose to him and he kissed her, trying to show her how much he loved her and longed for her, and she responded. They were not alone. Couples were glued together everywhere one looked. Finally Rose and Brad broke apart.

'Goodbye,' she said.

'Not goodbye, my heart, cheerio,' and Brad was gone.

Agatha was reading a magazine when Rose finally got back. 'Did he love the shoes?'

Rose pushed her left hand deep into her coat pocket. She had forgotten to remove her engagement ring. *Engaged.* When she told her parents, they would probably put an announcement in the local paper. That is, if Flora could tolerate the idea of both her daughters marrying foreigners.

'Shoes, Rose. Did he like them?'

'Of course, and we had tea at the Goring on Beeston Place. So elegant.'

'Not the Ritz?'

'No, another time we'll go there to a tea dance. But the Goring is fabulous too, and the food looked so pretty we were afraid to eat it.'

'But you got over your fear?'

'Absolutely, and I wrapped this one up for you.' Luckily the tiny cake, the one with a swirl of chocolate, was in her right pocket, and so was removed without Rose having to take her left hand out of her pocket.

TWENTY-FOUR

May 1944

May, purportedly the loveliest month of the year, brought with it a killing frost. Blossom died on the trees and disgruntled farmers and housewives eking out decent meals on fewer and fewer choices of ingredients saw their hopes of fresh fruits, jams and apple pies disappear almost overnight. To add insult to injury there was a drought, and many of those citizens who had been urged to 'dig for victory' looked forward to a summer without salad leaves, carrots, or peas fresh from the garden. Enterprising gardeners re-used bath water, and even put to good use water in which the family clothes had been rinsed.

'Think positive: soap'll take care of the greenfly,' declared the more optimistic.

Rose managed to keep her engagement and the magnificent ring a secret. All her friends knew that Brad had gone and, equally, everyone seemed to know where. The world was afire with rumours. The Second Front, the invasion of mainland Europe; it was going to happen tomorrow, in a week, a month, before midsummer. Had the Americans and their Canadian allies not been rehearsing their tactics for months in the waters off the south coast?

The enemy did not sit patiently and wait to be invaded, however. Occasional bombing raids were suffered in spring and early summer. Rose wrote long loving letters to Brad when time allowed and quick notes in between. There had been only one letter from Brad, and Rose kept it as close to his ring as she could. Their presence comforted and strengthened her.

She could not believe how much she missed him and worried about him. This, then, was true love – and yes, it was wonderful, but there was pain there too. She buried herself in her work.

'Rose? Miss Petrie, it is you?'

Rose recognised the voice immediately and smiled. 'Yes, it is. Dr Fischer, how very nice to see you.'

'Ah, you recognise an old man from the past.' He turned to his companion. 'Commander, I have had the pleasure of knowing this young lady since she was a child.'

'Had I answered my own front door more often, Doctor, I would have known her then too.'

'No? You are from Dartford?'

'Yes, indeed, but let us all reminisce later. Corporal Petrie, as usual I have no idea how long we'll be.'

'I'll be here, sir.'

He smiled and Rose watched them walk away. She saw how protectively the commander held his left arm out in case the elderly scientist stumbled. *Some nice blokes in Dartford – and in the aristocracy.*

How Daisy would love to hear about her meeting with the former German refugee who was, at last they knew, working on something very special, and for the British Government.

Rose had picked the two men up at Westminster Abbey, an unusual spot, but it seemed that the abbey reminded Dr Fischer of a cathedral in his German home town and, when he had time, he liked to go there, and sit quietly in the enveloping peace of the church. She had thought she recognised him, but she had not been as close to him as Daisy, who had been in the habit of seeing the old refugee every day; and besides, it was not her place to speak to her Very Important passengers.

She had finished *A Tree Grows in Brooklyn* some time before and had found another novel to read in the camp library. At first she had been rather disappointed in the book because she had seen the film just after she and her sister had left school, and had thoroughly enjoyed it. The book, again a classic recommended to the 'bright girls' like Sally, but one of which Rose had never been made aware, was called *The Thirty-Nine Steps*. Rose had expected a nice love story along with all the spies and murders, but there was no love story in the thin little book. The more she read, however, the more she enjoyed it. She was right there in the theatre with Richard Hannay, when a rap on the window alerted her to the return of her passengers.

I'll have to ask if I can tell Mum and Daisy that I've driven Dr Fischer, she thought as she opened the door.

'The War Office,' said the commander's voice.

'Sir.'

Rose drove carefully, her eyes and ears alert. These days one just never knew, what with bombs and assassination attempts, but they arrived at their destination safely.

'And what does Mrs Petrie think of this "austerity bread", Rose?' asked Dr Fischer as Rose helped him out of the car.

'Austerity bread? Sounds dreadful, sir – so far, she hasn't mentioned it.'

'Please tell her how I long to enjoy again one of her apple dumplings.'

'I will, sir. She'll be thrilled.'

Again Rose watched the two men. She remembered how her family – and especially her sister – had worried about their former customer. *Wait till I tell her how well he's being looked after.*

Rose had no idea what Dr Fischer's skills were, or what the project was that was so important that they had had to steal him away in the middle of the night to complete it, but she could see that he was completely at ease with the commander, who treated the old man with the greatest respect. But still she wondered what would become of Dr Fischer when the war was over. Would he want to return to Dartford or would he prefer to stay in London? Only time would tell.

She returned to the depot and was immediately sent out to deliver a sealed envelope.

'Selfridges' annexe. Just ring the bell on the door on Edward Mews – know where that is? – and hand it in. Possible they might have a parcel for you to deliver. Better use the old Morris; look like anybody.'

Wonder if this is an order for his mum's birthday present. Can't see the PM popping in to Selfridges . . . but stop thinking and get your job done, Petrie.

She delivered the envelope, was told to wait, and fifteen minutes later was given what she felt sure was the same envelope and was ordered to take it immediately to a familiar address on Palmer Place. There she was ordered to wait. She did – for almost an hour, and then was surprised when a man in an American uniform jumped into the back seat and barked, 'US Embassy, and hurry.'

Rose drove as quickly as traffic would allow to Grosvenor Square and drew up at the American Embassy. Before she had stopped the car, the soldier was out and was being waved on into the building.

As always, being near the huge building filled Rose with excitement. Would she one day soon come to this centre of power to ask for permission to enter the United States of America? She tried to clear her thoughts. Right at this moment should she wait or should she return to base? She decided to wait. A second car drew up, depositing men in uniform, one Canadian, one French. Then another car, which dropped off two men in civilian clothes – British, she thought, the suits more Savile Row than New York.

She had not noticed the marine approach her car until he rapped on the window. She jumped and wound it down.

'Your passenger requests that you return to base, ma'am.'

Rose thanked him and started the engine. Ma'am. Ma'am – she loved that word. It did not make her feel old but . . . sophisticated. That would be something to write to Brad about.

There was a thrill of excitement at the bottom of her stomach. Was this meeting anything to do with the great enterprise? Somehow she knew that whatever it was, it had begun, and her euphoria turned to fear.

TWENTY-FIVE

London, June 1944

The summer months passed in a blur of activity and rumour, but with no word from either Brad or his father. Every day Rose waited for news, but went to sleep each night telling herself that Brad was well but busy and would write as soon as he could.

And then it was June and the atmosphere was charged, expectant, waiting – but for what?

Rose seemed to be busier than ever, transporting her human packages here and there. Other ATS drivers were just as involved and there were rumours and hurried conversations – 'This is it, you mark my words. I heard as the King, God bless him, is going to be on the wireless.'

His Majesty the King? If this piece of gossip was true, then something of great importance had taken – or was about to take – place. Rose crossed her fingers and wished that she would not be driving at the time of his broadcast. Crossed fingers were no weapon, though, and she did not hear the breaking news bulletins.

It was WO Carter who enlightened her. 'Heard the news, Petrie?' He assumed that she had not and carried on without giving her time to reply. 'Seems the PM told Parliament that thousands of Allied troops landed on the coast of Normandy today. Put that in your diary, Petrie. Sixth of June 1944, the first day of the end of this damned war. Troops were dropped from planes but even more arrived by sea. The King was on the wireless but you and me has missed him. Sorry about that. Can't really believe it till you hear it, right?'

The next day, returning late from dropping a 'package', Rose heard a newsboy shouting. Did she hear the word 'invasion'? She stopped the powerful car and got out. 'What did you say?'

'We're in the land of the frogs, oh General. Buy the paper and read it for yourself.'

Cheeky monkey, thought Rose, remembering her young foster brother's early days. 'May I please buy a copy of today's *Daily Telegraph*?'

'Certainly, General. Thruppence to you; it's a tanner to anyone else.'

Rose handed him a sixpence and took the newspaper.

It was true. There was a huge banner headline announcing that thousands of Allied troops had invaded Europe.

Her immediate thought was of Brad. Those strange boats he had talked about? Had he sailed to France? She pictured him, jumping into the sea and walking, his rifle – she supposed a soldier would carry a rifle – above his head, struggling to keep his balance over those last few yards. She returned to the car and hurried back to base as quickly as she could, taking into account the blackout, the dimmed headlights. When she was finally free of all duties, she went to the cookhouse where she was given a cup of what the cook called 'Victory coffee'.

'Victory coffee? Is it due to today's invasion?'

'No idea, love. Have we won? This is,' he said, pointing to the white cup of dull-brown liquid, 'as far as I know, the latest idea from those as has our health at heart. Taste it.'

Rose did. 'That's vile.'

'Fussy. It's made from ground acorns; there's at least five future trees in that cup, all sacrificed to make you a cup of coffee.'

'I appreciate their sacrifice, but would prefer that this bilge at least smelt of tree. Got anything edible to go with it?'

'Beans on some mashed potatoes.'

Rose asked him to ensure that the food was hot; when he brought the steaming plate over to her, she thanked him and unfolded the paper.

She read avidly.

'Mulberries!' she shouted.

'What, love?'

'Sorry, nothing – this is delicious.'

The writer explained one of the startling developments that had allowed the troops to invade and Rose read the piece over and over again.

The people at the party were talking about a man-made harbour – not fruit, but a floating road that moved up and down with the tide and allowed army vehicles to drive off their ships and onto the beach. Rose could not begin to imagine the scale of the enterprise, the brains that had dreamed it up and worked out the plans.

Oh, Brad, my darling, where are you? What part have you had in this? What are you doing now? So many dead.

She left her food and her Victory coffee unfinished, and took the newspaper to her billet, where no one slept much that night.

The conversation next morning was of nothing but the Normandy landings.

Thousands of men and machines were now covering the entire length of the French coastline from Cherbourg to Le Havre. Was one of them Master Sergeant Bradley Hastings? When would she know? How did the people who write the newspapers find out? Telephone calls? Radio messages? Pigeons? Letters took so long.

Rose wondered if Sam was familiar with the French names. She would ask him in her next letter. Next letter? How would she address the next to Brad? 'Somewhere in France'? She said the words again, pronouncing them as best she could. Senator Jarrold would know how to say Le Havre and Cherbourg. Now Brad did too – if he was there and still alive, for the enemy had not waited for all the men to disembark and dig themselves in before opening fire.

Work, as always, was the best way to deal with the fear that was eating her. She would work and she would remain positive. She slipped the chain out from its hiding place, held the ring tightly and kissed it before slipping it back inside her shirt. That became her routine. The simple routine, the connection with Brad, kept her spirits up.

Rose would never forget the date: Tuesday, 13 June 1944. A red-letter day, a glorious day. Two letters – dirty, creased, the address smudged – were sitting like little birds of paradise in her pigeonhole. Two letters, the first communication from Brad in two months. She held them in her hand, smelled them in the faint hope that they would contain some trace of him, but they smelled of damp, and the code to show which had been written first had been obliterated by what might have been water.

'I don't care, I don't care,' she sang as she waltzed around the office.

'Well that's nice, Corporal. Glad you're happy, for you've got a helluva busy day ahead of you. You can read his passionate outpourings between packages.'

But so pleased was Rose to have her precious letters that she smiled beatifically at WO Carter. 'Oh, thank you, Warrant Officer. Busy is good, the more the merrier. Where would you like me to go?'

'You don't really want an answer to that one, Petrie.' He looked at the sheet in his hand and Rose knew that he was desperately working out how many jobs she could possibly do without falling asleep or starving to death. There was no such thing as a stated shift pattern for some drivers. They drove, day and night, until the 'packages' had been delivered. Two o'clock in the morning was no different from two o'clock in the afternoon. If there was a job, a driver was found to do it. Today he chose to take out his own spite on Rose, who provided him with absolutely no joy, for she never complained but smiled and thanked him.

She was smiling at him now, her letters in her hand.

'Get through that list as best you can without killing anyone, especially your passengers. Let me know at dinnertime how you're doing, in case I need to find a man to finish the job.'

'Will do, sir. I'll just check that I have some pennies. Which car?'

'It'll have to be the new Wolseley. Don't put a scratch on it. Dismissed.'

Rose saluted and hurried off. A quick look at the times and the places had told her that a single hold-up of any length could destroy the whole schedule. She refused to dwell on the possibility that Carter wanted her to fail. She tried to summon up a good swear word or a curse but, blaming her parents for her lack of the relevant education, she found herself muttering, '"Double, double, toil and trouble."' Where that came from she had no idea, but she decided that it had to have come from a book. Had she not read more books since joining the ATS than she had in the whole of her prior existence?

She was almost skipping as she drove out in the lovely car for her first pick-up.

For weeks it had been relatively simple to move around London; now, as Rose was held up or diverted, she felt sure that this was how it had been to drive through London during the Blitz.

'What's the hold-up?' she asked a policeman who was valiantly trying to handle the chaos.

'A bloody bomb last night or early this morning, love, but a new one, right out of the mouth of 'ell it is. Hit a railway bridge at Mile End and the line, blast it.'

'What do you mean, a new bomb?'

'This blighter arrived with no warning. Not a sound till it hit.'

'But the planes . . . ?'

'There weren't any. Seems the bomb's the plane. The explosion woke everyone up.'

'Many dead?'

'No idea.' He moved his right hand. 'OK, why don't you pull out and pass that milk van?'

Rose thanked him, restarted the engine and drove off, her mind full now of a silent bomb. She forced herself to concentrate on her job.

Each package she delivered that day was as silent as the thing that had come in the night. The day before her passengers had been talkative, positive, the atmosphere full of hope. But now each man was sombre, thoughtful, worried. Rose was late for some pick-ups and found her passengers aware of the difficulties but impatient. It was her worst day of driving.

All that cheered her was the knowledge that in the breast pocket of her tunic were two letters from Brad.

She knew that they could not possibly have come from France. She remembered the weeks of nervous waiting that the family had endured while hoping to hear from Sam. She prayed silently that she would never receive a telegram.

It was not until nearly five o'clock that she had time to sit and read Brad's letters. Her VIP had gone into the Palmer Street building and told her to wait. She had had nothing to eat or drink since six-thirty that morning and had had very little to eat the day before, and she was really hungry. She looked up and down the street for a WVS or Red Cross canteen but they were busy elsewhere and, assuring herself that food would be the last thing on Brad's mind, she touched the ring hidden under her tunic and took out her letters. The grubbiest had been written weeks before and talked about his hopes that they could soon meet in London. The diamonds against her skin proved that they had met, had walked together, had talked and had kissed – such tender kisses. Her love and longing bubbled up inside her.

She put the first letter away and opened the second one.

My darling Rose,

I'm writing this letter as we wait to begin the invasion of France and I may not be able to mail anything until we reach Paris. Don't fret if you don't hear for a while, my heart. My guess is I'll be walking!!! Right now I'm looking at your picture in my billfold and thinking of how lucky I am that you love me.

Forgive me, but I gave Dad your address. We'll be a while and if he comes back to London maybe you guys could keep each other company now and again.

We're being called.

I love you with all my heart and will love you for ever,

Your Brad

Tears were running down Rose's cheeks and she did not see her passenger return.

'Here, miss,' he said as he handed her a beautifully ironed handkerchief and half a bar of chocolate. 'My daughter always feels better after a good cry and a bit of chocolate.'

His kindness almost made her weep again, but she wiped her eyes and blew her nose on his lovely handkerchief, murmured her sincere but embarrassed thanks, and ate his chocolate.

To spare her further embarrassment he was now sitting on his seat, apparently engrossed in his papers. Rose started the engine and drove him as smoothly as she could to his next destination.

'Thank you,' she said again as she reached the address, and it was only when she returned to the depot that she realised she still had the handkerchief. *He wouldn't want a grotty hankie, would he?*

The new bomb that now rained down on London was called the V1. The British called it a doodlebug or buzz bomb. No one was safe. Among countless incidents, Bow in East London was hit, and some days later Victoria Station received a direct hit, but one of the most poignant tragedies took place on 18 June.

Rose had been sent to pick up a VIP at the Guards' Chapel on Birdcage Walk. She loved this drive, which took her past many of the most famous sites in London, including, of course, Buckingham Palace.

A service was taking place in the chapel, for Rose could hear singing, many manly voices raised in praise. She thought she heard a buzzing sound, not unlike the buzzing of a bee trapped against a window, but it grew louder and louder, completely drowning out the singing and then – dead silence. Rose's heart seemed, for a moment, to stop beating. There was a boom, and with an almighty roar, the roof of the chapel collapsed, burying everyone inside. She screamed in both horror and terror. The engine stalled, leaving her in the middle of the road; part of her consciousness noted that there were other vehicles in like state.

After that she reacted instinctively, but had no idea what she and the many others who tried to help had done or tried to do. Much later she was taken back to her rescued car by a Red Cross helper. The beautiful car was covered in dust. Carter would be furious, especially if there were scratches or dents under that dirt.

'It's a car, Carter,' she yelled across the miles, 'only a car.'

Later she was to learn that 121 guardsmen had died in the bombing, with nearly 150 more seriously injured, together with almost 200 members of their families. Huge piles of bricks and mortar and general devastation marked the scene for some time, as piles of rubble were doing all over London.

Rose grieved for the soldiers and she grieved for their families. Had some of the men been preparing to go into battle; had family members come up to London to participate in the service and to pray for their husbands, fathers, sons or lovers? Had they stood there singing lustily as their minds prayed that their beloved one would not die in battle?

Oh, Brad, war is so cruel and I miss you so much.

She knew that she must not dwell constantly on the horrors that were happening all around her. She resolved to carry on doing her duty as well as she could. She decided even to try to find some sympathy for WO Carter, who had said nothing at all about the car.

'Would have been a damned nuisance if you'd got yourself killed, Petrie. I haven't got time to train up another half-decent driver. Get yourself off to bed early. You'll be right as rain after a decent night's sleep.'

'Yes, sir, thank you, sir.'

She had reached the door when he called her.

'Have a hot shower, Petrie, and wash your hair; it's a disgrace.'

'Yes, sir.'

Again his voice stopped her. 'Heard from your Yank?'

'Too early, sir.'

'He'll come back.'

'Thank you, sir.'

She reached the door. She could not possibly have heard him say, 'If you were waiting for me, I'd come back.'

Could she?

In late September, an annoyed voice calling, 'Petrie, is there a Rose Petrie around?' sent her flying out of her billet.

'Telephone, Petrie, and don't hog it.'

'Thank you. No. Of course not.'

Rose practically flew across the ground.

The telephone receiver was sitting on the shelf. Breathlessly she picked it up. 'Brad?'

'Rose?' It was not Brad's voice.

'This is Rose Petrie.'

'Anderson Hastings, Rose, Brad's dad.'

Joy turned to utter despair. 'Oh, God no—'

'Rose, honey, he's fine. I pulled every string within reach and then his mom pulled a few more. What we know is that he's well and out there with his platoon. They promoted him, Rose, on the battlefield. I bet he's mad as hell, excuse my French, but he's Captain Hastings now.'

Rose was incapable of speech. Her legs trembled and she leaned against the booth for support.

'Rose?'

'I'm here,' she said, annoyed that even her voice was trembling. 'Thank you for telling me.'

'Rose, I'm in London for the next month. Do you think . . . I mean, would you care to have lunch in town one day so we could begin to get to know each other, maybe take in a show some time? Brad asked me to look out for you and we really want, his mom and I want, to get to know the girl our boy loves. Just till he gets back.'

'Mrs Hastings?'

'She's thrilled. She's already planning her share of your parties. She'll come over if Brad hits the UK before the US.'

How positive he sounded. He was Brad's father and he was positive, and she would be too.

'I'd love to meet you, Mr Hastings.'

'Call me Anderson. And, Rose, we can't meet in the Goring or the Ritz, I'm afraid.'

What a strange thing to say, thought Rose. Was he saying he would be ashamed or embarrassed to be with her in those beautiful hotels?

'That's all right,' she said.

'You see, my son told me very severely that the Goring is very special to both of you and he says, next time he sees you, he's determined to take you dancing at the Ritz.'

'I'm looking forward to it.'

'Have your sister and your brother managed to arrange their wedding dates yet? And isn't there an ATS friend too?'

How did he know?

'Yes, my friend Chiara's mother will marry next year, but I've heard nothing about dates.'

'Then, when I take you to lunch – and soon, I hope – I won't expect to see you wear your ring. I do hope everything goes well for each of them.'

'Thank you.'

'Good night, Rose. Welcome to the family from both of us.'

Rose thanked him, said good night, replaced the receiver and went outside.

How quickly it was beginning to get dark – earlier and earlier. Rose stood for a moment in the slightly chilly evening air and breathed deeply. Soon it would be autumn. Was that too early to hope to see Brad, or should she think of winter? Her mind and heart were full of hope. She would wait for Brad, and she would worry, she knew she would. She was a woman in love with a soldier who was fighting a war, but she would not be waiting and worrying alone.

Time to write to Brad and to her parents. There was so much that she had to tell them. Rose's hand went automatically to the place between her breasts where the beautiful ring rested. She closed her eyes, remembering, with such sweet joy, the moment when he had given it to her. They had laughed together at the idea of her wearing both his class ring and the engagement ring on a chain round her neck. 'I'd clink,' she had told him, as she'd returned his university ring. They'd raced to the station and there they had clung to each other until the very last moment.

'Not goodbye, my heart,' he had said. 'Cheerio.'

Cheerio. He was coming back to her. She had to be strong just a little longer, for surely the servicemen in France would be sent back to their last base. Soon he would be there with her. Oh, yes, there was so much she had to tell the families.

TWENTY-SIX

October 1944

At the beginning of October, Rose was given a weekend's leave. Before she left for the station she checked again to see if any letters had been delivered, but there was nothing. Nothing from Brad's father either, but she knew he had been recalled to Washington DC and so she was not really disappointed. The war had not ended on those blood-soaked beaches as they had prayed. But surely the men involved in that mighty push should be sent home. She tried so hard to think of other things but, when she was not driving, all she could think of was seeing Brad, or at least hearing from him.

She did not read on the train to Dartford but, as usual, fell asleep almost as soon as she sat down. Only the conductor's parade-ground voice alerted her when they pulled into the station.

She peered out into the darkness but could see only anonymous shapes.

Rose stepped down onto the platform and was startled to find her case taken out of her hand and a soft voice she had not heard for a very long time saying, 'Hello, Rose, we thought we'd come to meet you.'

'Grace, Sam, oh how good . . .' Rose got no further but burst into tears of joy and found herself wrapped in her oldest brother's strong arms.

'Best tell her, Sam.'

Rose's tears did not prevent her seeing the obvious affection and trust between her brother and her friend. She turned from Sam and hugged Grace, Sam's fiancée. Her heart lifted with joy at the thought that perhaps they were in Dartford to arrange their wedding.

'Dry your eyes, our Rose. Phil's home for the weekend and Mum's baking, so we'd best get a move on.'

Talking all the way, they were soon home, and Rose was thrilled not only to see her parents, her adopted brother, George, and the recuperating Phil, but a beautiful blonde girl whom she had no problem in recognising as Grace's Polish friend, the Land Girl Eva.

'Eva's been accepted at a terrific college, the Royal College of Music in Kensington.'

'Super,' said Rose, 'it's just across from the Albert Hall, very easy to reach, Eva.'

'It will be if Lady Alice's father can get her out of the Land Army,' Grace explained. 'Now that the war's over in Europe, there shouldn't be a problem, should there?'

'Nothing is over, sweetheart,' said Sam. 'There are thousands of Allied soldiers all over Europe – heck, isn't Sally somewhere over there?' Sam stopped as he saw expressions of joy wiped from his family's faces. 'We have to face facts. Until we hear officially, from the Prime Minister, from His Majesty himself, the war in Europe is not over.'

It was Eva who was brave enough to mention the war in the East. 'There is war still in my homeland in East Prussia and in Japan,' she said. 'But today is for us happy days, yes?'

'Of course, Eva,' said Grace, taking her friend's hand, 'and there will be war in this kitchen if Mother Petrie can't serve her wonderful dinner.'

Rose felt the heavy atmosphere lift, and the rest of the evening was full of talking and laughter; of good, if somewhat plain food; of plans discussed. Throughout this Rose sat, all too aware of the beautiful ring warm against her skin. At last, after Phil, helped by George, had cleared the table, Sam made a large pot of tea and carried it into the front room, and Rose steeled herself to tell them about Brad.

'Spit it out, lass,' coaxed Fred. 'You've been like a cat about to have kittens since you came in the front door.'

Rose followed the teapot and sat down beside Phil, who squeezed her arm with his good hand. 'Got a nice chap, our Rose? Not before time.'

'You know most of it already, but yes, Phil, I'm now officially engaged to a nice chap.'

'A Yank. I told you, Phil,' came in a loud whisper from George.

'Officially?' Fred was on his feet. 'Without a word to us?'

'Maybe Yanks do things different, Dad Petrie.' George's unwelcome comment was ignored.

'He couldn't come to ask you, Dad, Mum; he was part of the Normandy push – he's still there somewhere.'

'And so when did this take place, officially?' Flora was hurt.

'Before he shipped out, Mum.'

Flora turned away from the family and Rose looked at her mother's ramrod-straight back.

'Months, Rose, near six months, and not a word from you or from him.'

'Sit down, Flora love, you knew they was making promises last Christmas.'

'And you told Grace and me you were quite happy he's American,' said Sam.

Flora, who had suffered in so many ways since the beginning of hostilities, fought back gamely. 'I never said I were happy; I said I didn't mind. I'm a modern woman; I know the war's changed everything – and not for the better – but at least Tomas came to meet us. Never imagined for a minute my eldest daughter would get engaged without us ever setting eyes on the lad.'

'C'mon, Mum,' Phil decided to wade in on his little sister's side. 'Seems to me our poor Rose ha'n't seen much of the lad herself. He weren't over here on holiday. The Yanks practised all their manoeuvres constantly. That's why the invasion worked and I'm just glad Mr GI's still alive to marry my beautiful sister. His family in favour, Rose?'

Rose nodded. 'I've met his dad; in fact, I drove him,' she added, 'but without knowing who he was, Mum, and he didn't know me either.'

Flora walked over to the sofa where Phil and Rose were sitting and hugged her daughter. 'I'm sorry, Rose love. 'Course we want to hear all about the lad . . . and his dad. He in the army too?'

Rose looked around the spotlessly clean 'front room' where, since she was old enough to notice, everything important or special had been discussed and dissected. She realised that never in her wildest imaginings could she have envisaged saying the words that she was about to utter. 'No, Mum, he's a politician.'

Silence, broken eventually by George. 'Like on the council?'

'Like in Parliament, George.'

'Well I never,' put in Fred, 'and you've met him?'

'Without knowing who he was, but he telephones me, and when he comes back we're going to have lunch together.'

For a moment everyone, even the quiet Grace, was talking, but no one mentioned a ring. Rose, who had been willing to show it off, decided that dropping a United States senator into the room was enough for one evening. 'Could I hear about Daisy, Grace and Phil now?'

'Nothing much to say; we still plan to marry when the war is over, Rose,' said Sam. 'But when we do marry, Eva here is going to sing at the service, if she's not too busy singing in posh opera houses.'

'I will never be too busy to sing for Grace, who has done much kindness for me, and also for Daisy when end hostel . . . what is word?'

'Hostilities,' said Phil.

Eva turned to Grace and Sam. 'You will tell Miss Rose.'

'Tell me what, Grace?'

'Nothing much. You know your parents helped me find out about my family. There's no one left, I'm afraid, but we did find out about my mother and her parents. Long and short, there was over five hundred pounds accumulating in a bank account for me, and you remember the beautiful watch?'

377

Rose nodded.

'Well, I plan to keep the watch as it's an actual connection with my mother and my grandmother. I'm sure they wore it, but Sam and I want Eva to have the money for her studies – Sam says he's able to take care of his wife and I wanted to help someone, just like the Petries have always helped me.'

'They are too much kind,' said Eva, who was almost in tears, 'but I will repay, I hope, a little with music.'

'Lots of family weddings when the war's over,' said young George. 'Daisy and Tomas, Sam and Grace, Rose and her Yank. I'll be your manager, Eva, and take the bookings. Rose has an Italian friend getting married and you sing Italian things, and what about Sally? She's bound to get married soon. In love with a sailor, Eva, and I bet you know songs about the sea, or maybe he's an actor. Anyway, she's going to be in pictures, she'll meet all sorts – and we'll get you jobs, just see if we don't.'

'I'm sure Eva is delighted with your offer, George, but right now the rest of the family is hoping to hear her sing – if you're not too tired, Eva pet,' said Fred.

Eva sang in English; as her pure voice rang through the flat, Rose wondered that her sung English was so much more correct than her spoken English.

'Her singing teacher corrects her pronunciation,' Grace explained, 'but no one, except Lady Alice, corrects her spoken English, but honestly she is so much better than when we first met.'

'She's like a bird trilling away in the summer,' said George, showing an unsuspected romanticism.

Rose too was moved. 'I've only heard a sound like that at the pictures: just beautiful. You must be very proud.'

'I'm proud of Sam,' said Grace, 'and now we'd best get off to bed.'

Two days later, Rose was back at her London base. In her luggage was a carton of her mother's 'best tea' and a dozen scones. By eleven thirty on the third day, it was almost possible to wonder if she had ever been away. Had nothing changed, or was the atmosphere in London a little lighter than it had been a few short months ago?

I think I'm feeling what I want to feel.

The war was, most definitely, not over. The dignitaries she drove were the ones she had been driving for months. One day she was surprised and delighted to find Dr Fischer in the back seat of the new Wolseley. If only she had met him before her short visit home. For once, he was alone.

'Miss Daisy is married, yes, Miss Rose?'

Rose kept her eyes on the road. 'Not yet, Dr Fischer. They will wait until the war is over.'

He sighed. 'Sometimes it is better to seize happiness when it is within our grasp.' His voice changed. 'And you, Corporal Petrie, you have found a nice young man?'

Rose wondered if he could possibly know. In her mirror she could see a tiny smile move his lips and his eyes . . . yes, his eyes were tender. 'I have, Dr Fischer, an American soldier.'

'A new country, a new life. I too may go – for a while.'

Rose drew up outside the nondescript office building.

'Perhaps we will meet in Washington. My very good wishes to your family.'

No time to ask when he might be leaving, if indeed he would go. Rose thought of her twin sister, Daisy: little Daisy who flew Spitfires and other planes. Daisy loved the old German; there was no other word for her feelings, and Rose

379

knew that Dr Fischer loved Daisy too, like the daughter he had never had. Or had there been a little German Daisy?

Would she ever know? Secrecy was now such a part of everyone that no one chatted naturally these days. She thought of the hours she and her sister and their friends had chattered about film stars and dances and clothes. Now, impossible to think about anything other than Brad, Tomas, Daisy, Sam, Grace, Sally, and all the others, still doing their bit in their selected fields.

'Don't be gloomy, Rose,' she talked to herself as she drove to her next parcel pick-up. 'When you get back to base, write and tell Daisy all about Dr Fischer.'

She was on the point of finishing the letter that evening when the door flew open and a voice yelled, 'Petrie, phone call, and God, do you owe me; it's like Siberia out here.'

Brad, it had to be Brad.

Rose grabbed a coat from a peg, threw it over her head and ran out into the rain, unaware of who had called to her but throwing out a 'thank you' to be picked up by the wind and blown away.

Fit enough not to be breathless when she reached the empty telephone box, Rose pushed her mane of wind-blown hair into some semblance of order and picked up the receiver. 'Hello, Rose Petrie here.'

Her stomach dived downwards as a pleasant American voice said, 'Rose, honey, it's me, Anderson, Brad's dad.'

She had known that the call could not possibly be from Brad. How often had she told herself calmly that it would be months before Brad returned? 'Mr Hastings . . . I mean Senator.'

'Anderson's fine, honey. I just got back and wanted to call you right away. Have you heard from Brad?'

'No, sir.'

'Anderson, even Andy. He's written and his mom managed to get a call through to his base. Almost two whole minutes, but better than nothing. He's well, but won't be back in Merrie Olde England for a while . . .' There was silence on the line for a heartbeat or two and then he spoke again. 'Maybe not till next year, honey; transportation's needed for more important things than R 'n' R.'

'R 'n' R?'

'Don't you use that terminology? Rest and recreation. The Government won't send fit men home on leave while ships are needed to transfer the wounded or to transport units or heavy equipment to other theatres.'

'I understand.' What other theatres?, Rose wondered, but she would think of that later.

'I guess you're still delivering packages, Rose.'

'Yes sir.' She forgot to try to say Andy.

'But maybe some evening you would have dinner with me?'

'Yes, I'd love to.'

'I'm at the Dorchester, very new for London, but the restaurant isn't on Brad's list of "Don't dare, Dad".'

They laughed together and, after assuring him that she would be happy to meet him on the Wednesday of the following week, Rose said good night. She returned to her Nissen hut, her whole body alive with joy.

'Sorry,' she said as she hung up the very wet and much-too-small coat she had borrowed.

'No problem, Rose, yours covered me right down to my toes.' One of the other girls pointed to a wall peg, where Rose's coat hung dripping onto a day-old newspaper.

'Nice call?'

'Yes, a friend's father,' said Rose, trying to save her letter to Daisy from getting wet as she hauled off her damp clothes.

But at last the lights were out and conversation ceased and there was no sound but the sagging of bed springs and the occasional rattle as a burning log moved in the great stove.

He was well. He had written to her. She did not wonder where the senator would take her. He was Brad's father and she would enjoy getting to know him.

'Had we met here a few months ago, General Eisenhower might have been at the next table. He lived here, did a heap of planning. Place was crawling with Government officials and Service chiefs; it's a little calmer tonight.'

'It's quite lovely,' Rose said as the wine waiter poured white wine.

'Chef does wonders with rationing – but we don't want to talk about war; we want to talk about Brad.'

Rose smiled and he took that as agreement and over the very good meal he showed Rose pictures of Brad at all stages of his development. 'Mom and I thought you might like to have a couple – of his graduation, perhaps: doesn't he look real solemn?'

Very late that night, although she was well aware of the time of her first delivery next day, Rose sat pasting the black-and-white photographs into a notebook. Only a small candle gave her any light. Unfair, she had decided, to disturb the sleep of her colleagues by turning on a light.

The photographs certainly helped her remain positive over the next few months, but so too did the two long letters and three postcards that arrived a week after her dinner with Brad's father. Someone had kindly clipped them together, and so she read from the top, aware that they might not bring her up to date.

My darling Rose,

I wish I had learned how to train a homing pigeon. We have them here, you know, and those little birds are amazing. They fly through everything to deliver their mail and then fly right back to do it again. I guess you know I'm feeling sorry for myself, not getting answers from you, but I do get mail, honey, and every one of the letters you've sent me is right here inside my shirt. Paper's no substitute for my beautiful English Rose, but you're with me always, in these pages and in my heart. I never knew that being miles away from the person you love most in the whole world hurt physically, but boy, it sure does. There's an ache inside that just stays there, stuck, like when you're a kid and you eat something way too quickly because you're greedy and want some more – part of it sticks and just won't go down.

But honest, you don't have to worry about my table manners.

This has all got to end soon, darling Rose; it must and then we can plan our wedding and our life; not our lives but our life. Mr and Mrs, the Bradleys from Dartford, Kent, England, and Cos Cob, Connecticut, United States of America. Do you picture us, Rose, with three little girls who look just like you – I guess I'll spoil them – and one or two little boys; maybe they'll be cute little blonds too? My mom will tell everyone at the club that she's died and gone to

heaven, so happy will she be. I'll give you all five
names in my next letter – you can choose names too
and we'll discuss like a real partnership should.

I'm holding this paper against my heart. How I
wish I was holding you.

All my love,

Brad.

The cards said, 'Love you', 'Still love you', and 'Hey,
maybe our girls will be triplets', which made her both
laugh and weep, and the second letter spoke about a
baseball game his platoon had taken part in and she shuddered, wondering if he was really talking about a battle.

She had no idea where he was and so, now completely
and painfully aware of how her mother had suffered
when all three of her sons had been out of touch, she
wrote, firstly to her own mother and then to Brad's
mother, introducing herself and sharing the little he had
said – about baseball games.

Rose did not go home for Christmas. Like many others,
she was on duty. The war had not ended with that brave
push into Europe; if anything it had escalated, especially in
the once-mysterious East. Wireless broadcasts and newspapers told of unbelievable horrors in the Philippines, in
Burma, India and, slightly closer to home, East European
counties like Poland. Rose thought of Grace's friend, Eva,
and wondered too if Tomas, her twin sister's fiancé, had
ever discovered the fate of his family in Czechoslovakia.
The war would end but the suffering would go on.

An enormous, beautifully wrapped parcel arrived from
New York, a gift from Brad's parents. With the wireless

384

pouring out Christmas music and a special tribute to the missing American band leader, Glen Miller, and her colleagues looking on, Rose opened it and found tinned foodstuffs and, joy of joy, perfumed soap and shampoo. There was also a very elegant but very warm dressing gown, six pairs of nylon stockings and a lovely pair of fur-lined driving gloves.

'Wow, lucky you, how the other half lives,' wisecracked a fairly new recruit to this close ATS group.

'I take it you disapprove and won't want to share,' said Rose, as she arranged the tins on her bed. 'I haven't the slightest idea what some of these are,' she said as she picked up a tin, 'but we can have fun finding out.'

'Send it home, Rose.' The orders came from all corners of the room.

'No, girls. I'm sharing the stockings with my family, and maybe that tin of ham, but we'll have a party to welcome the New Year, the end-of-the-war year.'

There were cheers at that, and Rose looked at her gifts and saw that there was enough soap for everyone. 'Perfumed soap for the first bath of the New Year. Wonderful.'

Later she wrote to Brad's mother and thanked her, not just for the gifts but for the lovely welcoming letter that had accompanied them. She finished by saying how much she looked forward to meeting them.

But reports of torpedoed refugee ships, the emerging reality of the existence of concentration camps, food riots, as in some areas neither the vanquished nor the vanquishers could find enough food, and ongoing fighting filled the newspapers, day after day, week after week, month after month.

Among the occasional letters a card arrived from Brad saying, 'Guess where I am? Perfect place for a honeymoon?' Since there was a picture of the Moulin Rouge on the front, she assumed that somehow he and his platoon were in Paris.

The sixth year of the war came in with cold weather and optimism. Letters from family and friends seemed to echo the growing awareness that not even bad times last forever. Wedding fever gripped the Petries and their friends. Brad's parents announced their imminent arrival. Did that mean they knew something that Rose did not? Brad's letters were more frequent, as if whatever homing pigeon or mail service he was using was as excited and ready for the future as the brave young people whose letters they carried.

Dr Fischer never appeared, although she looked for him. Sometimes she found herself thinking of him and their conversation the last time they had met. Was he correct? Was it better to grab happiness when it was within one's reach instead of waiting until everything was absolutely perfect? Better to face facts.

'Grab it, Rose.' The voice was so clear she could swear he was in the room. Stan. But Stan, her oldest friend, was dead. She looked around; she was quite alone.

'Didn't I tell you the real man for you was out there?' The voice was quiet but clear. 'Be happy, Rose.'

There was silence. Rose was slightly shaken but, being practical, decided that she, Rose, had conjured up her old friend. She was tired; she was hallucinating.

'Petrie, get your own damned phone.' This voice was very real and belonged to her sergeant.

'Yes, Sarge, thank you,' she answered automatically as she grabbed her coat and ran to the telephone box.

'This is Rose.'

'And this is Brad. Darling, they're giving me a furlough – five days at the beginning of April. Will you marry me then? Somehow I'll get to Dartford, and you know my mom will swim the Atlantic if that's the only way she can get across. I know it's not—'

'I will.'

' . . . exactly what . . . Rose, did I hear you? Did you say . . . ?'

'Yes, Captain Bradley Hastings, I will.'

She heard him yell, 'Yippee,' and was sure half the camp heard it. She picked up the receiver again but he was gone.

No matter. Sometimes there really is no need for words.

If you enjoyed this book, why not dip into these other fantastic reads in Ruby Jackson's CHURCHILL'S *Angels* series?

It is 1939 and in the town of Dartford, Grace, Sally, Daisy and Rose are determined to do their bit when war is declared.

Grace signs up for the Land Army. Sally's dream of stage school is thwarted by the war, but she finds hope in an unexpected place.

Nothing has prepared the twins for the shock of the nightly raids on their home town. Rose signs on at the local munitions factory, but Daisy is still needed at home in her father's greengrocer shop.

When she meets the aristocratic flying ace, Adair, Daisy initially dismisses him as a 'toff'. But when Adair encourages Daisy to pursue her ambition of becoming a pilot, it seems all her dreams could be about to come true...

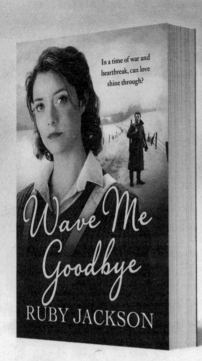

In a time of war and heartbreak, can love shine through?

Wave Me Goodbye

RUBY JACKSON

The four plucky girls from Dartford – Grace, Sally, Rose and Daisy – are still doing their bit on the Home Front.

For orphan Grace, it's a chance to start afresh. She's always had a soft spot for Sam Petrie, brother of Daisy and Rose, but realising that he is in love with their friend Sally, she puts her own feelings aside, and signs up for life as a Land Girl.

Mucking out and early morning milking come as a big shock and life is harder than she expected. But Grace is nothing if not determined and though their lives will never be the same again, the four girls know they will always have each other – no matter what the war throws at them …

Sally Brewer can hardly believe her good fortune when she lands a theatre job in London. But her hopes are stalled with the nightly hail of German bombs. Determined to play her part, she joins the newly-formed ENSA, the Entertainments National Service Association, and is soon raising morale all over the bombed-out city.

One night, Sally discovers a valuable ring sewn into the lining of a cloak. Intrigued, she tracks down the owner, a Naval Officer called Jonathan. There's been little time for love, and now she finds herself falling hard. But before long Jonathan is recalled to sea, and then Sally receives the terrible news that his ship has been destroyed. With only the ring to remember him by, can Sally face the future without the man she loves?

Ruby Jackson

A Christmas Gift

The W6 Book Café

Want to hear more from your favourite **women's fiction** authors?

Eager to read **exclusive extracts** before the books even hit the shops?

Keen to join a monthly online **Book Group**?

Join us at **The W6 Book Café**, home to HarperFiction's best-loved authors

Find us on Facebook **W6BookCafe**

Follow us on Twitter **@W6BookCafe**